DATE DUE

MAR 8 0 72015 MAY 0 7 2015		
SEP 2 5 2015		
MAY 1 3 2016		
JAN 1 1 2017		
FEB 0 1 2018		

Demco, Inc. 38-293

8/22

THE LOST SUN

BOOKS BY TESSA GRATTON

THE LOST SUN

THE UNITED STATES OF ASGARD
✦ BOOK I ✦

TESSA GRATTON

RANDOM HOUSE 🏠 NEW YORK

Text copyright © 2013 by Tessa Gratton
Jacket art: Photograph of boy © Geber86/Vetta/Getty Images;
photograph of trees © Fuse/Getty Images

All rights reserved. Published in the United States by Random House Children's Books,
a division of Random House, Inc., New York.

Random House and the colophon are registered trademarks of Random House, Inc.

Visit us on the Web! randomhouse.com/teens

Stars and Stripes . . . and Viking Gods
unitedstatesofasgard.com

Educators and librarians, for a variety of teaching tools, visit us at
RHTeachersLibrarians.com

Library of Congress Cataloging-in-Publication Data
Gratton, Tessa.
The lost sun / Tessa Gratton. — 1st ed.
p. cm. — (The United States of Asgard ; bk. 1)
Summary: "In an alternate U.S.A. (the United States of Asgard),
Soren Bearskin, the son of an infamous berserker, and Astrid Glyn, daughter of
a renowned seer, embark on a road trip to find Baldur, the missing god whose absence
has caused panic throughout the country." —Provided by publisher.
ISBN 978-0-307-97746-5 (trade) — ISBN 978-0-307-97747-2 (lib. bdg.) —
ISBN 978-0-307-97748-9 (ebook) — ISBN 978-0-307-97749-6 (pbk.)
[1. Fate and fatalism—Fiction. 2. Gods and goddesses—Fiction. 3. Prophets—Fiction.
4. Mythology, Norse—Fiction.] I. Title.
PZ7.G77215Los 2013 [Fic]—dc23 2012027695

Printed in the United States of America
10 9 8 7 6 5 4 3 2 1
First Edition

For Natalie,
who taught me everything
I needed to know
to write this book

+ + +

And once, you stopped
on a dark desert road
to show me the stars
climbing over each other
riotously
like insects
like an orchestra
thrashing its way
through time itself
I never saw light that way
again.
—*Dorothea Grossman*

+   +   +

Light up, light up
As if you have a choice.
—*Snow Patrol*

ONE

MY MOM USED to say that in the United States of Asgard, you can feel the moments when the threads of destiny knot together, to push you or pull you or crush you. But only if you're paying attention.

It was a game we played during long afternoons in the van, distracting ourselves from Dad's empty seat. Mom would point out a sign as we drove past—WELCOME TO COLORADA, THE CENTENNIAL KINGSTATE, bright green against a gray backdrop of mountains—and she'd ask, "Here, Soren? Do you feel the threads tightening around you?" I would put my fingers to my chest where Dad used to say the berserking fever stirred. "No," I'd say, "nothing yet."

And Mom always replied, "Good."

We both dreaded the day Dad's curse would flicker to life in me.

LEAVING WESTPORT CITY—COME AGAIN! "I hope it wasn't back there, my little man!" "No, Mom, I doubt it." CANTUCKEE:

HOME OF BLUEGRASS. "Soren, do you hear the clacking loom of fate?" "I couldn't hear anything over the banjos."

But I have felt it, four times now.

When I was eight years old, standing in a neon-lit shopping mall, and my ears began to ring. My breath thinned out and I ran.

Again five years later, when Mom stopped the van for gas and we happened to be across the road from a militia station. The sun was just barely too bright, cutting across my cheek. I knew what I was supposed to do.

Six months ago, I was in the dining hall about to take a long drink of honey soda when the air around me turned cold. I had time to get to my bedroom before this jagged hot fever began to burn.

And today.

It's Tyrsday afternoon, and so I'm in the library reading the thickest section of the *Lays of Thomas Jefferson* for my poetry and legends class, trying to ignore my excited classmates as they whisper back and forth about the famous new student arriving any moment now at Sanctus Sigurd's.

Perrie Swanson and her roommate huddle over a copy of the winter issue of *Teen Seer,* which isn't the sort of magazine I normally pay attention to. The headlines tend toward fashion and boy hunting: "Top Ten Ways to Make Runes Sexy" and "Dating and Prophecy: Things He Doesn't Want to Hear."

I definitely don't want to hear. But the cover features a girl my age against a shocking orange background, her eyes sad. Curls like licorice twists surround her face, and there's a necklace of large black pearls at her throat. Her hands are up, gripping ropes as if she's been caught on a swing.

The headline reads: "Astrid Glyn—Seventeen and Ready to Change Your World."

I stare back at her, as if she can see out from the glossy cover. I hear my mom's voice echoing against the metal roof of that old Veedub, *Is this the sound a knot in fate makes, little man?*

A commotion at the library window has Perrie on her feet, and she races over with her roommate stepping at her heels. I slowly stand, waiting until I'll be the last to arrive. Over the bobbing heads, I look through the panes of glass toward the front gate of the school as a silver town car pulls through, its windows tinted so dark the sunlight vanishes against them. The girl in front of me holds up her cell phone to take a picture, and on the ground outside, students pause on their way between classes to stare.

It isn't that Astrid has done anything remarkable on her own, but we all know of her mother. Astrid grew up traveling the country, like me, but she wasn't living in trailers and the backs of old vans. Astrid is the daughter of the most famous seethkona in a generation—a prophetess who read the fate of the president himself, and had private rooms in the White Hall in Philadelphia. But Jenna Glyn vanished one night about five years ago from the South Lakota plains, setting off a days-long search that eventually recovered her body. Astrid was on TV at the time, small and sunken and alone, and I'd wanted to send her a letter because I knew what it felt like when your parent died in front of the world.

I turn away from the library window and go back to the *Lays*. It will not be me who makes her feel like a specimen on her first day at a new school, no matter how my blood is rushing in my ears.

But the next afternoon she walks into our history classroom and stops beside me. She looks less glossy in real life, with messier hair. But the black pearls are the same. I stop breathing as her eyes level on the spear tattoo cutting down my left cheek. She might stare forever, and I might let her, if not for her roommate Taffy, who tugs Astrid into a desk.

All through Mr. Heaney's lecture I feel her watching me, feel the fever churning in my chest. It's good I've done my own reading on the Montreal Troll Wars so I don't have to worry about missing anything vital for the test.

When class ends I wait, as I usually do, for all the other students to file out so I can slip through the narrow aisle by myself. But Astrid remains, pushing Taffy on with a silent wave.

Even Mr. Heaney leaves us alone. He pulls a black cigarette from his pocket and marches outside to indulge in that particularly Freyan habit.

I slowly stand. Astrid's eyes are washed brown, the color of very old paper. She reaches toward me, her finger aiming for my tattoo. I don't move. If she touches me, I'll let her. I even want her to—a thought that makes me hot all over and tell myself it's only the berserking fever, not hormones or wanting.

But she doesn't. Astrid only holds her arm out and turns her eyes to mine. "I dreamed of you," she says in a voice as distant as clouds. Then she spins and is gone from the classroom.

The words sink down through my skin and embed themselves in my bones.

It's the end of my Thorsday morning run, and I'm coming into the courtyard in the center of campus, where a statue of Sanctus Sigurd himself rises out of a fountain. My eyes are on Sigurd's spear, which he lifts in a stone hand to defeat his dragon. Directly behind him the sun rises, split in two by the shaft of the weapon. I'm already slowing on the cobbles when I realize Astrid is there.

She sits on the marble rim, trailing her fingers over the thin layer of ice.

"Soren," she says without looking up.

"Astrid." I pause a few steps away. My breath hangs white in the air before me.

"Everyone here is afraid of you."

My stomach tightens, and I'm glad she doesn't follow the seethers' tendency of being long-winded. "Yes."

"Because of your father."

There's no reason not to be honest. I know who her mother was; of course she knows of my father by now. "And because of my tattoo and what it means."

Her gaze narrows to the rune she draws over and over again on the ice. She begins to smile, then stops, leaving only the promise of it in the corners of her lips. I wish suddenly that she would give that smile to me. "Doesn't it mean you'll be a great warrior, strong and sworn to protect New Asgard against her enemies?"

I could say, *That's what my father was, and it didn't stop him from murdering thirteen people and only falling when the SWAT team shot him.* Instead I roll my shoulders.

She looks up at me with the same mysterious not-quite-smile. It throws me off guard, not knowing what to expect. Which, I suppose, is exactly what I should have expected. If Astrid is a seethkona like her mother, she's devoted to Freya, the goddess of magic and fate, and of course she's so mysterious. So beautiful and alluring. It's in their nature.

"The seethers say," Astrid tells me, "that before the world existed there was only darkness and ice, and cold nothing waits for us when we leave behind the sun and stars to venture into death. That there is no light, and all is chaos. And a slice of that cold chaos is what lives inside berserkers. Lives in you, as it lived in your father, his father, and his father's father, all the way back to the times when Odin Alfather, King of the Gods, gave a bear spirit into a man that he might become a perfect warrior."

She speaks in a hushed tone, too intimate for two people who've only just met. I shut my eyes. For six months I've felt the frenzy burning, cutting up against my heart and keeping me from sleep, making my skin hot to touch. For six months I've struggled to lock it away. Yet here is Astrid Glyn summoning it with a few words—pulling on me. I don't know what to tell her, how to protest, and when she's next to me I'm unsure that I even want her to stop. "It doesn't feel like cold nothing in my chest."

Behind me, the dormitory doors open and footsteps tap lightly down the sandstone stairs. Astrid stands, ignoring the students who slow nearby, as if she knows they won't interrupt us. She says, "Tell me what it feels like, then."

She touches her own chest, low over her diaphragm, which is exactly the place on my body nearest to the fever. As if she knows, as if she feels it herself. And I remember suddenly that Odin stole his mad magic from Freya. If Astrid has the gift for grasping the strands of fate, for dancing in wild circles and asking question after question until the universe talks back, maybe she actually can understand. Maybe that's why I feel this way around her. Maybe it's worth it to tell her. I say, "Most of the time, like a million tiny flames. A fever."

Astrid smiles very softly and nods as if it's exactly as she expected. Then she walks around me, just like that, to join the group of girls who've been heading for the dining hall and breakfast. She doesn't look back. After she disappears through the heavy double doors, I have to tear myself away from the fountain, where my feet have frozen to the earth.

The best thing for me to do is go about my routines. To ignore the way I catch my breath when she passes, and the thoughts that shoot up about touching her hand. Nonengagement is the way to avoid getting upset, which can trigger the berserking, and once it finally overtakes me I'm stuck with it forever. I keep myself out of fighting, out of situations where most boys my age throw punches. I avoid falling for girls—until now they've made it easy by avoiding me right back. If I hold the madness off, maybe it'll fade. Maybe I can squash it, bury it for the rest of my life.

Only that won't happen so long as Astrid is making me feel this way.

I have Anglish and biology on Freyasdays, and as Astrid comes into biology carrying a brand new elf anatomy textbook, she notices me. She sits only two desks over. I stop breathing.

In lunch period, I glance across the dining hall to see her fingers at her chest, rubbing tiny circles against the button of her cardigan.

And my fever burns hotter.

The bench creaks beside me as my former roommate London slides in and slaps his laden tray onto the table. "You're staring," he says, digging into mashed red potatoes. He's a hand taller than me, and his skin is even darker than mine. I used to think it was the reason we were originally dormed together—Sanctus Sigurd's two charity cases—but he was quick to tell me his grandfather was the king of Kansa for one term, despite their race and allegiance to Thor Thunderer, the least diplomatic of all our gods.

I look back at Astrid, who's in the middle of a circle of admirers, with Taffy at her right hand. "Not at your girlfriend," I say to London as I push ham around on my plate. I stab two chunks at a time and eat them.

"I'm not worried about you and Taffy."

His mouth is full as he says it, and I make sure to swallow before answering. "What are you worried about?"

He picks up his mug of honey soda in one big hand. London is the only student on campus stronger than me, but we'd still had to quit sparring when the fever started keeping me up at night. He'd thrown a fit worthy of his patron the Thunderer. But it hadn't done any more good than when his parents requested that he be removed as my roommate. "The match," he admits.

I clench my teeth against regret. Last year we were co-captains of the school's battle guild, re-creating famous battles for competition. Next week is a campaign against one of the big Westport City public schools. Very calmly, as if it hardly matters, I ask, "What's our team's role?"

"The horde of greater hill trolls that swarmed into Vertmont ninety years ago."

"The Battle of Morriston."

"I'd love to go over some tactics with you."

"You know where I'll be."

"Staring at Astrid Glyn?"

I snap my head toward him.

With a great laugh, he says, "Soren, I think you'd blush if you could."

Swinging my leg over the bench, I stand. "I'll be in my room after devotions if you want to bring by the tactical map." And I go, forcing myself to keep my eyes on the path ahead, to not look back at her.

Fortunately, I have private lessons on battlefield history with Master Pirro all Freyrsday. He's a retired berserker who served in the president's personal bodyguard at the White Hall until a wound from the Gulf conflict gave him a limp that relegated him to teaching. Because he'd volunteered to act as my custodian when everyone else refused, the kingstate of Nebrasge agreed to subsidize my tuition here. Sanctus Sigurd's is a humanities academy, privately owned and meant for the kids of people who can afford to keep them out of apprenticeships while they're still young. If not for Pirro, I don't know where I'd be.

Anytime my focus drifts away from the immediate lesson, Pirro slaps a gnarled old hand against the desk between us. The backs of his knuckles are crisscrossed with scars. "Soren," he says in his gravelly way, "is the fever stronger? Is that what's distracting you?"

I can't imagine telling him I'm thinking about a girl, and only stare at the sharp blue of his eyes. They droop at the corners. He should have glasses, but he says that if a berserker can't do it with his own body, he shouldn't do it at all.

After a moment, he coughs and orders me to write out the best strategy for defending the city of Chicagland against siege.

It's nearly two hours before he's satisfied and I'm free. On my way home to my dorm, I hear Astrid call my name.

She stands in the arched doorway of the chapel, one hand on the edge of the heavy wooden door. Beyond her, the glow of candlelight transforms the edges of her hair into a halo. Taffy's there, hip cocked impatiently, along with two other girls from their year, waiting to begin their evening devotion. Last year Taffy's parents won a civil suit in the Nebrasge king's holmcourt that meant Sanctus Sigurd's had to put a Biblist cross up in the chapel for her to pray. But I hadn't heard of Taffy herself ever bothering before.

Astrid gestures for me to go into the chapel with her, and I almost laugh. But it would be a bitter, ugly noise, so I just shake my head and move off on my way. There's only one thing I've ever prayed for: to have this fever pass me by. Every Yule and Hallowblot, and every Disir Day since my father died, I've lit candles and made sacrifices to Odin that his particular curse not fall onto my shoulders. But my prayers never mattered. The Alfather didn't listen, and the madness curled its fingers through my ribs, clutching tight. It will never let me go.

"Soren." Astrid dashes across the lawn to me, making Taffy's and the other girls' eyes go wide.

I wait for her, unable to turn away when my name hangs between us.

"Do you ever come in?" Instead of reaching for me, she folds her hands together before her stomach.

I focus on them, on her small wrists. If I lost control here, with her, it would be so easy to break her. "Praying won't make my life better."

"That isn't what praying is for."

Because we have an audience, I don't ask what she thinks it *is* for.

Astrid goes on when I don't. "Your berserking is a gift. We need your strength to protect the people of New Asgard. To defend our values, our freedom against our nation's enemies."

It sounds as though she's been reading pamphlets from

the Hangadrottin War College. Why is she challenging me like this? Why does she care that I don't join in evening devotions? Can't she see the fear and mistrust engendered by this tattoo on my face? With half our year slinking out of the chapel to watch our encounter—some excited, some hostile, and one dashing off, probably to get a teacher—it should be impossible to miss.

"That is what they say," Taffy adds, coming up behind Astrid to take her elbow. "But not all the Alfather's berserkers can keep themselves from brutal murder."

Astrid, instead of shaking Taffy off as I suddenly want her to do, turns to go with her roommate, saying only, "Soren, you should come to my room tonight. I'm throwing runes, and I want to see what future is in yours."

I stand there, gutted, colder than I've been in a half year, as Astrid goes inside with the others, as the crowd melts away.

I tell myself I don't need to know my future. I won't go. I can't go.

I know exactly what she'll see.

My room is sparse: the walls empty, the floor bare, with only a trunk of clothes and a desk that should have pictures and mementos but doesn't. My father's sword, sheathed and silent, leans against a corner. The second bed was removed last year along with London, so I have space for indoor exercise. It's what I usually do, and will all day Sunday, too, as it's our break day from classes.

But tonight I only lie on the hardwood, staring up at the

ceiling, thinking about Astrid and my mom's destiny game, about how angry I was when I realized we'd been running away from the world ever since my dad died. Mom wasn't helping me listen for my destiny so that I could find it, but so that she'd know how to steer me away. I left her because I refused to run anymore.

If Astrid can read my future in her runes, how is it brave to ignore her? She might tell me the berserking is inevitable. But there's the outside chance I'm right, that I can fight it, and maybe Astrid will confirm that. She'll see me grown and free, living my life apart from the berserking bands, liberated from battle and killing and this always-present fever. Then I'd know I'm on the right path, that I'm doing what I need to.

I get to my feet and pull a school hoodie on, scrubbing a hand through my short hair. It's been about a month since London buzzed it, and it feels shaggy. The second I notice I'm worried about how I look, I frown. Astrid is making me crazy.

It's a quick walk between dorms, and early enough that I can walk straight past their RA's open door without checking in. Thanks to London, I know Taffy's on the third floor in a corner room, and I take the stairs three at a time, in large, slow steps.

The hall is brightly lit, with fewer scuffs on the walls than in the boys' dorm, and a newer carpet. All the doors hang open, but I don't glance in. At the far end, students overflow from Taffy and Astrid's room, their backs to me as they peer inside. I smell honey and candles, and am vaguely surprised at the hushed atmosphere.

A small girl leaning on the doorjamb, probably a second-year, notices me first; her shoulders jerk in surprise. She knocks into her neighbor, whose painted mouth makes a wide O. I keep my face solidly expressionless and stand in the doorway so I'm clearly visible.

At least twelve people are crammed inside, all on the floor but for Astrid, who's on the center of her bed like a queen, and Taffy, who's perched right on the corner. Taffy purses her lips, but Astrid smiles. "You came."

I tuck my hands into the front pockets of my hoodie and wish I hadn't. Light flickers on the ceiling from the candles stuck to the windowsills and desktop, overpowering the dim lamps. A bottle of honey mead is being passed around, and it occurs to me that I'm the only boy here. The other guests are in pajamas, sitting on their own pillows or wrapped in blankets. I tower over them all, and can't see a path I could pick my way through in order to get to Astrid. I study her, seated with her legs up in the middle of a web of red yarn and dark scattered runes made from sticks and bones and rock. She's got dark writing on her palms, and she's staring back at me.

For just a moment, we're alone. It's only the two of us, and in my mind I can hear her whisper, *You're a berserker, Soren. Fate is inexorable.* That's all she'll read in my future.

Several girls shift away from the door, away from me. They don't want me to brush past them, as if even that quick exposure might be deadly.

"I shouldn't have," I say, and Astrid's smile fades. Like I'm a child who's done something disappointing. A sick feeling

14

sinks down through my stomach. I gesture toward her company, wanting to say I can't let this happen with so many witnesses. But it's a ragged motion. Astrid nods sadly and I leave as quickly as I can.

It doesn't matter what she might see in her runes. My fate is sealed.

TWO

TODAY IS THE last day of winter, and across the country, people turn off televisions and the interweave. They hang lanterns in order to wrap hope and light around their homes and loved ones. They wait quietly for the sun to return, in order to welcome Baldur the Beautiful back to life with joy.

I usually spend holidays alone. But even for me, Baldur holds some appeal. There's a chorus of gods in the USA, brought over from Scandia by our founding fathers: Odin Alfather, the mad one, the god of war and poetry. Thor Thunderer, the sky god, who defends us against our enemies. Freyr the Satisfied, god of wealth and prosperity. His sister Freya, the Feather-Flying Goddess of magic. Frigg, Queen of Heaven. Tyr the Just. Loki Shapeshifter, who never stops moving or changing.

When we become citizens, we all dedicate ourselves to one, based on family tradition or personal preference. Or, as in my case, destiny of birth.

My dad used to tell me that Loki sometimes drove an ice cream truck in the town where he grew up. I've seen photos in *Os Weekly* of Freyr walking down a red carpet with a star-let on his arm, and of Thor Thunderer standing over the body of a slain mountain troll that ventured into a Montania town and slaughtered a family in their sleep. Odin regularly visits the House of Congress to give his approval to a new law. Frigg cuts the ribbon at a new hospital. Tyr oversees his system of dedi-cated lawspeakers. And through her seethers, Freya gives us the magic to seek our destinies.

Our gods are scattered throughout our lives, even when we live in a place as remote as Sanctus Sigurd's. But none of them is so well loved as Baldur the Beautiful.

He's the god of light, and is handsome and golden, strong and funny. At the end of every summer, he dies and his body is consumed in a great bonfire, only to rise again at winter's end. He gives himself to Hel for six months of every year, but lives harder and more brightly in the time he has with us on earth.

He is the only god who dies at all.

And that makes him the one most like us.

At school we prepare for the equinox by folding paper lan-terns and baking fortunes into clove-cakes. The lanterns will be strung, ready for the ceremony at dawn, and the cakes will harden overnight so that at breakfast we can each choose one to crack open and discover our future.

I'm with my schoolmates in the dining hall, at a table of my own, peeling apples and gathering the long spiral strips of skin for the girls to throw at sunrise. The shapes that the strips form on the ground will spell out the next year of the girls' love lives. Taffy asked me with a hard smile if I would cut the skins. "It's always better if a boy does it, Soren, but not one any of us wants."

Instead of rising to her bait, I took the basket and pulled a sharp knife from my boot. The only time she and London fight, it's over how mean she can be, but I tell him it's her way of including me. "Blow that!" he says. "You're my friend." But then he goes and sits with them and knows I won't follow.

As I lift a particularly red apple from the basket, I feel the fever spread in my chest, as though I've swallowed hot cider. The warmth spreads up my neck and flushes across my face. I hold tightly to the apple, staring at the pale glow of the TV reflected in its waxy skin. Then I close my eyes and a rush of empty blackness fills my head. There's a distant roar, and I wish I were only going to pass out.

The apple falls from my suddenly shaking fingers. I push my palms against the smooth table. All around me, students laugh and chatter, oblivious to the chaos swimming inside me, to the danger here. I have to get out. I have to be free of the hall before this power claims me and I destroy everyone.

But as quickly as it flooded through me, the fever trickles away. I'm left, gasping, in the center of all that noise and crowd, a husk of what I was only moments before. I abandon the basket of apples and even the knife, and push outside.

The fever has never come on so suddenly. I need to get to Master Pirro, because he'll know what to do. He's supposed to help me when it happens. That's why I'm here at Sanctus

Sigurd's—to be near a man who can control me, because my dad isn't available. But he's out at the perimeter of the school grounds, resetting the troll wards as he does at every change of season.

Panic stretches across my chest.

I need to calm down.

There's one place I won't be disturbed: the combat arena. Tucked back at the edge of the burial hills, up against the woods, it's where they teach us fighting, preparing us for the day we might be called to ritual combat in response to a lawsuit or claim of honor against us. But it's a formality these days, or a game. Most lawsuits don't end this way anymore—and the vast majority of people hire a professional to represent them in holmcourt, either a fighter or a lawspeaker. But the arena is where I spend my free time.

I stop beside the gate to tear off my shirt and kick away my boots. I shouldn't work out in my school pants, but I can't return to the dorms, whose common rooms are crushed full with students excited and babbling about the holiday.

And so I do what I do best: lose myself in exercise.

First I choose the slow, focused stretching program Master Pirro and I developed last year. He isn't happy with my decision to fight the frenzy, says it will bite me in the ass someday, but I can't do anything else. My father was a full berserker by the time he was thirteen, and I hoped when I turned sixteen and it still hadn't come that maybe it never would. But since I turned seventeen I've been sleeping less and less and I'm constantly plagued by these low-grade fevers. All I can do is train my muscles for skill and calm, prepare my mind to contain the wildness. Isolate myself, keep tight control, be ready.

When I'm warm and loose despite the chill air on my back, I grab a dull practice spear from the storage trunk and get set in the center of the arena. It's ringed by a plain fence, hung with round shields that we use to determine who wins. I haven't practiced with a partner other than Pirro since last fall because the school doesn't want me to harm anybody accidentally. But it would be such a relief to slam my spear against another's.

I dig my toes into the dirt and ground into a mountain stance. Deep breaths lead me into the routine: thrusting with my spear, turning, cutting, blocking against an invisible opponent. Always knowing where I am, how my body fits into the eddies of air, aware of the wind on my face and through the leaves of the trees behind me. The ground holds me secure, and I lift each foot as though I stretch roots connecting my soles to the earth. I'm between earth and sky, in a fluid dance of battle melding all things into one. I am in control. I am warm and calm, not feverish. I am Soren Bearskin.

Five repetitions later and I'm moving carefully through a serpent routine, my eyes closed and the spear horizontal to the earth. All I'm aware of is the air moving in and out of my lungs, the next step, and the smooth but rapid beat of my heart.

I feel her coming through the strands of wind.

I stop, and the earth and sky whirl without me until I suck

in a deep breath and push the energy down through my feet, my roots, and back into the dusty arena floor. I open my eyes.

Astrid watches me from the fence. The wind ruffles the hem of her skirt. She should be freezing, but this is what she's worn both times I've seen her out of uniform: flimsy dress and thin sweater, with that circle of black pearls around her neck. As though she exists in a world that's always summer.

"Astrid," I say, not moving from the center of the combat arena.

Again she doesn't bother with small talk, or even with complaining that I left her room so suddenly two nights ago. Leaning her arms on the top rail of the fence, she just says, "Every year on Baldur's Night, I try to find my mother."

I don't know what to say. Her mother is dead.

"I chew corrberries and breathe yew smoke, Soren, and I dance a seething dance to search for her. For anything that will help me find her." Astrid's voice is smooth and unconcerned, but there's something in the tension of her fingers where she grips the fence. This feels like a challenge. Like she's daring me to say it. *But, Astrid, your mother is dead.*

She lifts her hands, palms up, as if releasing some invisible balloon into the sky. "But every year I only see apples."

I frown. There isn't a single reason I can come up with for her to tell me this. "Apples?"

"Apples!" she laughs. The edge of her smile catches me, and I put down my spear. I walk to the fence and rest my hands on the gatepost near hers. Elf-kisses trail around her wrists: she's cold; she just doesn't care. "I was thinking, though." She tilts her head up, and the laughter falls away. I wait, still unsure what she wants from me. The fever sleeps in my chest, but restlessly.

"Maybe . . . ," she continues, lowering her eyes. She begins to reach for my hand, but doesn't. When she looks back up at me, she's determined. "Maybe you can help me go farther. You can help me find her."

"Me? Help you go farther where?" I'm trapped between wishing she *would* touch my hand and wanting to get away before my fever wakes again.

"Into the seething. Across the river of stars and through the roots of the New World Tree, into death." She counters the drama of her words with a wry smile. "Where all the wisdom of the world resides, you know."

"I didn't."

Her smile softens again and her hand shifts closer to mine. "Will you anchor me, Soren?" It's strangely formal, as a request from one warrior to another.

I focus on her fingers, wanting rather desperately to say yes without thinking. But my best defense is caution. "I'm not safe."

"You're the only person at this school with Freya's wild magic inside you, too."

"It's not her magic in me. It's Odin's." I take my hands off the fence. I've never had a conversation like this before, never said so many true, raw things.

"Soren." Astrid becomes as still as stone. With one finger she touches my face. As she traces the spear tattoo cleaving my left cheek, I nearly flinch away. "I am not afraid of Odin's berserk warriors. Especially a boy who has yet to raise his spear for battle."

Now I do withdraw a few inches. But no one has said they aren't afraid of me before. None of the students here, none of the teachers, not my mom, not even Master Pirro. Just this girl I barely know. "Why not?" I ask, unsure I want to hear the answer.

"You stand between the earth and the sky," she says, echoing my own thoughts. "So do I."

That feeling of knotting fate my mom told me about is hot around me, and Astrid presents such a certainty, as if she knows all the possible outcomes. As if she's really not afraid. I want to be unafraid, too. I want to, but I can't. I remember what happened to my dad. I say, "It's a dangerous place to be."

"Which is why I want help. Why I need you." Astrid takes my wrists, curls her fingers around them. Her skin seems to send ropes of cold up through my bones. The frenzy leaps in my chest, or I tell myself that's what it is: only the frenzy reacting to a seether, and not just me wanting this girl to keep talking to me. To keep holding my hands.

"Soren." She squeezes her fingers against my pulse. "Tonight will you help me build my fire, and stand ready while I dance?" Her voice is a whisper, mingling with the wind through the valley meadow.

I nod, unable to speak the words pressing against my teeth.

+ + +

As the sun sets, Astrid and I sneak out of our dorm rooms and meet at Sigurd's fountain. She carries a leather bag strapped over her shoulder and I have my own sharp spear. Together we walk into the darkness, toward the academy burial hill. As we climb the barrow, a slice of moon teases us with scant light, and the buildings of the academy below us are like dollhouses.

I stand, watching the shadows that press toward the campus. Every window blazes. It's a separate world in those school buildings, shallow and easy and full of hope. Normal. Nothing like the chaos out here.

Unrolling the leather seething kit, Astrid removes two thin vials and a pouch of seeds. One vial contains lighter fluid, with which she lights a small fire made of yew branches swiped from the Great Hall. Their acrid scent sharpens the night for me. Astrid spills the oily contents of the second vial onto her fingers. She draws runes on her forehead and in the palms of her hands. I smell something heady and sweet like honey soda.

"Be ready to catch me, Soren," she says, and reaches into the small pouch of tiny red seeds. She tosses three into the fire and puts one more on her tongue. As she chews, she closes her eyes.

I've seen seethers on TV. Usually there's a grand display: drummers and attendants helping the seethkona up onto a chair raised high over her audience. She wears elaborate clothing: calfskin boots, a necklace of boar's teeth, gloves from the skin of a cat. A feast is prepared, from the hearts of native animals. These things are to anchor her in the world, to firmly remind her physical body that she is of the animals, of the earth. When she's ready, she begins her song, and her attendants pick up the tune, singing it in rounds while the seethkona dances. Seekers bring their questions and needs to her, crying them out from beside the high chair, and the seethkona answers as she can, or as she pleases.

Astrid has none of these things. She has only her fire, her berries, and me.

I wait, and she starts to sway. There's no wind to rock her; it's only the magic. My fever churns, flushing under my skin. Astrid brings it out in me. She's everything I've avoided: desire and wild magic, like the embodiment of frenzy itself. Here in the dark, alone with her as she turns in the firelight, I can easily imagine her an avatar from the Alfather, sent to awaken his wayward berserker.

And so, crouching, I ground myself firmly. She asked me here to catch her, not to dance wildly with her. Not to let go. The fever churns, but I dig my fingers into the frosty grass.

She gives herself over to the wild darkness of the sky, dancing with her arms spread out, twirling and twirling. I remain solid, crouched on the earth with my spear for balance, watching her let go and dance. For the first time ever I wish I could do the same, but promise myself it's enough to catch her.

The hill below us is used to bury princes and jarls, the illustrious alumni of Sanctus Sigurd Academy. When Astrid stomps on the yellow grass, I imagine I can feel their bones stomping back.

Our small fire flares orange and red. Astrid spins, her eyes blind and mouth open in wonder.

And when her feet stop but her body continues and she topples down—I'm there. I wrap my arms around her and cradle her against the crown of the burial hill. Her heartbeat pounds against her skin, and I feel it. So do the bones below.

I hold her there. The fire grabs at my back.

Her eyes are closed, but shivering with dreams. She curls her fingers into my shirt and a dark twist of hair falls over her face as she turns into me. I hardly remember how to breathe, but her own breath has a slow rhythm, and I match mine to it. All through the night I anchor her in my arms, against the earth, while her spirit flies through death.

The dawning sun paints golden waves into the Missoura River at the edge of Sanctus Sigurd land, and Astrid wakes up. I've been waiting, focused on smoothing my thoughts. Her passion and the bright lights of the school and my own fever kept me company all night, but as the sun rises, I'm calm.

"Soren," she says.

Her open eyes are some sort of trigger, and I release her. She stretches and rolls out of my lap. My legs tingle fiercely as blood rushes into my calves again. "It's dawn," I say.

Astrid stands on unsteady legs, scanning the rolling hills, the thin spring woods, us and the silent buildings of the academy. "No movement?"

"Not yet." My body feels hollow and light without her weight, as if she anchored me as much as I did her. I want to touch her shoulders, grasp her gently against me again.

"Then we have a few minutes."

Inside the Great Hall, and in the dormitory common rooms, the students and faculty must be gathered in front of televisions to see Baldur rise. Everyone across the United States of Asgard will be watching the ritual in Philadelphia as his priests spread the ashes from his death pyre into the roots of the giant New World Tree. Cameras will flash, the seethers will sing, and everyone will wait as—slowly, slowly—Baldur the Beautiful climbs hale and whole out of his own ashes: new, golden, and alive. He'll stand, bewildered and smiling, and the crowd will cheer. The gods will sweep their favored son away, until he appears at Bright Home, in Colorada, for a massive feast.

My stomach growls. There will be a feast at the academy, too. Candied plums and turkey and a whole roasted pig. Everyone but me will drink blessed honey mead.

"I didn't see her," Astrid says, sinking to sit in front of me, blocking my view of the sunrise so that she's a silhouette, with the golden aura behind her. It's the first time her voice sounds like the voice of a girl, not a legend. As if overnight that other-worldly aura popped.

"I'm sorry." Instead of watching Astrid's eyes, I focus on her fingers. People give away so much with their hands.

Astrid says, "My uncle went to identify her body, and wouldn't take me. But I've dreamed of her alive, Soren, and that's all I need. Besides, if she were dead, she would be easy to find." Astrid's mouth presses into a thin line. "I could summon her spirit then, as I could summon your father."

I don't need the reminder that my father is definitely dead, shot twenty-three times by police bullets. I watched his body burn.

Astrid seems to regret her words immediately, and scoots closer to me. "This is what I saw tonight: Baldur sitting in a desert. Faraway cities and people with mournful faces. I saw the New World Tree with ashes at its base, and the ashes blew away in a violent burst of wind. They scattered and became hundreds of people reaching out toward me. I saw an orchard of apple trees, stretching to the horizon, as far as I could ever run or fly. The apples were every color of the rainbow and together they made a bridge leading away from the Middle World and into Old Asgard, where the gods feast and fight and laugh. I saw the tent revivals my mother loved and the White Hall in Philly when the president's personal seethkona invoked Freya's blessing upon my family nine months and a day after Mom disappeared. I saw the people's tears and I saw endless streams of mourners on every TV in the States. But I didn't see my mother."

We sit in silence while the sky changes from indigo to pink and then to gruesome orange in the east.

"Maybe," I say, "you should look on a different night, when there is not so much of Baldur in the air, and the expectations of the world."

"This was her favorite holiday, though. Because of the hope, she said. She never worked on it, though she should have, and never tried to do anything but be my mom. Not a seer or prophetess or holy woman. We would curl up in her bed with a tiny TV stacked between us on books, eating bacon and roasted apples."

It's the most normal thing she's ever told me. I say, "My father liked the Hallowblot, for the humor of it. He used to take me to sacrifice mice to the goblins and trolls, and said, 'This mouse lives only for a single moment: his death. Just like us, my bear-son.'"

"Bear-son. I like it. I was Mom's little cat."

It wasn't clever of either of our parents. Cats are Freya's favored beast, and all berserkers are known as bears. Instead it was a promise to both of us, a naming of our fates.

"Astrid—" I begin, intending to ask her if she ever thinks of not becoming a seethkona like her mother.

She lifts her head suddenly. "Do you hear that?"

Before she finishes, I do: a wail crawling up toward the clouds.

It comes from the academy, where all the lights continue to blaze even as the sky turns blue. The wail is joined by another voice, then another, in a keening that raises the hairs on my neck.

"They're all crying," Astrid whispers.

The windows and doors of the dorms and class buildings leak with pain. I stand and Astrid does, too. But neither of us moves. The wailing is such a contrast to the bright morning, to the rippling clouds blowing from the south. The Missoura River is a blue ribbon sliding through the prairie, dragging streaks of sunlight toward us.

I run, and under my feet the frosted yellow grass crunches.

Astrid is behind me, so I pause and hold out my hand for her to take. We fly together away from the barrow.

As we careen into the courtyard, even the spill of water from the fountain statue of Sigurd Dragonslayer is overwhelmed by the keening. It's all around us, as though the air itself screams. I remember what it was like to be surrounded by mournful wails and the smell of blood, in that candy-colored shopping mall, and I suddenly can't move.

"The dorm." Astrid jerks my hand, breaking me from my memory. We run across the courtyard and up the three sandstone steps to burst through the front door of the girls' dormitory. The crying splits my head. In the dark wooden common room, two dozen girls clutch pillows and blankets, lips parted to wail through their teeth. The cries layer over and over and I cannot stand it. I back away.

Astrid falls to her knees, pointing at the projection screen.

The New World Tree is there, towering seven stories high and shading the entire park. Valkyrie in their corselets and feather cloaks push back a mob of men and women. The angry crowd raises fists and yells, but I cannot hear anything over the awful noise that presses into my eyeballs. A reporter stands in front of the camera, microphone shaking. Her words are drowned out, but a message scrolls across the bottom of the screen in bright yellow letters: THE SUN IS RISEN BUT BALDUR THE BEAUTIFUL REMAINS IN ASHES.

THREE

WITHIN AN HOUR, the whole school's been assembled in the Great Hall. It's the largest building on campus, and the only place we all fit at once. Pillars hold up the high roof and a line of small windows lets in sunlight. Benches are arranged in concentric circles. As we watch the constant news coverage on ABS, various cliques gather into clumps: the vikers and the brains on opposite ends; members of the joy squad trying to cheer themselves up by painting posters for their next rally. The prayer keepers argue about whether they should be asking Freya to deliver Baldur back to us, or asking Thor to fight his way into Hel and drag the missing god home. Damon Alling, the chief of student government, is loudly explaining to his lawspeaker that this is the kind of thing that happens only under an Odinic administration, but he's just aping his father.

Travis, one of the stoneball jocks, catches my eye and rolls his in Damon's direction. I never played with the team, but sometimes I used to join them in the weight room. A handful of the guys will still occasionally toss the ball my way in the courtyard—from a fair distance. I shake my head at him and shrug—*What can you do?*—just as London sits down on the bench a couple of feet from me.

"So," he says, stripping off his gray school jacket, "do you think it's the end of the world?"

I glance at the wide-screen television at the front of the hall: an anchorman with black braids is interviewing a representative from Congress. Their words appear in captions at the bottom of the screen. The representative is talking about what actions the assembly is taking to find Baldur. "No," I tell London.

"Why not?" His hands flex aggressively. His enmity isn't directed at me, but at the world in general. Sometimes I think London wants me to go berserk, to give him a reason to fight.

"I haven't heard the Gjallarhorn," I say. "Without the horn's signal, it can't be the end."

As he considers my answer, my gaze wanders again, this time to where Astrid sits several rows ahead with Taffy and two girls from the Poets' Club. Their heads are together, though Astrid continually throws looks toward the small door behind the television as if she's expecting someone to walk through.

London points at the TV. There's a new woman being interviewed. She's got the catskin gloves of a seethkona. "She thinks perhaps Baldur's been swallowed by Fenris Wolf," London says, "and the wolf swallowing the sun is the first sign of Ragnarok."

Sighing heavily, I clap one hand on London's shoulder. "Then, London Roschild," I say, "we shall battle the hordes of Hel side by side."

A smile peels back from his teeth and London laughs. "I'm being foolish," he says.

I shrug. "Not all would say so."

London pulls a pocket dagger from his boot and a small cleaning kit out of his bag. "We're not canceling the campaign next week unless we have to, and I'm still short a rear guard on my team," he mentions as casually as possible.

I don't answer, and he isn't truly expecting me to. We've had similar conversations before. He knows berserkers aren't cleared to participate in educational war games. We're too much of a liability. As London polishes the dagger, I glance at the hammer charm on the chain around his neck. It's made of iron nails. Being dedicated to mighty, brave Thor doesn't keep London from fear. I wonder what it gives him.

And I wonder what dedicating to Freya gives Astrid. When I glance at her, she's rising from her seat, looking again toward the rear door.

Just then it opens, and Modra Hadley walks through. She's a sturdy woman with a dozen brown braids wound into a crown, and a cool blue circle painted on her right temple because she's devoted to Frigg the Cloud-Spinner, Queen of Heaven. And naturally unsympathetic to my situation. She knocks the foot of her cane against the wooden dais until we're all paying attention. Her vice-modra Amanda, a spindly young woman ten years older than me, scurries after, carrying a stack of attendance sheets and holding her cell phone to her ear. She's nodding frantically and keeps opening her mouth but can't get a word in.

Hadley taps her cane one last time, then gestures at the television, which is nearly as tall as she is. "Boys and girls, in two minutes the president will be addressing the country, and so will Gundrun Graycloak and Lawspeaker Howardson. Please be attentive. And after the address, will the following students report back to your dormitories, please. Your advisors will be waiting to help you pack a bag, as your parents have contacted the school in the last hour and will be arriving to take you home shortly." There's an immediate uproar, but Hadley gestures at Amanda, who hurriedly snaps closed her phone and begins calling out names over the noise.

Amanda's gotten through about two dozen, including Damon Alling and half his cadre of politically involved students, when the news broadcast is interrupted by a bright blue screen depicting the seal of Congress: a white eagle over a shield, gripping an ax and a spear in its claws, and above, the rune for justice. Professor Dayling turns the sound up as the seal fades and we're presented with the president and the lawspeaker sitting side by side at a broad mahogany desk at the White Hall. Lawspeaker Howardson is a woman with solid-silver braids and a stern mouth. She holds a replica of the Poet's Cup, symbol of her office, and as she begins to speak, she raises it slightly off the desk with both hands. The official words are in Old Scandan, but we all know them: *So the law is written, so the law is spoken, I give life to the law.* She passes the cup to the president of New Asgard, a middle-aged warrior I haven't paid attention to since he was elected by Congress two springs ago. His name is Adamson and he has dark hair.

There's a small raven pin on his lapel, indicating his allegiance to Odin Alfather. A ragged scar under his jaw twists as he offers his country a somber smile. "We of the Congress ask that our people across the USA not panic, but hold steady in this time of distress. We are doing all that can be done to search out Baldur the Beautiful and discover the culprit who stole him. Please remain calm and go about your daily business as best you can. The worst thing we can do is give in to fear. We are a people of courage, no matter which god we hold dear, and I personally ask you to remember that. The sun will return to New Asgard."

He continues on, giving us details about how the national army is coordinating with kingstate and community militias to conduct searches. An emergency hotline number scrolls across the screen, for phoning in any tips. After a few minutes of continued assurances, the president hands us over to the press room, where the beautiful Gundrun Graycloak stands behind a podium with the Alfather's triple-triangle valknot symbol behind her on banners. Gundrun is the chief of the Valkyrie, and she speaks on the gods' behalf to the current mortal administration of New Asgard. Over a dark pantsuit she wears the traditional swan-feather cloak of the Valkyrie, and there is a spear in her hand. "I bring tidings of comfort to the people of New Asgard from the Alfather and all the gods under his rule: Baldur lives, though we know not where he is. The ashes spread at dawn this morning over the roots of the New World Tree did not belong to the god of light, but were the ashes of a pig."

From beside Astrid, Taffy yells, "What's the difference?"

only to be shushed by her friends in the Poets' Club. A quiet snicker passes through our hall, though I frown.

Modra Hadley glares mightily and bangs her cane against the dais.

Gundrun Graycloak is saying, ". . . have questioned Loki, and Freya herself has vouched for his whereabouts. Do please alert your king's hotline if you know anything that might possibly aid in the search. I am authorized to inform you that Odin Alfather himself will grant a boon to any citizen of New Asgard who significantly helps to locate Baldur."

A collective gasp pops in the Great Hall. Even the professors and Modra Hadley show signs of shock and sudden greed. The stoneball players begin yelling to London and his battleguild team, trying to talk strategy; the vikers cheer from their end; and the prayer keepers send up a plea to Odin, no longer needing to argue about who will receive their appeal. In the chaos, I can't hear how Gundrun Graycloak finishes her brief speech, but it doesn't matter because I see Astrid push through the benches and head for the main doors.

I follow, thinking only about what she said this morning: that she saw Baldur in the desert and ashes blowing away from the New World Tree.

Just as the heavy doors swing closed behind me, I catch a glimpse of her skirts as she rounds the corner of the girls' dormitory. I jog after in time to see her vanish into the woods.

I pause between two tall trees, wondering if she wants to be alone, if I'll only be annoying her if I follow. But then I recall the expression of loss pressing down her mouth as she stood up from her bench, and I keep going.

It's cold in the shade. None of the trees have new buds yet, and the ground is dank with fallen leaves left to freeze over the winter. Thin branches clatter together in the wind.

Astrid follows a straight path, and I easily catch up to her where she's huddled at the bank of the creek. The water barely trickles around flat rocks and exposed roots. Astrid's head is lowered and she stares at the stream with her arms wrapped around her knees.

"Astrid?"

Her whole body jerks and she stands. "Oh, Soren." She relaxes.

"I don't mean to disturb you, but . . ." I gesture rather helplessly at the path she took. "You were running, and I thought you might need something."

Leaning back against a gray tree, she says, "I need a lot of things."

I don't reply, just study her. The corners of her eyes are red. I take a step closer. "What's wrong? Are you hurt?"

She smiles. "I'm not that delicate."

"Everyone has weak days."

"You?"

"I feel weak every day."

"I don't believe that. You wouldn't fight it so hard if you were weak."

"I fight it so hard because I am."

"No."

I open my mouth to contradict her, but she shakes her head. "Soren, I'm thinking about what Odin is promising, to whomever returns the Light to Asgard."

"A boon from the Alfather is a great thing," I say quietly.

She's staring at my eyes and I want to look away. She expects me to ask, *Do you think he would take away my berserking?* Instead I say, "He could tell you certainly about your mother."

A hiss presses out through her teeth and she turns away from me.

"You're going to try, aren't you?"

There's no answer. Her shoulders shake as a cold breeze flows around us.

"Will you start in the desert?" I ask. "As you saw last night when you seethed?"

After a drawn-out breath, she asks in return, "Do you love the gods, Soren?"

"Love them?"

"You don't wear Odin's symbols, or a hammer charm for Thor. You don't light candles in the chapel."

"What does that have to do with love?"

She turns back as a quick smile appears and vanishes on her mouth. But her upset is so clear in the rigid posture of her hands. "Faith, then. Do you believe in them? My mom used to tell me all I needed was faith. 'Believe in them, little cat.' It was the last thing she said to me, you know." Astrid's eyes are big, as though if she holds them wide open enough she will only see me, not her memories. "But I thought having faith in our gods was like having faith that the grass will be green or that gravity will hold me to the ground. There isn't anything to have faith in. They simply *are*. They're real. Their power is real, even if they choose not to use it sometimes." Her voice lowers and I'm not certain she's talking to me anymore. "And then one morning, the sun doesn't rise. Baldur the Beautiful does not do what he's done for a thousand years! I feel it like a hollow wound right here." Astrid jabs her fingers against her diaphragm.

"Why are you telling me this?"

"Because you take it seriously. Every day you live with the consequences of the gods in our lives. So many people ignore the gods' influence until it's convenient to pay attention. Until they need goblins evicted from their basement or can't decide what cancer treatment to accept. Taffy just wants me to toss the bones and weave prophecy to tell her if she'll pass her history exam, and all the girls look at me as if they expect my mother. Expect prophecy to fall out of my mouth every time I open it. You know it's work. You know it isn't a game."

I stare at her eyes, where her passion burns hotly enough that for a moment I am glad I can't feel it. If I were like her, my berserking would have awakened long ago. But if I were like her, I might not mind—and what would that be like? To embrace the wild battle-fury the way she embraces her spinning magic? For a moment I consider it, my eyes dragging down to her lips as I imagine kissing her, imagine putting my arms around her and drinking her passion up, and her courage, too.

"Soren, what are you thinking?"

I hear her only because I see her lips move. "I am thinking that if anyone can find him, it's you."

"Because of who my mother was." Her brow lowers, her eyes narrow.

"No." I step away. Otherwise I'll kneel before her. "Because you'll be the only one doing it for the right reason."

Her face opens back up, but she remains silent.

I leave her alone in the forest.

While the rest of the academy's students are forced to spend the afternoon in club activities and sports, to keep their minds off the outside troubles, I work out in the combat arena with Master Pirro.

Today he's grumpy and distracted, and I don't have to ask why. Nothing like this, like a missing god, has happened in anyone's memory. He wants to be out there, with the war bands, searching. Doing. It's what he's meant for, but instead he's babysitting a kid berserker who refuses to let the fury come.

I heft my ax between two stances, both defensive, while Pirro barks at me to shift my left foot back or roll one of my shoulders. It's rare enough for a berserker to live into old age, and while he's a great instructor, the years have cooled his battle-fire enough to make his bones creak and keep us from sparring often.

Out of nowhere, Pirro calls a halt and says, "Soren, I've talked with my old friend Karlson at the Hangadrottin. He might have a place for you after Disir Day."

I don't move; I stand holding the heavy ax stuck halfway through a swing. Most of the best generals of our time attended the war college, as did the president himself. If I wanted to be a berserker, it would be my obvious choice. I have the credentials: recommendation and family tradition. Dad graduated from there, but in the end it wasn't enough to teach him control.

Pirro grimaces so broadly it pushes all his wrinkles up over his eyes and I don't know how he can see through them. He lays a hand on my wrist, gently pressing down so that I lower the ax to the holmring ground. "You need to study with them, Bearskin, to prepare to join a commit and serve your god and country."

He speaks as if my berserking is inevitable.

Because I won't answer him, Pirro continues gruffly, "You need their . . . training. The kind I can't give you."

Conditioning, he means. The exercises they put you through to teach you how to kill not just trolls or goblins, but other men. For us it isn't only about learning to pull the trigger, but about coping afterward, when you come back to yourself and are surrounded by bodies of whatever it is you've murdered while you went berserk.

The thought of it sets the fever spinning, making my stomach turn over until I clench my jaw and press my tongue to the roof of my mouth. I take a deep breath through my nose and turn away from Pirro.

I want it gone. I want so badly to be free; it's like a magnet pulling at my heart. What if Odin could take it away? What if Astrid could really find Baldur, and win us the Alfather's boon?

Pirro sighs. "Think it over, Soren. Better to be prepared. When the rage fully takes you, your choices will be over."

Then he gives me permission to go up to my dorm to work on my Anglish paper. But I'm too restless to write. Instead I sit on the floor where London's bed used to be and concentrate on my breathing. It takes all my focus to balance the fever, to calm it by spreading the heat evenly through my skin. As I slowly breathe, Astrid's words whisper in my ears. *This is what I saw tonight: Baldur sitting in a desert. Faraway cities and people with mournful faces. I saw the New World Tree with ashes at its base, and the ashes blew away in a violent burst of wind.*

She could find him.

A boon from the Alfather is a great thing.

I can hear the trickle of Sigurd's fountain now. The Dragonslayer had the patronage of a god. I would if I accepted Odin's—as Pirro insists I must.

There was a berserker thirteen hundred years ago named Starkad who served Vikar the King. Starkad was known throughout the north as stronger than a dozen bears, wittier than ten poets, and quicker than Loki himself. He and his king went a-viking, drawing praise and glory to their names. But on the way home, their ship was becalmed in a shallow bay. They swam ashore to pray and make sacrifice. Starkad dreamed that in order to be free they must draw lots among the band and sacrifice the chosen man. Because it was a high honor to be killed for Odin's sake, and because they were desperate, the men agreed. Vikar the King drew the short lot. Again and again they redrew, but all three times Vikar was named to die. But Starkad was distraught—his king, his lord, could not be lost outside of battle, even if it was to the Hanging Tree. Again

Starkad prayed, and Odin himself appeared in his dreams and said to Starkad that if he himself cast a reed spear at Vikar as the king stood beneath the tree, the shaft would shatter and the symbolic sacrifice would release them all. Starkad awoke, relieved. That morning as Vikar stood with his neck in the noose, Starkad raised a reed spear and, with a call of praise to Odin, cast it at his king.

The reed pierced Vikar's chest, destroying his heart.

Such is the honor of Odin, creator of the berserk warriors.

Astrid suggested that I have no love for the gods, but could she blame me for not wearing Odin's ring about my neck? This spear tattoo is required of me, as a warning to others of what I am, but I refuse to claim allegiance to a god who would so easily betray his own. As he did my father.

When I open my eyes, the sun has set, and I've missed the call to dinner. But nobody will mind. They might even be grateful I'm not adding my presence to the anxiety pushing throughout the school.

There's a tap at my window, like a tiny bird pecking to be let inside. I glance over and see only blackness. As I stand, the sound reoccurs. The window doesn't open, but I put my nose as close as I'm able. Down in the dark stone courtyard is Astrid. She raises her hand and tosses another pebble. I put my hand to the glass and she sees me. She waves me down. Beside her is a canvas bag.

A louder knock on my door shocks me.

In two strides I'm there, tugging it open.

Taffy.

She pushes past me into the bedroom, then whirls on me as if I'm the one who barged into *her* room. "She thinks you'll go with her."

I look down at her, at the frizz of blond hair she's pulled back into a tight braid, at her snub nose and surprisingly pink lips.

"Convince her to stay, Soren."

"No."

Taffy moves nearer so that she's completely within my personal space, her crossed arms only a breath from my chest. Her eyelids flutter, the only sign she's not as confident as she wishes to appear. "Why not?" she demands, but her voice isn't as sharp as usual.

I glance at the black square of the window and imagine Astrid waiting beside the Sigurd fountain, calm and certain I'm on my way. She needs me, just as she did last night when she danced into the future. I was with her when she saw Baldur, and I should be with her when she finds him. "I know what she is," I tell Taffy. "I know what her power is, and what mine is."

She sucks breath in through her teeth. "You think she can do it. That you can do it."

"Yes."

For a dozen of my slow heartbeats, Taffy stares up at me, her lips parted. Then she lifts a hand to fidget with the end of her braid where it sits over her shoulder.

I walk to my trunk for my old backpack. I stuff in extra shirts, sweats, and my toothbrush. Taffy says nothing as I put on a dark blue hoodie and tie up my boots. I grab my father's sword and buckle the sheath to my back, then sling the backpack over it. I take my spear from the closet.

A light touch on my arm nearly puts me out of my skin.

Taffy flattens her whole hand against my shoulder and says quietly, "I should have peeled the apples myself."

My cluelessness must be apparent, because she grows angry again. "I was trying to apologize, Soren!" She snatches away her hand.

"Oh." It's barely even a word, but she draws a deep breath and nods once, accepting it.

"London would want me to say . . ." She hesitates, her chin down. The rest rushes out: "Thor's strength and Loki's luck go with you. But I'll just settle for"—Taffy lifts her face and glares—"God's blessings on both of you. Keep her safe, berserker."

My smile feels weighted down. But I promise.

It's easy to slip out past the RA, since he watches too much National Stoneball to pay close attention to his wards. Especially on a night like tonight.

Astrid waits on the front steps of my dorm, and when I push open the door, she smiles. Silently, we jog through the courtyard, keeping to the shadows next to buildings. Nearly all the windows pour forth light and the sounds of TV updates, and the majority of the academy is locked down waiting for news instead of engaged in the regular evening movement between buildings for study sessions or visits to friends in another dorm.

Because the main gate may be watched for signs of more parents arriving to collect their kids, we cut through the woods. When we pass the burial hill, Astrid scrambles up it, disappearing over the summit. She skids back down a moment later, an ashy yew branch clenched in her fist. It's about the thickness of her pointer finger. "A wand for luck," she whispers.

The trees envelop us, but I know the quickest path off the property from my long runs. Leaves crackle beneath our feet and an owl hoots. Flapping wings trail behind us, but I can't find the bird to identify it in all the darkness.

We push out through the edge of the woods into an open field. It lies fallow, and has at least as long as I've been here. Before us is a gravel road leading west into the nearest town. It will take nearly two hours to walk, I guess, and as we pass one of the troll-marked stones Pirro showed me last winter, I am very glad the hill trolls were driven out of this area long ago. I keep a firm grip on my spear, though, for there might still be lesser trolls and goblins haunting the empty land between here and town. Trolls rarely attack large gatherings of people, but their tenacity is the main reason most people in New Asgard live inside a city.

Astrid takes off for the road. "Do you have a plan?" I ask.

"In town, I'll wire my uncle for some money."

That's good, because I only have half a note and change.

"Then we'll take the bus to Omaha, where we can rent a car."

"They'll be able to track us too easily."

Astrid hefts her bag more firmly over her shoulder. "Richard won't tell anyone anything, and even if they use the credit information from the car place, they'll never catch us in time. This won't take more than a couple of days."

"Baldur is that nearby?"

Her smile is beatific. "You know I dreamed he was in a desert. There were layers of rock towering high all around him and a hill covered in little flowering cactuses. And a stone shaped like a mushroom. I didn't think of it until this afternoon, when I was writing everything down from the dreams, but I've been to that exact place. I know where he is. It's only eight hours from Omaha in a car. Less if we take the kingstate highways."

I regard her as we stand still at the edge of the gravel road. Despite being on a quest, and despite the frost on the ground, she wears one of her perpetual sundresses and a thin sweater. The string of black pearls hugs her neck. I don't know what pearls are good for, in the seethkona business. She's dressed for lunch at a New Amsterdam café, not for hunting a missing god.

And yet, without saying any more, I transfer my spear to my left hand and offer Astrid my right.

FOUR

WE DRIVE THROUGH flat farmland still sleeping off the vestiges of winter. As the sun rises behind us, it melts frost, pulling gray off the sharp spikes of harvested hay and turning everything around us into gold.

From Omaha, we took the rental car northwest on Highway 275 toward the South Lakota kingstate. Now the highway follows the Elkhorn River, a wide, sad thing dragging a line of trees with it. A hundred years ago this area was the location of constant skirmishes between the New Asgardian militias and native tribes. My grandfather's grandfather was captain of the berserk band stationed here, and I wonder if he stared at the same stretch of river.

Astrid's window is rolled down and the wind of our passing roars inside. It's midmorning, and she grips the wide wheel of our car loosely, drumming one finger against it to the rhythm of some song playing in her head. When she chose this car I was amazed, and suggested something more sensible than a heavy '84 Volundr Spark with tail fins and a manual transmission.

But she shook her head so that her curls flounced. "It's what Mom and I used to drive all over the country, Soren. Well, we had an '89. But this is very reliable."

Any vehicle painted bright orange seems less than reliable to me.

"You look worried," she says now. "We'll find him."

"It isn't that. I was thinking . . ." I look at her gentle smile and don't want to mention war, or anything hard and bloody. But she takes her eyes off the road to glance at me and lift her eyebrows encouragingly.

"There were battles here a century ago. I was thinking about what it would have been like to fight in them, with so much open ground. The tribes refused to send champions to fight, and so whole armies died." Their blood soaked into the ground, and after the militias won, enslaving the surviving enemy in Old Asgardian tradition, few settlers came. The area is still rife with ghosts and hill trolls. Not even the Thralls' War, which ended slavery, brought many back.

How can this be where we'll find Baldur the Beautiful? Why would he be here? I peer out the passenger window at the naked winter trees and waiting fields. A farmhouse stands like a child's block in the center of a field of razed cornstalks. Its blue paint peels, as if the atmosphere here is acid and has never recovered from war. I wonder if its inhabitants enjoy the danger of living in isolation. Or perhaps they have no choice.

"Are all berserkers so dire?" Astrid asks lightly.

I frown harder.

Her lips press together and she says, "I'll have to distract you, then. Concentrate. There may be an exam when I'm finished." The line of her mouth spreads into a smile. I lift one corner of mine in response.

And Astrid immediately launches into random facts: Her favorite holiday is Disir Day, six weeks from now, when there will be dancing and revelry, then the slaughter of cows and goats and cats in honor of the goddesses. She prefers tea to coffee, but a fine barley beer to anything in the world. She dislikes the flavor of coriander, but cinnamon reminds her of her mother.

When her mother disappeared, Astrid went to live with her uncle Richard in Westport City. "He's a seethmathr," she says, casting me a sideways glance to gauge my reaction. But I don't judge men for playing with Freya's seething magic. Odin did it himself. When I only tap my fingers on the door handle, she continues, "He makes good money at it, and most of his clients don't care that he's a man."

"Why did you come to Sanctus Sigurd's?" Astrid should have had her pick of masters in nearly any trade; she shouldn't have needed to rely on an academy education.

"I wanted to apprentice to Richard, but he was worried that we'd both be shunned if it was discovered I learned from him. We compromised by having me go to Sigurd's for at least a year, in order to convince people I'd had a semblance of a regular education."

She tells me of driving around the country with her mother, stopping to camp with dozens or occasionally hundreds of people. "The festivals were the best," she says. "When tents went up and you could buy anything, from hotpigs to bison burgers, and sit at craft tables to watch women weave bracelets, or watch quilting circles creating these immense blankets with ancient heroes and common gods on them. We bought a hand-scribed edition of the Eddas for my tenth birthday." Astrid rolls her eyes my way. "Once we met a peddler saying his sticks were straight from the New World Tree itself."

I laugh for her, though I'm reminded of the snake caravans Mom and I sometimes joined. Lokiskin who were always trying to sell false relics.

Astrid sighs quietly enough that I can't hear it over the wind, but only see the way her shoulders rise and fall. "And then there was the seething." She tightens her fingers around the steering wheel. "Gods, Soren. You've seen me seeth, but that was nothing. Mom had hundreds of followers, always giving her things to toss into the bonfires. She'd personally throw the stuff in, no matter how long it took, and then her chorus would circle around, blowing the corrberry smoke at her from every direction. I remember how exciting it was when she danced, and how hot my cheeks would get. I always knew the moment just before she hit the deepest part of the trance. Mom would stop, suddenly. And one by one the people would ask their questions. About crop failure, marriage, birth, the stock market, even vacation plans, Soren! Important things and totally not important things. But Mom answered all of them. She always knew."

I want to touch her. To just put a hand on her shoulder or her knee.

"She was loved," Astrid says. "I would like to be loved."

My mouth opens and I almost tell her that my mom abandoned me when I walked into a militia station to declare myself and accept the stigma of my father's name. Instead I ask, "Were you and your mother in this desert where we'll find Baldur?"

"Yes. We camped there. For the last time."

After that, she's quiet until we pull into Bassett, Nebrasge, for gasoline.

We fill the tank at an old-fashioned station. It's a white brick building with a striped awning. The pumps have no automatic shutoff and I try not to worry I'll spill gasoline everywhere after the trouble I had popping open the lid.

Astrid leans out the open window to ask, "Are you hungry? Looks like there's a diner down the road."

We park on the street and walk into the plain red storefront. A bell clangs over the door. There are two rows of Formica tables with peeling plastic chairs and a bar with yellow stools. We sit across from each other at a booth. Astrid barely glances at the single-sheet laminated menu before beginning to flip through the wheel of jukebox choices. I decide on the pulled-pork sandwich with fried potatoes. When the waitress comes, she smiles brightly and the wrinkles around her eyes gather. A bracelet of linked silver horses circles her wrist: she's a devotee of Freyr the Satisfied, god of wealth and joy. She introduces herself as Esmeralda and takes our order. Astrid asks about local sightseeing as if we'll be in town longer to spend more money.

The sun is bright outside, making the tiny town of Bassett bold and colorful. I'm quiet, sitting with my tattoo to the window so it won't be readily visible to the restaurant.

Our drinks are served and I don't turn my face when I thank Esmeralda. After she's scooted off again, Astrid leans across the table. "You don't trust anyone anywhere, do you?"

"It's that they don't trust me. When they see this." I flick my thumb over the bottom of the spear tattoo.

"Because you act as though you aren't to be trusted."

Scowling, I decide not to mention being chased out of a convenience store when I was only thirteen. "You've seen how people turn away at school."

"Taffy said you're the one who stopped hanging out with London. Stopped sitting with them at lunch."

"It was better that way, so he didn't have to be uncomfortable."

She pushes curls behind her ears. "What about *your* comfort? Wouldn't you rather have friends? You aren't a monster."

I clench my jaw. There are so many arguments I could make, about being kicked out of battle guild, not allowed to spar with my peers. The way the girls all pulled back in Astrid's own room the night she was reading runes. I ask, "Where exactly are we going after lunch?"

Astrid waits, studying me with narrowed eyes; then she leans back into the booth. "The Badlands."

"That's desert?"

"Yes. It's rocky and desolate and there isn't any civilization for miles and miles. Good place to hide a god." Astrid toys with the saltshaker.

"You think someone did this on purpose, then."

"Must have. Baldur's ashes didn't get up and run away themselves."

"Gundrun Graycloak said it wasn't Loki. Freya vouched for him."

She dashes salt on the table, lifts her glass of tea and puts it down on top of the salt. "He's stolen things from his brother-gods before."

"What do pearls do for seething?" I nod at the string of them hugging her clavicle. "Protection? Ease of trance?"

Astrid bites her bottom lip as she grins. "No." She laughs and caresses the pearls. "These are plastic."

"Plastic."

"Oh, Soren. Don't glower at me." Her smile doesn't fade. "Mom gave them to me, of course. Don't you have some silly thing from yours?"

"No."

She begins to speak, but her eyes slide over my shoulder. Her mouth forms a perfect O. Twisting, I glance back at the TV anchored over the bar. A sketched image of a desert valley is displayed across the monitor. A young woman behind the bar stands on tiptoe to turn up the volume.

". . . released from a massive seething dance performed privately in the court of the New World Tree. Seethkona Lilja described the image, and all six other seethkonas present agree that this is the place they saw in their dreams. Baldur was there, very much alone. No one has identified the location specifically, though the god of light is believed to be in the southern desert region, and possibly as near to Bright Home as the southern part of Colorada kingstate. Anyone with information is asked to call the tips hotline number shown at the bottom of the screen."

"Southern Colorada?" I turn back to Astrid. But she purses her lips in a mischievous smile and sips her tea.

One of the men sitting at a table across from us pushes his chair back abruptly. His friend is glaring at me.

I draw up straight and square my shoulders, but remain seated. With my eyes, I try to warn Astrid. The two men position themselves at the edge of our table, looming over us with fingers tucked into their wide belts. Both wear hammers of Thor, one strung around the neck, the other as a dangling earring. By the way they walk, I know that one of them, the man with the earring, has training in a war band. His hard eyes scour over Astrid, then dart back to me.

"Can we help you?" I ask, not allowing them the first word.

The smaller one shrugs. "We were just thinking, ya know, what is a guy like you doing in our nice little town?"

The muscles in my abdomen tighten and I must force my hands to remain flat on the tabletop. When I twisted to watch the TV, I displayed the tattoo for all to see. "Passing through," I say.

Now Astrid is going to witness exactly why I've been so wary.

"Well, isn't that nice to hear," the man with the earring says. As they hang over us, I see that neither of them is older than twenty-five. Neither stands lightly, and both have looser muscles than me, despite the hardness in the soldier's eyes. If it becomes necessary, I can get us out of the diner even without my weapons. Both sword and spear are back at the Spark; as one of Odin's, I can carry steel into any public place except for some temples, but that would have drawn immediate attention. My tattoo and my darker skin are enough to make me stand out.

The question is, are these two going to back down now that they've spoken to us, made clear they don't want us here? Or will they do something rash?

Esmeralda appears at the soldier's elbow, her smile strained. "Hey now, all, your sandwiches'll be right up. Oz, David, you getting to know our guests a bit? They're on their way up to the Black Hills."

The soldier catches my eye. I see the change on his face as the idea occurs to him. Thor's soldiers are as notoriously hotheaded as berserkers are mad. This one is going to challenge me, I know it. Fighting holmgang against a berserker, even a young one like me, will go miles for his reputation.

"Oh," Astrid interrupts merrily, "we were just asking this pig-faced troll-sucker to leave us alone."

My body flares hot with panic, and all the sound in the restaurant fades.

"What did you call me?" the soldier hisses.

"Not you, darling." Raising her voice further, she taps

the younger one on the stomach. "This giant's ass-wart was ogling me."

I shake my head, trying again to catch her eye.

But her grin only widens. "For the insult, I challenge you. You are not a man's equal, and not a man at heart." The ritual words sound like a blithe poem on her tongue, not a call to battle.

"I am as much a man as you," bites back the young man, accepting the challenge with equal ritual. His fists clench until his knuckles turn white.

"Oz," Esmeralda says. She seems as worried as me.

The soldier claps a hand on Oz's shoulder. He glances at me when he says, "We will meet in the holmring."

"A mark and a half from now," says Astrid. She asks Esmeralda, "Can we still eat?"

The waitress nods and backs away.

"This will be fun, little witch," Oz sneers. He and David stomp out of the diner. We're being watched by the handful of other patrons. One older man at the bar follows David and Oz. I sit, pressing my boots into the tiles below the table, trying to be calm. The quiet roars in my ears. I look at Astrid and she's sipping at her tea, her face unconcerned. Her chin is lowered, so she glances up at me coyly.

I slap my hands on the table, stand, and leave.

Outside, the noontime sun barely heats the air. The previously charming little town appears closed, narrow, and hostile to me now. A row of toy houses glaring at me all down the street. I reach the car and lean against it, bowing my head.

"Soren."

A growl bursts out of me. "What were you thinking?"

"He was going to challenge you."

I turn. Her eyes are shining as ever; her face is calm. "I could have handled them, Astrid. You know that."

"We can't risk it. You—you don't have your battle-fury under control. You were forbidden combat until after you come to full berserking."

"By Modra Hadley, who only holds sway at the academy." My entire body is tense. Even my teeth vibrate. "It wouldn't have been difficult to stomp their pretty asses into the ground."

Astrid clasps her hands together. "I'm only seventeen. The worst he can call is blood. Not death. But you—if you were entering the ring, you'd have to give your name. They'd know you, and he could have called to death despite your age. Besides, they'd have had guns at the ready in case . . ."

I close my eyes, seeing the kickback of a dozen rifles and hearing the thunder as my dad jerked again and again and then fell.

She puts a hand on my wrist. I grab her shoulders. "Astrid," I say helplessly.

"Will you hold my shields?" They're only more ritual words, but this time I feel like she's asking me for my whole heart.

My hands tighten on her. I lift her up so her heels leave the sidewalk.

"You're hurting me," she whispers.

I drop her as though she's caught fire. "I'm sorry." I shouldn't be here with her, where I can harm her so easily.

We stand still for a moment before she takes one step closer. "Soren Bearskin, will you hold my shields?"

Her voice makes me flush, because she still wants to trust me. Fortunately, there's an official response, so I don't have to find my own words. "I will stand at the hazel pole, Astrid Glyn, Freya's daughter, and hold your shields."

She takes my hands, the ones that held her too hard. I feel her skin cold against my fever, and as she weaves our fingers together, I stare as if they're miles away.

Astrid says, "Come on, our sandwiches are waiting, and I'll need the fuel."

FIVE

THE HOLMRING IN Bassett, Nebrasge, spreads out within a grove of white birch trees. The black eyes spiraling down the trunks serve as nature's witness. A shallow square ditch creates a border around the ring, and the grass inside has been stamped down into dust. I stand with Astrid at one corner, which is marked off with four tall poles of hazel wood.

Oz and his soldier friend David huddle together at the opposite corner. I study them, trying to determine how difficult a time Astrid will have.

All around us a crowd has gathered. Half the population of Bassett, I suspect. It's not every day a holmgang occurs, especially one involving strangers. Adults and children sit on lawn chairs or stand around drinking soda and cans of cheap beer. Cell phones are out, clicking images of the ring, Oz, and us. I want to glower and glare at the culprits, to hide my tattoo even though it's too late for that. When a guy my age turns on a handheld video camera, I can't help stepping forward.

Astrid places a hand on my elbow. "There isn't anything you can do, Soren," she murmurs.

She's right. I frown down at her.

Esmeralda found Astrid a pair of loose fight pants that tie at her waist and leave her calves bare. Astrid wears the pants and her own exercise bra and nothing else but the plastic pearls. After she dressed, I ran through stretches with her, and a quick warm-up. Astrid humored me, and waited until I was finished to remind me that she'd been training for holmgang all her life, just as I had. I gritted my teeth and had to acknowledge it. I didn't like it, but I reminded myself that for most people, holmgang is not life or death as it would be for a berserker. Many of Astrid's peers hardly even take it seriously, assuming they can buy themselves a champion to fight for them, or get away with only a scratch.

Finally, before coming to the ring, Astrid removed the seething kit from her canvas bag and unrolled it. A single long piece of leather with dozens of pockets sewn inside, the kit held all the ingredients necessary for the seethkona's trade.

"You aren't going in altered," I said, stopping her hand as it skimmed over the pockets.

"No, but I want a charm or two, and lavender oil will calm me."

"A charm?"

Pulling a round, flat piece of horn from one of the pockets, she said, "Yes, this one." She offered it to me.

The cool horn coin was rubbed smooth on both sides. A

streak of gray mottled the edge. If there had ever been a rune marked in, it was long worn away. "What is it?"

"Walrus tusk."

I wrapped my hand around the charm. Walrus tusk for heightened strength and potency. Thor himself prized such items.

"And this," she said as she gave me another.

A molar, the size of my thumb knuckle.

"From a hill troll."

The two charms together in my hand tingled warmly. I raised my fist to my mouth and said against my skin, "Myself to myself." It was the oldest of Odin's blessings, invoking the power found in self-sacrifice.

"Thank you, Soren." Astrid dabbed lavender oil from a tiny flask onto her neck. She took the charms back and tucked them into her bra.

The mayor of Bassett steps forward from the crowd to officiate. "Who challenges?" he calls.

Astrid replies, "I do. I am Astrid Glyn, daughter of Jenna, daughter of Ariel, all of us daughters of the Feather-Flying Goddess, Freya."

With relish, I watch Oz's face slacken. He knows the name of Jenna Glyn. Hisses and whispers flicker around the gathered crowd like a swarm of flies.

Swallowing his questions, the mayor waves for the guy with

the camera to keep filming and yells, "And who answers her challenge?"

"I do. I am Oslaf Smithson, son of Erik, son of Patrik, all of us sons of Thor Thunderer." Oz puts his fists on his hips. He wears only loose pants similar to Astrid's. In older times, the holmgang was fought in battle raiment and boots, often with helmets. But modern sensibility allows for less terrible holmgang, especially between young people, and it can be little more than a common spar. Even when it involves blood.

"As the challenged," the mayor continues, "you, Oslaf, may choose settlement and weapon."

"I choose blood," he snarls. The iron hammer of Thor is black against his pasty chest. "And small swords."

"I accept," Astrid says before the mayor can ask.

She returns to me so that I can hand her the first of three thin round shields—provided by the holmgang committee of the local 4-H club, Esmeralda confided quietly.

"You wouldn't have chosen small swords, would you, Soren?" Astrid whispers when she accepts the shield from me.

I raise my eyebrows. "No."

She grins, and then laughs. I can't help laughing, too. This is all so ridiculous: challenging holmgang in a diner, running across Nebrasge after a missing god, leaving school with a strange, beautiful girl. And now she's teasing me before entering the ring.

Our quiet laughter breaks some of the tension in the birch grove. Several pairs of eyes watch us warily. I look to Oz. He's glaring, and David stands behind with hands on Oz's shoulders, speaking quickly.

"Make it fast, Astrid" is all I say as she steps into the ring.

They're each given a small sword; Astrid chooses first. The sword is a short, fat one with very little crossguard. Roman style, meant for a one-handed grip. The mayor removes himself from the holmring. Silence falls and wind rattles the birch branches together. Astrid and Oz face one another. Her back swells with a deep breath. I wish I'd seen her fight before, so I'd know what to expect.

The mayor calls out, "Hear!"

Astrid salutes Oz with the tip of her sword, and he returns the gesture. They lower into fighting stances. Astrid is on her toes, ready to dart in or back. She should be faster than him, but I can't be certain.

Oz attacks with an abrupt charge, and Astrid dances out of the way. Her hair flings itself around her neck, curls bouncing. I curse myself for not telling her to braid it back. But she avoids the hit.

The same give-and-take continues for several moments as they attack each other and hurl insults like arrows. He seems wisely reluctant to insult her famous family, but Astrid has no such compunction. When she calls Oz's mother a troll-wife, he turns red and swings hard, slamming into her shield. It snaps in two and Astrid falls to the ground.

Oz backs off and spits onto the dirt.

Slowly Astrid climbs to her feet and comes to me with the pieces of her shield. I trade her for the second shield and toss the broken halves away. "Fast," I remind her. If he breaks all three of her shields, he'll be allowed a single blow while she's shieldless. For a blood match, he can choose any nonlethal cut he likes. And nonlethal is very different from noncrippling.

I swallow frustration. If this were my fight, the dullard would've been down in five seconds. But I remember that if I were fighting, it would likely have been against the soldier David, who might have given me more trouble. And called for death.

As they move in again, dog-calls come in from the audience, some yelling for Oslaf to pound the little girl into the ring floor. A few encourage Astrid. I know she can't hear, but I mark them in case we need aid leaving town when this is done. The air grows warmer and the sharp clang of swords clashing together again and again beats a pulse into the earth. I feel it in my chest, echoing among my ribs and pulling my heart into rhythm. I stare at Astrid, watching only her motions, not his. It's as though I am with her, moving with her, feeling the jar of steel up my arm, the skid of my toes on the ground, the wind in my hair as she whirls and slams her shield against his. She slips close, under his sword arm, so that he must angle awkwardly to get the steel pointed again at her.

I crow with triumph a second before she darts away again, slithering under his arm like a bride through the commit arch. She touches one of the hazel posts, the one opposite me. I see David leer at her, but she says something, and he glances, shocked, at Oz.

The young man stands in the center of the ring with his

shield low. A long red line cuts across his right side, under his rib cage. Blood trails down, making his side grin. It's not life-threatening but will need stitches.

The mayor ends the holmgang, and the crowd descends upon Astrid.

I lose sight of her and shove my way through, ignoring my instinct against physical contact. When I reach her, she's with the mayor, gulping water from a Sigg bottle. Her sword is gone. Her opponent is also gone, and I don't care where he's vanished to. I position myself at Astrid's left side and just behind. Sweat beads on her temples, streaking down to her jaw. But she's smiling. Questions fly at us, and I ignore them completely. Astrid gives the water bottle to a woman in bright red and holds out both hands for quiet. After a moment, the clamor dies down.

I spy the video camera trained on us still. I hope she's right about how quickly we can find Baldur and return him to New Asgard, because we'll be on the interweave in five minutes, and on the news this evening. Local at least, and national if they realize Jenna Glyn's daughter is hunting the god of light.

"People of Bassett," Astrid says, "I offer you the blessings of Freya and thank you for the honor of your holmring and hospitality."

"Stay for a feast, lady," calls a man from the edge of the crowd. "We loved your mother well."

"And she spoke often of the kindness of prairie towns. But I must decline, friends, for I am needed elsewhere."

They protest, and I'm amazed at the calm Astrid shows despite being in only bra and battle pants, her cheeks still flushed from combat. She knows how to stir a crowd, just as her mother did. Obviously, there is something mysteriously trustworthy about her: I followed her with hardly a thought otherwise. But when I search for what exactly it is while she answers questions and makes them laugh, I can't see it. She's beautiful and filled with joy—can that be all it takes?

When one asks who is the boy-berserker standing at her back, she glances at me and the smile falls from her face. "This is Soren," she says. I do not smile, or look out at the crowd. I watch her. What do I want her to say? What am I to her? I'm desperate to know, but unwilling to let the crowd hear it, too.

But she only smiles again for the people. "We must go, thank you!"

Together we make our way through them, out of the birch grove and down the hill to the gravel parking lot where the Spark waits in a sea of cars.

Several townspeople follow, and I turn around. One glare and a tilt of my face to display my tattoo is all it takes for them to slow and stumble to a halt. For the first time I am glad of the fear. It allows us to escape.

Astrid sleeps in the passenger seat while I drive out of Nebrasge and into South Lakota. She said to keep going until we reach Interstate 90. By the time we do, she's awake and the sun is setting. For dinner we opt for meat pies and cider from a drive-through in Chamberlain, and then we continue on until nearly seven. Astrid tells me we're only an hour away, but she doesn't fancy wandering the Badlands at night even if we could get into the national park. We'll go at dawn tomorrow, which will be Thorsday, only the second new dawn since Baldur disappeared.

The problem is that there's no town between where we are and the Badlands, so we would have to backtrack for over an hour. I wish Astrid told me our options before we came this far. It's unlikely we'll be found by trolls on these plains: most have been pushed north or closer to the Rock Mountains. But it never hurts to be wary. Smaller trollkin can hide among the trees, or even in city parks if they're careful or desperate enough.

Exiting the empty interstate, we end up on a parallel county road and find a place to pull off. I choose a cluster of white ash trees planted by some long-gone settler and marked with troll-warding runes.

With the car turned off, the ticking of the engine is the only sound. It's too cold still for many night bugs or frogs to be singing. This quiet is so complete I can hear myself breathe.

"The back bench folds down," Astrid says.

We get out of the front. The chilly air slides down my shirt and Astrid pulls her sweater tighter over the front of her dress. It's blacker than Hel's gate here, with no light pollution. I can't see anything now that the headlamps are turned off. Even the ash trees with their carved runes have faded into the night.

Arching my neck back, I stare at the spill of stars. It seems like there's more light than blackness. The Milk Path stretches like a smear from one end of the sky to the other. I look down because for a moment it's overwhelming, as though the weight of it crushes my shoulders. All that space. And a sliver of it alive inside my chest.

Astrid opens the rear door and I help her lay down the bench seat. "There's room," she offers, and I try to stretch out. She curls into a tiny ball to give me more space. I pretend to find a comfortable position.

"Thank you, Soren, for coming with me," she says before closing her eyes. I can feel warmth from her back against my side.

"Gentle dreams, Astrid."

She sighs lightly, and very soon is asleep. I quietly climb out and unlash my spear. But instead of exercising, I stretch along the cool metal roof. There I lie, with my legs trailing off onto the trunk, to watch the stars move all night long.

SIX

I KNOW I slept, because suddenly I wake up.

It's a surprise, and unlike my usual slow awareness that the night has passed while I was caught in a half-sleeping state.

The stars have changed. They fade into the rising tide of indigo that parades before the sun. Beneath me the roof of the Spark is frozen and the metal creaks as I move.

A murmur from my side startles me. I realize the warmth there is Astrid, and I can't believe I didn't notice whenever she climbed up here with me.

Her nose is tucked into my ribs and her knees are curled up so she sleeps with her hands folded in the center. I stare at the curve of her neck, at the costume pearls encircling it. Her delicate jaw and pale lips, the line of her nose, the limp dark curls hiding her ear. Her lashes are short and straight, almost flat against her cheek.

The thin pink sweater covering her shoulders and arms cannot be warm enough. I'm cold, even though I have this fever heating me from the inside. With only a little hesitation, I put my arm around her. It's a relief like lowering a sword I've kept at the ready for hours. Then she snuggles closer. One hand grips at my shirt and she sighs.

I think my heart stops beating.

There are stories of old heroes being born and reborn to discover loves from past lives, to suffer and struggle for them again and again. Sigurd Dragonslayer and the Valkyrie Brynhild, Ivar and Ohther, Starwolf Berserk and Lady Kate.

In that moment on the roof of the Spark, I imagine ages and lifetimes pile atop us, spinning us into the pull of destiny.

Astrid's eyes snap open. They're as pale brown as hundred-year-old photographs. "Is it dawn?" she whispers, though from the light she must already know.

"Yes," I whisper back.

"It was very cold in the car, without you."

"I couldn't sleep and didn't want to disturb you."

"I don't mind. I climbed up here because you were so hot."

"It is the berserking, boiling in my blood."

"And the insomnia, too."

I nod. And shift away, taking my arm back to sit up. I can't hold her and think of berserking at the same time.

Astrid sits, too, pulling her knees up to her chest. "If you welcomed it, would you still be plagued by sleepless nights?"

"I believe so," I answer, not looking at her. "My father rarely slept. It's one of the reasons they say we have such limited time to live, even if we're never defeated in battle. We burn up our energy and life in half the time because we never sleep."

"Has there ever been a berserker who did not die fighting?"

"Yes."

Her finger, soft as a butterfly wing, skims down my tattoo. It continues down to my jaw, drawing a line toward my chin. My body flares to life, threads of fire ripping out from that center of madness.

She turns her hand over so her knuckles rest against my face. "Soren," she breathes.

I push myself off the roof of the Spark and my feet hit the frosty grass hard. "The sun will be bright soon," I say.

More slowly, Astrid slides after. I offer my hand to assist, but she ignores it. "Yes," she says, brushing off her dress, "and Baldur the Beautiful awaits us."

The land is flatter than ever and filled with nothing. It's as though vegetation has been burned off, and all that grows now on the rocky plains are stubbly patches of grass. The sky rises away, pale blue, and enormous clouds billow in rows like ocean surf. The only trees cling to the edges of trickling creeks.

We brush our teeth and change into fresh clothes in the public restrooms at a commercialized trading post, built to resemble a long building from an Old West town. They have fountain drinks, syrupy coffee, and doughnuts. We fill up the gas tank, too, and Astrid has a five-minute conversation with the attendant about the attributes of the '84 Spark versus the '92 with its Deutsche-made engine while I hover nearby, keeping my tattooed cheek averted.

Back in the car, we pass turnoffs for the Lakotas Buffalo Reservation and several pioneer homesteads turned into kingstate monuments. There are bronze National Historic Site markers every five miles or so along the road. The quiet, the utter lack of people on the road, makes me feel watched. I continue glancing in the rearview as I drive, searching for pursuit.

"They aren't coming after us, Soren," Astrid says.

I frown. "We're missing from school."

"We're adults and can leave school on our own. Didn't you pass your citizen test?"

"Of course." She knows it. I had to before receiving my tattoo. "It's only so empty here. Makes me nervous."

"Can you imagine living this far into the plains? There are still pygmy mammoths and hill trolls, and the walled towns are few and far between. Mom and I never camped alone in this part of the country."

I glance at her, to see she's staring out her window with her fingers against the glass. "Like we did last night."

Astrid laughs and looks at me from the corner of her eye. "Mom and I didn't have a berserk warrior with us."

I only grunt in response. The anxiety continues to itch between my shoulder blades, and I punch on the radio to HM, the public news station.

Through static, the announcer's voice slowly emerges: ". . . quell the rioting in Shenandoah. Graycloak has dispatched permission to all the kingstates for militia members to carry open steel in the streets, against the wishes of minority leader Edding."

My palms are slick against the steering wheel as all my skin begins to tingle.

"It's likely to be defeated by Lawspeaker Howardson when she brings it before Congress, but a source from the White Hall claims that the president hopes this situation with the missing god of light will be resolved before Sunday's emergency meeting."

Astrid sighs through her teeth and her head lolls against the seat back. "They can't fix this with politics," she murmurs.

"They have to do what they're best at," I say.

A little laugh escapes her, and she lifts her head as the announcer says, "Thousands of pilgrims have flocked to Skald, at the foot of Bright Home, with signs declaring that Ragnarok has begun. They're gathered in the city parks mostly, and the militias are in a bit of a standoff there with religious leaders who insist on opening all the temples on Skald's Chapel Row. The Valkyrie of the Rock arrived on the scene yesterday afternoon with seven of her wolves, and to the surprise of the king of Colorada, she held a prayer service in the city center, asking the mourners and pilgrims to remain calm and only pray together."

A new voice, that of a woman, speaks: *"This near to Bright Home, our prayers will rise with the wind up to the Valhol, where Odin sits and searches for his lost son. We will give the Alfather our strength to stretch his reach over the mountains and prairie, from ocean to ocean of this great country. Baldur the Beautiful will be found, and will return to us with all the glory of the sun."* The radio announcer takes up the story again, adding, "On the heels of the Valkyrie's prayer, a spokesman for Ardo Vassing, prince of Mizizibi and well-known telepreacher for the Bliss Church, told the press he'll be hosting a three-hour televent tonight, beginning at the CST sunset hour."

Astrid leans nearer to me. "We'll have found him by then."

My tension only lets me flick fast glances at her, but Astrid's face is loose with expectation and hope. I push the gas pedal down another bit to flare the engine. There isn't anyone for miles to notice I'm speeding.

The morning news hour ends with Evelyna Salsdottir, the champion poet of New Asgard, reciting her award-winning verse, "Sunfall in Mesa Verde." It's about vanishing people, and the memories they leave behind, like the longest shadows cast as the sun sets. I've never heard it before, but Astrid murmurs the refrain along with the radio. When the last word fades under the buzz of our engine, she changes the station to iron rock.

"We'll be there soon," she says, and shuts her eyes.

I let the pounding rock shake the car. The rhythm travels up my hands from the steering wheel and into my shoulders, helping me relax. I drive through two and a half songs, eyes glazed on the black line of highway, before a high beep interrupts the music.

"*This is an emergency broadcast. It is not a test.*"

Astrid grips my knee, digging her fingers into my jeans. I jerk upright, the frenzy blinding me like a flash-bomb. My foot hits the brakes and we screech to a halt. It's a good thing there aren't others on the road.

"*Repeat: this is not a test. All citizens of the United States of Asgard are cautioned against moving outside of city centers. Greater mountain trolls have come down from Canadia and attacked a settlement in Vinland. This is not a test."*

I lower my forehead to the steering wheel and press in, letting the dull pain focus my fever there instead of that hot place where Astrid's hand holds my knee.

"All citizens of the United States of Asgard are cautioned against moving outside of city centers. Greater mountain trolls—"

She violently changes the station back to HM. The emergency broadcast is blaring there, too. Astrid dials the volume down and gently replaces her hand on my knee. The effort to be calm makes my bones tremble.

After a moment, the HM announcer cuts in, apologizing for the interruption in regular programming, and says, "We received the official statement from President Adamson, and it's true that Tyrsday evening greater mountain trolls crossed Leif's Channel onto Vinland, wreaking destruction along the coast, including burning down the village of Jellyfish Cove and the National Historic Site where Gudrid Traveler and her family first landed. At least fifty-six people have escaped the island, but over a hundred residents are not yet accounted for. The Mad Eagle and Flying Bear berserk bands were dispatched from New Scotland to stop the trolls before dawn. No herd has caused such a death toll since the renegade Rock Mountain herd that famously killed Luta Bearsdottir's family in the sixties.

"The captain of the Mad Eagles reports that the trolls left symbols of Ragnarok painted in blood on the ruined walls of the town, and it's been confirmed that the president's warning has been put into effect because he and Congress believe the troll-mothers will use our time of loss to create as much chaos as they can."

I switch off the radio. I can imagine how brutal those people's deaths were, and don't want to hear more details.

Astrid slowly gets out of the car, moving with exaggerated grace as though she's afraid of falling over. With her seething kit, she kneels on the gravel shoulder of the highway and braids some of the tall prairie grass into a circle. She sets the kit before her and lights a slim candle. "For all the children of Asgard who were killed," she whispers, and then repeats it more loudly. "May their spirits lift as smoke and find peace in the halls of death, wrapped in Freya's feather-warm pillows."

She uses her hands to waft the thin gray smoke up toward the sky.

It's said that all our prayers are gathered up by the wind, are seen by the stars, are captured in the claws of ravens, and given into the ears of our gods. But the gods have been remarkably vague about why and when they choose to turn their attention to individuals.

As I watch Astrid, I wonder if she thinks any of them are listening to her now.

But I suspect if I asked, she would tell me that the prayer itself has power, regardless of who hears it.

+ + +

We've been back on the road for only ten minutes when we begin to see hills in the distance, turned shadowy and violet in the late-morning light. We turn off the highway where a carved-wood sign declares the entrance to Badlands National Park. Astrid says, "Mom and I used to stop at all of those kinds of signs to take a picture." She sighs. "Uncle Richard has the album. It's just us, standing there grinning. Sometimes Mom helped me climb up to the top, and held my ankles so I wouldn't fall."

"Too bad we don't have a camera," I say.

She smiles wistfully.

I drive to the small booth in the middle of the road. A rack of heavy spears and steel shields leans against it. On either side, an eighteen-foot fence of reinforced logs spreads out, enclosing the park. There's probably a war band based near here for emergencies. I've heard that most such postings are considered cushioned ones, because it is extremely rare for any of the parks to see more danger than the occasional pack of wolves. Though given what's happened in Vinland, that may not be true this week.

We're greeted at the gate by a woman in a brown ranger suit, blond braids falling from under her hat. Her eyes barely pause at my tattoo. "You two should be moving along to a city. Didn't you hear about the trolls?"

Astrid leans over me and says brightly, "We won't be long."

The ranger purses her lips, but then shrugs. I hand over money for the seven-day pass and an overnight camping ticket.

"If anything happens, make for the visitor center. There's a shelter in the basement," the ranger says. She hands me a glossy brochure along with the change.

Astrid flips through it as I pull the car forward. "I wish I knew which of these hiking paths Mom and I took that last night," she says, holding open the page with a green-and-tan map crisscrossed by red roads and tiny dotted lines.

"Why don't you look outside and I'll just keep driving until you recognize something."

The dry prairie spreads out all around us, but ahead and to the side are tall spires of layered rock. The road winds us closer to the spires, and when Astrid points, I stop the car on the gravel shoulder. There's a footpath leading toward the edge of the prairie, where the ground cuts away. I open my door.

The path crunches under my boots as I walk out through the scraggly prairie grass alongside Astrid. At the end of the path, a small sign proclaims the Badlands to be twenty-two thousand acres square, butting up against the Lakotas Buffalo Reservation to the south. What we're looking at is the bottom of an ancient sea, where layers of sediment were deposited and pressed into stone. Five hundred thousand years ago the land began eroding with rainwater and streams; it was water that cut these fissures and canyons.

"I prefer to imagine rock giants hammering their homes out of the flat prairie," Astrid says.

"So do I." The canyons stretch as far as I can see: striped gorges flushed deep golden and orange by the sun behind me.

✦ ✦ ✦

We drive all afternoon, around Cedar Loop Road, which winds from one end of the park to the other. Mostly we're quiet. Astrid stares intently out her window or the windshield, occasionally telling me softly to stop. I do, and follow her as she picks her way down the first few steps of a hiking trail. Some are just boardwalks through the prairie, and we can see black dots on the horizon that must be bison grazing. Some trails cut down into the canyon, and each time, Astrid pauses before descending. "This isn't it," she says. At first she's calm when we head back to the car. But as the hours pass, she becomes more and more frustrated. The dazzling sun and our increasing thirst can't be helping. Her fingers curl tightly into her skirt and she frequently murmurs "Where is it?" to herself.

We hike a mile down the Castle Trail, surrounded by sharp stone peaks like miniature mountains. There's dust in my throat and my shoulders are tense. We're vulnerable out in the open like this. When Astrid halts suddenly, I nearly run into her. She says quickly, "Soren, I know this is the place. I was here with Mom the last night." Her lips press together hard enough that they turn white. "Where is he?"

"Maybe he isn't here. Maybe . . . maybe you were supposed to come here for some other reason."

"Oh, Soren." She looks away. "Are you interpreting my seething now?"

My instinct is to apologize. "Isn't that what seethkonas need sometimes? Someone . . . else? To interpret."

She nods. "Perhaps I will dream tonight. Let's go get something to eat."

At the visitor center, we first find the restrooms and then share a bag of potato fries and a couple of club sandwiches at the small café attached to the museum. Astrid doesn't finish hers, but insists I take it. I'm hungry enough not to protest. When we're satisfied, we tour the museum panoramas and watch a movie about the formation and now the preservation of the Badlands. There are fossils and stuffed examples of the ancient equines that used to roam the area, as well as swift foxes and black prairie dogs, which have been reintroduced.

We're alone but for a ranger at the information desk. This early in Wildmonth must not be high tourist time here, even when there's no troll advisory. As always, I keep my left side turned away from the ranger, even as we go straight past him into the gift shop for Astrid to buy a postcard.

She fills it out quickly, to her uncle Richard, and we drop it into the mail slot by the front doors on our way out. As the sun sets, dark shadows streak toward us and silhouettes of the rocky spires jut up against neon pinks and oranges that should not be natural colors. "It doesn't look real," I say, though I'm thinking about what we heard on the radio this morning: now is when Ardo Vassing, prince of Mizizibi, is beginning his televised prayer service. Astrid thought we'd have Baldur by now.

Coming to stand next to me, her shoulder nearly touching mine, she says, "What I like is how vibrant it is, how the sky burns, and yet it seems calm from this distance. Like a controlled explosion."

When I glance at her, she isn't watching the sunset. She's

staring at me. My breath shakes, but before I can respond, we're interrupted. "You kids need anything else? I'm about to lock up," calls the woman in the striped baseball cap behind the café counter.

Astrid dashes over. I take a moment to relax, to center the burn in my heart and push it slowly down and down into the desert floor. We meet back at the Spark and Astrid dumps an armful of sandwiches in little plastic boxes onto the rear bench. "For later. I know you're hungry," she explains before sliding into the driver's seat.

There is just enough light to easily find the Cedar Loop campground: a barren field with short black stumps separating each camp from the next, and tin-roofed picnic tables to provide shade in the afternoon. Only one space is occupied, by a truck hooked to a pop-up trailer. We choose a spot two tables away: near enough not to seem hostile, but not so close that we'll have to listen to one another snore.

"Too bad we can't build a fire," Astrid says when we're parked, tapping the visitors' brochure. "You can only if you have a closed grill or something. Because they don't want the whole prairie catching fire."

"You can set yourself to dream without one, can't you?"

"I can chew some anise."

"Anise?"

"It reminds me of my mom."

We watch each other; I'm thinking about my mother, too, and how she'd have liked Astrid's easy way of smiling. My own seriousness was a burden to a Lokiskin like her.

The sunset catches Astrid's hair the same way it did this morning, in that expansive moment when I held her in my arms. I remember how her eyes fluttered in her sleep, and ask, "What did you dream this morning, right before you woke up?"

She laughs once, raising her eyebrows. "Apples!" Dismissing it, she gets out. I follow. We both just stand there on either side of our car. The dusty ground has covered my boots in dirt. My shoulders are stiff and I need to go for a run, or find a place for at least one of my routines. I realize it's been thirty-six hours since my last workout, and suddenly my fingers are itching to hold a staff or sword. Surely I can find a flat spot tucked behind a rock tower, or just get far enough away that I don't upset the other campers here.

"Soren?"

Astrid has come around the engine to stand in front of me. Her head is cocked quizzically. "Soren?" she says again.

"Yes." My breathing picks up speed. "Um, yes. What?"

"Are you all right?"

"Just . . . thinking. I need to exercise. It—it keeps me grounded and reminds me about what I can do—could do—if I let the battle-rage take me. I haven't run through a routine in almost two *days*."

"All right. Go."

I hesitate.

"Soren, I'll be fine." She puts her hands on my chest and pushes gently. "Take your sword, fling it around. Go." The chill from her cold skin seeps through my shirt, making me tingle everywhere.

My voice barely finds a path out: "You should get into the car. It's only getting colder."

"When you come back, you'll be nice and warm, like my own big oven. There are some convenient aspects to having a fever all the time."

My desire to kiss Astrid—to lift her up off the ground so that all her weight rests in my arms, to hold her close and bury my face in her licorice hair—destroys every piece of my vocabulary.

Fortunately, she slips away to untie my spear from the roof of the Spark.

By the time I return, it's fully dark, and all my sweat has frozen to my skin. My eyesight is adjusted so I don't skid or stumble along the gravel road. It was difficult climbing out of the small gorge I chose, and I nearly put my hand into a tiny cactus. But my blood still sings with the edge of the battle-dance and even now I walk with a bounce in my step. I'm strong and in the middle of an adventure with Astrid. We have food and shelter, and if no showers, at least there are covered toilets on site. What else could I need?

I reach the Spark only to find it empty. In a moment of hot terror, I spin around, raising my spear. My body thrums with bowstring tension.

Then her laughter rings out from the neighbors' camp. Peering, I barely make out Astrid's silhouette against the background of their pop-up. She sits in a low folding chair. Red light from the embers of their charcoal grill highlights the springing curls of her hair.

Beside her and across the fire are two people: a man and a woman. The man is telling a story, using precise hand gestures.

As my heart resumes its regular pace, I put away my spear and grab a new shirt and my jeans from my backpack. Changing helps me feel less grungy, but I fold my dirty clothes to use again for exercise tomorrow. Taking a final calming breath, I head for Astrid.

They're all three laughing when I arrive. "Soren," Astrid says, holding out her hand. I take it and stand beside her as if it's where I belong.

The man gets to his feet. "Hi there, I'm Elijah Kelsey. This is my wife, Abby." He touches his heart with his right middle fingers in a greeting of respect. I nod and return the salute. "Miss Astrid has been telling us about your trip," Elijah continues, stopping abruptly when he sees my tattoo. A significant look passes between him and his wife; my body goes rigid. But Abby smiles at me, and her husband follows her example after a fraught moment.

Astrid squeezes my hand, tugging at me so I crouch beside her. She doesn't remove her hand from mine. It's like a gift. I struggle to focus past it in order to say, "Thank you for hosting Astrid while I was away."

"She's delightful." Abby bends down to pick a long skewer from its holder below the grill. "Marshmallow?" She offers me the skewer, along with a half-full bag of jumbo marshmallows.

I accept, and while my marshmallow blackens, Astrid tells

me that the Kelseys are enjoying a second honeymoon along the same route they took for their first twenty years ago.

"We were only eighteen," Abby says, pulling her bouncy brown hair into a braid. "We committed in a little chapel and had the papers signed by a tyr an hour later."

"All our stuff was in the back of the Volvo," Elijah continues, "and we just took off! Stopped at every monument and park and historic site in thirteen kingstates. Took three months, and you know, it was the best time of our lives."

"It sounds very . . . free." I pull my marshmallow out of the coals as it catches fire.

"Yes, exactly. Free and perfect." Elijah leans forward and his necklace spills out of the collar of his sweater. At first I assume it is a tiny hammer of Thor, but a figure hangs from it. A dead man. It's a crucifix. I try not to frown.

Astrid offers me a piece broken from a Selway bar. "Want some chocolate to go with that?"

"We have graham crackers, too," Abby says. I let her help me create a marshmallow sandwich and am glad that eating the messy thing gives me an excuse not to talk.

All I know about the Biblists is that they worship a god of light, who like Baldur dies and is reborn. Taffy said last year at the academy's Many Gods Day that most of them accept Baldur as their lord, or as an aspect of the same, and hide behind his sun sign. London, an adamant son of the Thunderer, asked later, "Isn't that disingenuous?" And Taffy only offered him a withering look. "How do you know Baldur *isn't* my god?" she said. "Because yours isn't real" was the particularly stupid response London came up with. Taffy threw her pudding at him and stalked off. I never asked what he did to make up with her.

I try to unwind, sitting with my shoulder against Astrid's chair. The Kelseys both attempt to not look at my tattoo again, making up for it with a lot of obvious eye contact. Though they've got firm smiles and a natural way of talking, their hands give them away. As Abby eats a marshmallow straight off the skewer, I see how tightly her fingers grip the metal tool. When Elijah asks what brings us out this far from school, he taps his hand against his knee in a fast rhythm. I tell myself it's only me making them so nervous, but I wonder if it might be more than that: we're in the middle of uncivilized land during a troll advisory, and the god of light they believe in above all others is missing. At least Astrid has her dreams, and I have . . . this burning fever.

Astrid tells them we ran off for time alone together, and surely my spasm gives her lie away, but instead they both grin at me as though I'm only embarrassed. Which is certainly part of it. I'm glad when the conversation meanders to their favorite national parks, then to our favorite novels, and eventually devolves into an improvised sort of trivia game where they ask if we can name all four of the Quarrymen and we ask if they know who starred last year in the movie *Helgard*.

The stars wheel overhead and soon we're all yawning. It must be near midnight. As the moon begins to rise, it casts pale silver light over the prairie, and we fall quiet. It is a moment of complete stillness.

I allow myself to enjoy the cool wind that cuts down my collar. It helps me stay calm, caging the fever behind my ribs. But as Astrid dozes with her head lolled to the side, she shivers. She'll be better off in the enclosure of the Spark. Besides which, for the last fifteen minutes Elijah has been casting glances at the pop-up.

Quietly I say, "I should get her back to our camp."

"Wait." Abby pushes to her feet slowly and stands at the low fire, with her brows drawn together. Her husband joins her, putting his hand on her back. I move in front of Astrid.

"Soren, we . . ." Again Elijah glances back at the pop-up, and the calm I've nurtured this evening cracks. I feel the fire in my spine, crunching between the vertebrae.

"Tell me your business," I say, quietly but with a hardness in my voice that makes both of them lift their palms to me.

Abby takes a deep breath, then smiles as she exhales. "There's no threat, young man. We have . . . strange news." Her eyes light up. "News we think you were meant to hear."

"What? Me?" I want to nudge Astrid with my boot, to wake her. But I wait to understand.

Elijah says, "It's your tattoo."

His tone is relaxed, but that doesn't make a difference to me. My hands become fists. "My father was a berserker, and I carry the curse."

"It's a spear." There is awe in Abby's voice.

I narrow my eyes.

"Three days ago we came here, to watch the sun rise on

the first day of spring." Elijah takes his wife's hand. "We had no radio on, and didn't know what had happened at the New World Tree. We behaved as we always do when the Lord of Light returns to life: we shared wine and bread and walked along the paths of nature. It wasn't until the afternoon that we knew anything was different."

It's almost as though I expect what he tells me next. My fists are already uncurling, my lips opening up when Elijah says, "A beautiful, golden man walked out of the desert, and he came straight to us. His eyes were like the sky itself and he smiled and my knees were weak."

"Baldur," I say in a rush of breath. "Where is he?"

Abby touches her fingers to her lips and says, "Here, but asleep—so deeply asleep, Soren, you can't wake him. When the sun sets, all the life drains out of him, and he won't open his eyes until dawn."

"Why didn't you say anything? Why are you still here while the rest of the world is so afraid?" I can't help but talk high and fast, shaking my head. I turn to wake Astrid. But her face is drawn and her eyes dart under their lids.

Elijah touches my elbow and I whirl on him.

"Understand." Abby touches my other elbow. There is such brightness in her eyes—faith like Astrid has. "He told us he was waiting here, for someone to come. For someone to bring him his spear." She nods toward my face. "What could we do but wait here with him? So he would have a bed. So that he would not be alone. And now, the spear has come." When a new smile splits her face, there's only the dim red glow of embers to show it. A thrill of fear cuts me, because I don't know if she's right or if she's crazy.

But she tilts her head and the moonlight fills her face. Abby Kelsey is calm and peaceful. Her smile is only friendly, and her hands have lost all the pent-up energy from earlier.

She says, "Soren, the god of light was waiting here for you."

SEVEN

INSIDE THE SHELL of the Volundr Spark, all I see is darkness within and without. All I hear is Astrid's quiet breathing. I sit with my back against the door and she curls beside me, head on my chest, arms tucked between us. Through the opposite window I watch the pop-up trailer. The Kelseys spread two zipped-together sleeping bags in the bed of their truck and have not moved in hours.

Astrid barely woke as I lifted her from the chair at their camp and helped her back to our car. We climbed into our makeshift bed and Astrid huddled against me, asleep again immediately. Sometimes she smiles and her lips move as if she speaks in her dreams. Her fingers tense and relax against my T-shirt with every new dream. Part of me wishes to shake her awake and tell her everything. But I think, *What if it isn't true? What if they're mad, or fanatical?* Selfishly, I don't want to risk ruining her peaceful sleep, or the way her soft hair tickles my neck. So instead of confessing, here I wait.

Tonight I have no desire to sleep. I never even close my eyes, but keep watch out the wide windows to make certain the Kelseys don't vanish in the night, don't take their wild story with them.

And if they *are* being truthful, if Baldur sleeps in the dark of their pop-up trailer, I must be ready.

I cannot miss the moment when he will emerge to face the sunrise.

The moment there is a first sign of light in the east, I whisper Astrid's name against her hair. "Wake up."

The silver line grows, flat and narrow against the prairie horizon.

Astrid shifts, groans softly.

"Astrid."

She sucks in a great breath and sits away from me. Rubbing her eyes with her fingertips, she says, "Yes? What? I was so comfortable."

"Watch with me." I point out the window toward the trailer.

"Watch what?"

"Just watch."

She settles back against me, at an angle so she can see what I see. I finally shut my eyes for a brief moment, knowing she watches for me, because I want to remember this feeling. Astrid's shoulder presses under my arm, and one of her hands rests lightly on my thigh. My heartbeat quickens, and to distract myself I ask, "What did you dream of?"

"You."

"Me?" This is the opposite of the distraction I hoped for.

"You rode upon the back of a great wolf, as black and large as Fenris Wolf, with a spear in your hand and a wild grin on your face."

I remain quiet, and assume the wolf is my berserking, except that I smiled in her dream. Thinking of battle-frenzy does not make me smile.

"There were also apples," she adds irritably. "Many of them, in that same orchard stretching into infinity, until the colors transformed into the Rainbow Bridge that connects this Middle World to Old Asgard."

"Perhaps it's Baldur's way home, across that bridge."

"Oh, perhaps."

The horizon is white now, fading upward into blue. There are no clouds, only the empty, perfect bowl of sky over the prairie. She says, "I hope we find him today. If we don't, I'll make a fire outside the park and dance a true seething."

"I do not think you'll need to."

"Why?"

Silently I point again at the trailer. The door squeaks open. I hold my breath.

A man walks stiffly down the two plastic steps and pauses, glancing toward the rising sun.

Astrid's hands fly to her mouth. Before I can say anything, she crawls to the door and pops it open, spilling out onto the ground.

She scrambles up and stands perfectly still, watching as he walks away from the Kelseys' camp until he's alone and free of shadows. Light catches his hair, and it blazes as brightly as fire.

I move to watch through the open door. His back is to us, and his arms stretch out, palms open and facing the sun. As if embracing it. I see his shoulders lift as he breathes deeply. I wish I could see his face.

All the prairie brightens, becoming a plain of dazzling gold and silver.

Astrid takes faltering steps closer, and I finally climb out of the car to follow her. She continues toward him, walking as if in a trance.

The sun is fully up, a silver-white circle against the sky, blazing in my face. It warms me despite the chill in the air.

He turns to her, and they face each other before me. Astrid holds out her hands and says, "Baldur. Prince. We've come to take you home."

The smile she gives him is so bright, it eclipses the sun.

I feel trapped in shadows, without her warmth against my skin.

"My name is Astrid Glyn," she says. "I dreamed of you here, Prince. And so we came, to lead you to your father at Bright Home."

"Astrid. An old name." His voice sounds human, unaffected, not at all godlike.

"My mother, who gave it to me, is a favored seethkona of your cousin Freya." Astrid offers her hand again, and Baldur takes her fingertips, raising them as he bows.

"It is honoring to meet you, daughter of magic," he says as she leads him toward me. My frenzy blazes up in something that feels like anger, and in a fleeting thought I regret my spear is not at hand. I lift my chin, straighten my shoulders to take whatever comes.

Baldur appears perhaps twenty years old, slimmer than me, but his movements are as graceful as any warrior's. Below too-long sweatpants his feet are bare, and his sweatshirt is two sizes larger than he needs. Swimming in the clothes, he looks like a little boy emulating his father. Perhaps we're wrong and he is not the god of light. That would explain my sudden resentment.

"Will you come with us?" Astrid asks him.

He glances at her. "I, too, have dreamed. I am waiting for someone to arrive, whom I shall know when they do, because of my dreams."

Her eyebrows rise. "What have you dreamed of?"

They're just before me now, and my doubts about him drain away. Up close, his eyes mirror the fading silver and gold of the dawn sky, and every line of his face is perfect. My knees shake.

"I have dreamed . . ." Baldur pauses when he sees me. His lips remain parted to speak, but no words break free. Dropping Astrid's hand, he takes the final three steps separating us. He's taller than me, and beside him I feel like a heavy mountain troll. He raises a hand, coming close enough to touch my face. But he does not.

"I have dreamed," he says, "of spears."

EIGHT

BEFORE WE LEAVE, Abby Kelsey warns me that a spear is always what kills Baldur the Beautiful.

I don't know enough about her faith to know if she means her god of light, too, but it's true enough about our Baldur. A spear was his first murderer, and in every year since then he has stood before a funeral pyre on the last night of summer and waited for such a weapon to pierce his heart.

Astrid jitters with energy as she delightedly packs Baldur into the passenger seat of the Spark. I take the keys from her to drive.

As I attempt to keep the car on the narrow road, I'm constantly distracted by the brightness of Baldur's hair. It's right there in the corner of my eye, reminding me that beside me is the most beloved son of the Aesir. In this enclosed space, his presence is as big as fireworks.

He rolls down his window and sticks out his hand, palm upward, as if to catch sunlight.

"What do you remember?" Astrid asks him, leaning forward from the back bench.

"Buckle up," I tell her.

She ignores me, propping her elbows on either front seat.

Baldur leans his head back. When he answers, his face is only inches from Astrid's. Even in the shade of the car, his sky-mirror eyes have not dimmed. "I only remember pulling myself free from the roots of a tree. The sun rose overhead and I spread out on the rocks to drink it in. Foxes came, and a coyote; then as the heat of the day swept through the ravine, I was watched over by tiny little birds."

"You did nothing? Just waited?" I say, glancing disbelievingly at him.

"I was weary, Soren. The weight of the sky held me pressed to the earth."

"Usually you hop right up and go with your father."

"Soren"—Astrid lightly smacks my shoulder—"this is different and you know it."

I tighten my hands around the steering wheel and stare out at the road. The asphalt draws us forward; it's like a black string winding through miles and miles of fields. We're headed south, hoping to find a highway Astrid recognizes, or a gas stop where we can purchase a map. Our destination is the mountain in Colorada atop which sits the great hall of Bright Home, where Odin holds his earthly court. At the foot of the mountain is Skald, home of the Valkyrie of the Rock, to whom Baldur must be returned. Though I remember from the radio news yesterday morning that Skald is overrun by pilgrims.

Into the silence, Baldur says, "I walked out of the desert and found those kind people waiting with a fire. They told me my name, and welcomed me. That first night I dreamed of battle and death, of . . . so many things. I can't remember them clearly. It's all impressions and darkness, leaving me feeling like I've left behind an entirety of some other life. I woke afraid and cold. The desert is very cold at dawn."

I would not have believed Baldur the Beautiful could feel coldness. Nor, I suppose, would I have believed he needed to eat, but he devoured the sandwiches we'd saved last night.

"What did you do?" asks Astrid, concern deep through her voice.

"I waited."

"Why stay there? Why didn't you call a—an eagle, or yell out for Odin?"

"It never occurred to me to do such a thing." Baldur shrugs. "I had—have—no memory."

"None at all?"

Baldur closes his eyes, and the hand outside the car fists. "When the sun shines in my face, I know that the sun is my friend."

"We're your friends, too." Astrid is gentle, her smile calm.

I want to ask more about his memories, for if he has none, how can we be sure of who he is? How can Astrid just accept this? My anger sparks against the cooler voice reminding me that when I look at his eyes, I know. I trust.

But he says, "The second night my dreams were the same, yet with more brightness. Feasting, perhaps, and battling with men I think were my brothers, or cousins. There was a warm family around me, though I know not their faces; that is the feeling the dream gave me. And as the dawn came, I held in my hand a spear of light." He smiles, eyes darting past Astrid's face to mine. I feel his gaze but keep staring at the twisting highway. "That is how I knew to be calm, and to wait. The spear I needed would come."

Astrid says, "He will keep you safe, Baldur. He'll keep both of us safe."

I clench my jaw. I do not want her promising things to this forgetful god, this man who charms her so easily. But I can't say anything because I know what she says is true. I will keep them safe.

Astrid runs into a gas stop to pick up a map and honey soda. She's the least noticeable of the three of us, and we want to not cause a stir. I wonder if the video that the guy in Bassett took of her holmgang made it onto the interweave, but I can't worry about it. There shouldn't be a connection between that and the missing god.

Baldur stands outside the car with me as I fill the tank, with his back to the store and his face to the sun. His shoulders relax and his spill of hair is like strings of gold. I allow myself to stare. The angles of his face are not what I expected. I thought I knew what he looked like—what he's supposed to look like. For my entire life I've seen videos of Baldur rising from the New World Tree, golden arms clawing up through the earth and twisting roots, then at the feast afterward being presented by Odin to the gathered mortal luminaries. Baldur always smiles brighter than the torches and shakes hands with the lawspeaker and members of Congress, staying near his father, Odin, but reaching happily to kiss babies and accept a glass of champagne.

I know exactly how beautiful he should be, and yet the more I try to remember what I thought he looked like before, the less I'm able to picture him. As if the man before me is so vivid he's erased all my memories, too, or perhaps I never saw him clearly to begin with.

He notices my stare. "Soren, why are you frowning?"

"I don't trust you." The bluntness startles me, and I look away.

A short laugh pops out of his mouth. "Just like a berserker. Tell me like it is."

"How do you know?" I shift closer to him, as though to loom. But he's taller than me.

"Know what?"

"If you don't remember anything, how do you know what to expect from a berserker?"

His eyelashes flicker, but he keeps hold of my gaze. "I give you my oath that I speak only truth. My oath, under the sun and to the edges of the world."

My neck hairs rise, shooting chills down my spine. I frown as fiercely as I can. "How do you know that oath?"

His eyebrows lift. "The words waited on my tongue."

I cross my arms over my chest. "They are old words, ritual words. For binding-by-light." I tighten my fingers into fists. The binding is one between commit-brothers, and I want to tell him that he must refrain from giving oaths he doesn't understand, but I am afraid my voice will shake.

Baldur's face releases into a bright smile. "Then so we are bound."

I am half-awed, half-infuriated, and so I turn my back to him before he sees me grimace.

From the other side of the car, he says, "I trust myself, Soren. These words, like the sun, they are things I know. So little do I know, that what is here I must accept, no matter the consequences."

Consequences. They rage inside me, that black chaos of night sky wedged under my ribs. There are some consequences so unacceptable we have to fight against them every day.

Astrid pushes out through the glass door of the gas stop. She clutches two giant plastic cups in one arm and a third in the other. A small bag dangles from her wrist. I go immediately to assist. When I take the two drinks, she bounces ahead of me. "I have a shirt for you that should fit better!" she calls to Baldur. He comes around to meet her, stripping off the too-large sweatshirt.

I try not to be annoyed that he crawled out of the dirt with muscles like he has, but it's difficult when I notice Astrid glancing away with a subtle blush.

What if she can't resist him? There are so many stories of

Baldur flirting his way around the country, pictures of him kissing young women in the perfect summer fling.

But what right do I have to want her to resist? Why should she bother just for me?

While he changes and Astrid takes the old sweatshirt, I climb into the driver's seat and set the honey sodas into the cup holders. Only years of practice controlling myself keeps the door from slamming closed.

Astrid tells me to continue the way I have been, past a handful of dust-covered houses and a gray building that's a grocery, auto-parts store, and burger joint at once. Whatever tiny town it is, I'm glad I don't have to stay. We're continuing to Highway 18, and taking that west to Ulriks, where we'll turn south again on 385. We'll keep zigzagging south and west down into Colorada. It shouldn't take more than seven hours. By dinnertime we'll be free of him. Back on our own to head home. Together.

I surreptitiously run through a breathing exercise, as best I can while folded into the front seat of the Spark. My hands on the wheel work for grounding, since I can't have my feet flat under me. In, counting the lines painted down the center of the road to twenty; out, counting to thirty. In and out, keeping focused on my body against the seat, my palms against the leather wheel.

Baldur, now clothed in a tight, long-sleeved T-shirt with

a Denver City Stoneball logo emblazoned across the front, drinks from his soda. The noise from his open window muffles the slurping.

A look in the rearview mirror shows me Astrid leaning back in the center of the bench. Her hair hangs all around her face, and I can only see her eyes. They are on him alone.

"Baldur," I say too loudly, even with the roar of wind, "I don't understand why you don't remember. You have to remember more than . . . more than dreams."

"He's been dead," Astrid says.

Both Baldur and I look at her, and I want to stop the car. To turn all the way around and grasp her shoulders, make her look at *me* instead of him. But I drive, resigning myself to simply shaking my head. "That explains nothing to me."

"Nor to me," Baldur says.

"Memory loss is associated with the dead." She leans forward and presses her temple against the corner of my seat, angling her face toward Baldur. "My mother was a seethkona, a prophetess who could dance into death and speak through the gates of Hel, Baldur. I witnessed her raise a man at his year-old burial mound once, and I've read accounts of other revenants. The dead must be grounded somehow into their old lives, or they may leave their memories in the comfort of Freya's embrace. I'm not surprised you're having difficulty. You'll remember more as you go, or you should. And there will be fits and starts of memory. Sensations you know, images or words you remember, but that you might not be able to place."

I think of the binding-by-light. "He's alive, though, not undead. Not a revenant. This memory loss never happens to him."

"Not under regular circumstances, no." She sighs. "Perhaps there's something the Alfather has for him, or my Freya, that will reinvigorate his mind."

"I feel invigorated in the sun," the god murmurs, hanging his hand outside the car. His fingers move like he's playing a piano against the wind.

"Let me try to help." Astrid squeezes Baldur's shoulder, and in the low, swaying voice of a poet she says, "Over two thousand years ago, the elder poets say, Odin the Wanderer fell in love with Tova, a woman of Freyr's tribe."

Baldur's fingers stop moving. He sets his soda back into the cup holder.

Astrid continues: "This woman Tova gave birth to a son named Pol Darrathr, the Arrow of Odin. No more beautiful man had walked the earth, nor any more accurate with a spear, or more joyous or friendly or strong. Pol gathered to him men of all kinds, forming a great band of warriors in Odin's name. He was bold and wise, loyal and true, and when he swore himself to a king on earth, none doubted his word. Across the land, princes and kings bowed to Pol and his king, and all who fought challenge against him fell.

"Until one day Pol's half brother by Tova came to join the commit, bringing his promised-wife Nanna. In moments, Nanna and Pol loved each other as vastly as the gulf between stars."

Baldur draws his hand inside the car and folds it carefully with the other in his lap. He stares straight ahead, his face expressionless.

"Pol and Hoder, his half brother, fought the holmgang over Nanna, and Pol cut Hoder to the ground but refused to kill him because of their shared blood. For this honor and loyalty, Pol was brought to his father Odin's side and called Baldur, an ancient word naming him a prince.

"The gods of Asgard welcomed the new Baldur, giving him an apple from Idun's orchard and mead from the Poet's Cup. Baldur married Nanna, and together they lived happily. Yet Baldur's brother Hoder was not satisfied. With Nanna's father, Hoder plotted to trick Baldur into death. The two called him from his home in Asgard, the Shining Hall, to join with them in a game of spear tossing. Baldur, being loyal to his brother and loving toward his wife's father, went. Never suspicious. Never wary. Always trusting."

Baldur's hands, so carefully folded in his lap, curl into fists.

Reaching to touch his shoulder in comfort, Astrid says, "As Hoder's turn came to throw his spear, he faced his brother. With a cry of rage, he cast the spear, driving it through Baldur's heart. The Shining Hall fell into shadow. In nine steps down from heaven, Odin Alfather struck Hoder, crying blood price for his most-beloved Baldur.

"Baldur's funeral was glorious. Every god came, every goddess, too, and half the warriors of the world. Giants came to honor his light, and trolls and sea monsters. Even Thor Thunderer put down his hammer so that the fiends and gods might mourn together. Nanna, wife of Baldur, walked onto the fire-ship and threw herself across her husband's still-bright body. Together they burned."

Astrid pauses to wipe her fingers across her cheek. When she continues, her voice is thick. "Odin rode his eight-legged horse to the black river that floods into Hel. There he met the witch-goddess Freya, seer of all and the queen of Hel's magic. 'Freya: lover, friend, teacher. My prophetess,' the Alfather begged, 'give my son back to me, back to all the world, which loved him dearly.' And Freya ruffled her many-feathered cloak to reply, 'So he is loved, yet so he died, Odin Deceiver, Old Man Dreaming.' 'Freya, you who rule half of death, who rule by love, who know it better than any god, tell me what I might do to win my son back from you.' The witch-goddess laughed and said, 'This thing only: make all the living world weep for Baldur, show their lam-entations and wailing with silver tears to call back the sun.' 'If I do this, he will live again?' 'If you do this, Odin One-Eye, you may have him half the year. For that he is half of your blood, and half of the blood of mortal men, he shall be half-alive and half-dead from now to the end of the nine worlds.'

"So Odin returned from Hel and sent all the spirits and men upon whom he might call, his wolves and ravens, his Valkyrie and Lonely Warriors, spreading the truth of Baldur and his death, that all the world might mourn. The earth tilted with the wails of grief, and soon the grass was wet with dewy tears. Everyone cried, everyone wept, except for Tova, the mother of Baldur and Hoder. It was Loki who discovered her, and the boy-trickster crouched before Tova and asked why she would not cry for her son. 'Because I have lost both my sons, yet no one weeps for Hoder.' Loki, a mother himself, frowned and offered Tova a tea he claimed was for betrayed mothers. Whispering thanks, Tova accepted. As she drank, Loki laughed, for the tea was poisoned. The woman perished, and so Loki returned to Asgard and declared that no living being on the whole of earth refused to cry for Baldur."

Sitting up, Astrid says, her voice free of tears, "Thus, with every spring, Baldur rises from Hel to bring joy and life and sunlight to the nine worlds."

As her words fade, the only sounds are the rush of highway, the thundering draft through the window, and the rumble of engine. I am not certain any of us breathes.

The first new word comes many miles later, when we've found Highway 18 and the sun reflects off a lake, glimmering in my eyes.

"And so," Baldur says, "I'll die again in a few months."

I squint against the bright flickering light, then flip the sunshade down. But the glare comes from below, so it doesn't help.

Astrid, from where she's rested back into the rear of the car, says, "Yes, but it isn't a thing to fear."

"I think . . . that it is." Sighing, Baldur stretches his hand back out the window to catch sunlight. His head turns away from me.

"You remember something?" Her voice rings with hope.

"No. Not really. Every word you spoke drew something

from inside me. Hints of memory, perhaps. A flash of face, the sharp clash of swords. Fire. I remember fire, and the spear. In my chest. It's all like a dream. Like these dreams I have had that leave me with nothing but the impression of who I might have been. But if I loved this woman Nanna so much, why can I not remember her?"

Astrid says, "It was hundreds of years ago, Baldur. She has never risen with you. No one expects you to remember."

The look he casts her over his shoulder almost makes me forgive him.

And I don't even know exactly what I want to forgive him for. In the silence my anger builds up again. Anger that he's forgotten everything. Forgotten us. Anger that he was missing in the first place. Anger that the gods couldn't find him—that Odin Alfather lost his own son. Anger that there are riots and city parks full of fearing pilgrims. That trolls paraded through Vinland and destroyed all those people.

Anger that he holds Astrid's attention.

My hands grip the wheel tighter again. There will be impressions of my fingers in the leather by the time we stop. This fury is not worthy of me, except that I always carry it with me, cutting up at my heart.

I hear Astrid shift behind me, but my gaze darts between the road and Baldur only. He watches me, a slight frown marring his face. His eyes reflect the same hard light as the far-passed lake. I clamp my teeth together and can feel my jaw muscles tightening. But I don't care that they can tell I'm angry. All my bones are tense.

"Soren!" Astrid pushes forward again, putting a hand on my shoulder. I shrug it off. My battle-rage shudders in my stomach, reaching out like a grasping squid.

"It is well, Astrid," Baldur says lightly. "Soren, stop the car."

"What?" Both Astrid and I protest.

"Soren, I need you to pull over. We can't resolve this while you're driving."

His measured words cause me to obey without thinking further. The wheels skid on the gravel shoulder as we roll off the highway. Astrid says, "Resolve *what*?"

There's a field here, old soybeans waiting for the new seeds to grow. Baldur pushes out of the Spark and I follow. The day is warmer than any since last summer. Everywhere the light of the sun fills the air with energy. I drink deep breaths and keep my eyes on Baldur. He strides out into the field, curving left toward a grove of trees. "Get your spear, Soren," he calls back.

A thrill roots me to the ground for a moment. My heart thunders more loudly than goblin forges, drowning my ears in the rhythm.

Yes.

Whirling, I run back to the car. Astrid blocks my way. "Soren."

I smile at her unkindly, and her eyelids flutter closed. Even then a voice is whispering in my head to calm down, to spare her this side of me.

"Soren," she says again, forcing her eyes open. She puts her hands on my chest, pushing firmly so I stop. "Be careful."

"Oh, I will." I step forward. She doesn't move.

"I won't forgive you if he hurts you."

Laughter bursts out from my bear-smile. If Baldur is a god, he has a chance! I take her shoulders and move her out of my way. I draw my spear off the roof and quickly unwind the wrapping. Astrid pops the trunk and gets her seething kit.

With the shaft of the spear smooth and strong in my hand, I start after Baldur. But Astrid does not follow. I turn. "You aren't coming?" The first true shadow of doubt settles across my shoulders.

Astrid folds herself down to sit, legs crossed, at the edge of the field. She spreads open her bag. "I will not go watch my allies try to murder each other."

"It's your duty to bear witness."

"Not to foolishness!" she snaps, eyes up and locking with mine. Her cheeks flare pink.

I don't know how to explain to Astrid why I need to do this. Why everything Baldur has said to me has led to this holmgang I'm fighting now, for Baldur to prove his honor to me, regardless of his godhood or his memories. I stare at her, so small beside the sedan, in a violet dress and thin gray cardigan. Her plastic pearls reflect the sun like black mirrors, and her fingers dance over the tiny pockets sewn into the seething kit, as if hunting for consolation.

When I turn from her and stride toward the grove of trees, I'm no longer furious. But not any less determined.

+ + +

Baldur waits for me with a straight branch in his hand. The trees form a thick curtain around us. Inside, all is quiet and still. The grass is sparse, the earth covered in wrinkled brown leaves. A ditch that must run with water after rain cuts through the northern edge of the grove. Although the trees are bare, their interlaced branches shade the ground. Only a few sun spots dapple the air, and Baldur has found the largest. The light shines on him even as he steps closer to me, following him like a loyal dog.

"I would prefer swords, I think," he says. "But this will have to do."

Because his feet are bare, I stoop to remove my boots.

"That is unnecessary." Baldur drops into a fighting crouch.

He attacks the moment he sees me ready. I smack at his staff with my spear, and we bounce off each other, then begin to circle. The dead leaves crunch under our feet, and a breeze makes the dry limbs overhead clatter together. Though I haven't stretched or warmed up, I hardly notice. I am so alive and ready to spar—to fight! I've not faced a real opponent in so long.

And what an opponent! He may not consciously remember who he is, but his body knows. I see his movements in his face as he steps forward to attack, see the feint in time to catch his true blow. I skid with him, the two of us spinning with our weapons locked together. I'm smiling—grinning—then laughing. His own lips press together into a determined smile and he shoves me back.

I land on my knee and one hand, spear raised to defend, but

am on my feet again in an instant, stabbing at him. He swerves in time, air huffing out of him. The butt of his staff knocks into my shoulder, and I whack my spear back into his thigh.

We pause, panting and staring at each other.

His fighting—his battle sense—reaches for mine, and in the cool spring clearing there's nothing in the world but the two of us. My blood roars in my ears, my arms are alive with wind, my heart aflame, and the spear in my hand is a bright bolt.

I've heard it said that a proper battle is fought between two champions, and indeed most wars in our past were decided that way. And I've heard that a great battle is one in which the warriors do not clash, do not oppose, but one in which they dance. Together, back and forth, giving and taking, reaching always for the sudden jolting moment when one weapon pierces through the other's defense and everything ends.

I dance with Baldur the Beautiful.

And I can barely keep up. I push myself, past the aches in my bones, past the screaming muscles: attack, defend, withdraw, dash forward to attack again, whirl back, trip away, and always the thud of our weapons together, the hard smack of my shoulder into his chest, his knee slamming behind mine to drop me to the grass. I roll and am up again and again, faster than he expects, to drive him closer to the dry creek ditch. He leaps over it and I follow—we push against the trees.

Suddenly I feel it stronger: the dark, waiting chaos. It burns inside me, promising that if I break it open the world will explode with light.

I falter. I push it down, shake myself free. I grip my spear in both hands and attack Baldur in a flurry of short snapping swings.

He says, panting, "You are holding out on me, Bearskin."

"No," I manage. Every snap of my spear he meets with his own. The staccato echoes through the grove.

"Stop." He brings his staff over his head and slams it down. I block and the reverberations rattle my teeth. "Holding." Again, his weapon crashes into mine. "Back." With the third blow my knees buckle.

Baldur flings his staff away and catches my spear in both hands. He shakes me and I fall.

My hips and shoulders hit the ground, and then my head, snapping against the yielding leaves. My vision bursts into black. I push my palms into the ground and open my eyes.

He stands over me, ready. The tip of my own sharp spear presses into the weak hollow just over my collarbone. His head blocks the sun, and all around his dark form the sky is alive with light.

"Now, Soren Bearskin, are you ready to take me wherever I need to go?"

I allow myself time to breathe. His arm is steady; the spear never trembles. I keep my eyes on his. He's sweating and his breath comes almost as hard as my own. He could kill me now; it would be his right. But his face is calm. Pleasant, even. He does not frown or grimace, but waits with mouth relaxed, eyes calm. With the infinite patience of the sun.

I say, "I am ready, Prince. Under the sun, and to the edges of the world."

His mouth widens into a wry smile and he removes the spearhead from my throat. "Then up you come!" With a jaunty laugh, Baldur offers down his free arm. I clasp it, and he heaves me to my feet.

My body is shaking. By the pattern of shadows against the grass, I know we've been in the grove for nearly an hour. A long battle. I need water, and perhaps to collapse for a day or two.

Astrid has rolled away her seething kit by the time we climb up the shoulder to the car. She sits against the front wheel, arms crossed, glaring at us.

Baldur and I pause, and we share a look. He smiles first, then I do, and soon we're laughing. I'm suddenly light-headed.

"You bastards," she sneers, shoving to her feet. Baldur leaves me where I can put out a hand to support myself against the car as the ground spins.

"Astrid, don't be angry." Baldur reaches to touch her arm, his voice gentle and pleading. "We didn't hurt each other."

"I might pass out," I insert, and for some reason am not ashamed to admit it.

Astrid opens her mouth but says nothing. Her lips press together and she glances between us, her expression slowly settling into resignation. "Well, good. Let's go." She pulls open the passenger door and waves her seething kit. "Baldur, can you drive? I'm working on something."

"Um."

I nod. "Man can fight. So, driving—that's like riding a bike."

Baldur frowns at me, his head tilted quizzically. But Astrid opens the rear door. "Get in, Soren. You're delirious."

"He's in shock," explains Baldur.

Astrid sucks in a sharp breath. "Oh, sweet swans, he didn't—"

"No. That sleeping bear was forcibly restrained." Baldur sounds irritated.

I scowl at him. "Lucky for you, or that cut on your cheek would be a crushed skull."

Baldur touches his cheek, smearing the small stripe of blood. His mouth spreads into a grin again. "I barely dodged that one."

"Freya's tits," Astrid whispers, clutching at Baldur's wrist. She drags his hand toward her face and stares at the smudge of red. "You're bleeding."

"So is Soren," he says, face falling as if he's been caught out in some untruth.

Astrid barely spares me a glance as she drops Baldur's hand. She reaches up and nearly touches his face, but then she clutches her hands back against her stomach, fingers weaving together as if she's discovered her own dark chaos lurking there and must press it back into her intestines. "Don't you see?" Her sepia eyes are wide.

It creeps up on me slower than the sun sets. *Baldur bleeds.* Baldur, god of light, stands before us with a slow trickle of blood marring the perfect gold of his face.

"What?" He puts his hand against his cheek, hiding the wound as if that will make us stop watching him like he could crumble to dust any moment.

Astrid steps close to him again and gently takes his hand away from his face. She holds it between both of hers and then lifts it so that his palm cups her cheek instead of his.

I sink slowly to my knees. I'm dizzy once more, and Baldur puts his free hand on my shoulder to steady me. The three of us are connected in an arrow, with Baldur at the point.

Looking up at him, I say, "You're mortal."

NINE

THE ROAD RUSHES below me, growling in rhythm with the wheels. Voices murmur near the edges of my consciousness. I could reach out and be awake, could share their quiet conversation, or I could sink back down into the nothingness of sleep.

I sleep.

"Soren."

The car is stopped, and a gentle breeze drifts over me. Fingers skim across my forehead, brushing hair away. Astrid whispers my name again.

I open my eyes. She's crouched outside the car, the door wide. Her face is inches from mine and seems upside-down.

She is so beautiful.

I don't say anything, but merely watch. Her hand stills against my cheek. Dark curls fall toward me, hiding the edges of her face and framing her eyes. I could tilt my head and touch my lips to hers.

Astrid draws in a long breath. "We're just outside Fort Collins. There's a motel here, and a string of fast-food places. I'm going to go book a room so we can rest for the night." The corners of her mouth turn down, and she blinks her eyes several times.

"What are we going to do?" I keep my voice quiet.

Again she sighs. "I tried calling the info line they've been repeating on the radio, but can't connect to anybody I trust. They just want me to leave a message and a number for them to get back to us. Can you imagine? 'I have Baldur, call me!'" She hums displeasure before continuing. "We'll get a room, as it's near dark, then go more cautiously in the morning into Shield. We have to be careful with our delicate prince now." Nudging at my head, she angles herself into the car. I begin to lean up so that she can sit where my head was, but all my body blossoms with dull pain.

"Soren?"

I must have grunted, because Astrid is behind me suddenly, propping my shoulders with her hands. She pulls me back down, arms cradling me. "Stop moving if you're in pain. Oh, that blasted Baldur. I didn't think he really hurt you."

Shaking my head, I push away, sitting up through the aches that pummel at my ribs. "I'm fine. I was just out of practice and wasn't stretched out well enough and—" I manage to sit upright, but she's still got her hands on my back, sliding them down my arm and trying to keep me from opening the door to climb out the other side of the car. "Stop fussing, Astrid."

I say it more sharply than I intend, and she jerks her hands away. We both wait, not looking at each other. I glance out of the car.

One side of the road is lined with squat evergreens. Shadowy foothills stretch behind them, pale toward the far horizon. We're the only people here. Cars pass by along the highway frequently, and I hear a radio from inside the gas stop. Just beyond it is a cluster of stucco cabins under a neon sign that reads: SIGYN'S KEEP-INN. I don't see Baldur.

"I'm going to go to the motel," Astrid says. "I just didn't want you to wake up alone."

She starts to get out, but I say, "Wait," and she pauses, glances back over her shoulder at me. Her eyebrows arc neatly, impatiently.

"I didn't mean . . . ," I begin, but don't know what I want to say.

Astrid shakes her head gently. "Don't."

I want to grab her shoulders and lift her up the way I did in Bassett, to make her listen to me. Where has our easy communication gone? Why do I feel like every simple word with her is suddenly a struggle?

But then Baldur emerges from a door along the plain concrete side of the gas stop. He has a key attached to an old license plate swinging in his hand. There are shoes on his feet, and he's got on a hoodie and jeans that fit. He jogs toward us, smiling. One of his free hands spreads out so more of its surface is in the sunlight.

Astrid hops out of the car and goes to him. Their hands touch and the turmoil in her expression brightens into joy.

That's why.

Yet when Baldur's glance shifts over to me, I find myself smiling back at him, too.

Astrid shoots past him then, toward the motel. As he approaches me, I get out of the car and finally stretch, allowing a grimace to spread over my face. Pain creeps around my head from the point where my skull hit the ground when he knocked me down. I roll my neck and let the waves ripple.

Baldur laughs and claps a hand on my shoulder. "When was the last time you were so thoroughly defeated?"

I shake my head gently. "I don't remember. No—" I raise my arms over my head and reach with my entire body. "It was Master Pirro, before I began showing the signs."

"Well, then, it was time."

His smile is infectious. At least my face doesn't hurt the way my ribs do. And one spot low on my right thigh. And the back of my skull. "Are you hurting, too?"

"Ah, yeah." Baldur rolls his left shoulder with a wince. "I've got a couple of bruises."

My lungs squeeze as I think that I could have killed him. Like I'm being bound up by knots of destiny.

"Thank you," he says.

"For what?"

He sets his hand back on my shoulder and regards me with the same expression he did when he held my spear tip against my neck: patient, serene, and very old.

"Thank you for teaching me to remember I know battle," he says.

Words tighten in my throat.

I want suddenly to drop to my knees and swear to him. I think of all the times I've seen men and women touch the hammer charm at their neck to pray for Thor's protection, or whisper entreaties to Freyr or Odin or Tyr. I think of the wails of grief on Tyrsday when the beloved Baldur did not rise from his ashes.

I feel that wail inside me now, because as I stare at him, I know the truth: he is just a man now, like me. Vulnerable. Breakable. I am standing here next to Baldur the Beautiful, who dies with the summer and is gone, dead, all winter long. He who battled me in holmgang, who took my own spear and laid me flat, who pushed me until I had to clamp down on my battle-rage or explode. Who knows what I am, and puts a hand of trust on my shoulder anyway. And if he dies now, he won't rise next spring. It would take the tears of the entire world to bring him back again.

I think of Astrid, crying in the woods because Baldur's loss felt like a hollow ache inside her, and then asking me, *Do you love the gods, Soren?*

Slowly I nod at him. "Let us get you home," I whisper, "so you might remember everything else as well."

Astrid returns, jangling keys. We move the Spark around to the lot next to our cabin and head inside without speaking. The room is very yellow, with striped wallpaper and a painting of the Rhine maidens with their five dragon rings cavorting at the bottom of a waterfall. I dump my backpack onto the geometric quilt. The heater clangs below the window as I turn the thermostat off and pull shut the curtains. The last rays of the setting sun vanish from the room. Baldur bends over the bed and skims his hand over the hilt of my father's sword.

"This is beautiful craftsmanship," he says as Astrid walks in with the last of our things.

I don't want to think about the sword. "You two should take the beds."

Astrid frowns. "You and I can share, Soren. There's more room here than there was in the Spark."

"I'm not going to sleep anyway."

"But you were passed out all afternoon. Maybe you will."

"I slept more today than I have in the last month."

Before Astrid can argue further, Baldur unsheathes Dad's sword with a harsh slick of metal. Flicking his wrist, he's got it in one hand with the tip pointed at me, the other arm up defensively. The pose is one of the first I learned from Dad when I was a kid. Baldur says, "Balls! This thing's got excellent balance."

The dull blade winks in the lamplight. I used to covet the sword. Called Sleipnir's Tooth, its pommel is painted with an image of Sleipnir, Odin's eight-legged battle-horse, on one side, and the ravens Thought and Memory on the other. The grip is wrapped in sharkskin, worn and soft from my father's hand. Carved into the crossguard are all twenty-seven of Odin's runes, for which he hung nine days and nights on the Old World Tree, sacrificing himself to himself. The fuller cut down the center of the blade is deep and as long as the blade itself, to give better flexibility and to keep the sword from breaking against bone. "It was my father's," I say.

Baldur raises his eyes. "And so yours now."

Mine, but with Dad's legacy staining its power. A reminder of what could happen when I lose control.

"An unused weapon is a danger to its owner, as much as to others." It's an old proverb, but Baldur sounds like he thinks he just invented it.

"Not sheathed," I reply, unable to take my eyes off the tip of the sword where it glints a fiery orange from the poor motel lamp. Baldur makes a face and turns his wrist over, so that the blade, too, turns. I stare a moment longer, feeling the heat of my frenzy churn, then I grab my bag and retire to the shower.

The water warms my aching muscles. I turn the temperature up until the entire bathroom is foggy and I can't see anything but the simple squares of white tile surrounding me. I let the water pound down over my hair and stream down my back. I breathe slowly, drawing the thick, hot air in and out, using the motion of the water to imagine all my fear and anger and tension melting out of me, running off my skin.

If all goes well, tomorrow I will stand before Odin and ask him to strip this rage from my blood. I won't have to calm down in showers, mistrust myself, or fear releasing my guard. I can travel with Astrid, supporting her, watching her, waiting to catch her.

It is so close, the chaos inside me. Yet this morning I managed to hold it back. It was there when I fought Baldur, and I might have let it go. I might have lost everything then, fighting against him. He wanted me to. Why? Why did he want to see it?

Does Baldur know something I can't? He gripped my father's sword so firmly, with such familiarity.

Suddenly I'm afraid. Never before have I trusted anything but the exercises. The repetitions meant to train my mind and body to respond to control, to calm. I want to trust him.

I want to let go.

The battle-rage stirs: warm pleasure in my stomach, fizzing and popping like carbonated water. With Baldur at my side, could I give in?

I press my hands flat to the slippery tiles and lean in, stretching my back and shoulders. Could I stop being afraid?

The water takes my hopes and fears spinning down the drain.

I emerge from the bathroom feeling lighter. The hotel shampoo smells like candy, which would normally turn my stomach, but tonight reminds me how starving I am.

Astrid sits cross-legged in the center of her bed, tying knots in a thick red string. Without glancing up, she says, "He just went to sleep."

As I look, I rub my towel over my damp hair. Baldur didn't even take off his new shoes or bother with the blankets. We should have put him on the floor if he was only going to pass out.

Astrid tucks her string back into her seething kit, grabs a

pile of clothes from the corner of her bed, and goes into the bathroom. I hear the water turn on immediately.

While I wait, I drop to the floor and run through several sets of push-ups, then roll over to hold a dragon pose until the water turns off. When I release, my abs burn familiarly. I scan the room, wishing there was a pull-up bar, or some weights.

Although the back of my head continues to ache, my ribs are feeling much better. My stomach growls loudly enough that Astrid hears it as she opens the bathroom door. "Sweet swans, we should get you some meat."

"Anything," I say, stretching down to grab my toes.

Astrid begins picking tangles out of her hair with the pointed handle of a comb. "I'm hungry, too. Is it all right to leave him?"

"They think there are only two of us, yes?" From my upside-down position, the blood rushes into my face and my skull throbs. I straighten slowly.

"That's true." She watches the sleeping Baldur, fingers lost in her heavy, snaking curls.

"But I can run out. If you're worried."

"Why don't you cover up your tattoo with the hoodie? You'll be less recognizable."

Scandalized, I only stare. It's illegal for me to hide the spear, even with something as natural as a beard. She knows that.

Scrunching her hair up on top of her head, Astrid holds it there. Her thin dress hangs from her shoulders down to her knees. The ribbons at the waist are untied, so it falls without shape. In the light shining out of the bathroom, I can see the soft outline of her body. I clear my throat and look away. "I'll bring something back," I say, wiping my suddenly sweating hands down my jeans.

The night sky is thick with mist. I can't see the stars, and it's been a long while since I stayed in a place without them. Walking toward the block of tacky shops and fast-food restaurants across the way from our motel, I feel trapped under the low-hanging clouds. To the southwest, the glow of Fort Collins lights the sky like a false sunrise, and my skin crawls when I think of taking Baldur into it. We'll have to listen to the news again, and make certain the situation isn't worse in Shield.

At the end of the strip mall is a run-down pub with a painted announcement of mead and drink specials on its huge front window. I duck inside, glancing around for a menu. It smells like grease and peanut-shell dust. The hostess doesn't even flinch when she sees my face, but smiles brightly and offers me a booth against a dark wall covered in old pictures of National Stoneball teams and champion poets.

"Can I get some to take with me?" I ask, turning my tattoo away, though she's already seen it.

"Oh, you know it!" She hands me a menu. As I sit down on the cushioned bench along the wall to peruse the menu, she leans over onto her podium to display her breasts better. "I recommend the ham-LT on rye, and also that Arnold with chips. But you look like a burger man."

I nod. I'm bad at flirting, and don't even try.

The hostess continues on as if my participation doesn't matter. "Why not taste our Jotun burger—it's a house special. With a kicking jalapeño sauce." Her eyelids are shaded with sparkling green. I guess she's about nineteen. Probably a part-timer at the Poets' College outside Shield, where the best story-tellers and lawspeakers in the world are trained.

"Sure, I'll take two. And a lavender tea, and . . . Can I get a quarter-bottle of your house mead?"

She glances at my tattoo. She could deny me alcohol, but instead she just grins. "You bet."

After putting my order in, I try to relax back against the wall. Some folks notice me; others ignore me completely as they shoot pool or glue their eyes to the flickering TV. Are they so unconcerned with berserkers here? Maybe the proximity of Bright Home, of the Alfather and Valkyrie, makes the citizens less wary. Maybe they've let themselves forget what we can do. I remember sharply what Astrid said in Bassett, that it isn't other people treating me like an outsider, but me acting like I expect it.

The loud conversation is so different from the silence I've gotten used to in the past handful of days. I watch a few min-utes of the stoneball game on the TV hanging over the bar, and try to pretend that I'm at Fort Collins for no other reason than vacation. Maybe I'm meeting a friend. Suddenly I wish Astrid had come, and that we could sit together over dinner and talk. Pretend to be normal. Like we weren't smuggling a god in the backseat of our car.

"So, honey," the hostess says, plopping down beside me. "My name's Glory."

She's close enough that her shoulder brushes mine. "I'm Soren," I say, after suppressing the urge to avoid telling her. I want to test Astrid's theory.

"You a student?"

"Not here. I'm not a poet."

Glory laughs. "What brings you to the Fort?"

"Pilgrimage. To the gate."

"Bad time for that, honey." She bumps her shoulder against mine. Such a casual, easy touch. As if I'm not dangerous. "With all the folks here after the prince, it's crowded more than usual."

"How crowded?"

"Like hogs in a pen. Everybody's dying to see him. They're camping out in front of the gate with candles and prayer bowls."

I frown, wondering how to glean more details.

She squints her green eyes. "I sure as snakeskin wouldn't go down there, especially if I had a pretty god like him with me— I'd keep him all to myself."

It's like she knows. But she can't. The way she looks at my tattoo, like she's hungry, makes my hands sweat. I grasp for a flirtatious smile, but I haven't the least idea how to move my mouth to achieve it. I manage only, "Have you heard anything about him? About Baldur?"

"Nope." Glory shrugs, and she frees me by rolling her eyes to the rafters. "Between you and me, I think he ran off to some island again, to soak up the sun like he did a few years back."

"Surely the Alfather would be able to find him, if that were the case."

"Suppose so."

We're interrupted when a group of older guys with gray beards comes in to be seated. Glory winks at me as she sashays through the tables to show them to theirs.

I wonder if it's the shirt, instead of my tattoo. As I was getting ready to go out, Astrid said, "You should always wear that shirt, Soren." I frowned at her like she was crazy, and it made her laugh. "I just mean the color complements your skin and brings out your eyes."

"Boys don't care about that kind of thing," I told her as I closed the door. But I sure wasn't going to forget she'd said it.

I'm staring down at my orange Metal Canopy T-shirt when Glory returns. "You don't seem like the light guitar type," she says playfully.

"I like things that calm me down."

"Get worked up easily, do you?"

What do I say to that? I stare at her round cheeks and the wine-colored lipstick making her mouth shine. "Everyone does, lately."

"That sure is true. But more so for guys like you." Her voice lowers, and her eyes linger on my tattoo.

I swallow the dryness in my mouth and manage not to lean away. "It is," I say rather gruffly, "an added concern."

She smiles slyly. "Have you ever . . . you know."

"What?" I hope rather desperately she's talking about sex.

"Well . . . you know what they say about men with a spear tattoo."

We eat babies? Go mad and destroy a dozen men in half a minute? Tear heads off trolls? I know a lot of the things that are said about berserkers, but I don't think they're what Glory the hostess means. I'm having trouble not biting down on my own teeth so hard my jaw will ache. Rescue arrives when a kid in a greasy apron pops around the corner with two paper bags.

I stand, smiling tightly at Glory, and take the food in return for very nearly the last of our money. As she picks coins out of the register, she scrawls a phone number on the corner of a napkin, with a spear sketched under it. I notice a tattoo on the underside of her wrist: a snake twisted into a figure eight, just like my mom's. She's a follower of Loki. That explains a lot about her attitude.

Just as I turn, the nearest TV catches my attention. There's a red crawl of news moving across the bottom half of the stone-ball game. It's the word *death* that grabs me. VALKYRIE OF THE ROCK CLOSES GATE TO BRIGHT HOME AFTER MAN LEAPS TO DEATH TONIGHT AT SUNSET.

Hurrying outside and back down the street toward Sigyn's Keep-Inn, I'm determined to come up with a plan that does not involve taking Baldur into the thick of chaos. Either Astrid or I can go, perhaps, and prove to the Valkyrie that they need to come to Baldur, in a safe location. I want it to be me, because I'm strong and can't be hurt by a mere crowd, but I know they'll believe Astrid more readily. I'm just the son of a reckless murderer.

My tattoo seems to burn on my cheek.

I was thirteen when the ink was pricked under my skin. In a concrete building, surrounded only by militiamen who remembered everything my father did, I'd kept my eyes open the whole time, staring at a scattering of dots on the wall. It hadn't hurt, not compared to everything that came before, but the sting so close to my eye threatened to draw tears. I refused to let it. I would not cry in front of those men, in front of the artist who scowled and cussed quietly to himself about boring, straight lines and dangerous children.

And I remember seeing it in the mirror for the first time—angry puffed skin around it. Reminding me of my dad. His tattoo had been the same black streak against his hard jaw, sharp cheek. A scar. Linking us together. *Take my sword,* he said. The last thing he said to me before calling out the Berserker's Prayer and running at the guns.

The cabin is dark but for flickers of candlelight reaching around the ajar bathroom door. I set the paper bags of food on the empty bed, glance at Baldur. His golden hair manages to pick up the little bit of light and glint like he's a copper statue.

"Astrid?" I call. Weaving through the dull smell of vacuum cleaner and moldy motel is a strain of acrid yew that I recognize from the night on the barrow at Sanctus Sigurd's. My boots are silent on the thin carpet and I pause at the bathroom door, brushing my fingers down it. "Astrid?"

Her sudden harsh breathing grates at my ears. I push open the door. Astrid stands before the soot-smeared mirror; she's drawn all over it with the charred tip of her yew wand. A hundred curving lines, repeated like waves. Obscuring her reflection.

Red wax has bled over onto the toilet tank from the thin candle she lit, and shadows dance against the tiles, turning the bathroom into a white-and-gray prison. Stepping all the way in, I move behind her and put my hands on her shoulders. Her brow glistens with sweat and her wide eyes stare into themselves through the soot.

"Apples," she says.

I see it, then, the orchard on the mirror. Black and white lines creating a portrait of apple trees across the glass.

She drops the yew wand into the sink and turns around, putting her sooty hands against my chest. I feel the cold seep through my T-shirt. Astrid whispers, "The gods of Asgard welcomed the new Baldur, giving him apples from Idun's orchard and mead from the Poet's Cup." She tilts her face up. "Soren, he needs the apple. Every time after he rises from the New World Tree, they give him one of Idun's apples to make him immortal. That's what grounds him back into his life."

The truth settles in my chest, quieting the rage there. "We have to take him to the orchard." It's even a relief, to think we can pass by Shield.

"Yes." She nods slowly. There are dark shadows under her eyes.

"You need to eat, Astrid." I turn her by her shoulders and

push her gently toward the door. "We can't do anything until dawn."

"You too." She catches my hand, and when I gesture at the mirror she tugs. "No, I'll do it after."

I pull back, leaning over to blow out her candle. We're washed in darkness and I think, *This is a perfect moment to kiss her. To draw her against my chest and put my lips against hers.* But she laughs lightly, just a wisp of sound, and lets go of me.

With the lamp between the beds on, we settle on top of the quilt, my back against the headboard and Astrid's against the wall. Our knees touch. I dig paper-wrapped Jotun burgers out and hand her the bottle of mead. As we eat, neither of us talks. Astrid wolfs her burger as if she hasn't eaten in days, and after swallowing the last of it, untwists the cap on the mead. Although I'm happy with the lavender tea, when she offers me the bottle, I accept and take a very small sip of the thick honey alcohol. It slicks down my throat, leaving a warm, pleasant burn behind on my tongue. I close my eyes and feel the uneven mattress springs shift as Astrid moves to sit beside me. She leans against my arm, her head on my shoulder.

I keep my eyes shut, hoping she'll fall asleep so we can remain like this for hours.

But she takes the mead back from me and raises it high enough that I hear it glug into her mouth. She sighs heavily. "Soren."

Because it seems impossible not to, I lift my arm so she can settle under it, and I hold her against me. She smells of ashes and honey. "I have been dreaming the answer for years, Soren."

"We're exactly where we're meant to be," I say, looking down at her dark curls.

"Exactly where we're meant to be," she repeats, her head turning so she can see Baldur. I glance, too, and his eyes flicker beneath his lids. His lips tremble.

My arm tightens around her. But Astrid touches my knee. "The gathered gods consent to find / why baleful dreams to Baldur come," she says. It is a line from one of the lays in the Younger Edda. The one telling of Baldur's death, and of the nightmares that plague him before it.

"We must keep him alive and safe, Astrid."

"We'll do what fate dictates." Her forefinger draws tiny spirals against my jeans. Through the material the pressure is just enough to tickle. "He's fated to be swallowed by Fenris Wolf someday, at the beginning of Ragnarok, when all the nine worlds will perish."

I smile wryly into her hair. "So long as Fenris remains bound, the hunger controlled, he'll be all right."

"Why am I not surprised you think that's the moral of Fenris's story?" Astrid relaxes into me, melting into my side. I close my eyes and imagine turning to stone here, never moving again, and it's a pleasant thought.

"That's not it," Astrid says. "That's not the point."

"Oh?" I'm barely listening.

"Long after the World Snake spilled from Loki's belly, and

after, too, the first queen of Hel passed the throne to Freya, Loki transformed himself into a she-wolf in order that he might hide in the wastelands between Gianthome and the Middle World. No one knew why he left, but it was suspected he must have once again angered one of his cousin-gods. For many wolfish generations Loki ran and hunted, played and slept with the pack of giant wolves as they ranged over the mountains and glaciers. And one night, when Loki climbed alone to the edge of a cliff where he could look out over the tundra toward Asgard, a band of frost giants came hunting. They destroyed the pack, spitting and roasting all of Loki's friends and playmates. A distraught Loki returned to Asgard to grieve."

I'm familiar with this story, of course, but some of Astrid's details differ from the basic version they teach in school. She adds depth to the trickster's desires, and I find myself feeling an ache in my chest because this is a Lokiskin version. Like my mom would have told.

Astrid continues, and the spirals she draws against my jeans heat up. "But Loki did not return alone. In his belly a wolf-child grew, and Loki fed it honey and blood for nine long years until the day the baby was ready to be born. Half wolf and half god, Fenris was as beautiful as she was monstrous. She grew at an alarming rate, eating constantly, anything that was set into her path. She ate so much that Odin asked Freya to look into the strands of fate and read the wolf-child's destiny. 'Fenris Wolf shall swallow the sun, oh God of the Hanged,' Freya told him. 'She will signal the end of the nine worlds with her appetite.'"

Astrid's hand stills on my knee. "The gods were so horrified and afraid of Fenris Wolf that they went to the goblins under the mountain of Asgard and asked the creatures to create a rope with which to bind her hunger. The goblins were cunning, and angry at Loki for some trick he'd played, and so they did what the gods asked of them, but only barely. They wove a thread of six impossible things, creating a rope that was delicate and beautiful. But Fenris knew it would destroy her. It would keep her from her ravenous destiny, and she knew that to fight destiny was like denying your own name. It took the trust of Tyr the Just, god of accord and honor, to convince her to close her jaw. And even then it was only because he put his hand in her mouth, and she was so hungry she bit it off. The gods used that moment of brief satisfaction to tie the binding rope about her neck." Astrid brushes my knee as though it's dirty. "But, Soren, the rope did not bind her hunger. Instead it transformed her into a girl. It keeps her small and human-sized, but with a hunger still as large as the world! Even today her hunger grows and grows, never satisfied. And perhaps it is that rope itself which, by binding her now, will one day make her so starving, so keen to eat, that she will devour our sun."

Her story fades, and I touch the back of her hand. I draw a spiral there, as small as those she's traced on my jeans. "You twisted that just for me," I say.

The shadow of a smile graces Astrid's mouth. "I worry about you." Her voice is slow with sleep.

I hug her gently, and watch Baldur sleep, too, wishing I

were tired, wishing I could curl on the bed with Astrid and let go of the day. But my palms are hot, and my heart beats beside the black night sky of the berserker's rage.

Baldur's hands clench into fists.

I hope he doesn't dream of burning.

TEN

BALDUR RISES AT dawn, and Astrid is curled against me, her back to my chest and her hair against my chin. I've been awake for over an hour, running through breathing exercises as they sleep.

The first thing Baldur does is walk to the door and open it. Sunlight streams in. I squeeze Astrid's shoulder and she stirs. Her fingers creep up to mine and her eyelids flicker open. We both watch Baldur bask, Astrid breathing twice for each of my own long breaths. Then she slips out of bed and goes to him. The wrinkles fall out of her dress, but her hair is mussed where she slept on it. She brushes her fingers down Baldur's back before disappearing into the bathroom.

He turns, smiling widely enough I can see his teeth. The sunlight gilds the edges of his hair and I fight back a tightness in my chest. I must keep him safe. "We know where to take you," I say, my voice heavy after hours of disuse.

"Excellent." He sounds delighted.

The shower turns on, and the bathroom sink. Astrid must be cleaning the soot from the mirror and the red wax from the toilet tank.

Baldur's hands settle on his hips. "Shall we have an early-morning spar?"

We choose the far corner of the parking lot as our battleground. It's away from the road and blocked from view by the bulk of the motel office. After stretching out, we start to jog the perimeter of the lot. An easy rhythm forms between us, and one and a half laps into it, Baldur asks, "Are you certain I'm the god of light?"

I falter, the toe of my boot catching on a patch of weeds pushing up through the cracked asphalt. "You have to be."

"Why?"

Slowing to a walk, I glance over. A frown pulls his brow together, and he's staring at me with eyes that hold the pale blue of the sky. "Astrid believes it."

That surprises him. "That's all the proof you need?"

I stop completely and turn to face him. "What do you want me to say? That you're beautiful as only a god can be? That the sunlight calls you like it calls no man? That you—" *Make me wonder what it would be like not to fear myself?* I can't voice it, not yet. "Something about you, Baldur, is different. I don't think that's in my imagination."

Baldur crosses his arms, but not in resistance or anger; his hands cup his elbows as if he's offering himself support. "In Astrid's story, I was a man, and then Odin made me a god by giving me the apple and holding me at his table. Now I am mortal and have no memory of sitting at the high seat. Even if I was once the god of light, can I still be so?"

The idea is like a cliff crumbling beneath my feet. I shake my head. "You have to be. But you know already it doesn't matter to me so much what you say, that it's in your actions if you're a god. And yesterday, you fought me over that very thing. Your honor was at stake, and you proved it true. The essence of you is here. If you're only a man, you're a good one, and I will still help you get to the end of this." It's the most I've said to him in one go, and I hope that proves to him I mean it.

He looks east toward the dawn. I would have to wince away from the sun, but he stares full on. That his eyes are immune to the brightness should be evidence enough. "Thank you," he says after a moment, and picks up the jogging again.

Three pensive laps later, Baldur asks, "What sort of god am I?"

How I wish he would ask Astrid these things. I continue at the same pace and say, "Warm and bright. A warrior. Everyone loves you, and although you have a reputation for loving back a little bit, erm, too much, few fault you for it."

"Too much?"

I twist my lips, not wanting to be blunt. But there's no helping it. "You fall in love with a different woman pretty much every year. Sometimes more than one."

"Oh."

The tone makes me glance at him, and he's wearing a

bemused smile. I roll my eyes. "See, you do remember." And I remember how Astrid watches him. *It won't happen to her.*

"Not really. Though . . . it always ends badly, doesn't it?"

"They have an exclusive support group, I hear."

Baldur laughs, and I find myself laughing a little with him. Not because it's funny, but because of all people, it's me explaining to Baldur what his love life is like.

We jog on, and I think about the kind of god Baldur is. A lover and a strong fighter, outwardly, but his rebirth in the spring is our most beloved celebration. The moment all of New Asgard waits and breathes together. As I lead us back toward the far corner of the lot for a spar, I admit, "You're hope, Baldur. That's what you are."

He has nothing to say to that, except he cannot meet my eyes.

To soothe us out of the serious conversation, I offer to teach Baldur a few sets of partnered yoga. For a beginner, he's well balanced, good at finding the energy flow. I shouldn't be surprised. In return, he shows me something he says he thinks must be his favorite boxing warm-up. "It feels like a favorite" is what he says. My training hasn't included much hand-to-hand, since berserkers in general don't have to worry about being disarmed. Odin's way does not include fisticuffs.

I relax into his instruction, finding myself enjoying the pattern of back-and-forth. It's been too long since I've relaxed as I exercised. I know not to go at him with full strength now, because I can't risk hurting him, but even just as men we're well matched.

Astrid arrives to watch. Clean and changed into a pleated skirt and violet sweater, she leans against the hood of the Spark. Her hair is combed straight back into a thicket of curls at her neck.

I am so distracted by her sudden appearance, Baldur slams through a punch I should have easily stopped. It lands against my bruised ribs and I double over. "Soren!" he says, shocked, and grips my elbow.

"I'm all right." I wave him away. "Maybe more sore than I thought. I should have stretched more."

Baldur is frowning at me in confusion. "I'm sorry."

"No, no. We should get going anyway."

Astrid is beside us. She touches my ribs, right over the bruise, then pulls away sharply. Ignoring me, she asks Baldur, "Did he tell you we have no idea where to go?"

"No." Baldur glances at me. "He said you did know where."

"I meant," I say, to Astrid as much as to Baldur, "that we know we have to take you to Idun's apple orchard, where you can eat one of the apples of immortality. But we don't know where it is or how to get there."

"Ah." His expression brightens and he puts one hand on her shoulder and the other on mine. "So it's both things."

Leaning closer to him, Astrid says softly, "We have a more immediate problem, however."

I spin in a circle, searching for trouble. The highway is quiet, the sky clear, and there's nothing in sight but a few cars. Even the gas stop is dark.

Astrid says, "We have no money. Just enough for some more gas. I don't want to ask my uncle to wire more, because it matters now that we aren't tracked easily. The front page of the newspaper in the lobby said an old woman was killed in Mishigam yesterday because her neighbors decided she was hiding something about Baldur."

I crouch, balancing with my fingers splayed and barely skimming the asphalt. It makes me feel less like I'll fall over. "And they closed the gate to Bright Home because a man killed himself there," I add.

"My god," Baldur says, horrified. He doesn't even know about the trolls.

Astrid touches his arm. "It's bad, but not your fault," she says. "The way to fix it is to get you home."

Baldur hisses through his teeth.

From the ground, I say, "I don't have money. All my father's went to his victims, and I have a state trust that pays for school. I can't touch it."

Baldur and Astrid stand so close their shadows are one thin blur reaching toward me. He asks, "Do I have marketable skills?" It makes me laugh. Just once, and with little humor. Baldur shouldn't need money. But we do.

Fortunately, Astrid has an idea. "We only need to find a market or festival site where I can perform a seething. A few hours, and we'll have enough to last a couple of days."

I raise my head. The sun glares just over their shoulders, a brilliant silver light between Astrid's head and Baldur's, turning them into dark silhouettes.

+ + +

Baldur and I shower and pack, then we're on the road with empty bellies and the half-full bottle of mead left over from Astrid's dinner.

We head north, edging along the red-and-gray foothills of the Rock Mountains, which stretch from the center of the USA into the Canadia Territories and Trollhome. Astrid remembers traveling between Bright Home and the great Dragon Geyser in Montania, and that there were plentiful campgrounds and trading posts. We're bound to come across a likely venue sooner rather than later. I only hope people are calm enough to admit us.

The sun shines through white clouds that billow tall like a separate range of sky mountains. Astrid turns on the radio. We need to know what's happening, and as the news reels off dire warnings about trolls, about angry people and desperate pilgrims, Baldur grows paler in the backseat. He scoots to the passenger side, where there's a hint of sun coming through the window, and presses his forehead to the glass.

The news hour ends on an upbeat, though, with a story of a girl in Philadelphia who climbed high into the New World Tree in order to tie a prayer card in among the bare branches. People saw her and reached in through the iron fence to hand her their own prayers, tied with ribbons and bells, which this girl then took with her back into the tree. For two days she's been papering the tree with colorful prayers, and the reporter says it has made the New World Tree blossom with hope.

Signs for Ashdown Fairground begin to appear before we cross into Cheyenne, but it's almost two hours before the flat grassland curves toward foothills again. The highway's not crowded, thanks to the troll warnings no doubt, and most people are going south, against us.

To distract Baldur from his dark thoughts, Astrid climbs into the back with him and begins telling him the story of how Freya agreed to teach Odin her magic only if he lived a mortal life as a woman for seven years. She mentions her mother, and Baldur interrupts to ask, "Where are your parents?"

She tucks a curl behind her ear. I struggle to keep my eyes on the road and not constantly stare at her reflection. "My father I never met," she admits, "though Mom made up stories about him whenever I asked. I'm not certain she knew his name, or his family. They spent a Yule night together, and she told me Freya herself arranged it, under the sacrificial banners, to enjoy the feasting and dancing, and to bring me into the world. Then my mother disappeared one night, Baldur, and no one has seen her since. They believe she's dead; everyone does. But I'll find her again someday, when fate allows."

"When fate allows," he repeats, making it more true. After a pause he says, "And you, Soren? Your parents?"

"Father dead. Mother . . . gone." I don't elaborate, and neither pushes.

We're nearly to a town called Laramie when the Ashdown turnoff beckons with its cracked sign. Someone has erected a temporary plastic arrow declaring the Half-Serpent Trading Company is in town for the semiannual bazaar.

A haze of dust billows behind us as I veer off onto the poorly kept county highway. Baldur leans forward, his arms hanging over the passenger seat. Through the windshield all we see is scrub and the wide-open sky, with snowy peaks far in the distance, until suddenly the ground drops away and we're curving down into a pocket valley full of color.

Cars loll in the bright sunlight like painted lizards, sprawling haphazardly in a field of crushed grass. Beyond is a gathering of trailers and tall tents, ringing a central open space that's been filled with booths and blankets. Surrounding it all is a high loop of green cloth, strung on poles and fluttering in the wind. It's representative of the World Snake, and this is a caravan of Lokiskin.

I slow the car and stop in the middle of the road.

"What's wrong?" Astrid asks.

"I haven't been inside a caravan like this in a long time." I stare down at the flapping green circle, pushing back memories of my mom, of long nights surrounded by firelight, drums, laughter, the sweet smell of leaf sticking to my clothes.

"You lived with a caravan?" Her voice is dry with shock.

"For a few months after my father died." I glance at Baldur, the only person in the country who doesn't know anything about Styrr Bearskin. He's watching me with those sky-mirror eyes. I wonder what will happen to them when it rains.

He puts a hand on my shoulder. "I'll wait in the car with you."

"No." I grip the steering wheel and touch the gas. Astrid needs me to catch her when she dances. "I'll be fine. They're just memories."

It's only ten in the morning, but already the bazaar is

running at full strength. I pull the Spark into a crooked line of parked cars and Astrid says, "I'll need to find the matria and make sure we can set down."

"Don't promise her more than ten percent," I say, handing her the key before climbing out.

I strap my father's sword across my back and untie my spear from the roof. Though they're incongruent with my jeans and T-shirt, I'm not willing to leave anything valuable in the car. Besides, there are likely to be plenty of armed Lokiskin, and I have a god to protect.

Astrid hands Baldur a pair of gray-tinted sunglasses she bought with our gas, and tells him to keep them on. "It's your eyes that really give you away," she says softly, her fingers brushing the back of his hand.

"We'll scout a decent spot." I take Baldur's elbow and steer him off.

"I need at least three circle meters," she calls after.

Together Baldur and I explore the bazaar. The Half-Serpent Trading Company sells everything from clothing to woven baskets, dipped cinnamon fruit, and used auto parts. Women, and men dressed as women, call out to us, offering deals for steel-polishing cloth for my sword and a new sweatshirt for Baldur. After we have money, we might need to take the girl up on that last offer. Mountain air is cold in spring, and Baldur, without immortality, is as subject to the cold as the rest of us. They all want us to buy food, and my stomach is in perfect agreement. Baldur leans over a table of carved idols, caressing the soapstone ravens and pigs and cats, and the woman selling them flirts with him until he laughs. It's such a bright sound, and the sun flashes suddenly from behind the clouds. Her eyes widen and she hushes. I guide him away before her suspicions take root.

The noise of tin whistles and twanging six-string banjos, smells of sandalwood and sharp cheese, all the colors and yelling and good-natured bargaining are both familiar and overwhelming to me, reminding me of times I've left long behind. It clutters my head, and the press of people makes my fingers twitch to close around the handle of my sword or grip my spear defensively instead of holding it loose as a walking staff. My shoulders tighten, and I can't settle my eyes from the hectic way they dart everywhere. I focus on my breath, on finding a location for Astrid to seeth. Baldur appears content to walk at my side, drinking it all in without touching.

The only thing I'm grateful for is that the Lokiskin seem to be less paranoid and desperate than the rest of the world. Maybe they assume, despite his alibi, that Loki stole Baldur, and so they have little to worry about. It wouldn't surprise me.

They do miss Baldur, though. A space has been created in the center of the caravan, where often there would be dancing as the sun set, a large fire, and much laughter. But this space has been covered with a wide blue cloth, and children are painting bright yellow suns on it with their fingers. Candles have been lit around its border, and two women stand, one with a bowl of paper scraps, the other with chalk and pencils. People take time to stop and write on the scraps, then hold them over this or that candle to burn the prayers. They whisper Baldur's name, every one of them.

Baldur freezes when he notices what's happening. He grips my hand and whispers, "They are praying for *me*."

I hustle him away.

"Soren," he continues urgently, "I am stripped down to my very core. There is nothing I can do for them. But I feel like . . . I should. I should reveal myself."

Pushing him against the red-checked side of a hotpig stall, I say, "Don't think about what you aren't doing. Focus on what we need."

"What of what *they* need? How can I be hope if I stand here and ignore them?"

His distress flickers off his skin, dancing up my arms to find my frenzy. I take a deep breath. "Baldur," I whisper, "please don't. Please stay with us. We— Listen." I hesitate, because I realize I didn't want him to know this part. "Your father offered a boon. To whoever brings you safely home. We need it, Astrid and I."

For the first time, Baldur studies me with something shadowed. Or maybe it's only the sun in my face, making me wince. His eyes fall to my tattoo. "I'm supposed to be with you," he says, as though it will always be the answer.

We find an open space on the edge of the bazaar where once there was a booth to flatten the grass. The space has been abandoned, probably because directly beside it is an animal pen. A dozen small ponies share a water trough and bales of hay. Their rough braying and musty smell aren't anything I'd like to be trapped beside for long. Fortunately, we only need a couple of hours.

Astrid finds us there, with a tall Pan-Asian man in a long green-and-blue robe at her side. His skin is only just darker than mine, and gold hoops decorate his eyebrows, one nostril, and both ears. Green plastic jewels dot his forehead in the twisted figure eight of the World Snake. He smiles, and behind red lipstick his teeth gleam. "Greetings," he says.

"This is Jon Shandrasdottir," Astrid says. "Matria of Half-Serpent."

Jon crosses his ankles in a short curtsy. It's long-held tradition that the leader of a caravan be a woman or put on the appearance of one, because of Loki's fondness for traveling the world in the guise of mother or maid. "Pleasure, friends," Jon says.

Astrid introduces us as her circle keepers, Soren and Paul, and says we've been welcomed to seeth for the morning. Fifteen percent of the take goes to Jon in return for the space, mead enough to begin, drummers from his family, and a basket of food. I raise an eyebrow at Astrid, but she waves me away. "I'll need half an hour," she tells Jon, "and then I'll be ready to begin. I'll seeth until the last seeker comes, or until I fall over, so long as your hospitality holds."

Curious eyes watch our company as Astrid begins her preparations—children of Loki with their green makeup and snake bracelets, as well as shoppers come from nearby Laramie. A small boy, about five years old, dashes through the pony

pen and climbs the fence to hang over and stare at me. He's in
muddy clothes and his dark hair needs a trim, but his smile is
true and his eyes wide with wonder. He curls his fingers in a
wave. My favorite thing about the caravans was the other kids.
We played hand-toe throw and always had enough for stoneball
pickup games. That was before the tattoo. I didn't stand out. I
was normal.

"Sam!" a girl calls from the shadow of the trailer attached
to the pen.

"Is that you?" I ask him.

The boy nods his head.

"Your sister's calling."

He holds out his hand. It shines with some kind of sticky
substance, but I take it. He uses my strength to haul himself up
onto the top of the fence. Carefully, we pick our way around the
pen, me on the outside, Sam walking along the thin wooden rail
as though it's a balance beam. His bare feet curl easily around
it. Several of the ponies trail after us, snorting and whuffling as
though we might drop carrots out our back pockets.

We reach the far side where the trailer backs up against the
pen, shading a second circle of fish tanks and terrariums, crates
and cages with rats and rabbits. Instead of hopping down, Sam
grips my shoulder and doesn't let go. I move away, holding my
arm out. He dangles from it like a monkey, laughing and kicking his feet. A smile pulls at my mouth before I can stop it.

"He isn't bothering you, is he?" It's the same girl's voice,
and I lower Sam to the ground as she climbs out of the trailer.
She's about fourteen or fifteen, I guess, in loose pants and a

tight green tank top. Her coloring is pure Asgardian: white-blond hair, pale green eyes, skin so light I see veins. The bridge of her nose is pink with sunburn.

"No, maid," I say respectfully. "Sam here is only using me for what I'm best at. Support."

She begins to smile, but her eyes find my tattoo and she stares.

"I'm Soren Rebeccasson." I offer the matronymic, hoping it will comfort her. We don't need frazzled nerves today.

"My name is Vider Lokisdottir." She squares her shoulders; her voice is even and she tears her gaze off my tattoo and brings it to my eyes.

"Snakes!" Sam says, taking my hand and dragging me toward a terrarium settled against the crunchy grass. He flips off the lid and reaches in. Two small snakes, both dark gray and green, crawl up his arms. He draws them out and allows them to twist half around his shoulders and into his hair. His mouth is open and he's giggling the whole time. Vider slips a hand into a separate terrarium and removes another, slightly thicker snake, with markings more golden and tan.

She offers it to me. "She's just a python, won't hurt you."

"Royal, isn't she?" I hold out my hand and let the snake make her own way onto my wrist. Her head is light as a feather, skimming against my palm, and her scales dry. As she slides up my arm to curl around my elbow, I run a finger down her back. The texture is both pebbly and smooth.

"You know snakes?" Vider leans back on her heels, lips pursed.

"I used to travel with a caravan. When I was a boy younger than you."

"But you're Odin's."

"My mother wasn't."

Sam skips over, offering Vider one of his snakes. She gently uncoils it from his neck.

I settle down onto a pile of dusty rugs. Here, in the lee of their trailer, the noise of the bazaar is muffled. Beyond the pony pen, I have an excellent view of Astrid as she weaves her circle. Baldur's hair gleams in the sun; he's found a chair somewhere and stretched out to soak in the heat. They'll call for me if they need me. Here I draw less attention, and the less attention we attract before she begins her seething, the better. I ask Vider and Sam, "How long have you two been in Half-Serpent?"

"Always!" sings Sam. I assume his parents have long traveled with the caravan. He probably was born here.

Vider shrugs and sits beside me. "A couple of years is all for me." Her shoulders relax, and she strokes the python on my arm. She said her name was Lokisdottir, suggesting she doesn't know her family, or else chose to put them aside when she joined the caravan. There are no good reasons for such a thing. But nor are there ways to ask.

Sam says, "Do you know how snakes were born?"

I do, of course, but say, "Tell me."

He embellishes a version I know well: Loki's belly squirming larger than the world with a hundred million snake-babies ready to explode, but when Freya cuts him open, only Jormundgandr, the giant World Snake, emerges to wrap around the earth. Sam's version includes gushing blood and birth fluids, and shrieking minor goddesses. The little boy cackles like an old man and wiggles his fingers like snakes. He pats my chest as he assures me it's the best story in the nine worlds. But Vider says, "Oh, so?" and after slipping the snake in her arms back into its glass cage, she gestures for his attention. Sam shouts and stamps his little foot in preparation for a fit, and I quiet him by promising him a bear ride if he listens. After twisting his face and considering, he climbs onto my lap.

Vider tells the story of the first berserker, for my benefit, I'm sure, though Sam clutches my shoulders and is riveted to each word that falls off her tongue. Her version says that the first warrior was eaten slowly and painfully by the bear the Alfather chose, and the warrior screamed and cried but did not run away even as his flesh and bones were torn apart and his soul destroyed and consumed by the bear.

It sounds terrifying to me, and Sam hides his face in my shirt. But Vider is calm and certain, as if she knows the painful sacrifice was worth it.

When she's finished, I say, "You should go to Poets' School." She eyes my tattoo again. "I'd rather be a berserker." "Why?"

"No one can hurt you," she says, as if it's the only answer.

Sam squirms down from my lap and dashes back over to the snakes. "I want my bear ride!" He begins closing up the tanks.

But I keep my gaze focused on Vider. There's brightness in

her green eyes, almost like a fever. If she were a boy, I would wonder if her father had been a berserker and the frenzy huddled under her ribs. But girls are not born to berserking, so it must be something else that causes the anger in her heart to mirror mine. "A berserker can hurt himself."

Her look is scathing.

"Or hurt others easily," I add.

She juts out her chin. "That's better still."

It's my turn to level her with my most fearsome scowl, which always cleared the hall at Sanctus Sigurd's. Vider Lokisdottir doesn't shrink back or cower, but she does lower her eyes and say, "The price for strength like that is worth it. And better than the deals of some other gods."

I want to laugh and tell her I never made any deal with Odin. That we are taking Baldur the Beautiful home, and I will ask my god to strip away his so-named gift. "I had no choice in this." I flick my thumb down my tattoo.

"I know." She shrugs, and when she lifts her head there's a teeth-baring smile. "We never do."

Sam jerks on my arm, throwing all his weight onto me to get my attention. I put my wide hand across his face and remain focused on Vider. Because I suspect that this girl doesn't need Odin to hand her the strength she thinks she's missing, I make an offer I've never considered before. "I can show you what gives a berserker strength."

Surprised, her smile falters. "Thank you," she manages.

I heave Sam onto my back and tell him to not let go of

my shoulders. His small hands clutch at my neck and his toes knock against my ribs. But he clings well.

We come upon Baldur stretched shirtless beside Astrid's circle, hands beneath his head and eyes shut behind his sunglasses. The sun shines off his hair and body as if he's made of silver. I can see a wicked purple bruise like a splattered plum streaking across his ribs on the left side. Where I slammed him with the butt of my spear. When we approach, he cracks open an eye. "Sun's warm if you care to join me."

"You're not exactly blending in," I mutter. Sam squirms and I lower him. He scrambles to Baldur and climbs directly onto his stomach.

"Oof," Baldur gasps, laughing and pulling the boy onto his chest.

"You're hot!" Sam declares, smacking his hands together.

I grab the back of Sam's shirt in my fist and lift him off the god. "And he's boring. You're better off with us."

"And what are you all off to do?" Baldur asks.

Vider says, quietly but firmly, "Soren is going to teach me where a berserker gets his strength."

Baldur raises his eyes to mine, lifting the glasses to see me clearly. Despite the sun behind me, glaring directly into his face, he doesn't wince or blink. His eyes are hot, and golden-white. "Are you," he murmurs.

Sam begins kicking his stubby little legs in the air, and I suddenly remember I'm holding him aloft. He grins, and flaps his arms like a bird. "Caw, caw!" he cries.

Sitting up, Baldur takes Sam from me, then sets him on the

grass. "Look over there at what Astrid's doing." Sam twists his neck and his eyes light up. "I bet she'll let you help."

Sam dashes off. I glance around to see Astrid weaving strands of red yarn, looping them around and setting the edges of a web under loose rocks. Sam bends to try to pick up a stone that probably weighs half as much as he does.

"What *is* she doing?" Vider asks.

"Setting up to seeth. I'm sure she'll read your future if you like." To Baldur I say, "Enjoy the sun." He grins at me and flicks a thumbs-up before resettling his sunglasses and reclining again.

Vider and I walk a bit away through dry, knee-high grass. The air coming off the distant mountains smells of pine and snow. I show her how to ground herself; how to imagine she's part of the mountains, that she *is* a mountain. I show her how to breathe so the air scours emotions from deep in your guts.

"This is the secret of the berserkers?" she whispers, eyes closed and face turned up.

"It's the first secret. Always know what you are, because with knowledge comes control."

"And breathing teaches me what I am?"

"It calms your emotions, your anger and fear. It draws the world inside your chest to balance out the rage," I say. "You are the rock, and the wind batters at you, flows around you and within you. But you are the rock. The mountain. You stand."

"I stand." She draws in another long breath. Wind ruffles her thin blond hair.

I try to breathe myself calm, too. But people are gathering outside Astrid's circle, watching her, watching us, and I open my eyes. Astrid slowly stands. Her back is to me, and she strips off her sweater so she's only in the pleated skirt and a tank top. She unbinds her curls and spreads her hands out. Thin catskin gloves, the mark of the seethkona, cover her hands. The sun caresses the muscles of her back. Suddenly my breathing is not calm. I am not peaceful or anything like a solid mountain.

I am fire.

I long to step close to her, but she would ignite me, and how could I ever control something like that?

She calls out, "I am Astrid Jennasdottir, child of the Feather-Flying Goddess." Her voice rings high. "I dance the paths of the past, the present, and the future. I see the strands of fate and understand the language of bones. I am here for seething, and will answer all questions as my lady deems fit."

Vider touches my hand, freeing me from Astrid, and we move closer to where folk gather in a wide circle, calling their friends, holding hands and putting shoulders together to create a wall of people. Baldur, joining us, lifts Sam up onto his shoulders.

"We have honey mead, seethkona," Jon says, flourishing a clear bottle of swirling yellow alcohol. A charm is tied to the neck with silver wire.

Astrid accepts it. "Thus is the first exchange, given and received. Who will step into my circle?" Her eyes scan the crowd and she turns slowly, mead bottle cradled in her arms.

A teenage girl speaks up, but not to volunteer. "You're Astrid Glyn, Jenna Glyn's daughter."

Astrid nods. Smiles and whispers shoot around the gathering, but before Astrid says anything, the same girl says, "I saw you on galdralag-dot-com. Fighting that dick in Nebrasge."

"I fought holmgang, yes."

"I saw your mother once," says another onlooker, a woman with huge gold earrings that dazzle in the afternoon sun.

A man in heavy eyeliner says, "The Seether of All Dreams would have known how to find Baldur."

Astrid's fingers go rigid. A snap of quiet surrounds her, and she manages to say, "I'm sure my mother would have been doing everything in her power to return him to us."

I glance at Baldur, who's edged to the back of the crowd, sunglasses still shielding his eyes.

"Why aren't you seething for him?" "Why are you here?" There's more than one of them crying these questions out now. I can feel the frenzy tingling in the palms of my hands, and I breathe down into the earth. Astrid can handle this crowd, but I am ready.

"I am here, to seeth for you," she calls, spreading her arms out like wings. "To be with you and to pray, to offer you the visions I can see in your dreams. Not just my own. Baldur is a part of all of us! Who will let me look into your dreams for him?"

Someone must help her recapture the focus of the crowd on the magic, and I owe her a fortune-telling. Before I can reconsider, I step into the circle.

She whirls to face me. Her expression is all smooth confidence, but I can just barely see the strain at the corners of her smile.

I stand across from her, the blood-red web pinned between us. "You've always promised to read my future, lady."

My voice seems to relax her, and she gazes at me as though she already knows everything my bones will say. "Welcome my friend Soren, daughter of Rebecca but son of Styrr." Astrid raises the mead and takes a long pull while her naming of me spins off into the crowd. They know who I am, too, especially if they've seen that video of the holmgang. Especially if they remember the day my father died.

Fear and anticipation hang in the air, like an acidic wind. There is Jon Shandrasdottir moving about, offering drums of all sizes. Some that fit in the palm of one's hand, some wide as tambourines, and some only half spheres covered over with painted skin, which cup perfectly in a person's lap. Vider accepts a bone-rattle.

I hear words fall out of the humming conversation: "berserker" and "danger" and "Styrr-Styrr-Styrr." We certainly have pulled their attention off Baldur completely.

Astrid holds the mead out to me in one hand. I accept, and drink the cool, sweet alcohol. We sit, and the circle of observers slowly follows suit. Then Astrid gathers the bones from a deep pocket in her seething kit and cages them in her fingers. Her runes are pieces of stone and wood, finger bones, and a rainbow shell. All carved by her own hand with the language of wisdom.

Standing, she shakes the rune bones. Eyes down, she begins to walk around the web counterclockwise. The drumming begins in rhythm with her footsteps. Her lips move rapidly. I step back so I'm not in her path. Around she goes, and after a full revolution she returns to me. Pausing, she lifts the runes to my mouth. "Breathe, Soren," she murmurs, eyes on my lips.

My throat catches and I cannot breathe as she instructs. I feel her magic, like a frenetic dance, shaking toward me.

The drums pound with my heart and Astrid laughs a breathy laugh. "Soren." She shakes the bones in her hands, and it also shakes loose my breath.

I sigh over her fingers, over the bones.

Astrid continues on with the whisper of a smile, until she's walked around the circle three times. Then she walks faster, three more times. The drumbeats speed with her. Little Sam claps his hands, and I'm surprised that he's perfectly in rhythm, but then, Loki's children love drums. It seems as though my breath and heart match the fast pulse, too, and I feel the fever of my frenzy rise. My face flushes, and sweat breaks out along my spine. Yet my rage does not flare; it only simmers, bubbling in time to the cadence of Astrid's dance.

She turns in place and continues to circle, like the earth around the sun, orbiting and rotating at once. I don't know how she doesn't fall, but her feet are sure. Her curls bounce over her bare shoulders and her eyes flicker beneath closed lids. Her lips keep moving, faster and faster as she whirls, and her cheeks are pink.

I've lost count of her spinning, of her revolutions, when

suddenly she stops. The drums stop, too, and Astrid casts the bones away from her, tossing them onto the scarlet web.

They slap the dusty ground, tumbling into clumps and spreading patterns.

Astrid crouches, hands out over the web, fingers splayed. She peers down, head swaying as if she's finally dizzy. Everyone is silent. I hear only a strain of distant tin whistle and stifled bazaar conversation, the wind in the field and everyone's breathing.

"There," Astrid points at one bone. "Torch! The burning ulcer. That is you."

I kneel across from her. I feel alight, feverish, as though something inside is truly burning.

"It kills you, as it kills all children." Her face lifts to mine, but Astrid is not in her own eyes. They are dull and reflective circles. "But it does not kill men." She nods decisively. "It does not kill men. This!" Her finger moves to point at a rune on the opposite edge of the web. "Ash tree. The sacrificial tree. You do not hang upon it; it hangs upon you."

"I don't know what that means," I say.

"I do." She nods again and waves her hand over the runes. "It means that you . . ." The lilt of her voice shifts, and it is more the Astrid I know. "You . . ." Her pause is long now, as she stares at one single rune: the symbol means journey, and is carved onto a curved yellow tooth. A dark frown ripples across her face as she contemplates it. One finger hovers in the air a mere centimeter above.

"Astrid?" I keep my voice gentle, unsure how far into seething she remains.

She blinks and shivers as though shaking off the dread. Her smile appears, small but true. "You're on a journey," she says, tapping the rune.

I laugh, just once. Out of disbelief. Even I know that much about the rune. But Astrid looks me in the eye and tilts her head to the left. All the people around us—I don't think she wants to say anything about this rune in front of them.

"A journey that will lead you to make a choice." It's a simple prophecy she offers me, and I wonder if just because it isn't the complete meaning of what she sees in the bones, it can't also be true. "Between two parts of yourself." Astrid touches my chest, just over my heart, and skims her fingers up to the strap holding Father's sword to my shoulders. I take her fingers in mine, drawing them away from the sword.

"My turn!" cries Sam. Astrid and I both jump. We were quiet too long, kneeling together in the web, its scarlet strings tangled with our feet and spreading out from us like a pool of bloody water.

The little boy's dash across the circle breaks the spell settled on the crowd, too, and many of them laugh or at least smile. Some hold up money, others clap relieved hands on their neighbors' shoulders. They eye me warily, but as I back away, a few nod. Most can't take their attention off the seether.

I join Baldur as Astrid gathers the mood of the crowd into her hands again, sweeping the people in the direction she wishes with Sam's enthusiastic help. Her smile and the grace-ful motions of her fingers as she plucks bones from red thread convince them she is a girl on the edge of wisdom again. She uses little tricks to flip her bones from hand to hand, and closes her eyes as she chooses her next seeker by spelling out his name in the air with a long bone of polished yew. A man in jeans and a Stetson steps forward, and the drums begin again.

For nearly two hours Astrid spins and dances, throwing her bones and calling out answers to questions of love and death. She translates messages from the grave, and offers riddles to all who ask. Sweat glistens on her forehead and upper lip. It trick-les down between her shoulder blades, and when the mountain wind blows, elf-kisses raise the hair on her arms. She shivers.

The bottle of mead is passed around to all the seekers who ask a question, and when it's empty, coins and notes are dropped or stuffed inside. We'll have to break the glass to get them out.

The crowd belongs to her. She connects them with her words and dance as if literally tying them together with red thread. They are a single creature, birthing out seekers one at a time, then sucking them back in. They move in perfect rhythm, feet stomping the heartbeat of the seeth.

I sit on the ground several feet back, where I can see Astrid but not be in the way. This is her element, her power.

Although at first Vider holds close and watches the seeth-ing with livid attention, she eventually creeps to me and settles near. On her other side, Baldur sits with his knees curled up and arms around them like a little boy. The sun shines on him and I can feel the warmth from where I sit. The energy of the seething seeps through the air, electric as a lightning storm. With Baldur the Beautiful so near, Astrid dancing her circle, and even Vider who does not fear the berserking, I am suddenly relaxed as I haven't been in ages. I belong.

It makes me careless. "Baldur," I say quietly, to point out the red-tailed hawk that perches on top of the nearest pole holding up the green snake flag.

He glances at me, loose and easy, but Vider freezes and her teeth snap together. "Baldur?"

And suddenly it's everywhere.

"Baldur." "Baldur the Beautiful."

The whisper weaves through the crowd and faces turn toward us. The moment people see him, thinking his name, they know. With the suspicion rooted, there is no other thing he could be.

I'm on my feet, dragging him up. "Astrid," I say as calmly as I can. She whirls around, confusion painted across her face as the attention of the crowd diverts to us.

Baldur puts his hands out. "Kind folk—" he says, trying to deter them, hand them back to Astrid.

"Are you Baldur, the missing god?" calls a woman with turquoise hanging from her ears and neck.

"Yes, are you?" Someone else echoes her cry. "Baldur!"

Jon pushes through a family with heavy hemp bags in their hands. "You said your name was Paul." His voice is quiet, like he wants to believe we did not lie. His green jewels flicker with their own life.

Others are faster to condemn us. "He said his name was Paul! It's Pol Darrathr!" The crowd presses forward in a wave.

Baldur blanches; he takes his sunglasses off. "I call on your honor, Lokiskin: hold back."

I glimpse Astrid ducking low to gather her seething bones, barely visible through all the brilliant colors of the caravan. Her hands flutter fast as bumblebees as she packs her things.

My spear is dug into the earth four meters back, but Father's sword remains strapped over my shoulder. I'm loath to draw it, but plant my feet. *I am the mountain.* I drag a huge breath. "Stop!"

The crowd falters, but then hands flail and voices rise again. No one yet breaks apart to approach him alone. Prayers sing out, and curses, too, hope and anger. Their collective voice turns the wind into heat. They're between us and the Spark. If we run, they'll overtake us. Baldur they'll hold safe, but Astrid—

I put my hand on Father's sword and flick open the strap holding it in the sheath. With a single sharp tug, I swing it free. "Astrid!" I yell.

She appears, shoving aside a man twice her size. She darts to Baldur, and I step in front of them. I hold out the sword and the sun makes it blaze. "Stay back," I say. "Or I will hold you back."

My chest constricts and I feel the rage poking out in all directions, an iron star tearing at my ribs. I bare my teeth, hold my father's sword high. I can't think about the blood splattering my face when he went mad. I can't think about these people splayed before me in a fan of death, cut down by my uncontrolled power.

I can only think of being the mountain. Being the solid wall between my friends and the storm.

I back up slowly; Astrid and Baldur the Beautiful back up, too. Until I reach my spear. I curl my fingers around the smooth shaft, warm from the sun, and jerk it free. "Go, now," I say to Astrid.

With spear in one hand, sword in the other, I face the crowd. They aren't angry or yelling, but hands reach out. Their faces are washed with awe. A half dozen have fallen to their knees, and there is a family of four holding hands and singing the opening of the Psalm of the Sun. "Don't go!" cries a woman. "Baldur!" yells the man beside her. And they're yelling again, begging him to stay, calling his name like a prayer.

We move toward the eastern side of the caravan, nearer to the parking lot. More and more people arrive to join in the noise, spilling out from the stalls, between trailers. They're circling behind Baldur and Astrid. Soon we'll be surrounded. I swing my sword, the arc of steel holding them back.

The voices mix together into a great swell of noise. Someone yells a curse at us for trying to take Baldur. Another accuses us of stealing him in the first place. "Hel-spawn!" he yells. I point my spear at the young man with Thor's hammer tattooed on his neck, but he points at Astrid and calls her Odin's whore.

I slam the butt of my spear into his nose.

The bone crunches and blood stains his lips and shirt. The crowd leaps back, and then in a sudden thrust they swarm forward.

"Soren!" It's Astrid, calling as she runs with Baldur's hand in hers. They sprint toward the Spark, which idles at the edge of the field with a girl behind the wheel. People grab at them, and Astrid punches at one. Baldur, the faster runner, pulls her along.

I sense the crowd around me, and I roar. My arms shake with the effort to hold on to myself, to not let go and destroy everything threatening my friend and my god. My yell is like a steam valve, releasing excess energy so I don't explode, warning others to stay back. The iron star crunches against my ribs, pushing to be free. Never has it been so close!

There are some men and women not trapped in the wild mob, newly arrived or broken free somehow, and they hold their fellows back. But too much magic was raised in Astrid's seething circle, letting loose all their fears and the anxiety and hope that here, now, here is Baldur the Beautiful—it is not enough.

They want him from us. From me. Their desperation pushes away the terror they should feel when faced with an armed berserker.

My breath is ragged, my mind spiraling away from rational thought, lifting high up into the air.

Astrid screams. I turn, weapons out, and see a man between her and Baldur, tearing them apart. But she grabs the man's hair and rips at it. Baldur helps, and they kick back the man and then another. The car doors are open. "Soren!" Astrid screams again. Baldur climbs into the car, dragging at Astrid, but she reaches out for me. I am far away, with half a generation of Lokiskin between us.

I see Vider through the car window, her hands on the wheel. I don't know how she knew the car was ours, but I'm not surprised. "Go," I say. She can't hear me over the crowd, but she sees my mouth and nods.

The tires spin and the Spark jumps forward. The momentum slams shut the door behind Astrid.

Kicking up debris into the faces of the crowd rushing after, the Spark speeds up the hill of crushed grass and away. A handful of people straggle in its wake.

And I am alone with them.

The world holds still for a long moment, and then a wail lifts up to the sun.

It's followed by mourning cries like the ones Astrid and I heard when Baldur failed to rise. Tears streak down a little girl's cheeks.

With Baldur and Astrid gone, the bubble of seething energy dissipates.

But I cannot back down.

There's Jon, the matria of Half-Serpent, touching his family, his soothing voice reaching out.

But inside me the iron star rushes faster and faster.

My vision wavers. I'm dizzy and wind-headed.

Astrid is gone.

Baldur is gone.

I lean on my spear. I'm a great, hulking, empty husk. Inside is only the fury, the empty night sky.

Voices murmur all around, some full of anger, others sorrowing. A laugh rings out, and then a new prayer: "The Laying of Loki," a ribald song.

I have to get out of here. I can't stay. I can't. My hands are sweating; my face is flushed. The fever sticks my shirt to my spine, sweat pooling in the small of my back.

"Berserker."

My eyes focus on a woman, my mother's age, with her hand out. She isn't smiling, but her brow wrinkles with concern. "Are you well, son of Odin?"

A laugh chokes me, and I stumble away from her.

Someone catches my arm, and I lash out, knocking the man off his feet. Though he was only trying to help.

My movements are stilted, my knees shaking. I tighten my fingers around my spear, and raise my sword. There are people backing away, scared now as they should have been then.

Good.

I turn my back to them, and I look at the distant mountains.

I lift one foot, then the other. Toward the mountains. The iron star wants out. The rage pushes all my heat away, energy dripping down my skin in rivulets.

I am on fire. My bones tremble and my teeth ache. I can't— I can't stop it.

It's coming.

The battle-rage is coming.
To the mountains.
I run.
I open my mouth.
And roar.
Feet on the earth, pounding.
Pounding.
The iron star breaks my skin.

ELEVEN

I WAKE COLD. And nauseated. My skin feels like wet clay, sliding slowly off my bones.

I'm on my back; the soft earth cushions my shoulders and hips. Father's sword is a solid line between me and the ground, bruising my spine. Red pine trees tower thin and needle-like around me. The world is dark on the forest floor, but high overhead a circle of sky shines indigo. A single star peers back down at me from the third heaven, the home of wind.

My memory is a black blur. I hold my hands up, though they ache and my muscles are slow to work as a winter fire. Darkness stains my palms, and my breath catches in my throat—but it is only dirt. Not blood.

Thank you, Mother Frigg, that I didn't hurt anyone.

The evergreen smell of earth and snow hangs tingling in the air. My breath puffs out in pale wisps. I close my eyes again and ache as I wonder where Astrid is now, and Baldur. I move my lips in another silent prayer that they escaped north and somehow are continuing the journey. *Let my sacrifice be worth it. Let them succeed even if it be without me.*

I expel a hard sigh, and am left with emptiness. I'm more tired than I've ever been, all my muscles loose. My thoughts dispersing across the forest floor.

I went berserk.

The frenzy found me, and I am fully Odin's now. No hope left that I might somehow beat it back, hold the rage steady. No hope that it might dissipate into nothing if I push it away for long enough. No hope that I can ask Odin to take it from me, because I've lost Baldur.

I am my father's son, now and ever. The tattoo on my cheek is a true mark.

Nausea crawls up my throat; tears threaten to spill over. But I swallow them back, hold in the anguish because I am so used to holding everything inside.

At least I got away. At least I didn't hurt anyone.

This time.

I don't know what I'm going to do now. Hike as far as I can, perhaps find a road or a town where I can beg change for a phone call. Because I frenzied, they'll take me in at the Hangadrottin, even without Pirro's request. Assign me to a berserk band.

And maybe—maybe when she's delivered Baldur, Astrid will visit me. I wish I could find them now, but I don't know where I am, or where they are. I can't see how I have any chance of catching up. They're on their own, as I am.

I try to convince myself it's better this way. Astrid is safer without me, now that I've lost my control.

Where is my spear? I turn my head and scan the ground for it. Nothing.

But someone leans against a tree several paces away. Just a shadow against a shadow.

I'm up instantly, on my hands and the balls of my feet, crouched to spring. I dig my fingers into the soft ground cover of old pine needles to keep balance as my head fills with clouds. "Who are you?" I demand, but my voice comes out low and yielding. I teeter and all around me the shadows of the forest scatter and dance. I blink. I breathe in the cold air, only wanting to sink down again and fall back to sleep. For a year. My thoughts are giant slugs creeping around inside my skull.

"You're weak, Bearskin."

The voice is a woman's, and familiar.

I squint, trying to make out her features in the deep shadow. Something glitters near her eyes. "Who?"

Her sigh echoes through the trees like a gust of wind tossing needles across the ground. "Sit back; I don't mean you any harm." She sashays closer and I recognize her wine-colored lips and green-glitter eyes.

Glory. The hostess from the pub. A daughter of Loki.

I collapse back onto the ground, knees up, arms slack. I don't have the energy to be surprised or angry or anything. Weariness is a long rope, pulling me into the ground.

"Now, Soren." Glory the hostess sits in front of me, legs

crossed, and takes my hands in hers. Her skin is soft. I smell bubble gum. But she isn't chewing anything.

"Glory," I say.

"Good!" She squeezes my fingers. "But it isn't my real name, you know."

I shake my head. I don't know.

Her eyes narrow, and suddenly the shadows suck closer to her face. She's dark and dangerous, and her mouth seems to grin as big as the moon. Her teeth are sharp, fanged and yellow. She drops her jaw open and a great pink tongue lolls out.

I shove away, yelping.

A peal of laughter snakes around me, and Glory is Glory again: only a pretty girl in a low-cut blouse, tight black skirt, and spike-heeled boots she could not possibly have walked very far in.

My back presses into the rough trunk of a tree, Father's sword poking my hip. I automatically take calming breaths, then notice my rage is not churning—it's been spent. I'm too exhausted.

The realization drops the ground out from under me. I sway, feel my eyes roll back. I dig my fingers into the pine-needle ground and order myself to stay conscious. I bite my lip, use the pain to focus.

"Here, now," Glory says. Her hands are on my face. "Rest, dumb beast. You're going to pass out again. You need food and water, and really you need a good lay."

I grunt, trying to edge away from her. Whatever she is.

"I've known many of your kind, Soren, and you're all the

same. After raging, you need meat or water or alcohol or sex. Sometimes all of the above."

Batting at her hands, I manage to hoarsely say, "Water."

Her laugh now is a deeper chuckle. It rolls down my skin. "Very well."

From nowhere there is a goblet in her hand. She puts the smooth edge to my mouth, and I smell perfect water. Cupping the goblet in both hands, I drink. The liquid is warmer than the air, soothing and peaceful and slightly honey-sweet. It tastes of flowers and springtime.

Long after the goblet should have been empty, I continue to drink.

The water fills me up, washes my nausea away. And I see more sharply, as if I slept for hours.

Glory sits next to me, also leaning against a tree. Her long legs are out and crossed at the ankle, her arms folded under her breasts, pushing them up toward the open neck of her shirt. I can see the edge of her lacy bra. I look away, down into the goblet, where three drops of water remain near the bottom. They glint with starlight.

"Give it here, boy."

She holds out her hand and I see the figure-eight tattoo on her wrist. The World Snake. I hesitate as an idea blossoms, then give the cup over. I raise my eyes to hers and ask, "Does it bother you that his image is the symbol of Loki's children?"

Her answer will tell me what I believe I already know.

Glory's lips curl into a tricky smile. She sets the goblet

down and laces her fingers together. "I have more than enough notoriety without my true face being burned into the skin of every orphan across New Asgard."

I am both surprised and not surprised. My throat is dry again.

Part of me wants to get onto my knees out of respect, but the rest of me remains too tired. And she's flirted with me, teased me, offered me drink. I was never any danger to her, and I can't imagine she'll tear my face off now. Though there was the time in Alta California she supposedly broke a man's neck for speaking ill of Tyr the Just. I say, "It is an honor, Fenris Wolf."

Her tongue slides across the tips of her teeth as she grins. "Just Glory, son of Odin. The only ones I allow to call me by the name my father gave me are those who want to screw me or fight me. And you don't. Alas."

"Wh-what are you doing here?"

Glory stands, confident and balanced even as her spike heels sink an inch into the carpet of pine needles. "I'm getting you on your feet. Shoving you back on your way." She thrusts down her hand.

Eyeing it, I wonder if she's been following me for days, or if it was only last night she happened upon us.

"Come on, boy." She wiggles her fingers. Her nails are polished with silver glitter.

I take her hand, but hold fast. "Why?"

"Why what?"

"Are you helping?"

She curls her fingers so her nails cut into my hand.

I don't move. "They say the world will end when Fenris Wolf devours the sun."

"Yum, yum." Her nails dig harder.

"I can't lead you to him."

"I *know* where he is," she snaps. Then she leans down, loosening her grip on me but pushing her face close to mine. I smell bubble gum again, and a thicker scent like old buried metal. "I knew as he slept with you in that little motel last night. If I wanted to kill him I could have. If I wanted to eat him . . . well." She tilts her head to the side and starlight glints off a thin ring of scar tissue encircling her neck. "I am quite bound, and won't be swallowing anything larger than a grape."

"Then why?"

"You are more stubborn than a rock goblin!" Glory lets go of my hand and throws hers up. "I want Baldur the Beautiful safely to the apple orchard, Soren Styrrson. I want him safe and I want my father released from the ever-watch the Alfather has set upon him."

I climb to my feet without her help, though my knees are unsteady. "Loki was given alibi from Freya herself. He is still a suspect?"

Glory stalks away from me, whirls, then stalks back. "Make no mistake," she says, her mouth inches from mine. Her eyes are hard and black as a dog's. "Make no mistake that it was anything but a god who kidnapped the sun. You think for an instant a *man* or *woman* might have done this thing? Never. It was no mortal who stole Baldur's ashes and flew them away from the New World Tree. A god of Asgard did this, and whenever that is the case, it's always my father blamed first."

I hold my hands up. "I believe you, lady wolf."

"Good. Then come." She holds out her hand again.

This time I let her help me. She walks beside me through the darkness, slow enough that I manage without terrible vertigo. We make our way between the pole-like trees. My boots crush needles loudly, while Glory's are nearly silent. She moves with furious grace, yet her hand is gentle in mine. "Glory."

"Change your mind about the sex?"

I clear my throat uncomfortably, and she laughs, just a quiet *huff, huff*.

I try again. "Why, if you know where Baldur is, are you here with me? Why not take him straight to Odin?"

"Are you being slow on purpose? I told you, a god did this, and I'll not return him to Bright Home ignorant of the culprit. Especially without his apple."

"Then why not take him to Idun yourself?"

"I don't know where the orchard is."

Shock stops my feet.

Glory tugs on my hand. "They don't tell people who've been fated to destroy the world, Soren."

"So your dad brings you your apple?"

"Something like that." She turns that snapping grin on me again. The darkness is nearly complete, and I realize I hear nothing but the sound of wind slinking through the pine trees. No insects or night birds calling out. None of the tiny noises a forest should be full of. It must be because of the wolf at my side. Though we see only a girl with glittery eye shadow, the forest knows her true form, and that if she could, she'd swallow it all.

Should I be more afraid than I am? Most like. But I'm tired, and the thing I've dreaded for the last five years came true today. I am a danger to all, and wouldn't mind too terribly if Fenris ate me up.

But here she is holding my hand and helping me instead. I ask, "How can Astrid get Baldur there, then? How will Astrid ever find the orchard?"

"Ah, Soren, that is finally a good question. And I have an excellent answer." Glory reaches up and pats my cheek, her hand lightly slapping my tattoo. "Astrid Jennasdottir doesn't need a god or her own shadow magic to find the orchard. All she needs is you."

Glory leads me to the edge of the forest, where a highway cuts through the abruptly flat grassland toward the northwest. A motorcycle tilts on the steep shoulder, looking like it will topple over at any moment. Starlight shines darkly off its body. She lets go of me and walks straight for it, lifts it in one hand, and straddles it. Her skirt rides up her thighs and she pats the seat just behind her. "Hop on."

I do, scooting up against her. My boots fit on thin metal bars protruding from either side of the engine. Glory wiggles her butt between my thighs and I close my eyes tight. My hands are fists against my jeans, and Glory laughs as she takes them and puts them on her hips. "Don't be a baby, Soren."

"You aren't making it easy." It sounds like I'm strangling.

"I don't like things *easy.*" To highlight her statement, she revs her engine. "Don't fall off."

The motorcycle jerks forward, leaping onto the highway. I clutch at Glory as her peal of laughter is snatched away by the wind. Cold air bites at my face and I tuck closer, my nose in her hair. The smell of bubble gum and old blood washes over me. With my eyes shut and my body tight to hers, it's almost like flying. The roar of wind, the feel of it pricking through my torn T-shirt, ripping at my hair, as if it's trying to pry me away from her, off the bike and back into the wild frenzy.

We stop in a town large enough for a handful of fast-food joints. Glory drags me inside the Jarl Burger and orders three meals for me and a cherry soda for herself. I try to protest, especially when the clerk gives my tattoo a dirty look. I tell Glory I'm more nauseated than hungry. She brushes me away, pays, and sits me down on a metal stool anchored to the floor.

We're alone in the fluorescent-lit dining hall. Behind Glory's head is a blurry pastel watercolor by some Frankish painter. In the stark lighting, her green eye shadow looks like giant bruises. With my darker skin and dirty orange shirt, I must stand out against the room's muted colors like a gratuitous Hallowblot decoration.

The first potato wedge I taste transforms my nausea into starvation, and before I know it, I'm halfway through the second burger. Glory watches me with a cocky smile, leaning back against the wall. I think of being in the diner in Nebrasge with Astrid, and wish it were her instead of Glory across from me. Except then she would know I'd frenzied.

My gaze slides to the big black windows. The edge of the town is alive and brightly lit with gas stops, more fast-food places, and a long windowless warehouse I suspect is a strip club. How far did Astrid and Baldur make it? Did they pass through here? I draw a breath as if I'll be able to taste them in the air.

It's so dark now, Astrid must be awake alone. Baldur would have passed out, no matter where they were. I imagine her sitting beside him, arms around her knees, cold and fighting sleep.

"You have quite the brooding expression," Glory says.

To avoid answering, I take another bite of the burger. A dollop of ketchup smacks down against the crinkled paper on the table.

"Thinking about your girlfriend?"

"She's not—"

Glory grins. "Right."

I stare at her as I chew. Nothing about her suggests immortality or great wisdom or explosive violence. None of the things I associate with Fenris Wolf. She's a teenager, overdressed— or dressed for that strip club—and impatient. Her painted fingernails tap against the side of her cardboard cup.

But she doesn't look away. Her eyes are dark green, almost

black in this light, and something in them makes me uncomfortable. I feel the pinch of my power again, sharp in my chest, as she stares back. She never blinks. As if she doesn't have to.

I swallow and put the last hunk of my burger down. "You, ah, said you've known other berserkers."

Her eyebrow cocks up as if to remind me I'm being an idiot.

"Do you know if we always pass out the first time?"

Glory pinches her lips together, and I see laughter in the way her eyes narrow.

Grinding my teeth, I clarify, "The first time we go berserk."

"No."

The answer is so quick and so calm, I grip the table. "Are you sure?"

"I've heard of some of you entering such a deep fugue state you black out, but usually a berserker doesn't go through it alone. Usually you have a father or uncle or commit-brother, and usually the frenzy is brought forth purposefully, in circumstances as controlled as possible."

I know these things. I've read all the literature. Seen the made-for-TV movies. It wasn't something Dad ever talked about, and when he was alive, I never thought to ask. It hadn't mattered. I knew I'd grow up to be a berserker, and when the time came he'd take me through it. He'd be there.

"You look disappointed," Glory says. She doesn't sound sympathetic.

"I thought maybe you might know something to help me."

"Why haven't you sought out a commit? There are several

well-known berserk bands that would take you in, despite your father's rather spectacular ending."

"I don't want to be a berserker."

"Much choice you have." Her upper lip wrinkles into half a snarl.

"You fight *your* destiny, don't you? You don't want to swallow the sun." I'm desperate for her to say it's true. That the bindings on her throat and wrists aren't the only things keeping the world from ending. There are no such bindings for me.

"Ha." Glory leans in, her mouth open in a wide smile so I can see all her teeth and her tongue. "What do you know about these bindings and how they stopped me from eating the sun, Soren Bearskin?"

"I know . . ." I take a breath and gather my thoughts. "I know you were brought to Bright Home as a wolf-child, and that you kept growing and growing, so the gods feared you would grow large enough to swallow the sun whole. They sought to bind you with chains, but you broke free. They commissioned ropes of goblin magic and you agreed to let them put the ropes around you only if they proved they meant you no harm. So, to prove it, Tyr the Just put his hand in your mouth. As they tied you up, you bit off his hand."

Her smile widens impossibly, until I think my eyes have unfocused. The strangeness of it on her human face turns my stomach. When she speaks, her voice reverberates in my skull with the edge of a growl. "This is what it was really like, Bearskin: There was my father, Loki, the boy-god everyone loved and hated in equal measure. He carried me over the Rainbow

184

Bridge to Asgard and put me into the gods' bower. They raised me on the mountain with kindness, though most feared the sharp fangs appearing where my baby teeth had been. Only Tyr brought me meat instead of fruit, and when I was my wolf-self, starving and running wild, only he brought me flowers instead of whips. He sang me songs to help me learn control, and taught me the language of peace.

"It was my own fault they remembered the prophecy that I would swallow the sun: I ate a feast's worth of sacrificial horses and pigs. I did it because they were meant for Freyr, who had kicked me and called me Loki's bitch. But all the gods saw then was my never-ending hunger. I was brought to the Shining Hall, where Odin and his brothers sat waiting. The gods of Asgard encircled me, made me gag on the sour and sweet and bitter smell of apples. 'We shall subdue her,' Odin said. 'With impossible things to keep the impossible at bay.'

" 'Wait,' Tyr said. He stood before me, sword at his hip. He is one of the elder gods, and if he has not the sharp wit of Odin, the loudness of Thor, or the richness of Freyr, it isn't because he is not strong. It isn't because he is not beautiful. He said, 'This wolf-girl is one of us. A child of Asgard. Shall we treat her so poorly?'

"I held my head high for him, the hunger gnawing inside my chest for bones to crunch between my teeth, or for one of his songs. I growled my starvation.

" 'Show us, brother,' Odin said. 'Show us that she can control herself. That she can resist the sun-sized need.'

"I thought, *No! I cannot do it!* But Tyr walked to me. I backed away, my body ripping and cracking. He was not safe from me! The transformation to wolf broke my bones and reshaped my teeth. It changed my tongue until I could not speak. But he was calm. He did not shake. My back bowed and he put out a hand. 'She will not attack,' he said to them. 'My word shall bind her.' And to me he lowered his voice: 'My flesh shall sate your hunger.'

"I opened my mouth to howl and he slipped his fingers past my teeth, sliding them along my tongue. I held my jaw open, my entire body trembling, and breathed in the apple-smell of him. I sucked it down my throat and into the hollow of my stomach. Until it was all I knew, all I wanted and needed in the universe.

"I bit down. The gods cried out in fury and horror as I drank Tyr's blood and crunched the delicate bones of his hand. He himself stumbled back, lips white, bleeding wrist spilling apple-sweet blood onto the floor of the Shining Hall. I swallowed his hand, Soren Bearskin."

Glory Lokisdottir snatches my hands where they grip the table. I can feel her hunger, can see the want in her eyes. Her teeth grow sharp—sharp enough to eat me. And she wants to. She lets me see it, lets me feel the churning hunger that is so like rage. It gasps and begs in her stomach, the way my frenzy cuts and spirals in my chest.

And then she closes her eyes, releases me, and sits back.

The Jarl Burger dining hall is silent. I hear sizzling meat, smell layers of grease and tomato ketchup. Fenris Wolf is a teenage girl, sitting across from me with her hands folded loosely on the table, her expression slack, with glitter decorating her eyelids and falling down her cheeks like dry tears.

When she opens her eyes again, I am struck by how weary she looks. This light finds the hollows under her cheekbones and makes the skin over her clavicle appear more delicate than spiderweb.

"Did you see, Soren?" she asks.

I nod. Her hunger is like my frenzy.

She says, touching her neck, "It isn't the binding that stops me from starving. These"—she turns over her wrists and the scars there shimmer like the rainbow in spilled oil—"these only keep me from becoming a giant wolf-monster."

"You control it," I say.

Her smile is back, but only half as bright. "I have help. I need help."

"From whom?"

"Tyr the Just. Weren't you listening? He gave me something to fill the void. He offered me something more potent and delicious than the sun. Himself."

"The memory of his blood keeps your hunger at bay?"

Now she grins again. "Oh no. I need reminders." Glory licks her teeth. "When I am too hungry, when I am too desperate to live so bound, when I would like to rend and tear and eat my fill of the world, I find him." She slides off her stool and stands beside me, hands on her hips, spike-heel boots tapping against the tiled floor. "I find him, and I kiss him." Glory presses close, her hand squeezing my thigh. "And those kisses are the only things keeping the sun in the sky."

I spend the rest of the ride with my cheek against the back of Glory's hair, my eyes wide open to watch the black lines of Cheyenne at night.

It's better I can't talk to Glory while we ride. I also can't tell how much time passes, and it's difficult to believe I'm huddled up against Fenris Wolf. That she seems to have decided helping us is in her best interest.

Finally, Glory slows her motorcycle in the middle of the highway. There aren't any cars, and I look out in every direction to see nothing but blackness and stars. The sky gapes overhead; the grassland appears at first to be a solid flat surface of sagebrush and sand. But as my eyes adjust to the stillness and shadows, I see the land rolls very gently, in wide plateaus and valleys. There could be houses or whole towns tucked away.

Glory says, "Hold on," and just as I do, she turns the bike in a quick U and drives slowly back the way we've come. Her head tilts up. She's smelling the wind.

All I smell is grass, exhaust, and bubble gum. But Glory finds an invisible turnoff, only a dirt road next to a green mile-marker sign. She kicks off again, but keeps our speed low. The engine putters and we rile up the dust. I want to bury my face in her hair so it doesn't get in my eyes, but I keep my gaze ahead. There in the distance is a small orange flicker of light.

A minute later she stops. She puts a foot down and says, "Get off. This is it."

I don't react. In the starlight I can only barely see her impatient expression. "That's where they are? That light?"

"It's a barn, I believe. And yes. I smell pine smoke and ash. Gasoline and old horseshit." She sniffs long, probably for my benefit. "Also Baldur. He's there. With two other girls. One with cotton candy shampoo and the other smelling of snakes." Glory grins. "A cousin of mine."

"Vider," I say, glancing off at the distant fire. Part of me is relieved she went with Astrid and Baldur, part of me unsure what I'll say to her.

"Mmm. Well, be nice to her, or I'll snap your fingers off one by one."

I remain on the bike, hands loose on my thighs.

Glory twists all the way around. "Off you go!"

"You aren't coming?"

Her smile is small and flirtatious. "I have to get my ass down to New Spain and pretend to smell Baldur there. Get them off your tail after today's fiasco."

I grimace.

"Yeah, it's all over the news, big boy. Baldur the Beautiful in the Cheyenne kingstate. Burn some pig fat in thanks that nobody recognized you."

Slowly I swing my leg off the motorcycle. I stand, swaying slightly as I adjust to being on solid ground. It isn't as though I've been sailing the ocean, but the day was so rough, the food not enough to refuel my losses. I wish I had my spear to use for balance, but it's long gone. At least it was only a practice weapon from Sanctus Sigurd's. "Thank you," I say to Glory.

She tilts her head and eyes me. "If you get Baldur safely to the orchard, you'll owe me nothing."

I put my fists against my heart. "I have sworn to Baldur, Lady Fenris, under the sun and to the edges of the world. Everything I do will be to serve him."

The corners of her mouth turn up mischievously. "A berserker sworn to the sun god? What fantastic gossip. Perhaps it will cheer my father."

Bowing, I give her my permission to tell Loki, though I cannot imagine she would care if I didn't. The idea of the god of fire and lies knowing my intimate business is so distant and far outside my purview that it rolls off my shoulders like rain.

Glory walks her bike around and makes to remount.

"Glory," I say, the false name falling out of me more naturally than her title.

She glances over her shoulder. In the darkness, she's only a shadow with green glitter at her eyes. "Soren."

"Tell me why they need me. Why me? Why can't they find the orchard alone?"

"Because you know where it is."

"But I don't!"

Glory shrugs. "Then you're all doomed."

I call out again, but she ignores me and climbs onto her bike. She leans over it, back arched provocatively and elbows out. The engine rumbles and she growls, too, as if in conversation with it. Then she's gone in an instant, leaving only a wake of dust and the smell of exhaust.

TWELVE

DAD'S SWORD CHAFES my shoulder as I walk toward the firelight. I can't wait to remove the sheath, to rub out my sore muscles and change into a shirt that isn't caked with sweat and dirt. My boots are the only things that aren't the worse for wear.

My pace picks up as I near the barn, eyes on that pinprick of light. I am so near to her. To Astrid. After being afraid I wouldn't see her again for weeks or months, if ever, knowing now how close I am makes me ignore the aches woven through my body.

Could wanting Astrid be enough to hold my frenzy in check? After today the madness has become my burden, my responsibility. A curse that I must tame again and again, every day.

Surely it can't be controlled the way Fenris Wolf keeps her hunger in check, with a need stronger than starvation.

With love.

I pause and close my eyes to trade the world's darkness for my own.

It's a thrilling possibility, but I don't know if I can embrace it. No matter how much of a relief it might be to think I only have to find something I need more than the rage, if it's true, and love can hold back the rage, doesn't that mean my father didn't love us enough?

Either Glory's solution doesn't work for berserkers, or Dad's need for us wasn't strong.

The barn is closer than I thought. It looms on the grassland, heaving to one side where the roof collapsed. Several of the windows are unbroken, and though dusty, the glass gleams dully back at the sky. The tiny fire is burned down to embers but still glowing like a dragon's eye, casting light at the Spark. There's a ripple from a nearby creek stirring the silence.

I approach quietly, but nobody curls inside the Spark, and there's no sign of any of the three near the fire. The barn doors hang intact, and the one I pull slowly outward hardly creaks at all. Inside is black, with thin shafts of starlight like ghosts in the rafters. Waiting for my eyes to adjust, I hear the flutter of wings overhead. The entire place smells of hay and must, and entering is like pushing into a deep, black sea.

Something shifts dryly to my left, where a mound of old hay rises gray and dark. I see their sleeping forms, and walk carefully closer as relief warms my skin. Vider has climbed to the top of the pile and splayed herself on her back with her face tilted up toward the windows. Her white-blond hair catches the starlight. Lower, where hay spills down across the dirt floor, are Baldur and Astrid beside each other. Her back is against his shoulder, and she curls tightly in upon herself. She must be cold. It's chilly even with the walls of the barn cutting the wind, and Baldur doesn't give off heat the way I do. It should be me there with her.

For a moment I bend down, as if to take my place at Astrid's side.

But my flushed skin reminds me the fever is alive. I could warm her nightmares, but at what price? The memory of the iron star tearing at my ribs from the inside holds me in place. I'm a berserker. A danger to all around me.

Astrid can never tame my frenzy—because she only makes the frenzy louder, stronger, and more potent.

Besides, I'm filthy and wide awake.

Retreating, I open the Spark and dig around in the trunk for my backpack. I move slowly around the barn through the crackling cold prairie to where the creek shines silver in the moonlight. My breath hangs before me and frost glimmers like diamonds from the tips of the grass. The water will be freezing.

I strip down and quickly wash dirt and dried blood from my skin. My muscles tighten and I clench my jaw as the icy water makes my bones want to crack. When I drink, the water cleanses away the last of Glory's death-sweet smell from my palate.

Most carefully, I wash the raw spot on my shoulder where

Dad's sword has been rubbing. The sheath wasn't meant to be worn with only a T-shirt, and I'm lucky the skin didn't break open.

When I finish, I stand alone and naked between the stars and the earth.

My outsides are tight with cold, but inside, the berserking fever churns. Tendrils of it worm toward my extremities, flushing up the back of my neck. I'm in no danger of freezing.

They say the berserkers used to run into battle without armor, sometimes without clothes, with only their weapons and voices at hand. They say the roar of a bearskin band was the most feared sound across a dozen countries. They say we cannot be cut down, cannot be controlled. Cannot control ourselves.

But more than controlling myself now is the need to understand why Glory—why the Fenris Wolf, daughter of Loki the Mother—insists that I am the key to finding Idun's orchard.

I dress slowly, back into my worn jeans, but into the last of my clean shirts. I sit cross-legged at the edge of the creek. I should pray to Odin, to the Alfather, whose gift this berserking is. I should abase myself, beg him for answers.

But I can't bring myself to do it. I swore myself to Baldur the Beautiful, and I still intend, if we succeed in returning him to Bright Home, to take for my boon the freedom from this battle-rage.

I can't ask Odin for help now.

The stars are reflected in the creek, winking at me as the

cold water ripples over gray stones. I tilt my head up to the sky. Here, I am between the stars of the sky and the stars mirrored in the water.

And there's this chunk of that sky in my chest. I wish it were a tether, and that I could tug on it until the stars overhead listen to me, until they answer my prayer.

If I fell asleep, perhaps I would dream the answer. But although I play a game to relax my muscles one at a time, to sink into the earth as though I'm becoming part of it, and I quiet my mind with the smooth sounds of the wind through the grass, I cannot sleep.

Stretched out on my back, I watch the stars curve across the sky. I try and try to think of how I can know but not know the location of the apples. All our destinies seem to ride upon my understanding. Baldur's, certainly—he's the lost god of the sun, depending on me for immortality. And Astrid's quest to find her mother will charge forward only if she wins Odin's boon. Even Vider is with us now, and I suspect she'll remain through to the end. Even if the end is here at this abandoned barn.

Sunk as deep as I am into thoughts, I don't hear the barn door open, or her whispered footsteps through the grass. She says my name with the harsh rattle of shock.

"Soren?"

I sit in a smooth motion. In the dark, her eyes gleam like

twin stars and I think briefly that the sky sent an answer after all. "Astrid."

She huddles in her cardigan, arms wrapped around her stomach. Her seething kit is tucked under one elbow. "You're here."

I do nothing but stare back.

"Alive?" Astrid chokes on the word.

I'm on my feet and gripping her shoulders. "Alive." My voice is deeper than normal. As if I dragged the word out from the pit of my intestines.

A tiny noise squeaks out from between her teeth and Astrid falls forward into my chest. She trembles and I put my arms around her, my nose brushing her dark curls.

"I thought I'd never see you again," she whispers.

"I'm here."

Astrid shakes her head against my chest. "No, you don't understand." She backs off, and my hands fall away reluctantly, fingers curling for her. "I read it in your bones."

My bones. And I recall the dread that passed over her as she stared at the journey rune, the rune she purposefully misread for the crowd. "What did you see?" I ask, more harshly than I mean to.

Kneeling, Astrid unfurls the seething kit and flattens her hands against it. "I saw that you'll be alone. You'll make your-self alone and . . . that means I . . ." Her voice trails off. She looks at me. Her eyes are a little wild and whirling in the dark, as they were when she seethed. "I thought I'd be there, too. In your bones."

"You have to be." Though only recently I was pulling away, was telling myself to keep back from her because I'm a danger, I never believed that we weren't somehow fated to walk together. I've felt it since the moment I first saw her. Knots of destiny.

"I didn't see myself anywhere in them. Like when I search for my mother, when I seeth for her and there's just nothing." Astrid is whispering, and each word is a new, sharp knife. "I thought it meant, when we drove away from you, that you were going to die. Because to the world she's dead. Because none but me believes otherwise."

I tug gently on her hair, to tell her, *I believe, because I believe in you.*

Astrid puts a hand on my face. "But you live. You live and you found us. That means only one thing." She sucks in a great breath and says, "I'm not part of your fate, Soren."

"No. You have to be. Look again." I thrust a finger at her kit, at the pocket that holds the runes.

She shakes her head. "I'm not. I'm not there." The words slide over her tongue like thick syrup. Her voice is low and raw.

I put my face close, inches from hers. "It isn't set. Fate doesn't have to be inevitable."

"Yes it is! Yes it does!" She wrenches back from me, but I hold tight to her elbows.

We stare at each other. I don't know what to say, how to untangle the longing and anger and frustration I feel, and put them into coherent sentences. How to convince her I won't let fate keep me away from her. I will win Odin's boon, divest myself of this frenzy, and be with her. If fate can't foresee such an outcome, it is only because fate is too narrow-minded to imagine a free berserker.

Astrid's rigidity slowly melts. "But maybe I'm missing something. I thought I wasn't going to see you again, and here you are." Her lips twist. "I'm not infallible."

I smile, too, just a little.

She takes my hands. "Why are you out here? Not inside where it's warm—where we are?"

"I couldn't sleep. Too awake. Too wired." I shrug.

Astrid pulls me down to my knees, and I sit so that she can slide between my legs. Her back settles against my chest and I wrap my arms around her. I close my eyes. The ground is hard and cold, but it doesn't matter because she's enveloped in my fever. She holds my arms close to her and tells me what the three of them did after escaping the caravan mob. "We drove and drove," her voice whispers up at me, and I'm glad I can't see her face. "I kept turning around to look out the back, even though it was ridiculous to think I could see you. I just couldn't stop hoping. When we got gas, I watched the road. Baldur and Vider broke open the mead bottle for the money, and I didn't even help pick up all the rolling coins. When we stopped for food, I didn't want to eat. I was so worried. But we had to go on."

"I know. It was the right thing. Baldur is the most important."

"He said to me, 'Do not throw away his sacrifice. Soren gave us this gift, and he expects you to use it.' And so I climbed into the car with them and tried not to think about the last sight of you I had. Blazing with strength and power. I wanted to go back. To take the car and drive back. All I could think of were the runes I read, of fate taking you away." A shudder presses between us. "And I held on to that image of you, painting it with brighter colors in my mind, so that I would always have you with me."

I say, "I'll bend fate to my will for that."

She laughs, and twists in my arms. One hand finds my face, her palm cool against my tattoo. "Soren, I half believe you could. You would stand there and simply not move until fate bowed away first."

Her smile shows off her teeth, and even in the thin starlight, she's beautiful. She scratches her nails gently down my face and back into my hair, just under my ear. I'm suddenly frozen. Her lips are centimeters from mine. I can feel her breath in my mouth.

"Astrid," I say heavily and fast, "I frenzied today."

Her little gasp and laugh cut through the air and I'm free of my paralysis. She pushes back from me, delight widening her eyes. "Soren! You went berserk?" Astrid shakes her head and looks me up and down. "That's what happened to you? That's how you found us again? The rage led you here!"

I think she's going to clap, and I catch her hands. I press them together. "I lost it, at the caravan, and ran for the mountains before I could hurt anyone. It was so awful, so dark and spinning— Astrid, I don't even know how to tell you what it was like."

"Like being caught in a whirlpool? Like your limbs will be torn free and—"

"And if I didn't hold tight, I would be destroyed." My chest pinches as I remember falling into the frenzy and losing myself. I close my eyes.

Silence is her only answer. I can feel her waiting, sitting back on her heels in the dark prairie. The creek teases me with its quiet babbling, like distant laughter or applause. I look.

Astrid is watching me. Her lips pull down into a pout; a line pinches between her eyebrows. "I was going to say: and all you have to do is let go."

I shake my head. "No. Never."

"It's the only way—give in to it and you can swim *with* the current. You can't fight the tide, Soren!"

"I want it out of me. That's all."

"You want to lobotomize yourself! Destroy everything that makes you who you are!"

"It doesn't define me."

Astrid laughs. A full, high-pitched laugh that tilts her face up to the stars. "Oh, Soren. You're either blind or a fool."

It hurts, but I clench my jaw and say, "I won't let it define me forever, then."

"It's your every waking thought." Astrid stands. "What will you be when it's gone?"

"Anything I want."

She shakes her head. "Can you imagine me without my seething? As anything but a seethkona?"

I stand as well. "I don't have to. It's what you want, who you are. You've embraced it."

"A berserker is who *you* are, Soren."

"Not when I ask Odin to take it away. Not then. I'll just be Soren, a warrior. I'll be able to fight at your side safely." I reach for her. "I won't have to worry about hurting you. I can be with you."

Astrid doesn't let me touch her. Her chin lifts and she says with an air of finality, of authority, "If that time comes, I won't want you to."

She leaves me standing alone at the bank of the creek.

Dawn arrives as a sky full of purple clouds.

Vider comes running around the barn, a grin splitting her face. Twin braids trail out behind her. "Soren!"

I push up from my meditative crouch and grimace. Every piece of my body aches. "Good morning," I manage. It isn't that I slept, but that I spent the final hours of the night unmoving, staring into the water until I imagined I could feel the earth turning beneath me.

"Astrid said you came in the night." Vider stops a few paces from me, her hands clenched together. She's wearing one of Astrid's cardigans, and already most of her flimsy pale hair has fallen out of the braids.

"I want to thank you, Vider Lokisdottir," I say, holding out my hand. "For aiding in the rescue of Baldur. I owe you a debt."

She bows her face and shakes her head so that hair falls over her eyes to hide her blush. "That isn't why I did it."

I don't reply, but only wait with my palm up. Wind fans her hair over her face and she claps her hand against mine. "Why, then?"

"I'm not certain."

"It was well done."

Her fingers curl firmly around my wrist and she peeks up at me. "Teach me more?"

It startles a laugh from me, and Vider puts her fists on her hips.

A workout is exactly what I need. And food. But food is where Astrid is, and I'm not ready for that.

Vider lowers herself down beside me and we begin some stretches. As I show her the proper stance for a triangle stretch, Baldur arrives. "Ho!" he calls.

It's such an old-fashioned greeting, Vider rolls her eyes at me.

But I welcome him on my feet, as I did her. Baldur shines, and his eyes mirror the purple sunrise behind him. I hold out my hand, but he embraces me like a brother. "It's the best news, that you returned to us," he says. "I had to come see for myself."

"Thank you, Baldur." At this moment, as the sky-mirrors of his eyes glow and he smiles at me with such simple, friendly grace, it's worth it that I lost myself to the frenzy. Further words dry up in my mouth, but he smacks my shoulder and says, "Are you ready for a spar? Is that what all the exercising is for?"

I look at Vider and tilt my head questioningly. She shows a ferocious smile that squints her eyes and reminds me of pictures of forest goblins I saw as a child. I hold up one finger and swiftly flick it at Baldur.

She catches my meaning before he does, and we attack together, with a strangely harmonized roar.

Baldur throws out his hands and laughs, letting himself be tackled. We all go down. It's a quick skirmish, and I'm against both of them when Vider suddenly switches sides like a proud daughter of Loki. She feints toward him, but inserts herself to block my attack so that Baldur is able to sideswipe me. Then she uses her disloyalty to get around Baldur and sweep his right foot out from under him. I catch him and pin him, and we're all gasping with laughter. Clearly Vider is the victorious one.

As revenge, we teach her some difficult blocks and tell her to repeat the string of movements over and over until her muscles know it better than she does. With a scowl of concentration she begins, and Baldur and I face off.

We're a few minutes into hand-to-hand, and my forearms are alive with pain from blocking his punches, when I notice Astrid coming around the barn. I try to ignore her, to focus on Baldur. He's an excellent boxer and I'm already sweating in the cool morning air.

I won't want you to.

Her words snake through my thoughts as she kneels by the creek, some ten paces downstream. I barely deflect the heel of Baldur's hand as it comes at my head.

I maneuver so that my back is to her. Baldur frowns as he realizes I've put myself at a disadvantage on purpose.

I focus as I dance around Baldur. My breath moves through

me like a calm but strong river, lapping at the edges of the frenzy.

"If you take me down, we can stop. You seem tired." Baldur falls into a defensive stance, on the balls of his feet, hands up.

"I'm not tired," I say. I attack again; he deflects again. We move around each other, jabbing and blocking. My boots grind into the field dirt and my arms ache. But it's distracting me. *I won't want you to.*

"Have you ever wondered," he says between heavy breaths, "what Astrid tastes like?"

"What?" I swing in and he blocks me. Our forearms jar together as I bounce back again.

"I suspect she tastes as good as she looks."

I aim for his nose.

Baldur deflects again, slapping me away easily. "Sweet as mead, sharp as vodka."

My stomach twists as though I'm starving, or about to vomit. I never should've reminded him of his womanizing. "She isn't yours to taste."

"Whose is she, then?"

I falter. Not mine so long as I berserk, by my will. Not mine when I am free, by hers. "Freya's." It's half a question.

Baldur catches my fist and flings me back. "I doubt Freya would mind sharing with a handsome cousin."

My breath streams out raggedly. I remember how Astrid looked at him that first morning. How her face lit up with awe and love. *Do you love the gods, Soren?* She could love Baldur in my place.

He would never be afraid of the frenzy.

The moment I think it, my iron star cracks open. It's so freshly awake, hungering to be free again.

Baldur skirts closer and I leap back from him. I shove a fist hard against my own chest as if I can keep the rage trapped; my other hand shoots out. "Stop. Baldur, stop."

"Stop what?" He spreads his hands and sneers. The expression, on his beautiful face, is terrible, like the sun burning black. I can hardly believe this is Baldur! I meet his eyes and . . . they're calm. As serene as the sky, as a quiet mountain lake.

"Baldur." I whisper his name. He doesn't mean any of it. The derisive mask is only that: a mask. I'm confused, and my hands lower as my rage quiets down.

His eyes narrow at the corners. He winces. Then his hands, too, fall to his sides. "Soren."

"Why did you do that?" I shake my head. "My battle-rage, it . . . You . . ."

Baldur sighs. Wind picks up through the trees on the other side of the creek, shaking free loose pine needles and scattering them into the grass. He closes his eyes briefly, and without their knowing sky-bright gaze he's only a beautiful man.

I step away again. "Why are you trying to make me berserk?"

His eyes pop open, pinning me to the spot. My heart stops beating as he says, "That is not what I'm trying to make you do." And then his gaze shifts. I follow it to where Astrid is rinsing her face in the creek. We watch as she dries it on her sweater and then stands. She glances at us, but the moment she sees me looking, she turns her back and hurries for the barn.

"What's wrong with Astrid?" Vider asks, coming up beside us. I don't think she's heard our conversation.

"Yes, Soren, what's wrong with Astrid?" Baldur nudges me with his elbow, as if I'm his little brother.

I open my mouth, then clap it closed again. Vider's eyebrows are lifted, her cheeks flushed from effort. Baldur's lips pinch expectantly.

"She and I . . ." I pause. What can I tell them? Nothing that doesn't make me sound exactly like what Astrid accused me of being: a fool.

"Go talk to her." Baldur bends over and grabs the roll of Astrid's seething kit, which she left out here last night when she stormed away. I take it reluctantly.

"She's mad at you?" Vider asks. Something I don't understand wavers like uncertainty in her eyes.

My hand tightens around the leather kit. "Yes."

Vider throws her arms up. "That doesn't make any sense! She was desperate yesterday afternoon for you to be all right, and now you are and she's angry?"

With a laugh, Baldur wraps his arm around Vider's shoulders. "Are you sure you're a girl?" he says, and receives a sharp smack on his hand in return. He takes her fingers and raises them to his lips. The smile he offers is smooth and perfect. I see the moment she meets Baldur's eyes, because the sunlight brings her to life, too.

I can't be upset with him. Not with the morning turning his hair to gold, and his laugh making everything brighter. I see ghostly chain mail hanging from his shoulders, and a silver helmet caught under his arm. It's some image of him I've seen on TV, I'm certain. He has gold rings in his ears, and bracelets lining his forearms like gauntlets. The memory wraps around my ribs.

We must get him to safety. And Astrid should be out here with us.

Grimly, I take my father's sword and swing the strap over my uninjured shoulder. Before I can give in to fear, I head for the barn.

The sunlight crushes through the fallen section of roof, filling the barn with yellow light. It transforms the dust motes into elf-gold.

Astrid has put on the exercise bra and pants she wore at the holmgang in Nebrasge, and she carries a thick branch in her hands as she silently moves through a pattern of combat. It's a dance we're taught as children, incorporating the seven basic sword strikes that are legal for holmgang. I stare at the muscles of her back as they move beneath her skin, at the appearance of ease with which she lifts the branch. Her form is excellent. I walk forward to take my place beside her. I mirror her movements, find the rhythm of her breath with my own. We do not touch; she doesn't even acknowledge my presence, but there's no way she isn't aware. Her pace never changes, and when she transitions into the seven-defense dance, she flicks her eyes at me briefly.

Both of us know this well enough to do it with our eyes

closed. All I smell is the dust of the barn, the dry hay and old, rotting wood. There's a gentle rasp as wind off the prairie pushes against the roof.

Our dance is warmth and lithe, and so soothing it never once awakens the frenzy in me.

When it ends, Astrid faces me. Sweat glistens on her face, as I'm certain it does on mine. I'm thirsty from the dry air, but we must speak before going back out to the creek.

"Are you finished outside?"

I nod.

"We should get going, then." She starts to go past me, heading for the doors.

I catch her hand. "Astrid, wait." Her hand is limp in mine and she keeps her body half turned away from me. "I only want to explain."

"Is my seething a curse?" Her eyes remain focused on the packed dirt floor.

"No."

She snaps her head up. "Our powers come from the same place, Soren. The same wild place inside us." She pushes a hand flat against my chest, right over my heart. "I feel it. I'm certain of it. Condemn yourself, and you condemn me, too."

"Your power doesn't kill people."

"Doesn't it?" Astrid removes her hand and crosses her arms under her exercise bra. "Did you know my mother seethed for the Congress just before the Mediterr Conflict? The president was unsure, and so was his assembly, if we should participate. She seethed, and she told him we must. He ordered troops into the desert and more than eight hundred died in that single year."

"Your mother was doing her job. She's supposed to read the strands of fate."

"And your father's job was to protect, to defend. To kill."

"Not unarmed families in a mall."

"Not his job, then, but his purpose, Soren. If it happened, it was meant to happen."

"You wouldn't say that if you'd been there." My voice is suddenly thick. I don't want to tell her more. I don't want to put those memories into words, or make her listen. Give that terrible hour more power over me than it already has.

But Astrid touches her fingers to her lips. "You were there?" she whispers.

I nod. They always leave that out of the television spots. No one cares that Styrr Bearskin went mad in front of his eight-year-old son.

She clutches my hands. "I'm listening, Soren."

Astrid tells so many stories. Surely I can endure telling her this one. And if it's a story, maybe it will be easier. I close my eyes. Images assail me and I open them again. Astrid's face is there. Her sepia eyes are level with my mouth, her face tilted upward. She has no expression on. No smile or frown, no expectation. She only waits, ready for me to fill her ears with my story.

At first I whisper. I know to set the stage because of how she's always told her stories to me. "There was music in the rest-room. A cheerful song about tricky goblins for the Hallowblot.

Father and I had been at the food court and I drank an entire giant cream beer float by myself, so I really had to go. If I hadn't, it might never have happened."

I remember that as I walked back to him, I stopped to stare at the clothes in the window of the Fashion Hole, thinking how you could never fight in them successfully. The tight green skirt especially, I was going to tell Dad about. And then I heard the first scream. Followed by his roar.

"I heard him yell," I say to Astrid. "And it was so wrong. Not his practice roar, but deeper and more—more raw than I'd ever heard. I ran for him."

My sneakers skidded on the tiles and I had to grab the corner of a trash can to keep from falling. It crashed to the ground, though, and I crouched behind it as a woman's body slammed down in front of me. Her neck was broken and her eyes wide and staring. Blood slipped away from her head. Coming at me like a red snake against the yellow floor tiles. The colors were so bright. All the memories are that bright. But I don't have to look at them as long as I can see Astrid. "He was killing people, pulling them apart with his hands."

She doesn't flinch.

I say, "It was so fast."

There were two boys, torn open and bleeding, still clutching hotpigs, then a man who tried to fight. Dad swung around and crushed his face with his bare hands. He did everything with bare hands! His sword still strapped to his shoulder. I tell Astrid, "I hid from it, my hands clutched over my ears. All the screaming drowned out the music and crashing.

Chairs and plastic tables were ripped from their bolts, and the bodies . . . But I don't know what made it happen, Astrid. What set him off."

The words are blocks of ice in my mouth, numbing my tongue. "I couldn't move. To help. There was so much noise, wailing in my ears. And then it was gone."

Only the tinny music floating down from the ceiling remained, the soft groans of death, and Dad's heaving breath. In and out.

I blink slowly, taking a moment to feel that panic again, the not knowing if it was safe for me to crawl out. Not knowing if he'd kill me, too. Then I focus on Astrid. "Of all things, I remember that the walls were decorated with plastic pumpkins and holly berries. Crepe paper streamers fluttered from helium balloons and I just stared at them until he stepped in front of me. I saw the fury in Dad's eyes, the twist of his lips and the bright flush tearing across his cheeks as he turned to me. I stepped back. Slipped. I landed on my butt, slapped my palms down into a streak of sticky blood. I scooted away, smearing it everywhere, sliding past a couple of girls with bright bangles glittering in the fake light. Their eyes were wide open. Their chests, crushed."

I suck in a shaking breath. "Dad said my name then, and his voice was rough from screaming. I couldn't look away from him." From the splatters of blood on his hands and across the T-shirt I'd given him for Yule the year before. "With his free hand, he reached down and grabbed the front of my shirt, dragging me to my feet. I gripped his wrist, terrified, and shaking all over. I clenched my eyes closed, until he said my name again. I fought against him and he dropped me. I sprawled on the flat tiles of the mall floor and gaped up at him. Dad crouched; his knees touched the floor. 'My son,' he said, putting his bloody hands on my face. I tugged away. I wanted to run as far from him as I could.

"He told me to take his sword, Astrid. It was still sheathed on his back. He'd never drawn it, even in the midst of his frenzy. He shook me, and I fumbled for it, unbuckling the strap holding it in the sheath. Dad said, 'This is the sword of a bear, my son. Always the bear, no matter who you serve.'"

My throat closes, and I swallow several times before I can speak again. Astrid waits, eyes grown heavy with sorrow.

I say, "Then—then there was this yelling that echoed toward us. SWAT called in by escaping shoppers and mall security." *Dad,* I begged. I don't know what I begged him for. My voice falls to a whisper again. "He released me and stood. He said, 'I shall not come into this hall with words of fear upon my tongue.' And he just . . . walked away from me, toward the line of police aiming automatic guns at him. He yelled the entire prayer. Then he—he just ran at the police, and they opened fire."

The memory of him jerking, then falling back, overwhelms me. I squeeze Astrid's hands hard enough to crack bones. But she doesn't wince.

Astrid lifts my hands toward her. "Soren." She breathes against my knuckles. "Tell me the rest of that prayer."

"I shall not come into this hall with words of fear upon my tongue," I say, "for Odin will welcome me. Death comes without lamentation, and the Valkyrie summon me home. Gladly shall I drink ale from the Poet's Cup, for the days of my life are ended. I die with a laugh." My eyelids twitch as I try not to blink. "Only he said, 'I am Styrr Bearskin, and I die with a laugh.'"

She holds my gaze. "I understand," she says.

I'm exhausted. My eyes are drier than birch bark, my ribs tight. My arms throb from the new bruises Baldur gave me, and now my insides feel raw, as though I've been throwing up. Astrid pulls me down to sit on the pile of hay. Overhead, thin clouds press into the round of sky we can see through the broken roof. It probably took about three minutes to tell Astrid that story, but already it's a memory that feels a hundred years long.

She holds my hand, lifting it up. I watch as she touches her lips to my fingers. As she turns my hand and presses her cheek to my palm. Her face is cool and so, so smooth. I want it to stay there, cupped in my hand, forever. But I tighten my fingers, gripping her face until I make white dents in her skin. "I could crush your skull if the rage was on me," I murmur.

"I'm not afraid of you."

"You should be."

"No. I do not fear death. Like the poem says." A smile teases up the corners of Astrid's mouth. "My death is woven already, and if it is meant to be by your hand, so it shall be. But it's unlikely. Your fate is greater than that." Her eyebrows arc up. "So is mine."

My hand slides down her neck. "Of course you think such things."

"I know them. I'm a seethkona, remember?"

"I remember." I run my hand over her shoulder and down her arm. Astrid shivers. I don't know if it's my touch or the breeze against her sweat-damp skin. "I know what you are," I whisper.

Astrid lies back onto the pile, shifting against the sharp ends of hay that poke into her bare shoulders. "Can you imagine me without the seething?"

"Of course," I answer automatically.

"Truly?" Her fingers crawl over the hay to my wrist, and tighten around it.

In the sunlight shining down through the roof, her eyes lighten into a color so clear it's like honey mead. The curling snakes of her hair spill all around her cheeks and neck, emphasizing the shadows under her eyes. Her lips are pink and slightly parted. I imagine her spinning, when her cheeks are rosy and her mouth open so I can see the tip of her tongue, when her eyes stare beyond this world and she laughs at what she discovers there. I hear her voice and that singsong quality that somehow blends seamlessly with the matter-of-fact quirk of her eyebrow, and I hear the hush of wonder when she knows something to be true because she saw it in a dream.

If she did not dream, and did not dance, who would she be?

A beautiful girl, but would she still be so strong? Would she be so full of wonder and passion?

What would the wind be if it did not blow? What would the sun be if it did not shine?

My throat tightens. *What would the mountain be if it did not stand?*

She sees it in my face, and she nods. Understanding shimmers through the honey of her eyes.

I whisper, "I do not want it."

"Oh, Soren," she whispers. Releasing my wrist, she pushes up again and wraps her arms around my neck. "I know," she says into my ear.

I hold her, dragging all of her into my lap and hugging tightly. I shudder.

"I know," she whispers again, and she does. She told me last week: "You stand between the earth and the sky." What she meant was, We *can touch the earth and the sky.*

Because of the wild magic inside us.

THIRTEEN

ASTRID AND I take a box of energy bars around to the creek. She slips her hand into mine as we walk.

We interrupt a punching lesson Vider is getting from Baldur, and the four of us sit together to eat and scoop up cold water with our cupped hands. The sun breaks through the clouds and warms my shoulders; the bars taste nutty and full of fruit; Astrid shifts so that her knee touches mine. It's nearly perfect. Vider huddles with her arms around her knees, picking her bar apart into crumbs that she puts carefully into her mouth. Avoiding the dried cranberries. And Baldur stretches out on his stomach so that the entire length of his back welcomes the sunlight.

There's peace all around us, and no one breaks it until we've eaten our fill. Astrid dips her fingers into the water and flicks droplets at me. Vider watches us from the corner of her eye, pretending to be focused on gathering the last crumbs off her knees with one licked finger.

Baldur sighs, drawing everyone's attention. His eyes are closed and his lips have relaxed into a smile.

"We need to decide where to go next," Astrid says quietly. "How to find Idun's orchard."

I suck air in through my teeth and launch into the tale of meeting Fenris Wolf. Baldur leans up onto his elbows. Vider presses her hands into her thighs and doesn't look up from them the whole time I talk; around her knuckles the skin turns white. I wonder why Fenris bothers her so much.

When I finish, Astrid touches my knee. "Do you know what she meant? Do you have any idea where the orchard is?"

"No. None."

"What—" Vider whispers. She clears her throat and says more strongly, "What is there to know about this orchard? All I know is that it's magical and hidden, that the gods go every year to receive their apples from Idun the Young."

"The orchard is charmed to stay hidden," Astrid says, and begins pulling at the grass. Little sharp tugs that rip it out at its roots. Her eyes are vacant as she looks into her memory.

Vider asks, "Why keep them in Mid-Earth at all, then? Why not in Asgard or Hel? If they're so worried about mortals finding them."

Astrid draws a rune in the dust. I know it: it means death. "It is said, in the old poems, that the gods tried that and it led to their first great battle with the giants. And now there's a pact among the gods that always a woman will guard the apples in the Middle World—sworn to the gods, and sworn to the apples themselves. She is Idun, the keeper of apples."

"So they say," whispers Baldur.

"Do you remember the way?" I lean eagerly toward him.

This would be so much easier if he suddenly knew how to find Idun.

His eyes close tightly and he shakes his head. "No. No, as I think on it, I see flashes of a face, of a woman with dark hair and dark eyes offering me a small golden apple in her palms. But the leaves obscure the sky and sun, so I can't tell where on earth she is."

Releasing a handful of grass, Astrid says, "They also say Idun has her own war band."

"Berserkers," Baldur adds excitedly. "I remember that! Idun's Bears, they're called."

"Great." I try not to glower.

She touches my knee again. And I remember something.

I'm sitting with my mother in the middle of a room covered in Legos. We've spent the entire morning building a Rainbow Bridge, and I'm excited because the Well of Mimir came with a special roundish Lego that attaches to the bottom of the well to look like Odin's Eye. The bridge spans two feet of dingy white carpet, an old grape juice stain acting as the clouds beneath it. Mom laughs as I reach my whole hand into the delicate well to push the eye into place. My hand is nearly too large, but I carefully withdraw it, then clap happily. She grabs me and drags me onto her lap and puts her chin on top of my head. One arm wraps tightly around me and the other reaches out for a ziplock bag filled with green and blue Legos. "This one is a serpent," she says. I touch her wrist, where the gray-and-green tattoo of the World Snake twists, nearly invisible against her dark skin. "Like this?" I ask. Her nod is soft against my hair. I say I want to wait for Dad. Mom kisses my temple with a smack. "I am always waiting for your daddy!"

Something about her tone makes me uncomfortable, and I squirm until she lets me go. I stand, which makes me taller than her because she's still seated, smiling up at me. In her nose and eyebrows are gold hoops that she told me she had to take out when I was a baby because I always wanted to tug. I still want to touch them, but don't. Mom holds out her hands, palms up. She wants me to put my palms against hers so we know we aren't mad at each other. She says, "I don't mind waiting, little bear. Your daddy gave up everything to follow me. He gave up an oath to a lady far greater than me, and a promise to his brothers. For me and for you, Soren." She wiggles her fingers playfully. I put my hands against hers, and she says, "We'll wait as long as we have to."

I stare down now at Astrid's fingers on my knee. "My father," I whisper, just as Astrid says, "Always the bear."

His last words to me, when he gave me the sword.

"Huh?" says Vider.

"I think . . ." I meet Astrid's wide eyes. If I hadn't told her that story this morning, I never would have let myself remember. "What if my father was one of Idun's Bears? That's why I'm supposed to know where the orchard is."

Vider asks where he is, and when I say he's dead, she flushes but offers condolences. I cannot remember the last time anyone told me they were sorry he passed into Hel.

"What about your mother?" Baldur says. "Can you call her?" The sun turns his eyes to gold.

I look down into my lap. "I haven't seen her in five years."

Astrid takes my hand. But I don't deserve her sympathy. I give her a sideways glance. "I never looked for her, Astrid. I never tried. I didn't care to, and I still don't."

"Why?" In Astrid's voice are all the years she's spent hunting for her mother.

"She doesn't want me. I remind her of him."

"She said that to you?" Baldur is aghast, and perhaps if I were still twelve and wanting her love, it would be endearing.

"No. But I know. She was arrested after I was tattooed, and charged with criminal negligence for not getting me training, for putting the public at risk. She was guilty, but she requested a holmgang trial, saying if she was good enough to win, she could have been teaching me herself. She did win, so the charges were dropped. I saw her for the last time at the trial. And after, she never came to collect me. I went into state protection, ended up at Sanctus Sigurd's with Master Pirro."

Baldur frowns at me. "It is too long to go without speaking. We owe our parents honor, at least."

I want to argue that he has left his mother, Tova, rotting in Hel since Loki tricked her into drinking poison. But right now I care more about what Astrid thinks of me. Her hand remains on my knee, gripping tightly. I hesitantly look at her face. I expect disappointment, expect her eyes to be filled with recrimination because all she wants in this world is to find her mother.

Instead she's staring beyond me. Twisting, I see what she's

looking at. Father's sword. The sheath is a long black bone half-hidden in the grass beside the creek.

Father.

The thought latches onto my heart and suddenly I'm terrified, but Astrid digs her fingers into my knee and I snap my eyes to hers. They're wide, the color matching the late-winter grasslands.

"What?" Vider asks.

My eyes are only for Astrid, because I suspect what she's thinking: on Baldur's Night, when she danced and I anchored her in this world, she said if her mother was truly dead, she'd be easy to find. *I could summon her spirit then, as I could summon your father.*

I shudder at the very idea.

Baldur says, "Soren?" But I'm stuck thinking of Styrr. Of my father.

I see him with blood splattered across his face, kneeling before me and offering his sword. He touches my face with fire-hot hands, then gets to his feet and faces the line of police.

My father. Swinging me onto his shoulders, where I sit clinging to his hair as he charges across a stoneball court. I laugh as his jarring gait bounces me hard against him.

My father. Screaming the Berserker's Prayer, running under garish mall lights and the Hallowblot streamers.

My father. His lips against Mom's hair.

My father.

How can I face him again, even in death? How can I agree

to have him dragged to the Middle World, where he'll be forced to remember? Where I'll be forced to remember?

Astrid's eyes are huge. Her lips part; she's panting shallow, fearful breaths.

I whisper, "Astrid."

"We can ask him," she says.

Vider's mouth falls open. My own dismay is reflected in the surprise coating her face. But Baldur waits beside her, golden in the sunlight. Calm, strong, and so vulnerable. For him, I cannot balk at difficult choices. Bad enough I've felt the frenzy and lost so much of my control. I will not fail him because of fear. I will not fail Astrid.

I clutch at both her hands. "Yes," I say. "We can."

FOURTEEN

IT ISN'T A ritual to perform in the daylight.

We have several hours to wait, and Astrid must use them to prepare her body and mind through meditation. I try to attend her, but she shoos me off and says I should rest. It will be the two of us alone, and she'll need all my strength to anchor her.

"What kind of anchoring?" I ask. "Will it just be to catch you, like before? Do I need to prepare, too?"

She taps a finger against her lips, then her hand flutters away. "All sorts of things can go wrong with a resurrection ritual. I could summon the wrong spirit. Whatever spirit I summon could possess me, or decide to tear us apart if I'm not careful. Your father might come, but be caught up too much in his final memories, in which case . . ." Astrid shrugs.

"In which case he'd be in the middle of a full killing frenzy," I say, stepping forward to loom over her. "Astrid."

"Or . . ." She puts her hand on my chest to back me away. "*Or* I could manage to produce nothing at all. Or simply lose myself in the darkness beyond the stars."

"I don't like this at all."

"It's what we have."

"I should try calling my mom on the phone instead."

"You said you don't even know where to begin with that. It could take days to reach her."

"But it's better than risking so much. This is insane!" I fling out my hands.

Astrid catches them and pulls them together. "I can do this, Soren. I only need to prepare, and I need you to help me. We can do this together."

I hunt for the truth in her eyes.

"I promise," she says, placing her fingers very gently over my tattoo.

What would it take for me to say no to her?

"I'm strong, Soren, and you know it. Especially with you at my side. My mother did this three times, and always with success."

My sigh is consent enough, and Astrid takes her seething kit south along the creek. I stare after her, nerves pulling me tight, until she is only a tiny figure against the grass.

Baldur comes up behind me. "I want to get closer to the sky." He's feeling alert, but his blood is running slowly, he says, and perhaps the sun will lend him vitality. He eyes the partially collapsed roof of the barn.

I frown, following his gaze. There's a patch of roof that appears solid from here, but I don't trust it. Before I can say so, Vider dashes inside. We follow to find her scaling the inner wall up to the hayloft. She discards Astrid's cardigan, and it falls softly all the way to the floor. "Vider, be careful," I call up.

"Don't distract me!" Her fingers grip a dark board and she lifts herself easily as a spider. She isn't even watching her feet, and her toes seem to stick to the wood. By the time she reaches the jagged hole in the roof, I'm half-convinced I could do it.

With perfect balance, Vider crawls to the edge. She crouches on hands and feet, then slowly rises. Her arms splay out and the wind catches the loose tendrils of her hair. She is all silver and green in the sunlight, skinny and graceful as an egret. In a few quick steps, she's around the gaping hole and standing directly over us, where a heavy crossbeam holds up the rest of the roof.

Bending over to wave down at us, she says, "I think this is sturdy." To prove her point, she jumps up and lands hard on the flat of her feet. The crossbeam doesn't even shake.

"Excellent!" Baldur removes his sandals and T-shirt.

I touch his arm. "This isn't a good idea."

"I want to be close to the sun. And"—he dips his head to seem more earnest—"I'll be careful. No tripping and ruining the mission, I promise." His eyes shine and I know I'd have to pin him to the ground for the rest of the day to convince him not to climb up there with Vider.

With a sigh, I release him. Briefly I consider climbing up, too, but I weigh more than both, and what would I do on the roof?

Instead I go outside again, where the grassland meets the creek, and do what I do best. Especially in a stressful situation.

I let myself fall into the empty place where I'm not thinking or feeling, only moving with the beat of my heart. My hands are shovels, scooping energy from the world, moving it up through my torso, over my head, around and around in a calm sphere. I dance my slow dance, allowing the chip of chaos to churn and crunch in my chest. I move where the energy wills, where my body naturally shifts from step to step.

It's easier, for some reason, than it has been before, to move the hot frenzy.

I've lost all thought of time, my senses are open and my body's energies aligned, when Vider comes hesitantly toward me.

She knows not to leap into my path or startle me, and keeps back a few meters. I'm glad she's here; I want to talk to her about why she's afraid of Fenris. Most Lokiskin don't know the gods any more personally than I know Odin.

Letting out a long breath, I settle into a solid stance and look at her.

All her pale hair falls around her shoulders and she watches me with hunger sparking her green eyes. There is a new, long pink scratch down her left forearm, and dust marring her cheeks. She says, "Soren, there's something I think you should see."

My eyes dart toward the roof, and she hurries to assure me. "Baldur's fine. Basking."

And I see the glint of gold where he lies splayed against the dingy white roof. "What's wrong, then?" I ask Vider.

"This way." She flicks her hand at me to follow, and leads me around toward the north face of the barn. Here in the lee, the paint is less bleached, less worn away. I can see the red it used to be.

The day is warming nicely, so that in the moments between one breeze and the next I feel the presence of spring. Vider crouches against the barn, where scraggly bushes clump together. She points at the dusty ground. I bend down with her and see that there are paw prints clustered. Small, and without claw marks. "Barn cats?" I say, glancing at Vider.

She's got her elbows resting on her knees in a very childlike pose, and frowns down at the prints. "That's what I thought at first. But look."

We walk ten feet north, through grass that scratches at my jeans. The paw prints fade, but the last two are definitely aimed in this direction. Vider pauses beside two stones, one knee height and the other just shorter, both of them huddled together as though seeking comfort. They're taller than they are wide, and oblong.

I turn a full circle, scanning the ground. No other rocks like these near. It isn't rocky ground at all, but rolling grassland. When my eyes hit again on the huddled stones, my stomach sinks.

Troll sign.

Here in Cheyenne, we're bunched up next to the Rock Mountains and the Bitterroots that stretch into the Canadia Territories. I've never been so near Trollhome. These are plains around us, but with the troll advisory, even if Vinland is far to the east of here, we're in clear danger.

And I forgot.

In all the intensity of the past twenty-four hours, I forgot to keep on guard against trolls. I stare north, and then turn slowly all around. The nearest trees are on the other side of the creek, and to the northwest where the water curves. There's no flash of paint that might be warning runes. We've been completely vulnerable.

Vider says, "These must have been caught out at dawn, on their way back to their den."

"I heard nothing."

"Neither did I, but I was sleeping pretty soundly."

"I was awake." I put one of my boots against a stone troll. I can't believe how stupid I've been to not keep aware of my surroundings, to neglect the dangers of being out alone, where there are no ranger patrols or warded trees.

Vider puts a hand on her forehead as a visor, peering north with me. "Maybe that's why they didn't make any mischief for us."

Scraping my sole down the rock, I nod. "At least they're small ones." Greater mountain trolls don't tend to fraternize with their littler cousins, which suggests we don't have to worry too much. But the small grass-wights can be as dangerous, if they have a large enough pack or a smart troll-mother. Once the sun goes down, these two stones will melt back into flesh— creatures with tooth-filled mouths and spindly arms.

And we can't pack up and drive away. We need the privacy of this barn and the flowing water for Astrid's summoning ritual.

I suck a breath in through my teeth. "We have to find their

den and bind them, or appease them. Run back to the car and grab some of the mead, and a handful of the energy bars. We can all manage without until tomorrow's lunch. Be sure to leave some mead for Astrid to use tonight if she needs it."

Vider runs off, and I go collect Father's sword. I strap it on, to my left shoulder while my right continues to heal. I'm less skilled at left-hand draw, but still better than most. I make it back to the troll-stones first, and carefully pick them up. Hopefully, returning them to their den will be step one of soothing any disgruntled troll-mother.

They're heavy, but I tuck one under each arm. Vider's eyes widen when she sees them, but she sets off first. There isn't a path, but it seems the grass is bent just enough for her to track them. I'm impressed. The caravans usually have well-established routes, and their territory is marked by warded trees and ribbons braided into leaves or grass. But still, it's the children's task in the caravans to do a sweep every morning for troll sign.

Vider's sharp eyes catch more catlike paw prints in the dirt, so we know we're heading in the proper direction. We veer farther away from the highway, which is hidden by a large roll of hill, and closer to the creek and the tall groves of evergreen and birch trees. Through the clicking bare branches, I see the farmhouse.

The trolls, of course, are why our barn was abandoned.

We stand in the yard. Vider's shoulder brushes my arm. My wrists are tired from carrying the hefty stones, but I don't put them down yet. The farmhouse is two stories, a single white rectangle with windows like dark eyes. The front door's been torn from its hinges and lies in the tangled lawn like a discarded toy. A porch swing hangs by one chain. Most of the structure, including the roof, appears intact. But across the face of the second story is painted a purple rune: *thorn*.

Do not enter here, it warns, *for I am inhabited by trolls*.

"I don't think we can bind this whole house," Vider whispers. "Not without Astrid."

And we can't bother Astrid unless we absolutely must. "Bring the mead," I say. I walk slowly forward, eyes on the doorway. I stop several paces from the shade of the porch to turn in a circle and show any wights peering at me from the interior darkness that I am unarmed but for my sword. Vider walks with her arms out, the mead in one hand, the bundle of bars in the other.

We proceed carefully. There's a large iron elf-cup right beside the front door. Like an upside-down bowl, with a tiny impression pressed into the top of its dome, the cup is made for offerings to the land-wights and goblins. This cup is bone-dry, and likely has been for years.

Vider knows what to do. She uncaps the mead and goes purposefully to the elf-cup. She drips just enough in to fill it, though one quick drop slips down to the porch floor.

A tapping sound begins, coming from inside the doorway. It echoes through the wood of the porch.

The steps creak mightily under me, but I ignore them to bend down and gently place the troll-stones on the wooden floor, where they're completely shaded.

Then Vider dashes to me and we back away.

"I am Soren Bearskin, son of Odin," I call. The *tap-tap-tap* stops immediately.

Vider says, "And here is Vider Lokisdottir."

"We bring you honey mead and cakes of nuts and berries; we bring you two of your lost, sun-frozen brethren."

The darkness through the doorway shifts. There's something—or many somethings—inside. Their claws click against each other, creating a sound like insects flying.

The larger of the stone trolls shivers. The shade cools it, and a thin layer of stone cracks where its head will be. Tiny crumbs tumble away. As it shrugs its shoulder, the smaller troll begins quaking as well.

The stone breaks apart and they wake. The larger has orange eyes as big as apples, thick shoulders, and a ridge of fur down its back. It bares square teeth at us, hulking over onto its fists. But the smaller crouches, looking like nothing so much as a cat with arms and hands instead of forelegs. Its whiskers twitch and it puts one of those hands against its compatriot. The angry troll closes its mouth, while the cat-wight smoothes its whiskers and hisses, "*Cakesss.*"

Vider unwraps one of the bars and takes it forward. I want to tell her to toss the thing its cake, but won't interrupt. She creeps closer on tiptoe, holding out the energy bar. The cat-wight reaches out, too, and Vider must go all the way onto the first porch step so that it has no fear of moving into the sunlight. "Here, little brother," Vider says gently.

The larger troll quivers, but does not move, as the cat-wight nibbles at the bar. Vider remains at the foot of the porch steps. When the cat-wight has eaten half the bar, it offers the rest to the other and then holds out its hand. It curls its claws in a gesture for *more, more.* I gather up the rest of the bars and bring them. Holding them carefully, I crouch down and let the two trolls pick them out of my hands. The orange-eyed troll stuffs them under its arms and trundles inside with them. It chants something guttural that sounds like *"Shiny-shiny-shiny."*

I say to the cat-wight, "We ask you to allow us the use of your barn for one more night. We have magic to attend to that requires this sort of earthly privacy."

It twitches one ear, and holds all its attention on Vider. She smiles and nods, affirming my statement. When the cat-wight holds out its hand, Vider does as well, and the troll wraps its thin fingers around her thumb. *"Come, come,"* it says in its sandpaper voice.

"Vider," I say, concerned she'll agree.

She ignores me just as the cat-wight did, and stands, bent over enough not to strain the little troll's arm as it clasps her finger. "I will bargain with your mother," she agrees.

"Vider," I say again, taking her other hand.

"I'm a daughter of Loki," she tells me. "And kin to such creatures. They will eat our cakes and drink our mead, and we will bargain. Wait here." The last she says slowly and firmly.

I glance at the dark doorway. I don't know if there are five more inside, or a hundred. I likely can't kill them all, and it would be insulting to the land here to try. We came to their territory, oblivious and rude as crows. I clench my jaw and glare at her. But Vider shrugs. She disengages from me and says to the cat-wight, "I accept the hospitality."

It leads her across the porch and she vanishes into the house.

For a moment, I don't know what to do. I hear nothing but the wind against the eaves and through the barren tree limbs. I grind one foot against the ground, hands on my waist. My fingers itch for a spear, or at least to draw my sword.

If there's a problem, Vider will scream. She's fast and smart and spindly. Even if she can't fight free, she will at least find a way to warn me.

I settle with my feet wide, my hands folded in front of me. Ready. Waiting.

I wait a long time.

The sun moves far enough in the sky that the shadow of the house comes noticeably nearer to me. I recite to myself the first seethkona's prophecy of the creation of the world, from Ymir's death to the naming of Ash and Elm.

Just as building anxiety threatens to crack my calm, and I can feel the frenzy spin faster, Vider's voice calls out to me, "Soren, would you come to the doorway, please?"

I'm there in two leaps, one hand pressed against the torn hinges. I blink to adjust my eyes. It is dim in the house, but not dark. Gray light filters through threadbare curtains. I smell mildew, wet rock, and the thick, musty odor of rotten wood. The door opens into what was a living room, though the sofa has been hollowed out, wallpaper hangs off the wall in long strips, and there are the remains of a fire just in front of the actual fireplace.

Trolls crouch and sit in every corner. They bunch up in the destroyed sofa cushions, staring at me with lidless eyes. Some pick their teeth with tiny bone-needles; some wear scraps of clothing. They are tiny beasts, many with the features of a cat in face or fur or long curling tail.

And Vider sits cross-legged among them, with the original cat-wight on one side of her, and a three-foot-tall and nearly-as-wide troll-mother on the other. The troll-mother is mottled green and gray like a dead fish, and her cat eyes are silver as Vider's hair. She wears what used to be an apron, and her flaccid breasts droop over a round stomach. But she smiles, and pats Vider's knee with one thick hand. "*Stay,*" she says, and the trolls clap.

Before I can protest, a troll near a stack of rotting books rolls a red rubber ball at Vider. Vider catches it and rolls it back. A bent Slinky shines, strung between two of the trolls, and there are other toys scattered all around. Vider catches the rubber ball again, and rolls it toward another troll. Vider says, "It's all right, Soren. I'll stay here with them tonight, and they will not bother you and Astrid."

My teeth are on edge. The trolls are small and childlike, but they have claws that could rip through Vider's stomach, and teeth that might crush her bones. Any moment they might change their tiny minds. Any moment the troll-mother might take that thick hand and cover Vider's mouth and nose so she can't breathe. Then they will still have Vider to play with, and I will return in the morning to find her bones charred in the fire, and her intestines—instead of that Slinky—strung between two of the trolls.

The choice is between fighting our way out and losing the location for summoning my father, or allowing Vider to do as the trolls wish. I remind myself she's a daughter of Loki. She's as close to trollkin as a person gets.

And I remember the look in her eyes when she first saw my tattoo. When she homed in on it and never let go.

I clasp my hands in front of me again, and bow. I hold my eyes upon the troll-mother's. "Very well, little mother. Our friend Vider Lokisdottir will stay the night in your den. At dawn, when the sun turns the world into stone, you'll send her back to us whole and unharmed, and we will abandon your barn."

She inclines her feline head and says, "*Yesss.*"

Vider, not moving from her seat on the carpet, says, "Please ask the others not to worry."

"I will. Be safe."

Her smile is shallow and her expression too still as she says, "I am in no danger. The trollkin are my kin."

I back out of the doorway and touch my hand over my heart for her bravery.

FIFTEEN

WHEN I TELL Baldur of Vider's decision, he looks past me toward the trolls' house. "Are you certain, Soren?"

His eyes darken and I expect the sky to follow suit, but it remains sharply blue. I move so my head blocks his view, and say, "It was her choice. She's Lokiskin, and the trolls will honor that for one night. We must have time to perform the ritual, and you—"

"Me," he says with a heavy sigh. His eyelids shut and his shoulders droop. "When the sun sets, I will be useless."

"We will do this for you. You're not yourself without the apple."

"I wish we could do it now." The almost-god twists to glance south after Astrid, and bitterness flavors his words.

"We can't."

When he looks back to me, his eyes are sad. "Nothing is worth doing that cannot be done under the sun."

+ + +

I've heard stories of seethkonas raising the dead; stories of sorrow and loss. Odin has done it himself, and Freya, too, for no one knows the secrets of the earth as well as those resting within it. I want to ask Astrid to tell me a story of resurrection that ends well for everyone. Do such stories even exist? But when she returns from her meditations, she is quiet, her demeanor smooth as a deep pool. I tell her about Vider, and she holds her breath a moment before nodding peacefully.

As the sun sets, my nerve endings prick and tingle. For better or worse, we are doing this thing.

With Baldur tucked in sleep inside the barn, as hidden as we can make him, Astrid and I walk south along the creek toward a place she found in the afternoon. Here the water bends to create a natural U and will act as a barrier to hold her power contained.

We have no flashlight, and make our way by the low moonlight as best we can. Astrid tells me my father's interment ship would be the ideal place for such a ritual, and barring that, a crossroads. But as neither is possible, my presence and our desperation will have to suffice.

We arrive, hopping over the creek to the opposite bank. Astrid says, "We need a small fire. Will you gather some wood while I lay out the rest?" She unrolls her seething kit.

Icy wind flows down through the trees, gentle and slow like the sky's caress. I pick my way among fallen branches, gathering them, hoping they're dry enough to burn without too much smoke. I take pinecones, too, and some of the top layer of needles for getting the fire started.

I kick clear a space where Astrid directs and build the fire, lighting it with starter fluid from her seething kit. It catches a little bit too eagerly. I decide to pretend it's not an omen.

Astrid has knelt and opened her bag to pull out the remains of the thin yew branch she took from the ashes of the fire we made last week on the hill. With it, she draws runes of binding into the dirt. She takes corrberries and chews them with her eyes closed. Then she drinks long of honey mead from a clear glass bottle, the last of those purchased with money from the caravan seething. When she lowers the bottle, she sighs mightily.

"Tell me what you're doing," I say, unable to bear the silence and not-knowing. Father's sword is strapped to my back, and my hand twitches to pull it free.

She holds my gaze. With the fire to her right, half her face is lit by wicked orange light, and the other half is in darkness. I see the gleam of her shadowed eye, and think she looks just like Freya wearing her Hel Queen face: half-alive and half-dead. She says, "The corrberry and mead invite me to step between the worlds. I'll call your father, and he'll be bound here by these runes." Astrid points to the nine runes she's circled us with. "And the water."

All her dire warnings from earlier flood around me. "But he'll be . . . himself?"

Astrid takes my hand and squeezes it, as if unable to promise any other way.

With a tangle of nerves like razor wire in my chest, I crouch beside her in the darkness, forcing myself to imagine my father's face, his wide shoulders and hard hands. Because he was a son of Odin, his body was burned upon a pyre and his ashes buried. That body is gone, but his spirit will remember the form, whether he resides now in the Valhol or in the depths of Hel.

A ghostly smile appears on Astrid's mouth. "Are you ready?"

"Yes," I say, but my head is shaking *no*. I don't want to see him; I don't want to hear his voice or pretend he isn't long-dead. "I don't know how to do this."

"You will know what to do, son of Odin." Her voice is breathy, already fading into the trance. Her eyes flutter closed. "I feel it coming." She points at one of the pouches. "If I stop breathing for more than twenty-seven seconds, smear this onto my lips."

Twenty-seven seconds is forever. "If you stop breathing." I reach for her, to grab her arms and end this, to keep her safe and not let her step out between the worlds. I need her in this world, with me.

But Astrid takes another swig of mead and stands up. "It is time." She drops the bottle into my waiting hands and then spreads her arms. "Freya, Feather-Flying Goddess, Queen of Hel. Hear me! Hear me!"

Astrid's voice rings through the trees, rolling up and down the prairie like a peal of thunder. "I am Astrid Glyn, daughter of Jenna, and your child. Hear me!" The creek gathers her name and carries it away to all the rest of the world.

My heartbeat quickens as she cries, "My lady, my mother of

magic, I call Styrr Bearskin from your embrace. I call him from his place beside your throne. I call him from his bed where he sleeps in your love. Styrr Bearskin. Styrr Bearskin. Styrr Bearskin."

The flames leap high. They crack and pop, and sparks flare up. But nothing happens. My father does not appear. Astrid continues calling his name.

Now that we've begun, it *has* to work. The longer she stays in this wild place without him answering, the more likely we'll be faced with complications. I look up at her, at the wind pushing back her skirt, at the glint of moonlight on the black pearls slicing across her throat. And I call on my war god, on the god of the hanged, for the first time in my life.

I whisper, "Odin, send him to us." I kneel and bury my fingers in the earth. "He died with your song on his tongue. He died with your rage in his blood. We seek Idun, we seek her orchard, and we need my father to save your son."

Astrid begins to stomp her foot on the ground in the rhythm of my heart. She continues to call his name. The wind shakes the pine trees and needles rain down over us. The stomping beat reverberates through my bones. I lean down and take out the tiny dagger tucked into its sheath in Astrid's kit. With it I cut a small chunk of my already-short hair, and I scatter the hairs into the fire. I hold out my hand and slice open my thumb so that blood drips down and is swallowed up by the flickering orange flames. "Father," I whisper.

Suddenly Astrid stills. Her mouth falls open and she collapses onto her knees. Her eyes are wide and unseeing. Harsh breath chokes in and out and her jaw twitches as though she is trying to cough something away. Her hands are rigid at her sides, fingers splayed.

"Astrid." I move toward her, to catch her, to lower her to the ground, but there's a shuffling sound from across the fire.

Twisting quickly, I see a figure rise from the earth, as though it was huddled there in a fetal ball. It stands tall, with braids falling over its shoulders and down a body clothed in jeans and a Silver Horse T-shirt. Dried blood is splashed hard across its chest.

Dad.

His eyes are black through and through, like chunks of coal. His face is stretched tight to his hairline and his lips are as white as his cheeks. But it is my father.

"Who calls me?" he asks, in a voice like dry sticks scraped together. His head tilts down. "My son. My Soren."

Astrid continues to cough in her trance, mouth gaping wide, but I can't move, because he says my name. My father says my name.

"Soren, why have you called me?"

He is so strong, so broad even in death. His hair is shaded gold by the fire, his face fierce. A perfect son of Odin.

"Soren, why have you called me?"

Stumbling to my feet, I stare at him. "Father," I whisper. I'm as tall as he is now. "Styrr." I wipe my sweating hands against my pants. "Son of Jul." With each naming his eyes clear, until they are the same green I knew so well. I can't speak past the hard stone in my throat.

"Soren." He smiles, the mischievous smile that spelled fun for me and trouble for Mom. Next will come his laugh, and I want to go to him and put my ear to his chest the way I used to, to hear that laugh being born in his heart.

But if I walk around the fire, I will not be next to Astrid. Her hard breathing drags at me. I can't leave her side, even to touch my father. Not when Astrid might stop breathing and I would be too far to hear. "Dad."

"You called my name, son, and I came."

I struggle to remember why we called. "Idun, Dad. Did you know her?"

And here it is: his laugh. "The Youthful Lady! Ah, what beauty and charm. Yes, I knew her."

"Where, Dad?"

"She called me her gentle bear, and loved me." Dad winks. "Don't go and tell your mom that."

His chuckles pace Astrid's choking breath. I don't have time.

"How do we find the orchard, Dad? How?"

His face freezes and he stares at me. "My son. My bear-son."

"Where is the orchard? You have to tell me, please."

"No one can find the orchard but one called by the Lady of Apples."

"No, Dad, we have to. We have to find it!"

He squints over the fire; his green eyes spark through the haze of smoke. "Did you take up my sword?"

I reach over my shoulder and grasp the hilt. "Yes, Dad, yes. I did. I took it from you and carry it still."

"Oh, my Soren." His eyes shut and his body jerks. Twice. Three times. Then again and again in rapid succession, the way it did when they shot him.

"Dad!" I draw the sword. It melts orange in the firelight. "Dad! Look! Your sword. I took it. I am your son and your sword is here."

He stops moving, but his eyes remain closed and he whispers, "I shall not . . . I shall not . . . with words of fear . . ."

I say, "For Odin will welcome me. Death comes without lamentation, and the Valkyrie summon me home."

Dad's dry voice joins me. "Gladly shall I drink ale from the Poet's Cup, for the days of my life are ended." He opens his eyes as we say together, "I die with a laugh."

The frenzy is alive inside me, cutting at my ribs to be free. To battle at my father's side. I'm reaching across the fire for him, to touch him and pull him closer or to go with him into whatever Hel is his. But Astrid's choking keeps me back. With massive effort, I tighten my hand on the sword. If he can't tell me where the orchard is directly, I have to find another way. As calmly and firmly as possible, I say, "Dad, I need to know where you met Mom."

His eyelids flutter and something yellow, but like a tear, drips from his lashes. "Leavenworth. It was near Leavenworth. They have amazing apples there. And you can see the Cascades."

I close my teeth around an exclamation of relief. *Please, Odin, let our guess be correct, that he met Mom while serving at the orchard. It's the only way I can be the key.* "Thank you."

"My son, I see the mark on your face."

It's my turn to laugh, a tight, fearful laugh. "I am truly your son, and a berserker."

"And in commit."

"No, Dad, I'm not in a band."

He raises a hand and points to Astrid.

I shift so I am mostly blocking his view of her.

"She is not long for this world," he says.

"No!" The word cuts through the fire and my dad staggers back.

Astrid's breath chokes off, then restarts in a ragged gasp. I touch her hair, winding my fingers into the curls. "Tell me, Styrr Bearskin, what will happen to Astrid."

"The Lady of Apples knows. She's waiting for you. For the bear, the sun, and the seether. One will die, one will forget, and one will be reborn."

"What does that mean?" My fingers are too tight in Astrid's hair, but I can't let go. I won't let go.

Dad is silent. His mouth presses closed and he stares through the smoke. His eyes darken, swirling into black coals again. I'm losing him as Astrid loses her breath. With one hand, he draws a rune in the air. And again. And again. "Only this," he says in a voice of sand. "The commit will break."

"You can't know!" I yell at him, and sweep one hand through the flames. I'll banish him; he has nothing to say that I want to hear.

"My son!" He flings out his arms. "My blessings on you. Your mother's wisdom guide you, your father's strength guide you, your heart's belief guide you. My blessings on you and your love!"

My father crumbles into ash.

The fire blows out.

Astrid stops breathing.

My knees slam into the ground when I fling myself down at Astrid's side. "Astrid?" I slide my arm under her neck so her head tilts back. Digging my fingers under her jaw, I find a pulse. It's slow and erratic.

I'm supposed to be counting. To twenty-seven. How long's it been? When should I use the ointment? Reaching over her supine body, I slide my hand over the bumps of the seething kit. Without the fire, it is so dark I can barely make out which shadows are the darkest.

The ointment jar pokes out of its pocket, the way she left it. I think. It must be the right one, and it's surely been thirty seconds now. Popping the tiny cork, I dump the viscous contents onto my fingers. The liquid glints darkly, coating my skin. "Astrid, please breathe," I whisper as I lean down and carefully spread the oil over her lips.

Everything smells of mint. The cold scent clears my head, mingling with the acrid fire fumes and the smell of wet earth.

Astrid's throat quivers under my hand, and she shudders as she sucks in a huge gasp of breath.

"Thank Freya!" I gather her up so she's half in my lap. "Astrid."

Pressing her forehead to my chest, she mutters my name. Her hands weakly clutch at the collar of my T-shirt. Her back is soggy and her curls tickle my nose and chin. She shivers.

"We have to get you inside," I say.

"Did it work? It worked." Her voice is hushed with awe.

My heartbeat picks up again, running fast. "Yes. It worked."

Astrid rolls her head back so she's staring up at the small scrap of stars visible through the clouds. "They're so far away," she says. "Can you believe I was flying past them? Through chaos and into death?"

I don't know what I believe about death anymore. It seemed and spoke like my father, but I don't want it to have been. Not with his words still ringing in my ears. *The commit will break. She is not long for this world.* But what I say is, "You did."

I carry Astrid back to the barn and help her down onto the pile of hay beside Baldur. A rafter high overhead creaks in the wind, and a low howl reminds me of Vider, trapped in that house where she plays catch with trolls.

The commit will break.

Was it worth it? Risking Astrid, letting Vider stay the night with monsters, just to hear him tell me we would fail and Astrid would die?

I know where to begin looking for the orchard now, but does it matter?

Astrid has already passed out from the effort of seething. I stand over her as everything falls quiet except for her soft breath, and all I can think of is the long space when she did not breathe. The idea of her never breathing again cuts so sharply, my breath turns into ragged little coughs.

Now there's nothing but darkness around us, not even thin silver moonlight or a single candle flame to chase the gloom away. I feel my chest will crack if I don't stop thinking about that moment.

"Astrid," I whisper. She doesn't move. I crouch and stroke two fingers down her cheek, even though I can barely see her face. When I reach the corner of her mouth, I pause and close my eyes. I remember the feel of the ointment between my fingers and her lips, still smell the fading scent of mint. With my eyes shut, I breathe her in. I breathe in mint, and faint honey, evergreen and cold wind. I breathe in smoke and sharp corrberry off her tongue, the memory of seething. I breathe in starlight.

Standing, I pace in tight circles, fingers curling in and out of fists. I want to tear the barn apart. To get into the Spark and drive as far away as I can. If I go, the commit will break early, and no one will die.

But I don't leave.

Astrid and Baldur need me. I must tell them what my father said.

And Vider is alone with the trolls. I must be there at dawn.

I spend the night pacing, listening to Astrid breathe because I'm terrified she'll stop again.

SIXTEEN

I HAVEN'T SLEPT at all by the time dawn begins to overcome the stars.

Astrid rustles the hay and I'm there immediately, kneeling at her side. "Astrid?" I whisper.

"Soren." My name becomes a wide yawn as she stretches.

"You're well?"

Her eyes pop open and she peers at me. It's still too dark to see easily, but soon the sun will rise. Soon Baldur will wake. "You're upset."

"Just—just awake. I have to go meet Vider."

Sitting up, she grasps my hand. "You're avoiding my eyes. What happened?" Her grip tightens. "Did he tell you where the orchard is?"

I spin away, go to the wall where a decrepit old scythe hangs. "He did. Near enough."

Her footfall is a soft shuffle through the dusty barn. When she touches my back I jerk from the coldness. My skin is alive with fire and fear. "Soren. Turn around. Tell me."

Unable to disobey, I slowly shift around. My eyes press closed and her cool finger traces down my spear tattoo. It sends shivers dancing up and down my spine.

"What did he say?"

All my father's words tear through my head and I try to form them into coherence. "He said Leavenworth, near the Cascades, is where he met Mom." I still don't look at her. "He said—he said that only someone called by Idun can find it, but that she's expecting us."

"Soren."

The coaxing tone pries open my eyes. Astrid's frown is gentle, and in the dim light her pupils are wide as holes to Hel. I whisper, "He said she's expecting three of us. The bear, the sun, the seether. And that . . ."

I can't say it.

"What, Soren?" She clasps my face. "Tell me."

"That our commit will break."

Astrid shakes her head. "It won't. It can't."

"It can, if—" The words strangle, and I pull away from her. My shoulders press into the wall, and the old rusting scythe swings on its hook.

"If what?" She doesn't touch me again, but waits with her eyebrows raised.

"If you die."

Amazingly, Astrid laughs. "Soren, I'm not going to die."

I jump forward and take her shoulders so fast, she hardly has time to gasp before I've lifted her onto her toes. "She is not long for this world," I whisper. "That's what he said, and he pointed at you."

Everything about her stills, as though she's become nothing but a hanging corpse already, and her eyes flutter shut. "No wonder I'm not in your bones."

"Astrid!" I release her with an abrupt little shove.

She only glances toward Baldur, who still lies dreaming, because the sun has not yet found his face. "It doesn't matter, for his sake."

I whirl and tear the creaking scythe off the wall. "We should never have raised him! We shouldn't have asked him anything, Astrid!" So great is my frustration, I throw the tool in a huge arc across the barn. It spins over itself and the blade buries a hand-span deep into the far-side wall. The long wooden handle quivers with energy. Little gray doves leap out of the rafters and fly out through the hole in the roof in a flurry of feathers. "It won't be worth it," I say, my breath heaving.

Astrid is there in front of me, and she slaps her palms flat against my chest. "Stop, Soren. Stop."

I lean into her cool touch, because it soothes the wild, ripping fury of the frenzy inside me. I want it out. I want to let it loose so that the fever consumes me, makes me forget about this rabid fear.

She points at Baldur. "We had to do this. It's for him, and there isn't any choice. Revenants are notoriously confusing and confused. Your father's warnings may not be literal ones. You have got to calm down."

"I can't. Not when I think about everything breaking."

"We won't break."

I grip her shoulders again. "You should stay here. If we end the commit early, you won't be in danger."

"No." She takes my hands off, puts them between us. "I will not willingly leave you."

"But—"

"*No*, you big troll. This is why prophecy is so dangerous. This is why we must be careful what we say to people, those of us who read the strands of fate." She shakes her head. "We don't know how what we say may bring prophecy into being."

"You were terrified of what you yourself read in my bones."

She twists up her mouth. "That was me. And I've read for you before. Looked into your fate." Her eyes wander away, avoiding mine.

"You have?" I say, my anger softening.

Astrid waves a hand, dismissing it. "Listen, seers can rarely see the entire path, but only little strands of it. Take Vider. Your father didn't mention her, did he? And yet Vider travels with us. You should go get her, and the four of us, a bear, a sun, a seether, and a—a little dragon, will travel to the gate of Idun's orchard."

"I don't like it. I don't trust it."

"You only have to trust yourself." She peers up at my eyes. "If he had told you that you would die bringing Baldur to Bright Home, would you leave Baldur? Would you leave us alone?"

My face crumples. I want to lie to her. Who is Baldur to me? What is he worth to the world? I think of her smile the first moment she saw him, and I think of him holding the spear point at the hollow of my throat. "No."

"So. Go fetch Vider. She's sacrificed for this, too. Baldur will wake, we'll pack the Spark and be ready to go when you return." Her mouth is relaxed now, her expression cajoling. Like I'm a child to be won to her side by charm.

I pull my hands from Astrid's as if they're burning. I turn my back to her. It's impossible to look at her face for long without seeing it the way it was last night: slack, choking, breathless.

She is not long for this world.

I gather up Dad's sword and stalk out of the barn.

The first rays of sun spread a path for me through the tall grass toward the farmhouse.

As I approach, the house begins to glow in the soft morning light. The broken porch swing creaks, though there isn't enough wind. Something must have waited in it, watching for me from the shelter of shadows.

I draw Father's sword, letting it catch the sun and send a shock of light like an arrow to the gaping doorway.

A shriek sounds, and then laughter titters from all the windows, from the wood of the house itself.

I don't wait, but charge up the stairs, panic pinching at my shoulder blades. Vider appears—a white ghost against the darkness—and is thrust forward. She stumbles and I catch her with one arm, dragging us back down the porch steps and into the sun.

She's deadweight in my arm, and I fumble to sheathe my sword. "Vider?" I take her shoulders and her head lolls back. She winces from the sunlight.

"Soren," she says, making one side of her mouth smile.

I heft her up into my arms. She's cold and I smell blood. But as I carry her, she doesn't tense or cry out in injury. When we're a good distance from the house, surrounded by fifty paces of sunlight on all sides, I crouch.

Vider's hair is free from its binding, and it trails down to the grass. A bruise forms red and brown on her left cheek and blood has dried just under one nostril. She opens her eyes and I am loose with relief to see all of her present there, aware of me and awake. She pushes away, twisting around to look back at the house. One of her hands is fisted around something.

"Are you all right?" I ask quietly.

"Rough play, that's all." Vider rubs her shoulder. Then she glances at her feet. Tiny round dots of red decorate the tops of them, as if blood dripped down and splattered there. The nose-bleed, I suspect. There's more blood, edging tears in her pants and tank top. A hundred tiny claws; a hundred tiny wounds.

But I help her up and she breathes deeply. No shaking, and her grip on my elbow is strong. "Did you speak with him?" she asks me, holding her other fist against her heart.

"Yes. Vider . . ."

"I'm fine. Hardly worse than I'm used to." She rolls her eyes and shrugs away from me, about to hurry past and force me to ignore the implications of that statement. I touch her back as she goes, in the center where I can always feel my frenzy burn.

Vider stops. Her chin is lowered, and she shivers. Silver-blond hair hides her face. I step so that I'm just behind her, and see that she gazes at her cupped palms.

In the center of them is a round stone the size of a cherry.

A slit pupil mars the face of it, and I imagine the eye glinting yellow out of a cat-wight's skull.

Vider snaps her fingers shut around it and walks on. This time I do not rush to catch up.

SEVENTEEN

WE DRIVE ALL day.

Astrid tells the others the basics of what my father said: Leavenworth. We're expected. She says nothing of the commit breaking, nothing of death. There's only one likely Leavenworth we can find on the map we buy with gas and breakfast. It's in the foothills of the Cascades, and we should be there by tomorrow afternoon.

I'm glad to use driving as an excuse not to speak. I don't have to look at anyone, but can focus on the road pulling us closer and closer to an end I don't want to reach.

Vider sleeps most of the morning away, curled on the backseat with her head on Baldur's thigh. Astrid dozes fitfully. I tighten my grip on the steering wheel to keep from nudging her awake every time her brow furrows or I hear her mutter in her dreams. Any touch might weaken my resolve, and I am determined to keep myself distant enough to see what's coming with open eyes.

Although Baldur remains awake with me, he doesn't roll

down his window to catch sunlight in his fingers as he did before. I turn the radio to a low murmur, and listen to a string of supposed Baldur-sightings across the country. In Cheyenne, where we were, they say he was seen with a berserker and a young seethkona, but there are also reports from Nordakota, Ohiyo, and even Laflorida. It's a relief that our rather loud encounter at the caravan two days ago doesn't seem to have put everyone right on our tail.

The gate to Bright Home remains shut, but there haven't been any more major troll attacks. A joint task force of berserkers and congressional soldiers caught up with the herd in Vinland, and slaughtered them.

Out here there's a lot of static over the radio waves, and there isn't much to listen to, other than the news station. I land on a replay of Ardo Vassing's cliché-laden sermon from the other night. He talks in powerful tones about waiting through darkness for the dawn and about the hidden roots of wealth that we see only when new shoots push up through the soil in the springtime. *"If we only love our brothers and sisters, if we only bring out the light within ourselves,"* he says, *"then Baldur the Beautiful will return to us."*

In the rearview, I catch Baldur staring intently at the dial of the radio. I click it off. His startled glance turns into a frown, and instead of engaging me, he looks out the window.

For lunch we stop in an Idahow town called Peccadillo. The welcome sign proclaims it the Smile Capital of the World, but the Spark is so full of tension none of us is laughing. I know it's my fault. I'm feeling wound tight and the sparks I'm used to holding under my skin are flaring up.

Astrid will go into the gas stop for food while Baldur remains hidden in the car. I don't think I should go anywhere, either, because of my tattoo, but when Vider jerks open the driver's side door and says "I need shoes," I share a quick look with Astrid and follow after.

We walk through the downtown with its red brick buildings, its striped awnings and green streetlamps. I stand glowering against the brick wall of a pawnshop as Vider darts in to trade a small copper medallion I think she may have pulled out of the air for boots and a pair of jeans.

As we return to the gas stop, the sun is behind us, casting our shadows ahead. We've been silent the whole time, but finally Vider says, "What's your problem?"

I grind my teeth and don't answer.

"Was it your father?" She flicks a glance at me. "I'd be upset if I had to see mine again."

As we walk, Vider skims through the crowd quickly, never touching, always avoiding notice. She pulls me along in her wake, so that even a bear of a man like me can slip through. I watch the side of her face as I consider my answer. The bruise has darkened. Did her father have something to do with giving her the crazed bravery to spend the night in a den of trolls and steal one of their eyes?

"Yeah," I admit. "I didn't really want to talk to him. And what he said was . . . bad."

Her eyebrows wing up. "If they're nacks in life, they're nacks in death."

"My dad wasn't like that. . . . I loved him."

"Lucky. Mine was."

"Is that how you ended up with the caravan?"

"Nope." Vider rubs the heel of her hand against her ribs. "I was born into that, but Dad wasn't. He was opposed to the whole caravan philosophy and took me away. Several times. You remember Sam? It was his mom who took me back, though she wasn't responsible for me."

In the caravans, Vider would have been raised by an extended family. Mother, father, aunts and uncles, anyone in the family by blood or bond. It's a wide-thrown support system, and it's one of the reasons the caravans have survived economically even into this century. "It must have been good then, having the Lokiskin to rely on."

She slides a look at me, her eyelashes low. "Sometimes, Soren, having more people watching out for you only means more chances to get hurt."

There isn't anything I can say to that.

We find Astrid and Baldur seated together at a wooden picnic table in the yard behind the gas stop. Snow-capped mountains rise in the distance behind them, the tips shining like glass as the sun heats the sky. A bucket of chicken waits, and bottles of honey soda weigh down napkins and paper plates. Baldur talks, using his hands to describe something. His fingers fan out like sunbeams.

I hold back to watch them, my friends.

I never thought of this as a commit before Dad said it would break.

There are several different sorts of commit rituals. Commitments can be made under nearly any god, though usually with Thor or Freyr, the gods of loyalty and strength, family and wealth. The most common are the commits of couples, and commits between battle-brothers or business partners. There are commits assumed between parents and children, and you never have to hold a ritual before a tyr for a family commitment unless you're stepping out of blood bounds.

And at the bare minimum, you only need to speak out loud that you are forming a commit with another, and it is so. The word is the bond.

Vider climbs up to sit her butt on the table and her feet on the bench, and pulls the bucket to her. She eats ravenously. Astrid wrinkles her nose and hands Vider a napkin before more delicately picking the skin off a drumstick. Baldur fishes through the pieces, discarding dark meat in favor of a breast. These are such little things, but they overwhelm me as I carefully sit down. Astrid pushes the chicken at me, but I shake my head. I'll eat it cold, when this feeling settles. My ribs are tight and it isn't the frenzy pushing out, but something from around me pressing in. From these people.

I cannot let us fail. We are bound together.

+ + +

For the night, we stop in a small city along the Face of Montania called Mimirsey. It's Vider we send in to get the room, for although she's young and hasn't passed her citizenship exam, Loki insists that a girl is grown as soon as she can be a mother. We hope Vider's adult status in the caravans will hold with the manager of a roadside motel.

When she comes out, she's excitedly twirling the key around her finger. "The guy told me Baldur's been confirmed all the way down in New Spain, by Fenris herself." She smiles and flashes change we didn't expect. "I convinced him a ten percent discount was in order."

"Enough for breakfast tomorrow," Astrid says, and Baldur tousles Vider's hair. She smacks his hand away with a sneer.

We pile into the double room just in time for Baldur to pass out. He does so, but first stands at the edge of the bed, staring through the western window to see the moment the sun slides past the horizon. Then his knees buckle and he sprawls onto the mattress. It's a melodramatic gesture, with his limp arms flung up over his head, and it makes Vider laugh. But by then the god of light is unconscious.

Astrid opens her bag, fishing through her clothes with a small frown. It's Moonsday, nearly a week since we left Sanctus Sigurd's. All my clothes, too, are filthy. I hold my hand out. "Give it here. I'll find an all-night Laundromat."

She hesitates, and I add, "I'm not tired."

With a little sigh, Astrid hands it over. I shoulder my backpack and, after a brief moment of inner debate, strap on Dad's sword, too.

I'd rather hunt for a Laundromat than show myself to the motel clerk for a recommendation, and I only have to walk about seven blocks to find what I'm looking for. It's empty but for a harried-looking woman who keeps stopping her folding to sing to a baby in a rickety car seat that's propped on top of a dryer. I get our load started and drop to the sticky tile floor to do push-ups.

After the woman leaves, I run small laps around the inside of the Laundromat, creating my own obstacle course. The rhythm of the machines is a good counter beat, and I measure my progress against it.

By the time I get back to the motel room, Astrid and Vider are asleep. I'm even less tired than I was before. I haven't slept for two days, and should try while I'm not feverish, but instead I sit on the thin carpet and eat the sandwich they left out for me. The TV is turned so low I can barely hear the canned laughter in the background of the comedy they left on.

That's why I notice Astrid's nightmare, an hour past midnight. The blankets of the bed she shares with Vider shuffle, and her breathing grows weighted and harsh. I glance around at her, from the foot of Baldur's bed. Her eyes flash wild under her lids and her lips are stretched thin. There's just enough white light from the television for me to watch a tear track down her temple.

I stand up. Baldur, too, is dreaming. His expression is steady but serious, and his eyelashes twitch.

Astrid whispers something. One word again and again.

Leaning down, I put my ear closer to her mouth.

"Soren."

My head cracks back hard enough to make me dizzy. "Astrid," I whisper, putting my hands on her shoulders. "Wake up."

I shake her, pressing my fingers into her bare skin.

Her eyes fly open and she sucks in a huge breath. I stumble back as she throws off the thin quilt and flees into the bathroom. The light flashes on and she shuts the door.

My heart beats fast as I sit on my heels in the dark motel room. Vider rolls over, tugging her pillow over her face, and behind me Baldur's breathing evens out.

A faucet turns on in the bathroom. I try to settle in front of the television again but can't even look at the bickering family and their illusory problems.

I go to the bathroom and tentatively knock.

Nothing.

After a moment, I push the door open.

Astrid huddles on the cold blue tiles with her back against the sink cabinet. When I enter, she shakes her head. "It was just a nightmare, Soren. I'm fine."

I crouch in front of her but don't move to touch. Her curls are frayed around her cheeks, her lips pale. "About what's to come?"

Her hesitation is a moment too long. "About death and

resurrections. It's to be expected. I did huge, dark magic yesterday, and there wasn't any good way to process it."

I can't believe she's lying to me.

I leave her there on the bathroom floor, and go outside with
my sword. I spend the night cutting at shadows.

EIGHTEEN

IN THE MORNING, bright sunlight makes my eyes burn, and Baldur volunteers for the first shift behind the wheel. Astrid and I aren't talking, so I'm in the back with Vider. She plays with one of the same copper medallions she traded back in Peccadillo, walking it across her fingers and making it disappear, only to pull it out of my nose. Despite the childish nature of the game, I play along with a plastered smile until Vider stops, narrows her eyes at me as if studying something beyond my expression, and suddenly claps. The medallion vanishes. Vider strips off the cardigan she's been wearing, pulls out her pockets, points to the empty carpet at her feet, the too-tight crease of the leather seats, and tells me I'll never find it.

I know it's a trick, but my shoulder blades prickle uncomfortably.

Within the first hour, we see dark clouds blowing over the low mountains to the north, directly before us. I'm glad of them, for the way the world seems to be echoing my own fear and anger. Then Astrid notices that Baldur has slowed our pace by ten miles an hour. She suggests a breakfast stop where we can trade drivers.

Baldur pulls into a twenty-four-hour truck stop with a star logo, claiming it's a good omen, and the girls go in for dough-nuts. Baldur and I mind the Spark. Vider suggests disguises if we're so worried, but both of us recoil. Me because it's illegal, and Baldur because, he says, pretending to be something he isn't is dishonorable. I'm not sure either of the girls agrees, but they go, murmuring to each other.

I begin a set of push-ups against the trunk. Baldur crosses his arms over his chest and watches me. Occasionally his eyes flicker east. The sun shines freely on his face now, but it won't be long before we're entirely beneath the storm clouds.

With a heavy sigh, Baldur sinks down to sit on the dirt with his back against the rear wheel. He unzips his hoodie halfway down his chest and leans his head against the bumper. Every time I push away from the trunk, the car shakes slightly, mak-ing his head knock as if he's agreeing with my silence.

I slow my push-ups. I've lost count anyway, and I did some-where around a thousand of them throughout the lonely night. Bringing my feet under me one at a time, I crouch next to him. Maybe my prickly mood is seeping into him, but maybe there's been something new in his dreams, too. "Baldur? Are you all right?"

He pops open one eye. It's a darkening blue, and gray swirls around his iris. "I don't think I like rain."

"We'll get through it."

Baldur shudders.

"Is there something else bothering you?" I stare at the shine of sunlight making his hair so vibrant it seems plucked from a cartoon. Yet with his eyes tightly closed and his hands tense against the earth, he's more like a man than a god now. He said it himself: he's stripped down to his core. I wonder what it's like for him, to have no memories of being a figure of power and light, to have us and the radio and everyone insisting that he's the hope of the world, when all he remembers is being a man alone in the desert. When all he has is a passionate seethkona and an uncertain, angry berserker.

"Soren." He pins me with a gaze gone more gray in only this short moment.

It isn't a time to be informal. His voice and my name hum along my spine, setting the frenzy to spin. "My lord Baldur."

His gaze does not falter. "What is the boon you would ask of my father?"

"That he strip the berserking power out of my chest," I say quietly.

Baldur nods, and the heat of his gaze cools. "Thank you for telling me."

He already guessed. He guessed because he's known men for hundreds of years, and the knowledge of our motivations resides in his heart, if not in his memory.

My god of light continues: "When you're no longer one of Odin's crazy warriors, Soren, will you serve me instead?"

A rock drops into my stomach. "As a priest? One of your sun priests?"

Baldur laughs. "The sunburst tattoo wouldn't work with your spear."

I rub the tattoo with my thumb. Even if Odin can still remove the frenzy, I'll always have this. "What would you have of me, then—how would I serve?"

"As my friend."

Picturing Baldur as I'm used to seeing him—as a god with sparkling women and dashing men at his side, surfing in Baja California or dining at fancy clubs in Chicagland, always with a happy grin, often with sword in hand and occasionally covered in goblin gore—I find it impossible to think he wants for friends. But instead of wondering aloud or disagreeing, I calmly say, "Friends don't serve. They just are."

His smile turns sly. "You serve Astrid."

I open my mouth to deny it, but can't. Even now, with my father's prophecy hanging between us, I won't leave her side. When I lower my head in surrender, Baldur laughs again. "So, Bearskin, son of Styrr, that is what I want from you."

"You won't have to ask," I promise, setting my loose fist against his knee. Baldur spreads his hand over my fist, but not before I see something uncertain, something slick and worried, pass through his storming eyes. "Baldur? What is it? What is it you're afraid of? That we won't get you to the orchard? That we'll fail?"

"No," he says firmly, gripping my hand. "I never doubt that." Baldur leans forward and I see a curl of lightning in his left eye. "Nothing could stop you, Soren."

I place my remaining hand over his, so that our hands are stacked in a solid pile, and try to ignore fear that thickens in my blood at his certainty. *The commit will break. She is not long for this world.* He doesn't know what our success may cost us.

"Soren, I'm afraid of . . ." He's whispering, and I hear the rush of a semitrailer barreling past, and then, beyond it, a far rumble of thunder. I wait, proud of him that he does not shut his eyes, that he holds close and confesses. "I am afraid that I will eat this apple and everything will change."

"It won't matter." I tighten my fingers so they don't shake while I reassure a god with what may very well be a lie. "I'll still be your friend, and so will Astrid and Vider."

I see the girls, as though summoned, exit through the glass doors carrying greasy bags and a twelve-pack of honey soda. Baldur sees them as well, and pushes up to his feet. He casts one look over his shoulder at me. "It's possible, when my immortality and memories return me to my better self, that you won't want to."

I take over driving, because I'm in the mood to maneuver through a storm.

My instinct is to tell Astrid what Baldur said. To share the burden of it with her. He and Vider are playing a license plate game in the backseat, though Vider is winning by several letters because Baldur obviously doesn't enjoy looking outside. His eyes are pale gray. The underside of the cloud sheet rolls in bulbous waves, and the wind picks up from the northeast, batting at the side of the Spark.

As I drive under the grave clouds, I can't shake Baldur's fear. Yet the more I think on it, the more certain I am that we know his essential self. All that's been torn away are the extraneous things. When the layers of Baldur the Beautiful are returned, we'll still recognize him as ours.

Astrid turns on the radio, and Ardo Vassing is speaking, filling the space with his deep, scratchy voice. She says, "I met him once," and twists the volume louder. He's got an accent from the Gulf, thick and soothing. He leads a meditation before his wife starts a choir singing.

Exactly then the rain begins, splashing against the windshield all at once, blinding me. Astrid reaches across to turn on the spindly old wipers.

For half an hour, I drive through the spill. Then with a hard crack the world is lit with eerie light. Thunder and lightning so close together they must be on top of us.

"This is horrible," mutters Baldur. I glance in the rearview, and he's paler than usual. His eyes are heavy and black.

I have to watch the road, especially as the wind strengthens again and the car in front of me turns on its flashers. We're crawling, but steady. Rain blurs everything and the wipers can't keep up. More thunder, and lightning nearly blinds me.

Vider says, "Maybe we should pull over."

"On the shoulder, we'd be a hazard to everybody. Better to keep in the slow line," I answer.

Between cracks of thunder, the rain on the metal roof is

loud. Astrid flips off the radio, which I didn't even notice was still on, and then she reaches across the gears to grip my knee. My whole body shivers, and I squeeze the wheel.

I won't lose her. I can't. Fate has always been a thing for me to fight. This tattoo on my cheek is a mark of possibility, and everything I've done has been to keep it from coming true. How can I fight any less hard for Astrid's life?

The storm can rage around us, but I refuse to stop driving.

As the first break in the clouds beckons ahead and the rain fades to gentle but constant, Astrid tells us the story of how Thor Thunderer lost his hammer and Loki Serpent-Mother helped him get it back. Though we've all known the story since we were babies, as it's a very popular one with kindergarten teachers and picture book writers, to Baldur it's new again. By the time she comes to the part where Loki convinces Thor to dress up like the goddess Freya and go pretend to marry the giant Thrym, the last of the storm has vanished from Baldur's eyes. Astrid's impression of the stalwart god simpering for Thrym and attempting to behave as a lovesick wife has Vider in stitches, and even I find a smile when Astrid puts on a crackling voice for Loki to tease his thundering friend.

This is worth sacrifice, too, I realize. Not only Astrid and Baldur, but Vider as well and the easy laughter among the four of us.

I want to point it out to Baldur, that this is who he is, no matter how memories may add layers and history onto him. This, right here, laughing with three friends, this is the meaning of the god of light.

Through the last drops of rain, I drive into the Washington kingstate.

Astrid takes over the wheel once we're through Lilac, the last big city before the Cascades. We have about three hours to go, and the land around us shows no sign of mountains. It's so flat and cut-down for farming that the sky overwhelms the horizon, stretching high overhead and all around. There's more sky than land, and I have a disorienting sensation that the car is upside-down and any moment real gravity will kick back in and we'll fall up off the road and into the deep sky.

Baldur says, only half joking, that he'd like to spend the remainder of the drive strapped to the roof where he can properly soak up the sun.

As we approach the mountains, whatever brief release of tension the end of the storm gave us begins to recede. We sit in silence but for the roar of wind from the open windows. Baldur has his arm dangling out into the sun, but his fingers are still.

Evergreen trees sprout up here and there, only to vanish again, giving us back to the vast, flat spread of grassland. There are only three colors: black highway, golden land, and blue sky.

We cut south and my ears begin to pop. It's just after noon, and when we fill up the gas tank at the start of the foothills, the attendant confirms we're less than an hour out from Leavenworth.

Less than an hour away from the end.

At first the mountains just seem like piles of dirt, so worn with erosion, and so lacking in trees. There's nothing but rock and round, tangled bushes. The highway follows a river for a while, and Baldur trades seats with Vider so he's on that side, where he can watch the sun reflect against the water.

Slowly the mountains grow, and we see signs for Leavenworth. As we pass through a town so small it has no fast food, Astrid sucks in a sudden, hissing breath. She points ahead to a bright red sign: APPLES AND CIDER, BY THE BUCKET OR JUG.

It's only the first.

Between us and Leavenworth are three dozen orchards. Apparently, apples are one of Washington's most prized resources.

The frenzy churns in my chest like an ulcer.

Astrid's knuckles are white on the wheel.

There are apples and orchards everywhere, and we have no idea how to find the one we're looking for in all the hundreds of valleys and gorges the foothills create.

After a few moments of anxious conversation, we decide to drive to the middle of Leavenworth, find a quiet place, and Astrid will cast her bones.

When we do pull into town, I'm momentarily distracted from the ache of worry. It seems Leavenworth has fashioned itself into a Bavarian village, complete with gingerbread trim on all the downtown buildings, cobblestones, dark wood balconies against whitewashed storefronts, and a handful of hotels and restaurants with names like Baron Haus and Die Ritterhof Motor Inn. Despite the cold mountain air and the fact that most of the trees haven't even begun to show signs of budding, tourists are plentiful. We drive past a pub with a large hammer of Thor hanging over the door, and in a small manicured park there's a gazebo sheltering a statue of his wife, Sif Longhair. It doesn't surprise me that the Giant-Killer is so popular here. Mount Rainier, only two hundred kilometers southwest, has long been a trouble spot because of the goblins who enjoy the heat from the volcanoes and use the natural gases and steam to power their forges. My father used to tell me that it's well known among berserk bands that the worst place to do battle is a volcano. Luta Bearsdottir, the only lady berserker of our century, died at the foot of Sanctus Elens, years before I was born. That was in the last elf uprising, when the volcano burst with the anger and power of battle, and they say Luta was skewered on a giant's spear when heat and sulfur leached away her ability to frenzy.

"There's a nice spot," Vider says in a tight voice, drawing my attention back to the town. We're passing another park, this one well covered with trees and perched on a rise that drops away toward a river.

I say to Astrid, "Why don't you pull into that lot up there, and we'll walk back around to the park."

She doesn't respond. I assume she's only concentrating

on the traffic, on the pedestrians who seem more than willing to step into the street without the aid of crosswalks. But instead of signaling to turn into the lot I indicated, Astrid lets the Spark shoot past, heading out of the city and straight into the mountains.

"Astrid."

Baldur leans up, too. "Astrid."

Nothing. She stares ahead and her expression is relaxed. Her hands are now loose on the wheel.

I touch her arm and she blinks, but nothing else changes. "Astrid," I say more sharply.

She frowns. "I know where to go."

"How?" Vider whispers. Her head is just by mine, because she's slid up to the edge of the back bench to grip my seat.

"I've seen this place, almost."

"Almost?" I ask.

Astrid looks at me. Her sepia eyes are full of dreams. "Last night."

I wait. We all wait as she steers us around a curve. "Every time I shut my eyes since the barn, I see them. Apples. And it isn't like before, when I would dream of the orchard and thousands of apples stretching out. Of the Rainbow Bridge made of apple blossoms." Astrid shakes her head. "This—this is closer."

I don't want to hear how this ends. I don't want her to know where we are, to be called by this orchard. Even if it's the only way to find it, it's also evidence that her fate—all our fates—will end there.

"They're surrounding me," she says, barely audible over the engine. "I'm in the center of a wilderness of apple trees. Not well tended and manicured, but ancient trees with twisting branches and heavy old apples. The entire ground is littered with them." Her hands twist around the steering wheel, creaking against the leather. "I can't get out. I don't know where you are, any of you, but you're far away from me. I'm trapped and surrounded by them."

Fear is a chip of ice cutting at my throat.

"Dreams," Baldur says, "are sometimes all we have."

We're silent and still as Astrid drives us between two mountains.

There's a solid rock wall to the right of the Spark, and silver-capped rapids just off the left shoulder. I can't be sure, but it seems too rocky and cold here for apples to be plentiful. Then again, these are apples originally from Old Asgard, a world of harsher climes. Astrid hasn't said anything for fifteen minutes as she weaves the car along the highway. I think of what she described, of a choking apple orchard and piles of dead fruit. I want to reach my foot over and hit the brake. Stop all of this from happening, as dread forms a thick shell around me.

"There will be a turnoff soon," she says quietly.

We curve long, and I hear the rush of the rapids, and Astrid says, "There."

She points ahead, to the right, but all I see is the steep slope of the mountain. The trees are not thick enough to be hiding a road.

"There's nothing there," Vider says.

But despite our being alone on the highway, Astrid flips on the turn signal. The heavy clicking fills the car.

"There's nothing there!" Vider says again, digging her fingers into Astrid's shoulder.

"Yes," she says. "There is."

My entire body clenches and I feel the burn of frenzy under my heart. Baldur takes Vider's hand.

The Spark slows. I do not close my eyes. Astrid turns the steering wheel and the bright orange nose of our car is three feet from the side of the mountain when the mountain vanishes.

One moment there is a gray-and-brown wall of stone, the next we are driving down a narrow dirt road. So narrow, in fact, that pine needles scratch the roof and Baldur rushes to roll up his window. There's nothing to see ahead but more trees.

Vider crows in delight. I allow a smile of relief until I notice that Astrid is so pale there are freckles I've never seen before standing out under her eyes. Her breathing is shallow and elf-kisses travel up and down her arms.

"Astrid," I say gently, circling her wrist with my hand, "slow down. I can drive."

"No," she whispers. "We're almost there."

Silence reigns again as Astrid drives down the sun-washed road. Somewhere ahead is the orchard. And before it the berserkers' camp. Soon I will stand on ground where my father walked; soon I may meet men to whom my father was sworn.

And for the first time in my life, berserking and my father are the least of my worries.

The frenzy presses dull spikes against my heart.

From behind Astrid, Baldur reaches up to touch her neck. He grasps one of Vider's braids in his other hand. She in turn hangs her fingers on my shoulder. I put my hand on Astrid's thigh.

We've united ourselves.

I take a long, slow breath, as if I would draw energy up from the strong earth; only now I draw balance from my friends.

There's an old nursery prayer: *May the ties that bind us be strong; may our journey together last through the end of all.* I repeat it to myself, again and again, as we drive toward this end.

The road ends abruptly when the ground cuts away, revealing a resplendent valley so bright with gathered sun I blink and lift a hand to shield my eyes.

Astrid stops the car, and we all leave the Spark to walk to the edge of the cliff.

As in a painting of Old Asgard, everything here is saturated with color, glistening as though each surface is covered in sequins. There's a wild green field within the bowl of cliffs, a waterfall spilling sky into three streams that flow across the valley. Nine buildings gleam white and gray on the far side of the meadow, and three holmgang rings are cut into the grass before them. High overhead, tall pennants snap in the wind.

Most are white with the stylized bear of Odin and a harsh black spear that mirrors the one on my face.

But one pennant rises higher than the others: a white triangle with a broad golden apple shining like its own sun.

Astrid shudders and leans back against me. Her hands come up and find mine. She is hot and trembling.

For just beyond the buildings, where the surrounding cliffs break open into a passageway farther up the mountain, there's a hundred-foot iron fence, and beyond it a million apple trees.

Where we stand, leafless winter trees wait like gray ghosts between the dark evergreens, but there in the orchard, it's already summer.

"There's a path," Vider says, skipping forward on the loose gravel. The path cuts down the cliff face, just wide enough to be considered a road.

I collect my father's sword from the trunk, strap it to my back, and rejoin the others. Baldur gazes longingly at the weapon. But I will keep him safe until we deliver him into the arms of Idun; he doesn't need a sword.

"Come on!" Vider drags at us with her voice, hopping farther down the path.

Astrid follows her, and Baldur and I take up positions behind Astrid, one of us at either shoulder. It strikes me as strange, because we're here for Baldur; he should be the one at point.

The path is steep, and loose rocks and dirt make it unstable. As we follow the narrow switchbacks, I wish I still had my spear. There's no sign of a lookout, and I don't think this way is often used. The berserkers must travel to and from the valley by other means. I pause halfway down and stare out toward the base. The buildings are clustered around a long feast hall with a pair of double doors so bright they reflect the sun. One other building is large and hangar-like, and perhaps hides a heliplane. On the wind I smell burning fat and smoke, and as I near the base of the cliff I hear the low of a cow.

But there's no sign of people.

I catch up, and at the bottom of the cliff we move into the dry, crackling grass. The fields are wild here in the valley. Wind blows through, shaking the evergreens along the mountain-sides, bending them in waves.

"There's no one here," Vider says, falling back to walk with us. And she's right: there is all of this beauty, but it waits empty.

We're a solid line, walking abreast beside one of the thin creeks. As we approach the base, there are more signs of civilization: satellite dishes anchored to several roofs, all aimed in the same direction; electric lights; an ATV parked beside the barracks; a fitness center with attached indoor pool where overhead fans slowly twirl. For this berserk band, no expense has been spared.

At the center of the ring of buildings, we pause and stand before the doors of the feasting hall. They're iron and wood, carved with teeth and claws, and inlaid with glass circles colored like apples and blood.

But there's no one here.

Where are Idun's Bears? Is this how they protect the orchard?

The four of us spread out. I listen as hard as I can, but hear only the sound of my boots on the courtyard stones and Astrid's low humming. I recognize the melody, but not the song.

Vider goes to one of the flagpoles and grips it. She kicks off her shoes, and Baldur gives her a boost. We tilt our heads and watch her climb until she is higher than the roofs, the bear-and-spear pennant whipping just over her hair.

"They're waiting by the orchard gate," she calls down to us, pointing beyond the feast hall.

Astrid says quietly, "They're expecting us." She glances at me with trepidation pinching the corners of her eyes. I think of her apple nightmares, and all her apple dreams. Part of her has known for years that we were coming.

As Vider slides down the pole, Baldur says, "They'll know what we need." He catches her and sets her on her feet. And then he strides away, heading where Vider pointed.

I go after him immediately, staying at his right shoulder. We come around the feast hall and the yard spreads out before us. A hundred steps ahead is the black iron gate to the orchard, and standing between us and the fence are nine warriors.

My breath jerks. Even Baldur pauses.

The men range in age from young and golden to hoary with years. Each one carries a black spear and wears the uniform of a berserk band: black pants, and sleeveless black shirt belted at the waist and open at the neck to reveal an iron collar. The berserkers require no metal armor. Even naked they're powerful. Their tattoos split their cheeks in two, and many have more ink decorating their forearms. Only one, a young man with red-gold braids, smiles welcome. The rest glower, focused not on Baldur or Astrid or Vider, but on me.

They will be my future, if I can't ask Odin to take away my power: to be marked with a band, to commit with them. I fiercely resist the urge to draw my father's sword, and the berserker in the center, with steel-gray braids snaking under his chin and the silver embroidery of a captain, says, "Son of Styrr. We did not know it would be you."

The whisper then goes through their line: "*Sleipnir's Tooth.*"

It's the name of the sheathed sword slung over my back.

I try to quell the shaking that begins in my ribs and grows to fill all my body. These are Idun's Bears, and they serve her. They serve the gods and by extension Baldur, too. No matter what they think of my father and no matter what they think of my uncollared neck, of my sword, they will continue to serve the interests of Idun.

Stepping in front of Baldur, I say, "I am Soren Bearskin, and I have come to deliver my lord to Idun's orchard."

Astrid and Vider press close, and Baldur lifts his face. The sun shines its final rays of golden light before dropping behind the mountains, and he glows.

The captain answers me, "I am Alwulf, son of Robert, and so is your lord delivered." His mouth stretches into a smile, and I begin to relax, to believe they will stand aside and allow the gate to open.

Until he cries, "Hail, Hangatyr!"

I don't know why he would call on Odin then, but all the surrounding berserkers echo his words. Their shout vibrates in my chest, their battle-rage calling to mine with a welcome I've never felt before. It distracts me for a moment too long, and Alwulf has raised and loosed his spear before I understand.

By then it's too late, and the wicked shaft pierces Baldur's heart.

NINETEEN

BALDUR, GOD OF light, falls back with a single cry.

I leap over him, roaring all my shock, and charge for the captain.

For the first time in my life, I reach intentionally for the rage, and I tear it open.

I explode like my own sun.

But these are berserkers, too, and they're prepared. They grab at me, too many of them. Faces everywhere, black collars and hard hands. I scream and throw myself away from them, but cold liquid splashes over my mouth, and the scent—the scent invades me, transforming my muscles into gelatin.

I fall with a single cry.

There is Astrid, body bowed across our god's, blood smearing her dress and painting her neck. She reaches out to me, gripping Baldur's shirt in her other hand, as if she could pull us all together.

It's the last thing I see.

TWENTY

THERE'S A UNIVERSE of time between closing my eyes and opening them.

I lie on a thin mattress in the corner of a barracks room that's been reinforced as a brig. The door's made of iron, with a small slot at the bottom for food and a barred window at eye level. Fluorescent light glares through, displaying the metal lattice that covers the whitewashed walls. The fortifications don't mean a full and strong berserker could be held captive here if he wanted free, but breaking out would cause a lot of noise, and the rest of the band would have plenty of warning.

There's a single window high up in the wall, and beyond it I see only stars.

For one long moment I allow myself the luxury of stillness. My chest feels hollow, as if not only has my frenzy been stripped away, but my lungs and heart and stomach and liver as well.

Baldur.

I clench my jaw and close my eyes. Two tears fall down my temples, scalding my skin.

Everything we thought was wrong. *Baldur is dead. Baldur the Beautiful is dead.*

I'd rather it was me, and I know Astrid will be thinking the same.

Again I see him fall. Again I see the black spear shaft rising out of his chest like a monument.

The world will never be the same.

I shake all over and know, the way I know that the moon will rise, that I will kill Alwuf Robertson, the man who murdered Baldur. My frenzy will consume him; I will bury Sleipnir's Tooth in his heart.

It occurs to me suddenly that just because I am alive doesn't mean Astrid and Vider are, too.

I'm on my feet so fast the ground tips over, and I crash back to the mattress with a yell.

Dizziness swarms my head and I take long breaths. The spinning is akin to my frenzy, only distant, buzzing about my ears and stealing my balance. This is the result of their drugs, not grief. I know grief, and it is a chasm.

Gripping the sides of the mattress, I sit up slowly this time.

And then I stand, because I have to. I plod to the door on heavy feet. My body wavers and I slam into iron lattice, catching myself with my palms.

"Son of Styrr?"

The voice is not one I know, but he speaks in the old wolf tongue berserkers teach their sons. It's only a memory to me, but it echoes with my dad's voice.

A moment later a face appears at the barred window.

Youngish, twenty maybe, with dark green eyes and braids that hold red even in the poor lighting.

The one who smiled.

"Tell me where Astrid and Vider are!" I roar at him in Anglish. I'll not share the little I know of the berserk language with him, or any of them.

The berserker jumps back, his hands up. He's weaponless, and no longer in uniform; instead he wears a half-buttoned Western shirt and jeans.

"Tell me where your captain is, so that I may take his blood for justice."

"Peace!" he says, his hands out. There is no smile now.

I slam my fist into the door. Pain slices up my wrist as my knuckles break open and blood smears. "Not until you answer me!"

"The girls are unharmed. One is in the orchard, the other I don't know where."

I curl one hand around the metal bar and lean back with all my weight.

"I don't know!" he insists.

The door creaks and I shudder with it. It doesn't break. Yet. "Stop!"

"Let me out. Take me to your captain. Now."

The berserker slips closer. "I can't. But I will tell him what you say."

"Tell him he is not a man at heart."

His eyes widen. The fluorescent lights glare back at me

from inside them. "It was no unjust murder, but in the line of our duty. Holmgang is too much blood price!"

"The line of *duty*?" I shake the door again.

"Yes! We are Idun's Bears, we obey her, and she told us: Kill the golden one and lead the seether into the orchard."

"You killed him because she told you to?" My voice cracks. I shake my head and feel tears tearing at my eyes again. A useless sob shoves through my teeth. "I will call holmgang on her, too," I cry. I don't care if she is Idun; it doesn't matter who she is if she caused Baldur's death.

"You loved him," the berserker says.

I suck air in through my teeth. "What is your name?" I wish to know it so that when I kill him, I will do so with the proper words on my tongue.

The berserker lowers his hands. He knows exactly why I'm asking, and draws himself up. His tattoo is just like mine, but stands out harshly against his paler skin. "I am Henry Halson of the Lone Star Henrys. I've known of you for years, Soren Bearskin. I admire this sword of yours, despite your father's stain." His eyes lower to where I guess my sword leans against the wall outside my cell. My palm itches for the soft sharkskin grip.

"You know who I am," I say, forcing out the words. "But do you know who it was your warlord killed?"

"My lady's enemy," he says calmly, softly. I read sorrow but not regret in the curve of his frown.

I will make him regret it. I return his frown with a smile, a teeth-baring sneer as horrible as I can force it. "You murdered Baldur the Beautiful."

"No." Disbelief etches lines around his mouth.

"Yes. *Yes.* Recall the sun on his face, recall the reflection of the sky in his eyes." Tears fall from my own eyes, each one hot with frenzy. "That was Baldur the Beautiful, the god of light, who we were bringing here to receive an apple from Idun."

My heart is breaking against the prison door, and it's all I can do to grip the bars and hold myself on my feet. "You know he was at large in the world."

Henry Halson presses himself into the wall across from my door. He doesn't want to trust me, but he must know I would not invent such a lie. I see the hardened skin under his iron collar, where it's rubbed and rubbed for all his years in the war band. The skin shines in the fluorescent light, standing out as he grows pale. "She ordered us to kill him," he whispers.

"Let me out." I will go after Alwulf, and then find Idun herself and cut her down beneath my sword. Sweat trickles along my brow as I think of my weapon in hand, as the fever embraces me again. The chip of starlight under my heart is burning and hot. I am ready. I want it now; I want to destroy everything around me.

But the berserker Henry Halson is gone.

Closing my eyes, I lean my forehead against the cold bars. I am glad it's dark outside. Any hint of sunlight would burn.

He died without remembering who he was.

I failed so completely.

Turning my back to the door, I slide down to huddle against

it, arms tucked to my chest, knees up. Here is my battle-rage, here is my power, and it is useless to me.

I must get to Astrid. I need to get to her, alone in the orchard, alone with her nightmares. Her grief must be explosive.

Like my fever, which is so near the surface, roaring in my blood. It dances over my skin like candle flames.

I don't know how time passes, as I crouch and shake with the power I no longer wish to hold tight inside. I would rather it rip me apart and escape, tearing down everything in its path. There are no innocents here; there are no people in this valley who are not culpable.

Because Baldur is dead.

Someone asks quietly through the door, "Is it true, Bearskin?"

"Yes," I say, the word practically a growl.

"Baldur—"

"*Yes.*" I pound on the door and hear the thump of running boots.

My hand throbs anew. I cradle it, welcoming the pain as an echo of my heartbeat.

Outside the barracks, light flares. Firelight. I hear a yell, but it isn't angry. More like a summons. They believe me.

I need to see him, to close his eyes and touch the wound in his heart. I want to wrap him in armor and set him onto the pyre. There's no telling what will happen to him now. He died forever once, and it took the entire world weeping to bring him back.

The scrape of the lock brings me to my feet. I peer out through the tiny barred window, but see nothing. Backing away, I tense and wait.

After a moment—too long for a key—the door slowly creaks open.

It's Vider.

In two bounds she's crossed the space and launched into my arms. I catch her, holding her dangling off the ground. Her hands clutch at me and her breath is hot on my neck. There are tears, too, smearing between us. She smells like smoke and hay and cow poop, and I guess she hid in their little barn, probably in the rafters. I hug her until she groans, and when I put her down she draws a huge breath but doesn't let go of my wrists. Her eyes are pale green moons, round in her narrow face, and all her hair floats around her head. I step back and eye her up and down. She appears whole and well.

"They didn't hurt you?" she whispers.

"No." I touch the bruise on her cheek left over from her night with the trolls.

Vider ducks her head. "I ran, when they—when they killed him. I'm no good to fight, and they were taking Astrid to the gate. I slipped out between two of them and heard their captain yell not to chase me. That I didn't matter." She thrusts up her chin. "Don't matter? Well." Her hand reaches out and she twists her fingers into my T-shirt. "This'll show them."

I put my hand over hers. "It will. You did the right thing. Your strength is in"—I glance at the open door—"sneaking."

"They're all gathered in the field now, arguing about something. Astrid hasn't left the orchard gate, though she's on the other side of it. I could pick that lock, too, but they'd see."

"No. They'll let me in to her." I take Vider's hand and exit my prison. The fluorescent light tightens my eyes, but I see my sword leaning against the wall. I swing the sheath over my shoulder, but free the sword. The runes etched into the cross-guard shine, and Sleipnir seems to wink at me.

"How, Soren?" Vider asks as she trails me. "How do you know?"

"Because they're berserkers, and I'm a berserker. And I know how to make them."

We leave the barracks unseen, which is easy because Idun's Bears are gathered in a circle of torches between the village and the iron gate. I stop beside the feast hall and count all nine figures moving through the darkness and flames.

And there is Baldur laid out nearby.

They've given him a white blanket to lie upon and a clean shirt to wear. The blood has been washed from him, his golden hair braided, and the spear that killed him laid beside his hand. I stare at his shape, wishing to convince myself he only sleeps because the sun shines on the other face of the planet. But his chest does not rise or fall, and no nightmares turn beneath his eyelids.

I look at Alwulf, their captain, who threw the fatal spear.

He will die by my hand. I curl my fingers tighter around the grip of my sword.

"Vider," I whisper.

She leans in.

"I'm going to kill him."

"I will hold your shields," she answers immediately, her fist pressing between her breasts.

"No."

Her quick look of betrayal and surprise has me taking her elbow. "Stay hidden, and no matter what happens to me, you keep yourself free of them so you can tell the world."

Her fingers pinch into my arm. "Let me help you."

"Help me by staying hidden. Promise me."

Her lips purse as if she's sucked sour candy.

"Promise." I bend so that our eyes are level. I hold out my arm to her, hand open to shake.

Her eyelids flutter and there's a glint of tears, but Vider clasps my wrist and shakes once. "I promise, Soren. Take this."

A round, hard stone is suddenly between our hands. I uncurl my fingers and the troll's eyeball is there. In the dark, Vider's silver hair is ghostly, and I think about how brave she was to walk into the troll house alone. And now the prize she claimed is a charm she offers to me to take into battle. "I will spill his blood onto this," I say.

Quick as lightning, Vider kisses me. Her lips press mine, and then she flits away. I cannot see her path through the darkness.

Sword in hand, I walk with measured pace toward the gathered berserkers. Some still wear their uniforms, but most have changed into casual clothes, likely believing their part was complete. I scan their faces and hair for the red-gold gleam of Henry Halson. He's there across from his captain, fidgeting with the end of one braid. I'm pleased to see the upset pinching his face.

And there is the man Alwulf, who killed Baldur.

I stand in the darkness at the edge of the torch circle, and stare at him. He glowers around at his men, and I know from a place deep inside me, even farther down than the home of my frenzy, that this choice is irreversible.

If I challenge him to holmgang, berserker to berserker, I will die or I will kill him, and in doing so become everything Odin could want. Berserkers are meant to fight and kill and die.

It doesn't matter anymore that I won't have a chance to ask a boon of Odin, because we failed to deliver his son. After this, I couldn't ask for the frenzy to be taken away. It will be mine. With this act I am about to perform, I will ground it into everything that I am. I'll become the bear, to avenge my fallen lord, and to accept what Astrid has always told me: my power is a dance. I am its partner, not its slave.

Just then Alwulf says in a hard voice, "It doesn't matter who or why, but only that we obeyed our lady."

I want to yell how much it mattered. I want to drive my sword through his chest right now.

Instead I plant my feet and yell his name: "Alwulf Robertson!"

The band turns to me as one, surprise and wariness marking their postures.

"Well," Alwulf says, striding toward me. "You're free, Styrrson, and your sword hungry for blood."

"I want Astrid, now."

"She's there, boy." He swings his hand out, gesturing through and behind the warrior band.

The iron gate slashes in black streaks between me and the silver-green apple orchard. All is gray and shadowed, but I see her standing. Her white hands curl around two bars and she watches me from eyes like gaping holes. Her hair spills free and she's lost her cardigan, shivering cold in only a pale violet sundress. Surrounded by apples.

"Let her out."

There's a rumble from the warriors around me because I order their leader, but thanks I am sure to my news of Baldur's death, they don't immediately stand behind him.

Alwulf laughs, and his gray braids tremble with it. "You are a fool. She's where she belongs, delivered into the orchard as our lady commands." To his warriors he says, "Take him back to his cell."

Several move to obey, and I lift my father's sword. Calm settles over my shoulders. I aim the point of the sword at Alwulf and say, "You are not a man's equal, and not a man at heart."

Silence falls.

Even Alwulf is taken aback. His cragged face slides into

surprise, but it only takes a second for him to snap out the response: "I am as much a man as you."

I push the words out from deep within me: "Meet me, then, Alwulf Robertson, for my right to blood price for my fallen lord."

He barks a laugh. "To settle this the berserkers' way," he says, "there is only death to choose."

It is good, for I would not have let him walk away.

His eyes slide down my sword. "And I look forward to battling against Styrr's blade."

"So be it," I say, my voice quieter than I'd have liked.

The words are echoed by all the warriors in the circle. *"So be it."*

The holmgang is set for one hour later, at midnight. A berserker with short hair like mine suggests waiting for dawn, but I tell him I'd rather cut Alwulf down where he stands than wait for the sun. Alwulf says he'll humor my eagerness, since we all know how lack of control runs in my family.

It takes every ounce of will and knowing Astrid watches from the orchard gate to prove him wrong and walk away.

Henry Halson appears before me and offers to hold my shields. I grind my teeth and look toward where Astrid stands as still as a statue. "Yes," I say to him, and he leads me into the fitness center where I can borrow his holmgang pants and take time to stretch. The garish white light makes my head throb, and we use the locker room between the weights and pool as a place for me to change. It smells of chlorine and wet shoes, and the concrete is rough under my bare feet.

"May I?" Henry asks, his hand hovering over my sword as I strip. I pause with my T-shirt balled in my hand and study his expression. It's clear and slightly deferential. I nod and he whips the blade free with a relish that reminds me of Baldur.

I turn away as I remove my jeans, not from modesty, but to hide the sorrow I find impossible to keep off my face. The troll eye gets tucked into the toe of my discarded boot.

"This is an amazing weapon," he says in the wolf tongue.

When I've tied on the thin holmgang pants, I look back, searching my memory for the right words of response. It's been too many years since I've spoken like a berserker. Pirro rarely bothered, for it's meant as a way to let us communicate war plans and secrets. Just another thing to set berserkers apart.

But I turn to find Henry balancing my sword like a circus performer, with the pommel in his palm and the tip straight up. It barely wavers and he adjusts his arm only minutely to accommodate.

"That's how you judge?" I say in Anglish, low and threatening, thinking of all the death this sword has seen.

With a flick of his wrist, he's got it held properly by the grip, and I barely saw the motion. He smiles as if he can't help it. "I can feel its . . . flavor and poise."

I only stare until he flips it around and offers me the hilt. As I take it, he says, "Thank you. I've wanted to hold it since I was twelve."

"Why?"

"I came here to replace your dad."

"What?" I sit on the long bench between rows of lockers. We have a few minutes.

Henry straddles the same bench several paces off from me. "After he was made *wulfheart,* the Bears were down a man. I had just come into my power and so was directed here from Tejas."

I realize I'm shaking my head. *Wulfheart* means Dad wasn't reassigned or released—he broke commit.

"You didn't know?" Henry frowns. "I'm sorry. I assumed..."

"I was only a kid. They didn't tell me."

He pulls a grimace. "And you haven't joined a band, so who would have since then? I see."

There are jagged pieces of confusion trying to connect in my mind, but I can't fit them together. "How is it possible?" I say. "You can't be that much older than me. When he left to commit with my mom, that was over eighteen years ago."

"Oh, no." Henry puts his hands on his knees as if he's holding himself back. "He was a Bear until that summer, only nine years ago, just before he killed all those people."

"No."

He only nods.

"Why, then?" I ask. "Why was he cast out if it wasn't for leaving to be with my mom?"

"Idun ordered that he return. That he leave his family and his wandering ways and return to the valley to be her captain." Henry's eyes flick down, and he's tugging the end of his braid again. I want to swipe with my sword and hack the braid off so that he stops revealing his nerves. "Your father refused to leave you. And Alwulf, who was Idun's second choice for captain, banished him for denying her."

I think of my dad the way I've seen him most recently: dead, with coals for eyes. He chose us over his goddess.

"It's why Alwulf won't back down about—about Baldur," Henry rushes on. "When we learned who it was he killed, the rest of us, or most of the rest of us, wanted to call the Alfather here, to ask him to come. But Alwulf ruined your father for not obeying Idun, and so he will only say, 'This is the will of Idun, and we do not thwart her will.'"

I can barely breathe, and cannot speak. Air rushes harsh and hard in and out of me. I should be glad I've been hollowed out already tonight, so this information can't bowl me over.

Henry shakes his head. "But if it—if he was Baldur—that cannot be the will of the gods. He—" He steps over the bench and grasps my shoulders. "Alwulf is my captain, but Baldur is—was—my god. The son of my Lord God." His fingers tremble and press into my bare skin. "We're berserkers, but we're not mindless the way others say we are. This is too complicated for unthinking obedience." A laugh shakes out of him.

I grip his hands, grateful for his grief. Here, maybe, is a berserker I could someday fight beside.

He says, "What else does Odin teach us but never to be blind to consequences, Soren?"

Consequences. Another word for the threads of fate. The reason I'm here, to claim blood price for Baldur, and maybe— maybe to avenge the wrongs Alwulf did to my father.

Slowly I nod, and he tells me, "Alwulf wants to kill you."

"I want to kill him, too." In my sword I see the reflection of my tattoo, and I grip the hilt tighter. I look up at Henry, at his same tattoo, and I say, "One of us will get our wish."

Dressed in only the loose black pants, and with my father's sword sheathed again on my bare back, I walk across the cold, dark grass to the orchard gate.

As I approach, Astrid pries her hands off the bars and reaches out, pressing her body into the gate so that I can clasp her fingers as soon as possible. They're like frozen sticks and she winces as I squeeze them. She shivers in her thin dress and slippers. I wish I had a jacket to offer her.

We say nothing for a long moment, then I step forward to wrap her in my arms as best I can with the iron rods of the gate keeping us apart. My Astrid. I whisper to her that Vider is safe, that I'll get her out, that I'm so sorry. I'm so sorry I didn't protect him the way I promised. She trembles in the cold, pressing into my fever. I stare beyond her into the orchard. The trees are thick and tangled, not laid out in rows but growing haphazardly and wild in their unnatural summer. Thick branches with bright green leaves twine together so that under them it's blacker than a cave.

"Soren," she whispers.

I cup the back of her head in my hand, cradling her face against my neck. "Astrid."

"It isn't your fault."

I'm silent.

"We're here for a hundred reasons. I can feel them piling up on top of me."

"I know."

"It was meant to be."

My arms go rigid around her.

"It has to be fate." There is a question in her voice, something I've never heard before.

Astrid Glyn, with wavering faith.

"But, Soren," she says, "every time I think of him, a new cut slashes inside. I don't know how this could ever be right."

I twist my fingers into the bottom of her curls. "I'll start by killing Alwulf Robertson."

Astrid tilts her face up and the moonlight spreads silver into her hair and eyes. I could almost imagine she mirrors the night sky the way Baldur mirrored the sun. That's who they are to me: my sun and my moon.

She says, "I never wanted you to have to kill."

"It's what I am."

"But not who you've wanted to be."

"It doesn't matter now. For Baldur I will do this, and for you."

"Soren."

I wait. Her eyes dart everywhere. Up at the stars, to the iron gate between us, to my eyes, to my mouth. "Soren, I dreamed last night that it was you I resurrected. You were dead but I needed you so much I brought you back."

"Oh." The single syllable is a world of realization. We both thought the other would die tonight. We both were so wrong, and now there is guilt weighing on top of our sorrow.

She says, "I'm afraid. I can't lose both of you."

"You won't."

"Their captain is strong and knows his frenzy so much better than you yours."

I say, "But he does not have you," and I kiss her through the orchard gate.

It's a kiss I have longed to take. A kiss that gently tugs at Astrid's seething power, at the wildness inside both of us. It's sweet and feels like a confession: I love her. Knowing that, I can temper my own frenzy; I can see all the sides of it. I sense it whirling, the form it takes and the way it clings to my bones.

Astrid whispers against my mouth, "Make it fast."

I smile, recalling the holmgang in Bassett, Nebrasge, where I spoke those same words to her. May this one go as much in our favor as that.

The berserkers call me with pounding shields to return to the circle of torches. I avoid staring at Baldur's body, and instead look toward the shadows of the buildings ahead. I know I won't see Vider; she'll be too good at hiding for that. But it's better than looking at the grayness on his cheeks.

When this is over, if I live, I'll see him. I'll approach him with news that his blood price, at least, is paid.

Alwulf waits as nearly naked as I, with two berserkers at his shoulders. One is as old as he, the other in his prime. Each holds a set of circle shields. Hawthorn poles have been erected to mark the quarters. In the torchlight everything is riddled with shadows and orange stripes.

The remaining four berserkers stand at the corners, and two step closer to Henry and me as we reach the edge of the torch circle.

"Who challenges?" calls the last berserker, who remains evenly placed between Alwulf and me.

"I do," I say. "I am Soren Bearskin, son of Styrr, son of Jul, and brother of Baldur the Beautiful, the god of light."

There are murmurs at his name, and even Henry is surprised: they expected me to say I was a son of Odin.

The berserker directly across from the first speaker, who resembles him too much to be anything but a brother, says, "And who answers the challenge?"

Alwulf stands forward. The sword in his hand catches firelight and throws it at me. Scars hook down his chest in a pattern of thorns, and his left shoulder is covered in mottled burn marks. "I am Alwulf Goodspear, son of Robert, son of Jerome. All of us sons of Odin, the god of madness."

Madness. Only another name for the battle-rage. I take deep breaths, pulling energy from the ground, and imagine it spilling down from the stars overhead. My bare feet are planted. I am the mountain, between the earth and the sky.

As Henry offers me my first shield, he puts his hand in the center of my back, and touches my frenzy. I shudder and lean into his hand as the connection snaps alive between us.

"Use it, Soren Bearskin," he whispers. "All of us will be with you, and all of us will be with him. So it is when berserkers battle in the ring. It is not only a battle of skill, but of power."

All our frenzies unite in a lightning web. I feel them individually: Henry, his rage so full of joy; the brothers, who push and pull like the moon and the tide; one who is hollow with fear; one with a center of peace; one and then another whose powers divide themselves again and again as they struggle between me and their warlord. One who grieves. And finally Alwulf, alive with strength and desperation.

Is he afraid of me?

I hold my sword aloft and yell.

All of them join me, in a growing roar, and I look beyond to Astrid, distant and small. She watches through the iron gate, one hand in constant motion as she draws a rune again and again in the air. The same one my dead father drew.

And then the berserkers yell *"Hear!"* and I leap into the holmgang ring.

When I battled Baldur, it was a dance. I held back; I tried to fight him with only skill and muscles.

This is different. I reach in and unlock that iron star.

Power rips through me, but I am a vessel for it, created to channel every bit of it, created to burn and exist.

It moves with me—I move with it—and when Alwulf and

I come together we explode. Our swords clash, ringing through my bones. I swing again and he blocks, both of us roaring, because we cannot hold in the energy.

I focus through it, drawing it with me as I draw my sword. As I draw my arms and legs, as I know the motions of the dance, the rhythm of attack and defend, the jar of swords and the pain of sudden bruises. His blade cuts against my ribs and the heat of blood only gathers more power to me. I knock him back with my shield, and we catch together, chests heaving, blood and sweat in our eyes. He's tied back his long braids but the iron collar marks his neck.

We fight, and we fight. All around the holmgang ring. My shield cracks in two, but we do not stop for a new one. Alwulf throws his away, and we meet again, swords ringing together like bells.

This dance is hard and pounding, and the weight of an entire berserk band's frenzy presses at me. My body is clear, though, and my every motion sharp. I'm certain of my rightness, that this battle is mine to be won. He killed my lord. He destroyed my father. He imprisoned Astrid. All these are his crimes, and I am here to cleave them away, to set his blood free into the ground and release him, release myself of the responsibility. That is the blood price.

My frenzy is Odin's hand, his own madness inhabiting me, guiding my sword. I bare my teeth as I fight, and my vision darkens. I am dizzy and burning and so near to losing my hold on what is happening.

The frenzy pushes at me, and I let go.

It courses through me in a rush again, sudden and fast, and I'm a tunnel for it. My ears go deaf from the roar of a hundred furious screams, and Alwulf falters.

The frenzy is mine.

I dive at him, knocking his sword away with my hand—my bare hand—and he falls back. I'm on top of him, a knee on his chest, the point of my sword pressing into his throat.

My arm shakes. Alwulf's eyes roll wildly and blood trickles from the corner of his mouth.

All I have to do is press in.

I remember Baldur standing over me, ready. The tip of my spear pressing into my neck. I remember how his head blocked the sun and the sky behind him raged with light. *Now, Soren Bearskin, are you ready to take me wherever I need to go?*

And I remember how calm he was despite the hard breathing and sweat of the moment. He patiently waited for me to say *I am ready, Prince. Under the sun, and to the edges of the world.*

Then he let me up.

That holmgang ended in mercy—a thing Odin does not believe in.

But I am not sworn to the god of madness.

Tears blur my sight and one drops hot and hard onto Alwulf's chest.

Closing my eyes, I close my heart, too, and the frenzy fades. Because I wished it to, because it is my tool. I am not its slave.

I stand up, taking my sword.

"New shield?" Henry calls, voice wavering with uncertainty.

Staring down at the captain, I say, "No. This is over. I serve the god of light; your life, Alwulf, the rest of the years, is a gift."

He grimaces, tries to sit, but can't. I've defeated him. Henry Halson says, "So be it."

"*So be it,*" the rest acknowledge, in scattered voices, repeating it one or two at a time until, finally, the three words rasp from Alwulf's own lips.

. Shakily, I go to where Baldur's body rests. I stare down at the pale gold of him, dull under the night sky, and lifeless as a doll. Down on one knee, I touch my hand over his heart, feeling the loss of him hollowing me out again.

Cold wind blows off the mountains, smelling of snow and evergreens. "I am your man," I say to his lifeless face. "There may be the wild frenzy inside, but I am not a killer. Astrid knew. You knew. I am berserk, but can choose what that means. I serve the sun, and that—" My voice thickens too much for talking. I want to lie down beside him, to remain here all throughout the night and, when the dawn arrives, myself light the fire that will consume him.

"That," I whisper, "means hope and life and love. Those things you forgot, but still were."

My hand warms the skin over his heart, and for a moment I can almost imagine it will beat again.

But he is dead, his murderer defeated. And I am not finished.

Astrid is in the orchard, and so awaits Idun, the lady who ordered Baldur killed.

As I move toward the gate, Henry and two others approach.

One is the older man who stood at Alwulf's side, the other the berserker in whose frenzy I sensed so much sadness. Both of them blond and blue-eyed as berserkers should be.

Henry says, "Take this, for it will get colder before the sun rises."

The older berserker holds out a coat of bearskin, and the sad one offers a cloak trimmed in fur.

"Thank you." I put the coat on over my bare, bloody chest. It's heavy and warm. Henry hands me my boots. I remove Vider's troll eye from the toe and tuck it into the coat pocket. As I tie up my boots I say, "Wait for me." I cannot add *before you burn Baldur,* but they know.

I throw the cloak over my arm for Astrid, and walk to the orchard gate.

TWENTY-ONE

THE HEAVY BLACK lock opens easily, and I step onto the orchard ground. Berserkers swing the gate shut behind me. The moment I'm trapped, I sense tranquility in the air itself: I've walked onto hallowed land.

Astrid appears, and I open my coat. She slips in against my bare chest, uncaring that I have been bloodied so recently. I wrap the cloak about both of us, and we breathe in slow unison, heating all the crevices and shadows between us.

As she thaws, tears gently fall from her closed eyes, as if her sorrow was ice and now it melts in the heat of my bitter victory.

All around us are the whisper of wind through leaves, the quiet creak of branches, and the crackle of fire as the berserkers outside light more and more torches to place along the fence. The glow will guide us into the deep darkness that is Idun's orchard.

Finally, Astrid opens her eyes and says, "That was well done, Soren. He would be proud, and I am honored." She wipes the tears from her cheeks.

I go onto my knees and kiss both of her hands. "I want you to come out of here with me, but you can't, can you?"

Astrid tugs the cloak closed around her shoulders. She turns and looks into the trees. "This is what I have dreamed."

"I know."

"For years."

"For your whole life," I say, thinking of how my father was here before I was born, how this orchard is the cradle for all the threads linking us to the past.

"It's been pulling at me," she says. "But I would not go without you."

I put my hand on her shoulder and squeeze. "As it should be, Astrid Jennasdottir."

Together we walk between the trees.

It's not long before we leave the torches behind, and the only light we have filters silver and pale from the moon. It's barely enough, but Astrid knows the way. Her fingers curl around mine and I move beside her, a strong shadow. Our feet make sharp snaps against the cold orchard ground.

The trees are ancient ones, their thick limbs heavy with leaves but mostly bare of fruit. Here and there a round apple shines, out of season, and colored unnaturally bright in the moonlight. But there are no more than a handful of apples for every tree. Fruit and leaves have blanketed the ground, though we walk along a clear path through the low-hanging, looming branches. It's quiet; even breezes do not penetrate the thickness here. I think once or twice that something watches us, paces us through the wild apples.

It isn't long before weariness creeps into me. I've exploded with frenzy, fought for my life, lost a friend. All I wish to do is curl up in the roots of a tree and sleep for several days.

I doubt we've walked more than a half kilometer yet into the antique orchard when a clearing appears through the branches.

Moonlight streams in, and onto a slender figure in a white cloak. A cat perches delicately on her shoulder. She stands before a small golden tree, no taller than me, but hung with tiny, wizened apples. A half dozen would fit easily into my palm, and they're every shade of gold.

I free my sword and say, "Idun."

But the lady draws back her hood to look at Astrid, and Astrid says, "*Mom.*"

My arm falters as Astrid rushes forward and Idun spreads her hands to welcome her daughter into an embrace. The cat leaps away, making room. They hold each other tight, and Astrid is shaking. Idun, known before as Jenna Glyn, closes her eyes, and I can see the finality, the penance, marked across her face as she hugs her daughter.

I wait outside their embrace, hanging back with my sword point hovering just over the earth. All I can think is: *Astrid's mother is alive, and she had Baldur killed.*

Astrid leans away and puts her hands on her mother's face, peering into it. "You haven't changed," she whispers, but Jenna says, "Oh, my little cat, you have. You have. Everything has changed."

"What have you done?" I ask, stepping forward. I wish to tear Astrid away, to impose myself between.

"Soren." Astrid reaches for my hand and for her mother's, and she connects us. "Soren, this is my mother, Jenna Glyn. Mom, this is Soren, my . . ." She blinks and shakes her head before saying, ". . . my everything."

Jenna's eyes widen in horror, and I don't mind because I dislike her, too. Vehemently. She is like an older, harder version of Astrid, with the same thick licorice curls, the same eyes that hold the moonlight like bottle glass, the same lips and cheeks, as if nothing of Astrid's father found its way into Astrid.

Except, perhaps, honor. For this woman had Baldur killed.

"Oh, Astrid," she breathes, her mouth trembling as she stares at me, as if I am news she has dreaded for a hundred years.

"What's wrong, Mom?" Astrid is smiling. "Sweet swans! I've found you here; I've always been meant to. I knew you weren't dead!" A laugh pours out of her, like bubbles in sparkling mead. "Mom! I can't believe it—you're Idun . . . but you're human. You're mortal, aren't you?"

"Yes. I am. But it is always a woman—or a girl—who guards the apples. True youth burns only in one who will someday die. The apples grow brightest when tended by one who is young, but will be so only for a time." Jenna's eyes close again, and she takes her hand away from Astrid, to press against her own chest.

I say, "Remember what the berserkers were ordered: 'Kill the golden one and lead the seether into the orchard.'"

There is a moment of fraught silence as Astrid remembers. I see the image of Baldur's broken self flash in Astrid's eyes, and I see her face fall to pieces. It cuts at me, because I made her remember, I wouldn't even let her have five minutes of happiness with her rediscovered mother.

"You left me to become the Lady of Apples," Astrid whispers. "You're Idun."

Jenna lifts one hand to gently cup a wrinkled apple of immortality that dangles near her from the small golden tree. "I am."

Astrid puts one foot forward. "And you told the Bears to kill Baldur."

"I did," she admits, her voice hushed and sorry. Not at all what I expected. She should not regret it; she should be triumphant. I grip my sword tightly and go to Astrid's side. I take her hand and weave our fingers together. "This was your mother, Astrid, but is no longer."

My cruel words cause Jenna's eyes to shut again, and tears plop onto Astrid's cheeks.

"Listen, Astrid, child of the Feather-Flying Goddess," Idun the Youthful murmurs, opening her eyes and pinning her daughter to the darkness of the grove. "And listen, Soren Bear-star, child of Odin and brother to his son. Listen to the story of Jenna Glyn, called Freyasdottir, called Seether of All Dreams. I will tell you what became of her, if you will listen."

She pulls back from us and kneels on the soft grass growing between the roots of the apple tree.

Astrid tugs my hand. My sword arm trembles, but she

caresses my knuckles, my wrist, her fingers flickering under the cuff of the bearskin coat. "Soren," she whispers.

I sheathe my sword. When Astrid turns to face Idun again, I wrap my arms around her from behind, making myself into a shell for her. Into support and anything else she might need. Both of us look to her mother.

"Once, many years ago," Idun begins in a voice of memories, a voice both lighter and more dreaming than Astrid's, "there was a seethkona who devoted all her life and energy to her lady, Freya, Queen of Hel. She traveled with her brother, with a parade of friends and followers, around New Asgard to tell the fortunes and read the bones of all with the courage to ask. Such was her fidelity to Freya that when she saw in her own fate the face of a daughter the goddess longed to see born, this seethkona did not hesitate to get herself with child."

Within my arms, Astrid is still. She stares at her mother's mouth, and I wish I could reach out and snatch the words before they find their way to Astrid's ears.

"Although her brother and friends and followers all wished to know the name of the father, the seethkona would only admit that he was beautiful and kind and filled with magic. When the girl was born, the seethkona and her daughter traveled the country together, with joy and promise, with all the magic to be found in this Middle World. The seethkona taught her daughter to see power, to dance the wild dance of fate, to carve bones and listen to the song of the past. In her daughter the seethkona saw the entire world of happiness made into flesh."

Idun's telling falters, and she tilts her face up toward the sky, as if she might find the tale's thread woven in the stars. For a single moment, a twinge of sympathy touches me. Astrid sighs.

The cat slinks into Idun's lap, butting its head up into her fist until Idun relaxes her fingers and continues, with the cat's purr as undertone. "For twelve years they were content, and more than content, until one night in the most barren place on the prairie, the seethkona woke to hear a low call. She reached out with her skillful fingers and plucked the strand of magic out of the sky. It was a summons, and because she was versed in the language of the gods, the seethkona heard it, though it was never intended for her ears. It was a call for her daughter, from a distant orchard where the apples yearned for a new lady, for youth and brightness and all the wild power a girl of such heart and strength could offer."

Now I know where Astrid learned to tell a story—I am so caught up in the words that it isn't until Astrid stiffens against me, until her sharp gasp snaps me into the moment, that I realize exactly what her mother is telling us.

Idun leans forward and says, "But the seethkona snared the call in a net of magic. She would not let her daughter go. She would not have her child of magic forgotten by the world, plucked from the strands of fate as if she'd never been, to serve in isolation. And so she kissed her little girl good night and vanished into the desert." Idun sighs, her eyes alive with need. "She followed the thread of the call into the mountains and through the orchard, to where her goddess Freya waited beneath a small and golden apple tree. 'Where is the girl we have called?' Freya demanded, blazing with a darkness from beyond the stars. The seethkona dropped to her knees and said, 'All things you have asked of me, I have given. But my daughter is only a child; she has not lived, has not loved. I beg you, let me serve in her place.'"

Astrid turns her face into my shoulder, and one of her hands slides under my coat. Her fingers dig into my ribs where blood has crusted, and I welcome the fresh jolt of pain. It reminds me of all we've been through tonight.

Idun continues her story: "The goddess was tempted to dismiss her seethkona's plea outright, but Freya is never one to lose an opportunity, and so she cast another spell. A spell to show her all the possibilities of the world, all the changes and fates that spun out from this single moment of choice. After studying the weave, she struck a bargain with the seethkona. 'You shall guard the apples in your daughter's stead for a handful of years, so that she may live and love. But there will come a day when a light will disappear from the world, and you will know your time is ending. You will peer into a cup of visions and see what you must do for me.'" Idun sighs again, and her lips stretch into a flat line that is almost a smile and almost a grimace. "Because she was desperate and willing, the seethkona agreed without thinking. She agreed out of loyalty to her goddess. She agreed for love of her daughter, and Jenna Glyn died. She became Idun. Me."

"You should have told me!" Astrid cries, shoving off my

chest and at her mother. She lands on her hands and knees, the cloak weighing her shoulders down. Her head hangs. "I would have loved you all the more. But now . . . now . . ."

"I could not, little cat." Idun takes Astrid's face in her hands and raises it. "To become truly Idun is to step out of Easte, to be forgotten. To have your human destiny pulled out of the weave of the world. You will no longer exist in the hearts of men."

Denial scalds my throat. "No one has forgotten you," I say forcefully. "There are memorials and—and television specials."

She lifts her gaze to mine. "I am sorry, young man. It is a tradition the lords and ladies of Asgard firmly hold, so that no one will know with any certainty who Idun is. To protect the apples. So Freya created for Jenna Glyn a seeming death, in order that no one might suspect what she had become. Who I have become."

"Astrid knew," I whisper.

"She needed a mother. She needed those memories of me, and so did the world, to make her who she is. And she believed I lived because she has always had faith as strong as a mountain. Because she is not wholly of the Middle World. She has always been destined to be Idun. She could not forget me; she needed to yearn for me and needed to hunt for me in order to play her role in Baldur's disappearance. That is the only reason the name of Jenna Glyn lived on, though to the world she had died. So that Astrid would seek out Baldur. But, Soren, when my daughter steps into her new role, you will forget her."

The thought of it does the one thing I have been unable to

do for myself: it makes me cold. The fever freezes in my blood and my ribs become a cage of ice. To lose Astrid is to lose everything I've become, everything I've learned to love. She changed me, showed me how to find strength in what I feared. Without her I would not have known Baldur or hope. I would still be a boy carrying the weight of my father's crimes around my neck. If I forget her, will I forget all of it? Not only my Astrid, but Baldur and Vider and the faith and strength I've chosen to wrap around my shoulders?

I would rather die. I would rather fight all the universe.

It cannot happen.

"No." I take Astrid's arm and drag her to her feet. "It will not happen."

Idun begins to speak, but Astrid puts her back against my chest. "Soren will not bend, Mom. He will stand in the way of fate until fate bends around him."

I grip her shoulders, relieved and afraid in equal measure. Idun watches, her pale eyes flicking back and forth between our faces, and she murmurs, "It was not supposed to be like this. I did not see it all."

Before Astrid or I can respond, the cat suddenly arches its back and leaps up into the apple tree, scrambling into the closest of the ancient branches. Although it disappears into the darkness, all three of us track its shadow, searching for sign of what startled it.

We don't wait long.

Out of the thick branches tumbles a person, her silver hair catching and tearing on the twigs. She lands hard and grunts, putting her hands to her head where a small trickle of blood sprouts like a tendril of grass.

"Vider." I release Astrid and crouch, just as the cat bounds down, too, and puts its front paws on Vider's chest.

Vider coughs and groans, but her eyes fly open, bright and startled. "Sorry!" she gasps. "But I *was* hiding!"

Behind me, Astrid makes a noise that's half a laugh, half a sob. She touches my shoulder and then reaches over to offer Vider a hand. Vider takes it, and with our help she slowly gets to her feet. We are three standing before Idun, where we should have been four. I don't have it in me to be angry that Vider broke into the orchard and followed us. I am glad for her hand in mine.

Idun takes us in, looking closely at our faces, her daughter's last of all. "There are many who love you. Whom you love."

"Yes," Astrid says, passion slurring the word.

"It wasn't supposed to be this complicated, little cat. I didn't see any but you and Baldur. It was only meant to be you and Baldur."

A new voice, low with authority, says, "I knew. I saw."

Where the cat was rises a lady. Her skin ripples as the fur disappears, and she stands before us with eyes the color of storm clouds and hair the color of rain. As I watch, half of her face darkens into blackness, the skin there tightening to fit against her skull until she appears half-dead.

Astrid and her mother, Idun, fall to their knees.

It is Freya herself, Queen of Hel and mother of all magic.

Vider shakes and slowly goes down, and I—I feel nothing. It is dangerous and crazy, but I stand.

She glides toward me, her closeness a pressure in my inner ear. "Soren, called new Bearstar, son of Styrr who lies well in my deathbed, self-sworn brother of Baldur the Beautiful. Will you not kneel?"

Her beauty is frightening, not like the overwhelming sunlight of Baldur, but insidious and creeping into my imagination so that no matter how long I stare, it is never the same shade of half-perfection. I bow my head and lower myself onto one knee. "Dark Lady," I say, surprised my voice is as firm as it is.

For the briefest moment her fingers skim down my tattooed cheek, and I am a thousand kilometers into the sky, surrounded by stars and the bright cold of death. My frenzy bursts into life and she draws it through her fingertips. I shake and shudder, but her lips against my ear whisper a song that brings me back into myself, into the apple grove.

Even in such a moment, my strongest thought is for Astrid. "Lady, please," I say, "if Astrid is to be Idun, can you not give her the same seeming death you gave to her mother? Let us not forget her, and still make it impossible for the world to guess what has become of her?"

The goddess with two faces puts both of her hands on my cheeks. Cold spins down over my skin, locking my bones. But there is sympathy in the turn of her lips. "Bearstar, no. Many exceptions were made for this already. Jenna-become-Idun could never leave the valley, for she would be recognized even in death. And so for five long years our apple ritual has been missing its linchpin, and my fellow gods agreed to humor my manipulations for only so long."

"I don't understand why you did it, then," I whisper. "Will you tell us what future you're trying to bring about?"

Her fingers slide down my face. "I serve fate, Soren Bear-star, not my own needs. And yet here"—she gestures gracefully toward Jenna Glyn—"here is a woman who served me well and faithfully, with love. If I could give her the desire of her heart for a few small years, is it so difficult to believe that I would not? Have you no faith at all in the love of your gods?"

"What of the desires of *my* heart?" My voice makes me sound like a child again.

"Your heart is not mine to attend, berserker."

All the words in the world seem empty.

"Freya."

It's Vider. She kneels with her hands clasped, her head down so that all her white-blond hair falls over her face.

The goddess moves to Vider, and my entire body sways at the relief. Freya sets one hand on Vider's head. "Daughter of Loki. I know what you wish to say."

She plucks a hair, making Vider wince. Then Freya blows on the strand, transforming it into a tiny silver sparrow. With a toss, she launches the bird into the night sky. It soars upward, disappearing almost instantly. "Go on," she says.

Biting her lip, Vider gets to her feet. She glances at me but lowers her eyes fast, then looks at Astrid, who has not risen from her knees. Vider heaves a breath and tells Idun, "I'm available."

"No," says Astrid immediately. And Idun's mouth opens slightly. She watches Vider with admiration.

"No one will miss me," Vider retorts, digging her fingers into her hips and again glancing swiftly and briefly at me. "Not, at least, like you'll be missed, Astrid."

"Vider!" I grab her wrist, thinking of how quickly she sacrificed herself to the trolls, how easily she'll give herself up from the world now. "You aren't worthless! None of us is staying here."

Astrid remains kneeling, and says to Freya, "It is not so easy as refusing, is it?"

"No, wise girl." Freya kneels before Astrid and holds out her hands. It reminds me of my mother, of how we would gently touch hands to show we weren't angry. "It is not so easy as refusal. You are Idun. There is no other path for you."

I lash forward, but Freya slams her hand into my chest, halting me before I can push between her and Astrid. I cannot move; I cannot speak. I am paralyzed.

She is Queen of Hel and I have no power over her.

"You will choose to stay," Freya says calmly to Astrid.

Astrid shakes her head. "You will have to trap me here, for I will not choose to give him up."

Ice creeps through my heart from Freya's hand. It tightens, breaking my iron star into small pieces. She could kill me in a moment, could take me away from Astrid and hardly think twice.

I gasp but keep my eyes open, wide and locked onto the goddess's.

Freya smiles at me. "You carry courage about you like a second skin, Soren. But I do not need *your* death for my leverage."

Astrid sucks air through her teeth, covering her mouth with one hand. I don't understand, but Freya gently pushes me back. I fall from her magic, collapsing to the cold ground, and Vider is there, holding my head up. She catches my eye and shakes her head. She doesn't understand, either.

But Astrid shudders. "Oh," she moans.

From beneath the golden apple tree, Idun, Astrid's mother, whispers, "It was only supposed to be you and the god of light. I did not see there would be others, others who would divide your love. Others to make the choice more terrible. It was only going to be you and Baldur. Everyone falls in love with Baldur."

"But Baldur is dead," Vider cries, fury splotching her cheeks. Her fingers dig into my scalp as she holds my head in her lap.

Baldur is dead. I'm dizzy and light as I begin to grasp the key Freya has offered. As I push up, I remember the story of Baldur's rebirth that Astrid told us in the car so many days ago:

Odin rode his eight-legged horse to the black river that floods into Hel. There he met the witch-goddess Freya, seer of all and the queen of Hel's magic. "Freya: lover, friend, teacher. My prophetess," the Alfather begged, "give my son back to me, back to the world, which loved him dearly."

Freya holds all the power over Baldur's death. It matters not that he ate no apple, for even if he is only a mortal man, Freya is the Queen of Death.

"You would bring him back," I whisper.

Vider, in her shock, drops my head. Astrid stares at me, and I see all those lifetimes of destiny in her eyes—the lifetimes I imagined joined us, while I held her on the roof of the Spark.

"Once upon a time," Freya and Idun say together, as Idun's eyes shut and she holds her palms out flat as if she channels a great seething magic, "it took all the world weeping to return the light to the sky." Their voices echo in the apple orchard. "But tonight, only one girl need make one choice, and dawn will come."

Vider pulls at the cloak hiding Astrid's hands. "She'll do it anyway. She won't let the world be without the sun. Odin wouldn't let her."

"Vider Lokisdottir," Freya says, hissing like a cat and turning so that the side of her face black with death shines in the moonlight, "you of all here should understand the length and depth of a god's temper."

Shrinking back, Vider says, "Against one, maybe, but not against the world."

Freya smiles. "I love the world, and I love Baldur the Beautiful. I would happily hold him in my embrace, keep him sleeping in my underworld bed for the next thousand years, little goblin. I see fate, and you cannot know if the fate of the world I have seen rests better if Baldur remains in ashes."

The air thickens, and I feel pressure in my ears again as Freya stands. "All the threads of fate are twisted here, in this moment," she says, "and even I cannot know how Astrid Jennasdottir will choose."

But I know.

I climb to my feet, and I go to Astrid. She takes my hands and there is such sorrow in the fall of her mouth. *Do you love the gods, Soren?* she asked me in the woods at Sanctus Sigurd's. Now I would like to answer, *Not nearly as much as I love you.* But she knows it, as she looks at me. Likely the whole universe of stars can read it in my face.

I wish I could choose to die in his place, that it would make this easier. Better to die with her name on my tongue than live a hundred years without even the memory of her. Without the strength she makes me feel, without her love to help me control the rage. I don't know if I can do it without her.

But Baldur.

Staring into my eyes, Astrid says, "Yes. Bring the sun back. Here I shall remain."

I pull Astrid into my arms, holding her as if I can impress her so deeply into my heart that no magic in the nine worlds could make me forget.

TWENTY-TWO

FREYA TOUCHES US both. "It is time to go to him. Odin will come with the dawn. You will receive your boons, and the moment you step out of this valley, all memory of Astrid will vanish."

It is a worse feeling than ever the sharp frenzy was. It bites and gnashes, and I can't think of a thing to say. I won't recognize myself in a few hours.

Idun plucks a leathery apple from the golden tree and tucks it into her daughter's hand. "When he rises, give him this, and you will become the Lady of Apples."

Astrid takes it, not looking at her mother. She gives her other hand back to me, and it's Vider, always willing, who asks Jenna, "What will happen to you?"

"She's coming with me," Freya says. "My most devoted, my beloved. Women will call on the spirit of Jenna Glyn for generations, and meet her in the seething dance."

I don't care, and by the way her hand in mine remains loose, the way she turns from the apple tree and begins the walk back to the orchard gate, I know Astrid is convincing herself not to care, either. If we had more time, I might try talking her into forgiveness, but I'm selfish for her touch.

The gate looms like a giant's iron mouth. Torches flicker, and in the far east a line of silver illuminates the mountain peaks.

Henry and his berserkers have been busy. They've set Baldur upon a pyre, and at each corner a bowl of herbs burns, sending acrid smoke into the predawn light. All nine berserkers stand at attention with spears and shields. Even Alwulf is there, blood dried on his neck, holding himself tall with his spear.

Their vigil is soon to end.

Freya goes ahead of us and, with a swooping gesture of her arms, makes the gate flow open. Every berserker sees us then, and as one they bow low.

The Feather-Flying Goddess glides over the meadow to where Baldur's body lies. Idun follows close, and the three of us after. Vider was silent for the entire walk, and now I hear her footsteps pause. But Astrid and I go on.

There's no spectacle of magic to his resurrection. Freya merely bends over his head and kisses him. Perhaps she speaks, perhaps not. Astrid holds my hand so tight.

Then Vider is at my other side, slipping her hand into the pocket of my bearskin coat to remind me where the troll eye rests.

No one moves, though Henry Halson glances at me. His face is joyful; I wish I could be as glad.

Baldur's eyes flicker.

To our left, Jenna gasps, and then collapses.

Astrid cries out and runs to her mother's side. She kneels. Her hands hover over Jenna's shoulder. But the sun slips over the mountains just then, and Baldur takes a deep breath.

"Idun," Freya says, in a summons not to be ignored. Astrid touches her mother's slack lips and stands. I can see her shaking as she walks to Baldur and Freya. The sunlight catches her curls, highlights the gold in her eyes. She is so beautiful.

A murmur goes through the assembled berserkers, but they're too controlled, or too afraid, to approach.

Astrid says, "Eat, Baldur."

The god of light opens his eyes. I strain forward, longing to see him closer, to look at the dawn reflected there in all its silvers and pinks.

He sits tentatively, rearranging his weight on the pyre. Though he blinks with confusion, he takes the apple Astrid offers. His fingers brush hers and she smiles. It is the smile I know from the first moment she saw him, when she recognized the godhood in his glance.

I cannot forget that smile.

It seems impossible that I should stand, but my legs remain solid as Baldur puts the small apple between his teeth. He closes his eyes as he eats, and when he swallows, a smile creeps over his mouth. His skin glows from internal radiance and the sun fills the valley with golden light. They are twins, Baldur and the sun, and I blink. It's hard to stare at him now, to study him in any detail. There aren't any shadows on his face to give his cheeks or lips depth.

But I know his voice.

"Idun!" he laughs. I squint as he holds his hands out to Astrid. Uncertainty flits through her expression, but she takes his hands and helps him from the pyre.

"This is different," Baldur says as he stands tall and surveys the valley. Despite myself, I feel warm and comforted. Parts of me that turned themselves to stone crack open.

"Aunt," he says to Freya, who remains cool and still, "are we in Bear Vale? Where is my father?"

"Yes, Prince," she replies. "Your father will be here momentarily. You've had quite the adventure."

"You remember nothing of the last few days?" I say, my voice breaking.

Vider echoes my dismay. "No, Baldur, you idiot."

He frowns at her, likely unused to such abuse. The frown changes from displeasure, though, into confusion again. "You . . . and . . ." He glances at me. "It is like a dream. I remember you as if I've spent days dreaming of you."

It is what he said before, only then we were reality and his godhood was the dream.

Astrid stares at him like he's a ghost. And I realize that what I feel, the horrible betrayal of forgetfulness, is what she will face in me. She sees Baldur and knows that soon she will look at me and I will not know her. My heart twists; my fever blossoms hot. *No.*

Tugging away from me, Vider steps close to the god of light. "I'm Vider," she insists. "And this is Soren. You were teaching me to fight, and that's Astrid—not Idun, whatever they say—and we've driven hundreds of miles to get you here. There were trolls and . . ." Vider trails off as Baldur's eyes widen.

"It sounds incredible," he says, his mouth widening into a grin. He spreads his hands. "You must tell me everything. Trolls, you say?"

He's giddy and bright, so pleasant, and with none of the sorrow or fear I'm used to. I look to Astrid and she's looking back at me. Baldur the Beautiful lives, and so the sun will be safe in the sky. But the man who became our friend is only a dream.

Freya brings Astrid before the berserkers, introducing her as their Lady of Apples. They all nod, unquestioning, as if the forgetting magic permeates the valley already. Then she instructs them to move Jenna onto Baldur's pyre, and tells them they should prepare for the Alfather to appear.

While she speaks, Baldur pesters Vider to tell him more of the story. He says she should go with him to find something to eat, because he feels like he hasn't eaten in a week. His smile is half-cocked, and when I realize he's flirting with her, I start for them. But Astrid catches my hand. "She can take care of herself," she murmurs. I turn to her and she takes my face, drags me down, and kisses me as if she can breathe only with my help.

It's overwhelming and painful, and I twist my hands in her hair. Her nose crushes into mine, and she kisses me hard enough I feel her teeth. It is not pretty, but a mess of kissing. "I will never forget you," she whispers, "and somewhere inside, you'll know."

Words die on my tongue as a cry echoes up from the gathered berserkers: *"Hangatyr!"* *"Alfather!"* Odin is coming. It's time.

I jerk away from Astrid. "Astrid. My boon." I laugh as I kneel and grab her around the waist. "My boon."

She lowers her eyes and puts one hand over my heart. "You must ask him for what will make you happy. What will make you live a long life, with love and peace and—and happiness."

"Yes." I smile at her, and I feel the fever waking again. This time I welcome the warmth of it, as a comforting power, a familiar storm.

We gather in a crowd, shielding our eyes from the bright morning sun as a great eagle soars over the mountains and spirals down. A nine-foot wingspan at least; his feathers glint bright as gold. Flanking him are two ravens and a red-tailed hawk.

Astrid clutches my hand, and I wish I had a moment to tell her what I'm thinking, but Vider finds us again. She casts a look of horror toward Baldur where he stands beside Freya, hands on his hips, in the white shirt the berserkers gave him but the same jeans we bought at that gas stop just outside Fort Collins. "I can't trolling believe it," Vider hisses at us while the eagle banks back. "You're giving up everything for a nack-brained surfer with about as much in his head as the World Snake."

I put a hand on her shoulder and say, "He is Baldur the Beautiful."

"Remember when he ran away to Fiji a few years ago?" Astrid adds with a little smile. "With the whole corps of the Bostown Ballet?"

Vider huffs and crosses her arms. "We should have left him in Mimirsey."

She continues shooting him furious glances. I watch him, too. Before we arrived in Leavenworth, Baldur asked me to be his friend. And he expected, too, how changed his memories would make him.

Nerves fist in my guts as I think of having my memories torn away.

The eagle's wings snap, pushing at us with a sudden warm wind, and all the layers of feathers fold into a broad coat, rather like mine, that settles over Odin's shoulders. He seems so modern, in black jeans and scuffed boots. His silver hair is braided down his back in a thick rope, and his wide hands hang relaxed at his sides. From here, his empty eye socket is only a shadow. I'm used to seeing him like this, appearing casually with Congress or beneath the New World Tree. Unlike Thor, who will not give over his armor, or Frigg, with her love for the old weaving ways, Odin has always been a god who changes with the times.

The berserkers go onto one knee in unison, saluting with spears held high and a sharp yell of *"Hangatyr!"*

Their call suspends in the air a moment, while the two giant ravens duck down from the sky, laughing loud enough that I wince. One lands heavily on Odin's shoulder, and the other flaps up to perch on Jenna's pyre. The red-tailed hawk lands on the ground, shaking its feathers.

And then, suddenly, Odin's single eye slides over me and in the empty socket next to it I see the frenzy. Odin scowls fiercely. His hair spreads wild around his head. He takes a spear and stabs himself with it so that his heart's blood spills into the valley with a hiss of steam. Red is everywhere, drowning me in heat.

I blink and the vision is gone. Nothing changed, except my fever is awake. Burning.

My knees tremble. Here is Odin the Mad One. Odin Dark-Bringer. Father of the Slain. No matter how he plays at being a man, at aiding us when we request it, pretending to be nothing but a figurehead, this is the Alfather. Poetry comes from the pinpoint of black at the center of his heart, and the piece of sky in my chest was born in him, too. The battle-rage flares along my skin and shakes through my bones. I hold tight to it, knowing if I let go so near him, I could scorch the earth with my fury.

I was so unaffected by Freya, but I fall to my knees before the god of berserkers.

Though Vider and Astrid kneel as well, Odin doesn't even

glance their way, but zeros past me and onto Baldur. In three large strides the Alfather is before his son, embracing him tightly enough to wrinkle his coat. Baldur claps Odin hard on the back. As Odin pulls away to study his son, tears fall onto his godly beard. "My son, my arrow," the Alfather says in a voice like the crashing of waves.

"Father. I am well; no need to worry." Baldur says it like a child. And he opens up to swing his arm toward us. "These are the friends who brought me here, Father. Soren and Astrid and Vider."

Freya inserts herself, and quietly says, "Astrid is Astrid no longer, but Idun, Lady of Apples and Youth."

I stand up, holding Astrid's hand tight as all the power of Odin's attention focuses on her. He comes, one arm about his son, and it takes all my energy not to back away. I avoid looking at his eye socket. The shadowed hole gapes there in his face, daring me to try again.

"So," he says to Astrid, "you are the new keeper of our immortality. And here with Baldur." Odin's smile is a wicked one, belying the plain coat and jeans, making him more like the raven on his shoulder. "That must be quite the story. You will come with us to feast, and tell it to all my children. For they are your cousins now, girl."

Astrid's hand shakes in mine and I feel the stress in her arm as she hangs on to me, as she barely manages to remain upright. "Alfather," she says. Her voice is empty.

Odin laughs. Both the raven perched on his shoulder and

the raven on the funeral pyre laugh with him. "You are too old to go easily with this, are you not? When you were a child, you'd not have feared me so."

"There is much to fear in dancing so close with the gods," she replies, a little of the familiar snap in her voice.

"Only too true, lady." Odin bows to her, much to my astonishment, and Astrid puts her free hand to her heart and returns the gesture.

The Alfather's gaze travels to me again, and his single blue eye takes everything in. Not just my bearskin coat and tattoo, but the edges of my frenzy and all the desire I've ever had to cut it from my heart. His stare leaves me breathless, as if he has reached in and filled my lungs with lightning. "Soren Berserker, newly named Bearstar. Son of one of my most wayward warriors. I see my son Baldur in your heart. I see you raise your spear against him."

I quail at his words, and now it is my turn to hold myself up by the touch of Astrid's hand. "Yes, Alfather," I say.

"I also"—Odin tilts his head as the raven on his shoulder clacks its beak—"understand that with that spear at your throat you swore yourself out of my service and into his."

"I did, lord." I glance to Baldur, where surprise makes his eyes even brighter. The god of light watches me and slowly smiles.

"Interesting." Odin turns finally to Vider. A single barking laugh launches from him. "Vider! No wonder that layabout wanted to come."

Vider flushes so hard her delicate skin turns pink from

collar to crown. Frowning, I look beyond Odin to where stands a boy I've never seen before, with a bush of violent red hair, wearing sunglasses and a T-shirt the color of the hawk's red tail feathers. No hawk is to be seen. The boy waves. Winding between his fingers is a strand of Vider's white-blond hair. The strand Freya transformed into that little bird when we were still in the orchard.

Ignoring the boy, Vider raises her chin and says to Odin, "We were promised boons."

My heart stops and Astrid lets loose a tiny groan. But on the Alfather's face shock is followed fast by amusement, which is lucky for Vider.

"So you were, trollkin. Let it not be said that all of Loki's children mince words." He crouches, and his raven spreads its wide wings for balance as Odin brings himself down to Vider's level. "And what is it, child, that you ask of me?"

There's no drop of hesitation before she says, "I would be your berserker, with your madness in my stomach, as wild and strong as Luta Bearsdottir."

The red-haired boy cries out, "Vider!" and jumps forward. He throws off the sunglasses and strides toward us, with every step aging until he is about fifteen. Her age. Freckles stand out stark against his suddenly bloodless face and he's reaching one pleading hand to her. "What are you doing?"

I recognize him now: this is Loki himself, patron of caravans. And Vider knows him personally. What else did she not tell us?

But Vider ignores the god of thieves, holding her eyes on

Odin's pale blue gaze. The Alfather ignores the boy, too, and says something. I only see his mouth move, but no words issue forth. Vider, though, must hear them, for she releases my hand and covers her mouth in the most fearful gesture I've ever seen her make. Tears fill her eyes but don't spill over as she nods. "Yes," she says, and her hands lower to her belly, as if she will feel the growth of the frenzy there.

Astrid squeezes my fingers and I look with her past Odin to where Loki sinks to his knees. The strand of Vider's hair is still caught in his hand, and I wonder what part he played in all of this. I remember that Fenris Wolf told me it had to have been a god who stole Baldur's ashes, and although Loki was given alibi, the alibi was from Freya herself, who is clearly involved. Had Glory known? Was she warning me? Or is her faith in her father more than it should be?

Odin says, "So be it."

Loki casts a baleful glance at Freya.

"Vider Bearskin," the Alfather intones, "the fever will grow to fill you, and you will writhe with madness and power. From this moment, not berserker born, but berserker made." Odin places a hand on Vider's white-blond head. She bows, shivering, and that is all of the passing of power.

Loki jumps to his feet and claps his hands. He is a fire-red hawk, screaming as he flies up.

"That shall be your burden as well, little warrior," Odin tells Vider. She purses her lips angrily and says nothing.

"And so," Odin says, standing again. He holds out a hand to me. "What is your wish, Soren?" Amusement glints in his eye.

"Immortality? Shall I bring you to the Valhol and make you one of my Lonely Fighters?"

I open my mouth and think for a moment what a thing it would be, with Vider asking to become a berserker, if I were to ask to be free.

But it isn't what I want anymore. I take a deep breath and say loud enough that Freya is certain to hear, and perhaps the gathered of Idun's Bears as well, "I want to remember Astrid."

I feel her tense beside me, going as still as stone. I don't breathe, either.

Odin frowns thoughtfully. The raven on his shoulder ruffles its feathers and tilts its head at me.

The moment drags out, and I cannot think that he will refuse. It is really so simple a request. Only memory. Only to hold her always in my heart. Nothing more. No power or immortality. Nothing to bend the laws of gods or men. *Please.* Just a memory.

And he says, "So it is done."

All the air falls out of me. "Just like that?"

His smile now is almost tender. "Just like that."

Astrid grips my arm and stares at me for a split second, then she reaches for Odin. With more courage than I have, she touches the Alfather's hand. "I want him."

Freya walks over and slides her fingers around Odin's braid. The two gods watch us—one blue eye and two gray as the moon. Freya smiles as if this was her intention all along, and on Odin's cheek a scar slowly blooms, cutting it in half under his missing eye. Just like my tattoo.

The weight of their consideration is the only thing anchoring me to the earth. We are all the beings in the world, me and Astrid and Odin and Freya, and everything hangs between us until Odin finally agrees. "Four days a year you may have him. Once at each quarter of the sun. Every other day, you will serve your apples."

"Thank you," she whispers, and closes her eyes.

And like that, our destinies snap together again.

TWENTY-THREE

IMMEDIATELY WE'RE SWEPT away.

Because most of us are incapable of transforming our-selves, Henry Halson offers up the berserk band's heliplane, a long black machine with two rotors and the face of a grizzly bear painted on its nose. Odin barks a laugh and accepts, clapping Henry on the shoulder with such force the warrior shakes.

Vider and I are taken into the heliplane with Baldur and Odin, and one of the berserkers to fly it. We're given headsets, but Odin ignores us, talking instead with Baldur the whole ride, in Old Scandan. I can understand maybe one in twenty words. Vider presses her face to the window, and I lean back in the hard leather seat with my eyes closed and hold the image of Astrid in my mind. I believe in Odin's word this once, because of all the witnesses, but as we lift off the valley floor and soar over the Cascades, I can't help the crawling fear that it was a lie. That I'll forget her. I whisper her name to myself.

Our ride lasts less than an hour, not enough time to fly to Bright Home, and yet that's where we are.

The helipad is halfway up the mountainside, and as I disembark I see the black roof glinting in the sunlight at the peak. Bright Home perches among snow-capped cliffs, its golden pillars and silver doors brighter than the ice.

Here, tucked back into the evergreens, is a network of old-fashioned longhouses, looking like luxurious halls out of an epic romance, with carved double doors, and round shields decorating the roofs. Torches burn with silver light, paved red paths connect the halls, and a lake shimmers in the center. The air is cold and thin, yet somehow I feel safe.

And I continue to remember Astrid's name.

I'm separated from Vider and put into the hands of a host of women who lead me into one of the halls. The inside is divided into a lobby and guest rooms, making me think of the kind of resort vacations they advertise on television. The women hardly talk, but give me no choice about being bathed and dressed. They trim my hair and present me with a tunic-like white shirt to wear under the bearskin coat Henry Halson gave me. I pull on leather pants softer than cotton, and new boots that match the coat. Finally, the women fit golden and copper bracelets around my wrists and shove rings onto my fingers. I'm being made into a proper-looking warrior, and when they belt Sleipnir's Tooth across my back, I stare at myself in the mirror. No one from Sanctus Sigurd's would recognize me if not for my distinctly non-Asgardian skin and eyes, and the tattoo gouging down my face.

I can't tell how much time has passed before I'm thrown back together with Vider in the lobby. She's been cleaned up, too, and put into a berserker's uniform of black so that she will fit beside Idun's Bears. Her silver-blond hair is braided in a crown. Her eyes are reddened with pain.

Because of the tattoo.

It's harsh and black against her left cheek, the delicate skin around it inflamed just enough to turn pink.

I reach out and brush my fingers down her temple, not too close to the fresh ink. Vider raises her chin and forces a tight smile. "This is what I want."

Her hand slips into mine, and we wait in the center of the marble floor while attendants and Valkyrie rush around us.

Baldur's Feast.

I've watched it on television; I've skipped it to practice with myself in the holmring. I never thought to find myself a guest.

The Bright Home feast hall where it takes place is nine times larger than the Great Hall at Sanctus Sigurd's, and at the high table are nine thrones, each for one of the most powerful gods of Asgard. Stretching out from it like multiple legs are long tables where the rest of us sit: minor gods and the president of New Asgard, the lawspeaker I saw so recently address the country, along with other blessed members of the Congress and specially chosen representatives from local assemblies. There are Valkyrie serving everyone honey mead in golden cups, and Lonely Warriors bring forth roasted boar. Berserkers chat with a handful of Thor's generals, and high priests of every Asgardian temple have assigned seats. There are film stars and that telepreacher, the prince of Mizizibi, we listened to on the road. I'm overwhelmed by the press of people, both famous and obscure, and by the presence of so many gods. TV cameras and flashbulbs crowd in the corners, and there's a constant stream of reporters tapping the guests' shoulders for attention and in hopes of an interview.

I whisper Astrid's name.

The roof arcs up into an illusion of the afternoon sky, with a false sun moving slowly across it. The torches here are silver, too, and everything is gilded or carved in intricate detail with the histories of our greatest heroes. When the attendants lead us in, I concentrate on breathing, on keeping my mouth closed. Thinking of Astrid. Gundrun Graycloak herself greets us and shows us to our seats just below the high table. Many eyes turn to us, though they don't know who we are. I hunt for Astrid or Baldur and find neither—Odin is not yet here himself, nor any of the leading gods.

I'm too nervous to eat. I sip the mead Gundrun offers, sharing most of it with Vider. The boar smells of cloves and pepper, and makes my mouth water. I don't know where Astrid is—the loss twists my stomach. But at least I know her name.

When the gods arrive, they each carry in a massive plate of food: candied fruits and apple dumplings, roasted potatoes, buttery rolls, and whole cooked crows and swans with their wings spread. There is Odin, of course, and his wife Frigg the Cloud-Spinner. Freya in her half-death mask hand in hand with her brother Freyr, who is the god of wealth and plenty. They laugh together, though I don't see what's funny. After them

Thor in a shining corselet with his fiery hair blazing, and Tyr the Just, missing his right hand because Fenris Wolf devoured it. There is Loki, looking fifteen and glowering.

Baldur enters, and a roar of approval lifts the roof of the hall. So many cameras go off I'm blinded, but I'm smiling, too, because Baldur is here and alive, and this is what I've seen through the lenses of those cameras for my entire life, only now I'm here. And I was part of what made it happen.

A hush falls. I look to the high table.

Astrid.

I remember her name.

She stands in a white dress, still with her black plastic pearls about her throat and her dark curls tumbling down over her shoulders. She carries a basket of large, beautiful golden apples, and suddenly I realize a secret: the gods never show their believers what the real apples of immortality are. We aren't supposed to know they are wizened little things; we're meant to believe they are these brilliant, round fruits that Astrid hands now to the gods: one to each, ending with Baldur. The god of light kisses her hand and takes a bite of the apple.

Another rousing cheer lifts through the hall, and Astrid herself quiets us with an open palm. She says, "Welcome to life, Baldur the Beautiful."

I am light and alive, laughing with happiness because she is so beautiful there with the table of gods. She glances out into the crowd. She finds me, and smiles.

+ + +

The Alfather brings Vider and me to the high table and weaves a story of heroism that is so false with Astrid's absence that I can hardly keep my expression even. But I glance at Vider, and she shows no sign of doubt.

This is the version she remembers. How will I ever speak to her again?

We're inundated by hands held out to shake. Microphones are thrust into our faces. I don't trust myself to answer in a way the Alfather would like—I can't strip Astrid from my story even for show. Fortunately, the reporters know of me and prefer to focus on the so-named redemption of Styrr Bearskin's son. They're more than willing to fill in blanks for me. And here is Vider, the first female berserker in decades, sucking their attention as well.

Baldur himself saves me with a charming smile that slides half off his face, and extracts me from the welter of attention.

When we're a little ways off, Baldur tucks closer so that I can feel the sunlight radiating from his face. "Soren?" he says, uncertainty pulling up the end of my name.

I cross my arms so that I don't forget he's changed, so that I don't offer him a spar or tell him to leave off flirting with Vider. When he pauses and looks up at the false sky, I take the opportunity to look at his eyes. It must be a crystal evening outside, with not a hint of clouds. The blueness deepens the longer I stare into it, and Baldur's hand is suddenly on my shoulder.

"In my dream, it was you who reminded me who I am," he says.

Startled, I blink at him. I remember what it felt like to

watch him die, to believe he would never again hold the sun inside him. I rush to say, "I promised you I would serve you. You didn't know if I would want to, and I do. If you . . ." I shake my head. "Not that you need it."

Baldur laughs, and the entire hall gets brighter. The flashes are like miniature sunbursts, the golden pillars glare, and the snap of the pennants hanging from the ceiling is like applause. "Soren, you know how, when you dream, sometimes you don't remember anything but what kind of dream it was? Frightening or hilarious or just strange? How there's only the feeling of it like a ghost in your mind?"

I nod once. We've had this conversation before.

"Good. Because you'll understand this, then." He puts his other hand on my other shoulder. We face each other. "I don't remember everything that happened, and I'm looking forward to the tale. But I know, I *feel*, that it was good. Even if I did die. It was a damn excellent dream." He pauses, takes a deep breath, and says, "I need you."

He holds his right hand out, and I grasp it. "Under the sun, and to the edges of the world," I promise.

"The binding-by-light?"

"If—if that suits you, Baldur."

He nods once, and slowly. "It does. Under the sun, and to the edges of the world."

His father calls him then, and he claps my arm before jogging through the throng to Odin's side.

+ + +

I want to leave, but don't know how or whom to ask, and so I hover at the edges of the feast, finally finding my way outside. The sun sets in a great swath of purple, peering out between the peaks. I walk among the evergreen trees and breathe deeply, planting my feet flat against the earth. *I am the mountain.*

"Feeling dangerous?" asks a voice behind me.

I turn, and there's Glory, crouched on all fours in a dark bodysuit.

"I would like to go back to the orchard," I say, "and wait for Astrid there."

"Who?" Glory says with a wicked grin.

I tighten my jaw and say nothing.

"I'll take you," Fenris Wolf says, her green eyes glowing neon, "and happily cause some panic when they realize you've gone."

"Did your father steal Baldur's ashes and hide him in the desert? I was told that it had to have been a god."

"That last part is most certainly true." She rises to her feet and walks closer to me. Even in this dim purple light, the green glitter on her eyelids sparkles. "If he did, it was to repay an old favor."

"To Freya."

"Probably. That witch plots out strands of fate centuries forward." Glory's tricky smile tells me that's as close to admitting the truth as she'll get.

I toy with the stone troll's eye in the pocket of my coat. "Tell me about Vider."

Glory's mouth curves down and she spits onto the bed of pine needles. "She was Lokiskin, and now is one of you."

"And Loki's upset about it."

She puts her lips inches from mine and whispers, "Wouldn't you be?"

I can't even be sure Glory and I are talking about the same things, but I think back over everything she's said to me and wonder if our meeting was coincidence after all. "Why did Vider make the choice she did?"

Glory's breath sighs across my mouth and she leans back. "Here is all I may say: My father prefers to be a boy himself, you must know, and often adopts a playmate from among the caravan children. When she was a young girl, Vider was who he loved best. But one day, Vider grew up. It didn't suit either of them."

It turns my stomach. The worst part of it is, by choosing Odin, Vider has not found a place any more stable. She's a ber-serker now, and it's the most volatile profession in the world.

"Poor Vider," I whisper, and Glory laughs.

All I want now is to be away from here, to be with Astrid.

"Let's go," I say to Glory, seizing her hand.

Astrid once dreamed of me riding a wolf the size of a bear, but she could not have predicted this.

I spread across the warm, rough back of Fenris Wolf, half god, half giant, and dig my fingers into her thick fur. My eyes are closed and my cheek presses into her. I feel her massive wolf-muscles work as she leaps across the sky.

We're running so fast, with stars barely overhead and the

earth far below, and the exhilaration draws my frenzy along with a frantic heartbeat. Glory growls, the sound vibrating against my entire body like a cat's massive purr. This is better than a heliplane, better than an orange '84 Volundr Spark with tail fins, and I cannot wait to tell Astrid. To describe the stomach-dropping motion of flight and the rich smell of earth and bubble gum coming off Glory's fur. The pristine chime of silver chains ringing at her neck.

In the end, I'm alone in the dark.

Glory leaves me in the valley beside Jenna Glyn's pyre. I thank her, and she steals a hair from my head so that, she says, she'll always be able to find me. I'm both comforted and unsettled by the idea, but I lift a hand in farewell as the giant wolf leaps again into the sky and disappears between the stars.

The feasting hall of Idun's Bears is alight with noise and fire. Henry Halson and his berserkers must be watching the festivities at Bright Home and sharing in their own feast. All the country is probably doing the same.

I take up a vigil, standing or kneeling or pacing slowly around Astrid's mother's pyre. The former Idun, Jenna Glyn, the Seether of All Dreams, is sunk into the bed of wood, and when I catch a glance of her out of the corner of my eye, her licorice curls make me think it's Astrid.

All night long I watch.

Mostly I stare up at the stars and center myself with long breathing exercises that Master Pirro would be proud of.

As the eastern sky begins to show traces of dawn light, I walk to the Bears' feast hall and take one of the torches from its sconce. With it I set Jenna's pyre aflame.

The fire consumes her, warming my face and hands. I think of the Berserker's Prayer, but can't sing it for Jenna. Instead I say, "May you find the sun, even in death, Jenna Glyn."

"Thank you," Astrid says behind me. She slides her hand into mine.

"Astrid!" I turn, gathering her up off her feet. I brush my cheek along hers. "How did you get here?"

"Got a lift from a wolf. She says if you ever change your mind about me, give her a ring."

I set Astrid down. She remains in her fancy Idun costume, her curls snaking all around her cheeks. The ankle-length dress leaves her shoulders bare to the cold, and her mother's plastic pearls cut a line of black across her throat. I kiss her forehead and then her lips. I kiss her closed eyes. In the orange light of her mother's funeral pyre, her face is shadowed, half-living, half-dying. "You're mine tonight," she says. "In the morning I will learn to tend my apples, and count the days until the solstice, when you will come to me again."

"It isn't so bad," I say, encircling her with my arms. "Only three months between. That's hardly time to do anything of import or have good adventure to tell you."

"Says the man who rescued a god in the course of eight days."

I shrug. Astrid traces the line of my spear tattoo. "I love this, have I told you?"

"I knew." I kiss her softly, reveling in the freedom of it, of touching her how I want, of kissing her and not being afraid. She slides her hands under the bearskin coat. "Will you do something for me tonight?" I ask.

"Anything."

I skim my hands down her arms until I find her hands. "Dance with me."

Astrid laughs, throwing her head back until she's laughing up at the stars. She weaves her fingers into mine.

The sun in my chest ignites.

Her hands tug at me.

We spin.

Our feet stomp the cold earth, and the bones of the world stomp back. Neither of us solid, but both wild and dark and yearning.

Between us is a piece of the sky.

ACKNOWLEDGMENTS

THIS BOOK WOULD not be what it is without the usual suspects: my first readers, Maggie Stiefvater and Brenna Yovanoff; my agent, Laura Rennert; and my editor, Suzy Capozzi. Not to mention everyone at Random House Children's Books who has supported me through the last year, especially Jim Thomas, Mallory Loehr, Nicole de las Heras, Paul Samuelson, Jenna Lettice, Sonia Nash Gupta, Rachel Feld, Nora McDonald, and Michael Herrod. There are so many more who I haven't had direct contact with: thank you!

Thanks as well to Kim Welchons, Myra McEntire, and Victoria Schwab for answering my panic and giving me exactly what I needed at the right time.

My Web designer, Chris Kennedy, might possibly be more excited about the United States of Asgard websites than I am. Bless you.

Thanks to La Prima Tazza in Lawrence, Kansas, where I'm sitting right now, drinking all your coffee and taking up an outlet.

I wouldn't have imagined this world without Professor William Lasher and his Old English classes at the University of Cincinnati. In 2005, everything about academia and politics was depressing me, but translating my own *Beowulf* got me through it.

Will Callahan, thanks for taking those classes with me and passing me notes scrawled in Old English.

Mom and Dad, Sean and Travis, this book is a love letter to our family road trips: rough with camaraderie and American history. Thank you.

And always, Natalie Parker.

ABOUT THE AUTHOR

TESSA GRATTON has wanted to be a paleontologist or a wizard since she was seven. Alas, she turned out to be too impatient to hunt dinosaurs, but is still searching for someone to teach her magic. After traveling the world with her military family, Tessa acquired a BA (and the important parts of an MA) in gender studies. While in school she studied Old English and translated *Beowulf*—leading her on a wonderful journey through the sagas, which in turn inspired her to create the United States of Asgard. Tessa lives in Kansas with her partner, her cats, and her mutant dog. You can visit her online at tessagratton.com.